ARCHIE WILDE

and the curse of

Baldizar

Archie Wilde and the curse of Baldizar

Published by The Conrad Press Ltd. in the United Kingdom 2021

Tel: +44(0)1227 472 874
www.theconradpress.com
info@theconradpress.com

ISBN 978-1-914913-06-8

Printed and bound in Great Britain by Clays Ltd, Elcograf S.p.A

Typesetting and Cover Design by The Book Typesetters
www.thebooktypesetters.com

Cover illustrations by Elmi Terjavjainen

The Conrad Press logo was designed by Maria Priestley.

ARCHIE WILDE

and the curse of

Baldizar

ROBIN HUGHES

To my darling wife Trudi, thank you
for your unwavering belief in me and
your constant encouragement to
let my imagination run riot, and
to never give up.

Also, to my wonderful children Mel
and Tom because it was your fun-filled
childhoods that inspired me to write
children's stories in the first place.

Part 1

REVELATION

Chapter 1

O ur tale begins on the planet Hexx, ten years past, during that most celebrated of festivals, Atunka Gaar. It was the final hours of the three-day celebration, and the drunken, raucous crowd that had swollen the amphitheatre to near bursting point was in high spirits, singing, cursing, laughing, and brawling.

For the lucky few, it was broad smiles and heavy leather hip purses swollen with spungold, their winnings from the prior day's gladiatorial games. However, the majority had purses as empty as their rumbling stomachs and sore heads. But such trifling concerns, along with many a black eye, split lip, missing tooth, and bruised ego, were swept away by the electric atmosphere of tense expectancy, for it was the festival's climax, the return of the chosen ones.

Across the bloodstained arena floor, upwind from the stench of the terraces, stood the main stage. The mighty timber construction occupied one third of the mammoth wooden stadium, the great amphitheatre of Garrknock. Rising like a sentinel at its crown, its fearsome head high in the sky, stood a titanic image of Jagdar, the one true God.

To its right, nine members of the council of the power ten genies, the ruling body of the known genieverse, sat upon high-backed wing chairs, arranged in the formation of a peak less pyramid. The two cosmic genies, Order and System, took their place at the front, followed by the three stellar genies, Star, Nova, and Quasar. Lastly, forming the foundation of the council, were the elemental genies, Earth, Wind, Fire, and Water.

To the left of the all-seeing likeness of Jagdar, Baldizar, or El Supremo, sat alone. Unlike the other genies' lavishly bejewelled chairs of the finest spungold, his was as black as a moonless night. There was nothing pretentious about its simple form, yet there were rumours, whispers in the dark, that its touch was as cold as ice, perhaps even as cold as the heart that sat upon it.

As the elected ruler of the council of the power ten genies and all their subjects beneath them, it was Baldizar's draconian laws that bound the genieverse together and his wisdom that led all species on the path of righteousness. The El Supremo's authority was second only to that of Jagdar himself.

The voice of the watchtower bell in the nearby Fortress Hexx rang out the last candle mark before sunset, its ever-attentive guards scanning the skies with their nearascopes.

'Look!' screamed a voice in the crowd. 'Up there! They're coming!'

All eyes and sensory organs turned to the heavens. There, high above in the clear, cold, red-tinged sky, was a solitary dot. Shocked gasps could be heard throughout the theatre as the solitary dot swiftly became a spiral of black smoke.

'Jagdar's teeth!' the mass of goggling creatures cried in horror. 'There's only one!' The swaying crowd, bubbling with excitement, strained to hear the distant screams, wrought of agonising pain and absolute exhaustion, of the rapidly approaching, twirling speck of black above the murmuring wind.

'Whoever that poor creature is,' yelled someone in the crowd, 'they're not falling—they're plummeting out of control.'

The more sensible and sober in the crowd, fearing that it could be a messy landing, immediately struggled for the exits. But the theatre stalls were so tightly packed in the expectation of a spectacularly bloody finale that it was impossible to move.

High above, somehow, the distraught creature managed to find the strength to pull up from his suicidal fall. At the very last moment and with two of his four wings blackened and smoking, the creature screeched into a low, swooping curve just above the awestruck crowd. In fact, so low was his entry to the arena that his claws scythed the heads off several of the taller spectators. A rapturous chorus of applauding approval came from those unharmed by his flaying talons. It was entertainment of the highest calibre.

Crashing at great speed, the creature ploughed into the dirt arena floor with a heavy, howling thud. A loud, unified 'oh' erupted throughout the theatre at his obvious pain. However, the fleeting moment of compassion was swiftly replaced by cold, cruel laughter.

Carried by momentum, the pitiful creature desperately clawed at the dirt, his talons gouging deep ruts in the ground as he bounced along awkwardly. His screams of agony echoed throughout the amphitheatre, until finally, his battered body fell flat and slid to a crumpled halt.

As the dust settled, so did the crowd. Even the ever-present Zephyar, demigod of all winds, seemed to hold his breath. As a cohesive mass, every living creature within the walls of the great amphitheatre of Garrknock—spectators, guards, prisoners, gladiators, and genies alike—turned with hushed reverence towards El Supremo.

From his throne of hellish black, the lone figure, completely encased in scarlet armour, rose regally to his feet. Standing ten feet tall from his flame-crested, horned helmet down to his huge metal boots, his appearance proclaimed his ruthless craving for absolute obedience. Deliberately pausing, he allowed the murmuring mob of lowlife scum a few moments to wallow in fearful awe at his majestic magnificence before striding purposefully down the creaking stage steps. His long cape of scarlet billowed from his wide shoulders, whilst his heavy iron boots left crisp, deep imprints in the compacted dirt. On his helmet, his impressive black-and-red mane waved in the cold breeze as he swaggered towards the fallen creature.

Forever skulking in the shadow of the red giant, the human known only as the professor followed dutifully behind.

Lying beaten, broken, and bloody on the arena floor, the challenger feebly tried to focus his bloodshot eyes on the approaching figure. Stamping to a halt before the wretched creature, El Supremo solemnly raised two of his four gauntleted hands high in the air. As if cut by a knife, the stalls instantly descended into silence, followed by a volley of bony clicks as thousands of heads craned forward as far as their scrawny necks would allow, ever eager to witness the contestant's final moments. Their excited breath hung like mist in the cold, late-afternoon air.

Kraknar was a proud Karralian mantis warrior, but even as he lay half dead and groaning in the dirt, his befuddled senses quickly realised that it was Baldizar himself who stood before him. Twisting his bulbous insect head through two hundred seventy degrees, he viewed his battered body with anguish. His normally glossy green skin was pallid and clammy, his skeletal armour all cracked and splintered. The stump of his rear forth leg was still bleeding, as were the multitude of other deep lacerations that covered his body. Of his two large front legs, the left was mangled at the knee, the tips of the shattered bones standing proud from the weeping flesh. His two main wings were scorched, black, and withered, and to add to his misery, the chilled, dry air of Hexx made it almost impossible for the tropical creature to breathe.

Normally, Kraknar would have stood twice the height of El Supremo, as he had at the start of the race. *Had it only been twelve candle marks? It seemed like a lifetime.* Openly grimacing, he pushed aside the torrent of pain and struggled upon his good right leg, holding his head aloft with as much dignity as his ebbing strength would allow.

'M-M-My,' Kraknar croaked, coughing harshly before clearing his parched throat of clotted lumps of foul green blood. 'My El Supremo,' he eventually rasped, 'I am the sole survivor of the race. The others, I have left dead and dying on Bleak, at the claws of the beast. I alone kneel before your glorious personage, and in the name of Jagdar, I beg you to spare me.'

'Have you answered the riddle?' asked Baldizar in a cold, clinical tone. 'Have you found what I seek?'

Kraknar's head fell in shame. 'I have not, my El Supremo.' Then he uttered in a pitiful tone, 'By the horns of the one and only true god, Jagdar, I beseech you to have mercy upon this humble creature today, on this day of days.'

Amongst the cheering, bloodthirsty crowd, a lone creature, caped in pristine sky-blue cape, held high a hand, its thumb defiantly skywards. 'Spare the maggot!' he cried. 'Mercy for Kraknar!'

His bold, treacherous words shocked the crowd. But his repeated pleas for lenience quickly fanned the latent sparks of defiance that lay dormant amongst the muttering mob. Soon, the air was loud with new cries as the voices of the mob filled the great amphitheatre of Garrknock with rousing chants for mercy.

Baldizar stood in silence, viewing the foolishly brave crowd with seething contempt. Behind him to the south, the second sun of Hexx kissed the horizon, its fading light bathing his crimson armour in a fiery wash, its brilliance magically illuminating the mosaic of ancient silver symbols etched upon it.

The Karralian mantis warrior understood El Supremo's silence. Staring up into his metal visor, Kraknar watched through its eye slit as the supreme genie's black eyes suddenly turned volcanic red. With inbred dignity, he recited a final prayer to his god, Jagdar, then bolstered himself as best he could, ready to embrace his fate. A choked breath later, the ornate spungold collar that hung about his neck, his sign to the genieverse that he was a maggot, a contender in the race, constricted swiftly upon itself.

With a neat, bone-crunching *pop*, Kraknar's head toppled from his shoulders.

Baldizar raised one of his size-twenty-four iron boots high, its seams of acorn-sized rivets and horned toecap gleaming in the light of the second sunset. Poised to drop, he let his boot linger above the head of the failed mantis warrior. Glaring at the cheering crowd, his thin, cruel lips suddenly smiled as he dropped his boot. It fell like a steam hammer, crashing down with a heavy, crunching thud.

The crowd fell silent, hardly daring to breathe.

In a loud, tyrannical voice that reached out to all listening, El Supremo proclaimed, 'I am Baldizar, supreme genie of the council of the power ten, and your El Supremo.' He twisted the heel of his boot, grinding the shattered skull fragments deep into the dirt. 'There shall be no mercy for failure!'

A slim, ghost-faced man in a grey suit stepped out from Baldizar's shadow. He walked with furtive mouse steps over to Kraknar's body, drumming the tips of his fingers together whilst tutting in obvious frustration. 'My El Supremo,' he said with a heavy sigh, 'I had high expectations for that one. His special training went well.'

Baldizar scowled. 'Obviously, your special training techniques weren't special enough!'

'He was the best choice from all the volunteers that you managed to procure.' Instantly, the professor regretted his choice of words and accusing tone, as he watched Baldizar's huge horned helmet rotate one hundred eighty degrees. Although it was cold, the professor suddenly found himself sweating profusely.

Baldizar's red, scolding eyes narrowed. Even with his visor closed, the professor could clearly imagine a corner of his mouth twitching at his blatant insolence. A single metal gauntlet shot out, its long fingers curling about his scrawny neck. 'Careful, Professor,' warned Baldizar, his metal finger tightening, 'or your usefulness might suddenly expire... along with your life!'

'A thousand apologies,' croaked the professor meekly.

'I don't want your pathetic apologies!' roared Baldizar, casting him down upon the hard earth. 'I want that dagger!'

The professor vigorously massaged his neck, trying desperately to gulp air into his lungs. He felt himself trembling under the gaze of Baldizar's cruel eyes, which were a boiling, volcanic red, scarred with pulsating black veins of rage. He knew that he'd just strayed into the last-chance saloon, and the bartender's name was Death.

Then he had a brilliant idea. 'Of course,' he said in a loud, purposeful tone as he scrambled awkwardly to his feet whilst tactfully staying out of range of all four of Baldizar's hands. 'There might just be another way!' With a shifty sideways glance, he breathed easily as he saw that his words were having the desired effect.

Baldizar's eyes were slowly returning to a cold, simmering black, his initial rage giving way to curiosity. 'What other way?' he demanded. 'Explain yourself.'

'Well, my El Supremo,' he continued, the tremble in his voice slowly subsiding, 'it's obvious that we can't train a creature to the standards needed to both survive the race and find the dagger.'

Baldizar leaned forward inquisitively, engulfing the

professor in his long shadow. 'Yes.'

'So why don't we grow one from scratch?'

'Can such a thing can be done?' hissed Baldizar.

'Oh yes, my El Supremo,' he answered in a flash. 'And what's more,' he continued creepily, 'you can personally design his every required quality!'

Baldizar's metal head turned to face forward. 'Make it so!' he ordered. 'Use your knowledge of the ancient black art of technology and bring forth your living abomination.'

The professor's whole body sagged with relief. *Yes*, the voice of his conscience sneered from the dark recesses of his mind, *once again I outwit the bartender.* But as he turned, ready to escape to the safety of his laboratory, two large metal gauntlets clamped over his shoulders.

'Professor, the next festival of Atunka Gaar, in one decade's time, will be my last chance to legitimately take control of the genieverse.' He exerted just enough pressure in his metal fingers to make the human wince with pain. 'By the curly horns of Jagdar, earthling, I promise that if your monster fails me, and I have to declare war on the council to get my way, you will be its first victim!'

Chapter 2

The statue of Jagdar stood proudly, as it had for centuries. It was taller than a hundred-year-old oak tree and had a wider girth than a bull elephant. Its four celestial faces were ever ruling, its eight eyes ever watchful—Jagdar was the one true god.

Many millions of years ago, the granite monolith had been birthed of molten lava from the very heart of the planet. Over countless eons, it had cooled and hardened—then nature's titanic forces thrust it skywards to become the building block of a mighty, snow-capped mountain range.

Then, in the near distant past, it had been brutally hacked from its mountainside by eager hands with primitive tools. For countless decades, the savages laboured tirelessly, fashioning it with muscle driven hammers and chisels, then smoothing it with endless leather and sweat. On the appropriate day, proclaimed by the druids, as foretold by the stars, their beloved and most sacred statue began its final journey.

Dragged by hordes of whiplashed slaves, on log rollers lubricated with their dying blood, it was moved slowly away

18

from its mountain home and through unforgiving forests and swamps, until it was manhandled deep into the land of the dead. And so it arrived at its final resting place, the great sand sea, where it was enshrined to stand forever dominant over all those who came to worship in the very heart of the sacred valley of the one true god.

For centuries, it had stood the test of both time and nature, its smooth crystalline surface having been scorched by the twin suns of Hexx, lashed by driving rain from colossal thunderstorms, scoured by unrelenting desert dust devils, and frozen by merciless night-time frosts. And yet, to all those who fell on their knees in breathless adoration before it, its crisp lines and silky smoothness could have been created that very day, for its chiselled image remained as powerful as it was on the day it was unveiled.

Nearby, a pack of sabre-toothed skunks stopped devouring the half-eaten carcass they'd found when day suddenly became night. Pairs of small red eyes squinted at the strange object that had blocked the twin suns high in the sky. Rows of poison spines sprang up on their backs, poised at the ready at the unexpected arrival of the mysterious apparition.

Of course, when they were younglings as a troop back in the burrows, the old ones had told tales of the giant white fluffy things that on rare occasions roamed the skies. Mystical creatures the size of mountains appeared as if by magic, their billowing forms casting weird and wonderful shadows on the ground. However, this one wasn't like those—it was giant and red with gleaming golden horns.

When the roaring started, so too did the panic. Curiosity became terror as the wind became angry, and dust devils appeared, forcing the pack to beat a hasty retreat to the safety of their burrows.

It was a four-day trek by Boombelly engine to the statue, longer by foot or hoof. Because it was deep in the great sand sea, all journey times to the temple were at the mercy of the fickle Hexx weather—except, of course, for Baldizar, ruling El Supremo, high genie of the council of the power ten genies, and owner of the biggest and most powerful sky cruiser in the genieverse.

Designed by the professor, the cruiser, dubbed the Crimson Raptor, was truly a mechanical marvel but also a monster, depending on whether one was pleased to see its arrival or running in fear.

Constructed from materials sourced from the planet Earth, the sky cruiser, at two hundred paces long and with a beam of one hundred and a draught of fifty, was truly massive. Powered by electricity, each of its four huge inboard engines had eight forty-foot-long propeller blades, giving it total dominance over all creatures of the air. From upon high, the Crimson Raptor brought Baldizar's laws and punishment to all creatures below.

Its appearance was like that of a giant flying beetle, its armoured skin so robust and smooth that even the sharpest spear and arrow failed to scratch it. It had six downward curving gold-tipped horns, which, apart from inducing the fear of Jagdar into any creature that saw them descending upon them, also served as stout landing legs. The bridge was shaped like a rugged angular head, with two smaller but nevertheless vicious-looking horns. Its reflective black bridge windows were purposely designed to mimic one huge intimidating eye.

To further encourage his craft's fearful reputation amongst the gutter species, the professor, just prior to the Crimson Raptor's unveiling, had Baldizar's network of spies purposely spread rumours that it was armed with a fantastically new, awesomely devastating weapon. This weapon was known only as the Wrath of Jagdar.

On the underside of the raptor, just aft of the bridge and emblazoned on a pristine white circle in crimson and black, was Baldizar's personal emblem, the image of his war helmet with its six curved black horns. This likeness informed the council of the power ten genies in no uncertain terms that he was extremely comfortable using the illegal ancient black art of technology. It also proclaimed to all creatures, no matter what their species, that Baldizar, their El Supremo, was the real authority in the genieverse.

After a short journey from Fortress Hexx, the Crimson Raptor found the ancient temple in exactly the location where the sky cruiser's navigator predicted it would be. Slowly circling the valley, the pilot picked out an appropriate landing site and gently manoeuvred the giant down. As it neared the desert floor, the thrust from its four powerful electric motors blew up a tremendous dust cloud that temporarily obliterated the view in all directions. With the grace of a dancer, the pilot manoeuvred his ship into a position facing the idol before gently touching down. The six giant curved horns, each moving independently, stabbed deeply into the cold hard ground, filling the valley with the sound of crushing rock.

With the dust settling, the main gangway was lowered, and Baldizar disembarked, followed by his entourage, and walked the short distance to the valley entrance. There, the supreme genie stopped atop a sand dune and studied the temple below.

The ancient idol, sited in the sacred valley of the one true god, was an ideal location for the trial of the professor's so-called wonder weapon. Staring indifferently at the huge statue, Baldizar mused contentedly, *there'll be no genie spies to go running back to the genie council here!* With one of his heavy boots, he kicked sand blasphemously towards the statue. 'Pathetic creatures,' he said with a sneer. 'After all the great achievements that I have shown them, some gutter scum still openly worshipped that absurd deity, Jagdar.' Their undying allegiance to the so-called one true god baffled his cold, logical mind—it also niggled him like a stubborn, inaccessible itch.

Shaking the repugnant notion from his mind, he focused his thoughts back on the forthcoming test. To his left, standing a respectful pace behind was, as always, the professor. Dressed immaculately in his strange grey suit of Earth design, he stood silently watching, his lips pursed, his long bony fingers entwined together. Of course, the power ten genies council, along with every other inhabitant of Hexx, quietly mocked his lacklustre appearance. But if one stood before the cunningly devious human, he would see his courage evaporate faster than the morning mist.

Oddly, though, considering that the planet Hexx was cold all the year round, he was known for his permanent aroma of sweat. When quizzed about this, he protested that it was an undesirable side effect of his nervous energy, but others saw it as a betraying sign of weakness.

To all those that had met him, he was considered weirdly dangerous and to be avoided where possible. His knowledge of the ancient black art of technology made him important to El Supremo but gained him no friends amongst the chieftains and the general populace. However, if any of them had dared to peer more deeply into those beady, greedy little grey eyes, they would have been shocked. Because there, masked by a glaze of meek servitude, were the burning flames that betrayed his wicked ambitions of a treacherous empire-builder. In his hands, caged inside his long bony fingers, he tenderly cradled a small control box. His eagerness to start was almost palatable.

To Baldizar's right, at ease on his six powerful legs, waited Meggladar, his Chief Artisan. This centaur—half man, half Gadalakk horse—with nearly two centuries of accumulated knowledge was considered the finest engineer throughout the genieverse. He was also very superstitious. So, when by chance, a rare and very lucky Skallenian ruby moth just happened to flutter out of nowhere before them, Meggladar naturally assumed that Jagdar himself was bestowing their endeavour with blessed good fortune.

The moth, about the size of a baby's hand, danced mesmerizingly before Meggladar's grinning face before fluttering off towards Baldizar. In a lightning flash of metal, a crimson gauntlet snaked out and snatched its frail body from the air, its metal fingers mashing it to a pulp. The professor, normally uncaring about any creature, cringed awkwardly, unsure what to do. Meggladar, however, forgot himself, openly gasping in horror at such an evil act but instinctively snapping his mouth shut, fighting back bile.

Baldizar watched their reactions with cold silence then simply discarded the tiny, mangled creature's body with a flick of the wrist. 'Professor,' he hissed, 'begin the demonstration!' He viewed the war machine set up on the plain before him with uncertainty. Indeed, the creation, which the professor called Phalanx, looked impressive. Its cylindrical iron body and smooth domed top gleamed in the morning sun, but he wondered how it would fare against the timeless strength of granite. Turning slightly, he glared sideways at the fretting man and added, 'For your sake, Professor, this had better be impressive!'

Professor Ratchet Madspanner bowed dutifully to his master then excitedly shuffled away to the side. *Oh, I'll give you a demonstration all right,* he thought smugly, *one that will blow your egotistically primitive mind away, whilst of course neatly fulfilling the next stage of my plan.* He'd hated Baldizar from the very first moment the obnoxious tin man had plucked him from his severely damaged space shuttle all those years ago. However, being a master schemer, Madspanner knew that being close to the main man, albeit in a secondary capacity, was just where he needed to be. He was high enough up the chain of command to get what he needed, yet low enough to slip under the radar when necessary.

With great pleasure, he pushed a small button on his remote, and a sudden thunderous staccato roar shattered the peace of the whole valley. Standing calmly with a broad smile upon his face, he watched with glee as Meggladar reared up in fright, whinnying hysterically whilst Baldizar recoiled fearfully, his four metal arms gesticulating wildly in the air.

The first 20mm armour-piercing tungsten bullet hit the statue dead centre. The resulting explosion blew a dinner-plate-sized crater deep into the granite effigy, sending chips and dust billowing into the air. The machine's angry roar was so intense that even with his helmet on, Baldizar thought that his head would surely split. But even though the pain that assaulted his ears was unbearable, he found himself ghoulishly hypnotized by the sheer destruction that he was witnessing.

In the space of a dozen breaths, the Phalanx fired 4500 rounds at the granite statue, pulverizing it. After exactly sixty seconds, it ceased firing, its long smoking arm of six rotating gun barrels whining slowly to a halt. As the smoke cleared, Baldizar stared in awe upon the terrifying machine. Then, smiling, he looked towards the great statue of Jagdar, or rather, at its claws and knees, for everything else had vanished.

The professor found himself drilling a hole into the cold sand with the toe of his left shoe, such was his agitated excitement. He could almost feel Baldizar's restrained terror at the weapon's awesome power. He boldly sneered at the back of Baldizar's helmet. *Ten more weeks,* he mused. *That's all I need for victory to be mine. Beware, tin man, you pompous, draconian buffoon, for this usurper who stands in your shadow now will soon be ready to strike at that cold, wizened heart of yours!* As he stepped forward to speak, he noted that Baldizar's rigid metal body showed no outward signs of remorse at the profound act of heresy. 'The demonstration pleased you, my El Supremo?'

Baldizar's normally calculating mind was suddenly a maelstrom of evil thoughts. *If the black art can do this to solid granite,* he wondered, an audaciously evil grin forming on his lips, *then maybe, just maybe, the great god Jagdar himself is not as indestructible as he thinks.*

'The Phalanx gun will be disassembled and reassembled by Meggladar and his crew of engineers in its new site, as per your instructions, my El Supremo,' the professor said, not waiting for Baldizar to answer.

'Meggladar,' barked Baldizar harshly, watching with pleasure as the centaur snapped smartly to attention and briskly cantered over to him. 'It will fit, won't it? I don't like complications!'

'The dimensions of its new location are snug, my El Supremo, but I am confident that its reassembly will prove no problem.' Meggladar struck the ground repeatedly with a fore hoof in a sign of confidence. 'Your command will be obeyed, my El Supremo.'

'Good,' hissed Baldizar. 'And my other command?'

Meggladar glanced across at his busy team of engineers, who had already started to dismantle the weapon. 'My El Supremo, when the task is complete, I will personally execute them all myself.' There was no hint of remorse in his voice. 'There will be no careless talk!'

'Good,' hissed Baldizar. 'You're dismissed.' He watched the centaur salute then gallop away to join his crew. After a moment, he turned to the professor. 'Make sure that your weapon is installed in the great amphitheatre of Garrknock at least one moon before the festival of Atunka Gaar.'

'It will be so, my El Supremo,' the professor replied.

Baldizar turned to walk away then suddenly stopped. 'Oh, and one last thing,' he added. 'When all the necessary preparations are completed, kill Meggladar!'

Chapter 3

COWSHOT CHILDREN'S HOME.
DRUDGE ON THE MARSH.
SATURDAY, 24TH OCTOBER 2015.
8.30 AM.

S tars exploded in Archie's head as he fell onto the porch roof with a bone-rattling thud. The impact punched the air from his lungs.

'Hey, you up there!' shouted a gruff voice. 'Stand up slowly and keep your hands in the air, where I can see them!'

Struggling to breathe, Archie tried to stand but only managed to roll awkwardly onto his knees. 'G-G-Give me a minute,' he gasped. 'I can't breathe!'

'Take your time,' growled the voice. 'But I'm watching you!'

Kneeling like a dog, Archie shook the dizziness from his head. The first thing he saw through bleary eyes was the fallen length of drainpipe. Suddenly, it all came flooding back: the arrival of armed police and the Royal Navy bomb-disposal squad, his liberal use of illegal smoke and stun grenades, and of course, his attempted heroic escape along the window ledge. *It's good I stashed all my more illicit Internet purchases in the scrapyard,* he thought smugly, *or those coppers would have found them all by now!*

'Come on! Shift yourself, lad!' urged the gruff, impatient voice. 'You've had long enough!'

Wobbling unsteadily to his feet, Archie stared down at a very angry-looking SWAT-team police constable whose rifle, between retching coughs, was aimed squarely at his chest. The poor man's eyes were red and sore-looking, his nose streaming.

Archie tried to swallow, but his throat was too dry. 'Einstein's underpants,' he cursed anxiously, 'did my grenades do that?'

Staggering uneasily forward, Archie accidentally kicked the section of rusty drainpipe. He watched in cringing horror as it rolled off the porch roof, landed with a splash in a big puddle, and sent a wave of dirty water flying up to hit the scowling policeman square in the face.

'Oh God, I'm dead,' he gurgled pitifully. Archie watched in horror as the policeman's face turned an angry purple, his trigger finger tightening. He felt his whole body start to shake uncontrollably. *This can't be right,* screamed his mind. *You're only fifteen. You're too young to die.* After a few tense seconds, Archie sighed with relief as he watched the policeman's trigger finger relax.

'Climb down *now!*' the policeman commanded through gritted teeth.

'Y-Y-Yes, sir, Constable, sir,' said Archie meekly. 'Whatever you say, Constable, sir.' However, as Archie moved towards the edge of the roof, he suddenly noticed his homemade electric cattle prod lying on the floor, its tip immersed in a puddle. He causally touched an empty pouch on his SAS-style vest. *It's open,* he thought. *It must have fallen out when I fell.* Suddenly, he froze, his senses on edge. The puddle of water about the tip of his cattle prod was lazily flowing to the gutter then down the drainpipe before issuing into a large puddle at the entrance to the porch, the same puddle in which the incredibly angry policeman before him was very obligingly kneeling.

With no hesitation or regret, Archie flicked his right foot just enough to click on the electric cattle prod on with the tip of his boot.

Two things happened instantly. One, the copper leapt up and did a freaky four-hundred-volt-induced dance, and two, which Archie didn't foresee, his trigger finger clamped down hard.

Archie dropped flat, hugging the porch roof as gunfire filled the air, a hail of bullets zinging in all directions. Several police-car windows exploded, whilst inside the orphanage, children and coppers alike dived for cover as flying lead blew mini craters in the walls of the entrance hall, ricocheting off the iron stair rails with shrill pings.

As quickly as it had started, the gunfire ceased. The magazine was empty.

With an adrenaline-fuelled leap, Archie launched himself off the porch roof, landing with a solid thump on the roof of the nearest police Range Rover. He laughed victoriously at the sound of chaos coming from inside the building as he dropped safely to the ground.

'You'll not get me now, coppers!' he shouted brashly over his shoulder. 'Freedom's mine.' From a large pocket in his vest, he plucked two flares, igniting them with a quick twist before lobbing them backward into the porch. Within seconds, the air became thick with billowing purple smoke.

With chaos reinstated, Archie happily sprinted through the open orphanage gates and dashed out into the road, oblivious to oncoming traffic. On the far side, he took a well-practised running jump up onto an old stone mile marker and hurdled clean over the top of the thick bramble hedgerow. Landing with confidence on the two hay bales he'd placed there earlier, Archie rolled off and onto his feet then dived backward under the cover of the thick hedge.

Panting heavily, his moment of glory was short lived, as he suddenly felt the mass of brambles begin to shake violently. Fearing that it was the police, he scrambled forward, lurching up onto his feet just as a multi-coloured blur came bulldozing through the hedge.

Tripping over Archie, a hysterical figure tumbled headfirst into the long, wet grass, his arms and legs waving hysterically, his clothes torn to ribbons by the vicious bramble barbs.

'Archie,' Boff said, 'what have you done?'

Archie stared in disbelief at the panting, sweaty heap sprawled on the grass before him. Boff was a freaky-looking boy who resembled a ten-pound sausage squeezed into a two-pound skin, but although loathsome and frequently annoying, he was Archie's best and only friend.

'You cow pat, Boff, why did you follow me?' he asked as calmly as possible.

'Orphanage,' gasped Boff, frantically stabbing the air in the direction of the road. 'Look at the orphanage!'

Archie sneaked a peek over the hedge. For several seconds, he stared indifferently at the scene of chaos outside the orphanage. There was still a lot of screaming and shouting, although oddly, there seemed to be a column of black smoke emanating from one of the police cars. *How very odd*, he mused. Dismissing it, he turned back to Boff and asked again, 'So why *did* you follow me?'

'I wasn't going to follow you, you dunderhead,' Boff blurted angrily. 'But after you torched that police car, they spotted me climbing down from the porch roof and started yelling at me and pointing their guns. I was scared, Archie. I panicked and ran.'

Archie looked confused. 'I didn't torch a police car.'

'Oh yes, you did,' he snorted, gulping down several breaths, 'when you threw those last two grenades!'

'Those were smoke grenades, dummy,' laughed Archie.

'Oh yeah?' Boff scoffed. 'Well, I watched one bounce off a copper's helmet and fall straight through the shattered windscreen of one of the police cars.' Scrambling onto his knees, he looked nervously over the hedge. 'The grenade that went into the car wasn't belching smoke like the others, Archie. It had a bright-red flame on the end!'

Archie quickly and calculatingly brushed his hands over the many compartments and pockets in his SAS vest, the fingers of his left hand coming to an abrupt stop at a thin, empty pocket that should have been full. 'Oops.' He smirked ruefully. 'Wrong flares!'

'Wrong flares?!'

Archie ignored him and dared another peek. 'Oh deary, deary me.' He laughed, grinning at the fiercely burning police car.

The pair of them ducked instinctively as the patrol car exploded before their eyes, the blast shaking the hedge violently. Blown clean off the ground, the Range Rover flew up into the air, arcing in a slow somersault before crashing back to earth, right on top of another police car.

'Flipping heck.' cried Archie, punching the air victoriously. 'Two for the price of one. Rebellion rocks, coppers.'

Boff's jaw dropped open in disbelief. 'Archie, you've just destroyed two police cars, and people might be injured or worse.'

Archie looked at Boff with cold, uncaring eyes. 'Does this look like the face of someone who really gives a damn? They're the cops, the bronze, the soldiers of authority,' he growled. 'They're paid to take risks.'

'What about Sniffy, Moses Pete, Moon Pie, and the rest of the kids who live in the orphanage?' growled Boff, glaring fiercely at his one-eyed friend in disbelief. 'They're not!' Just for a second, Boff glimpsed a flash of remorse in the boy's single sapphire-blue eye. Then, like a spark blown out by the wind, it was gone.

'Children playing childish games,' Archie remarked, staring at the fire. 'It's time to grow up—I had to! I didn't have to be a rocket scientist to realise that I was the only child in the orphanage that all the visiting families *didn't* want to take home!' With that, he turned and stomped off along the edge of the field.

Boff had never seen the angry side of his friend before—even the odd eye patch he'd had all his life seemed to glow with rage. It was scary.

The field was huge and freshly ploughed, so a direct route across was out of the question. With all the rain that had fallen the night before, they would have been bogged down within a couple of strides, so the pair hugged the perimeter, jogging at a steady pace for nearly two miles. Occasionally, Archie hesitated, listening in the direction of the orphanage before quickly moving on again, eventually stopping in front of a huge old oak tree. Moments later, Boff came staggering along, finally crashing to the ground at Archie's feet, his sweaty face the colour of a ripe tomato and his heaving chest gasping for air.

Boff watched, intrigued, from the wet grass as Archie immediately busied himself by searching the ground to the side of the tree. Using the toe of his boot, he probed the soggy grass in several different areas before unearthing the end of a thick, dirty rope. He grasped it tightly with both hands and gave an almighty tug. The damp soil resisted just enough to make Archie work hard for his treasure, but eventually, after a loud sucking squelch, he wrestled a six-foot cylinder up from the mud.

'Wow!' exclaimed Boff excitedly. 'What's that, and how did you know it was there?'

Archie pulled the cylinder clear of its shallow hiding place and hurriedly brushed off the clumps of sticky dirt. 'Because I put it there six months ago,' he said over his shoulder.

'Why? Hey, wait a minute!' hissed Boff, all the dots in his mind suddenly joining up. 'You were expecting the police to call, weren't you?'

'Firstly, this is one of my many hidden escape pods.' He grinned. 'And yes, I sort of had a feeling that the cops would come calling soon.' Chuckling, he turned back to the cylinder. 'Considering my nefarious activities of late, I'm surprised they took so long.' He brushed the dirt from his baggy, brown, oil-stained three-quarter-length shorts and old red sweatshirt. 'I've been pushing my luck at the orphanage for some time now, so I made some preparations, just in case I had to leave in a hurry.'

'A hurry, my foot.' Boff struggled to his feet, eyeing the long silver cylinder suspiciously. 'And just how do you propose to escape in that?'

'Watch and see, cow pat. Watch and see.'

With a loud metallic snap, the cylinder sprung open like a giant pea pod, revealing a rucksack, a green army motorcycle helmet, and a funny-looking machine with two small wheels. Boff stood wide-eyed with fascination as Archie lifted the small machine out with practised ease, plopping it down on its wheels. Then with the flick of two catches, he unfolded a set of handlebars and a small button seat.

'Why, it's a toy scooter!' Boff said.

'Actually'—Archie was a tad annoyed by his ignorance— 'this is an original World War Two Welbike!'

Boff thought for a moment. 'Yeah, like I said, it's a toy scooter!'

'The Welbike, you dodo, was devised by the boffins at Station IX for use by the special-operation executives during the war. This particular one was actually dropped into German-occupied Holland during operation Market Garden by the Sixth Airborne Division.' He paused momentarily, awaiting Boff's acknowledgement of these stupendous facts, but Boff didn't respond.

'This model weighs seventy pounds and has a ninety-eight cc, two-stroke, single-cylinder engine with a twist-and-go transmission, giving it a top speed of thirty miles per hour.'

Slowly, Boff's thick red eyebrows knitted together in a vague form of frowning acknowledgement. 'Judging by its drab-green colour, I rather suspect that all this is military equipment?'

'What have I just said, you plonka?' Archie frowned, shaking his head.

'Where did you get this lot from?'

'eBay of course, my irritating friend. Even someone as dense as you must have heard of it.'

'So, what has this miniature heap of junk got to do with our escape?' asked Boff, ignoring his friend's snarky remark.

Laughing, Archie swung the rucksack onto his back and mounted the tiny machine. His eyes were cold, and his expression clinically detached. 'What do you mean, "our escape"'.

The sound of voices on the far side of the field stifled Boff's shocked reply. Both boys turned in unison to see a tiny group of madly gesticulating black-clad figures vigorously hacking their way through the hedgerow.

'Blimey, they've spotted us!' said Boff.

The Welbike's tiny engine coughed sweetly to life with the second kick. Twisting the throttle, Archie revved it several times to warm it up before letting it settle into a funny putting rhythm that sounded a bit like an angry bee in an empty tin can. 'Yeah, they've seen us,' he said.

In the distance, two of the figures raised their rifles. 'Flipping heck!' cried Boff in dismay. 'They're going to shoot us!'

'Don't be stupid, Boff. We're only kids from the orphanage.' He'd barely finished speaking when a high-calibre bullet struck the oak tree's trunk, inches from his head, its loud crack shattering the peace of the countryside. 'That was a warning shot,' offered Archie, twisting the accelerator. The little bike sprang forwards.

'Hey, Archie,' Boff cried in horror, 'where are you going? What about me?'

'What about you?' Archie laughed callously.

Boff glanced back at the mob of coppers who were squelching their way awkwardly across the field towards him. 'They're nearly halfway across,' he squeaked. 'What am I to—' When he looked back, Archie, perched on his tiny chugging bike, had already reached the farmer's gate. 'Archie!' yelled Boff. 'At least tell me where you're going!' Even from a distance, Archie's mocking laughter was offensively loud.

'I'm off to where no one will find me!' shouted Archie as he rode through the open gate. 'Sayonara, fathead!' They were the last words Boff heard as he watched the boy chug off around a bend and disappear out of sight.

Cursing aloud, Boff glanced anxiously back at the ragged line of quickly approaching mud-splattered coppers then ran to the open farmer's gate. 'Jagdar's teeth,' he said, 'I hate that damn kid. Ten years I've known him, and he runs off and leaves me.' He slammed the farmer's gate shut, rattling its big iron catch. 'Some mate he is!'

Chapter 4

THE HOLLOW MOON
OF OOOZALIUM,
THE ANTARES GALAXY.

Exploding fireworks filled the starry sky over the fabulously wealthy metropolis of Balaskadar, second city of the hollow moon, Ooozalium. It was carnival night.

On the tree-lined boulevards, an excited throng of creatures cheered and laughed as they watched a spectacular parade of dancers, acrobats, clowns and fire-eaters. The boisterous procession threaded its way through the streets of the city, flowing like a living ribbon of jovial light, colour, and sound. Voices were happy and full of laughter, whilst stomachs gurgled in anticipation of the mouth-watering delights to come. The night air was heavy with the tempting smells of toasted exotic flowers, tasty snacks, sweet meats, curries, and hot spiced wines.

In the packed quadrangle, the rich mingled freely amongst the poor and the wretched with no fear of molestation or robbery because it was the festival of the summer solstice. It was the only day of the year when it was legal to eat the famous snorting Gimbal mushrooms of Fargg, a delicacy that when chewed slowly induced a blissful state of sweet serenity. It felt a lot like getting drunk on Best Majestic Gutstrangler grog but without the brain-busting four-day hangover.

Also, of course, there was the fact that the second largest and without doubt the meanest force of minotaur chieftains in the known genieverse was garrisoned on Ooozalium. As a police force, the chieftains were second to none. The average minotaur stood seven feet tall, with a barrel chest rippling with muscles and arms and legs like hairy tree trunks. Adorning their massive, shaggy, black-haired bulls' heads were two creamy white horns, the tips of which were stained with the blood of those silly enough not to come quietly. Inside their dense skulls were brains just adequate to understand and obey orders and dumb enough to take head-on the unruliest of angry mobs. The image of an aggressively snorting chieftain standing with hands the size of bunches of bananas, resting on the pommels of a broadsword or battle axe, was indeed enough to dissuade even the most zealous brigand. Crimes of any kind were rare.

Ooozalium's reputation was legendary as a place where heaven and hell were two sides of the same coin. On its surface, living in colossal lavish palaces and dining on the finest foods that spungold could buy, lived the Harshniks, the keepers of Ooozalium. They were a race of creatures so draconian and powerful in the world of business that even the ruling governmental authority was loathed to pry too deeply into their affairs, even regarding the questionable liberty and acquisition of those helpless wretches who found themselves shanghaied and enslaved in its labyrinth of hellish mines.

The council of the power ten genies who governed the rest of the genieverse, led by their El Supremo, turned an obliging blind eye to the suffering and torment that went on unseen in the vast mining complexes inside the moon. So long as the supply of delicious Gimbal mushrooms continued to flow, the awkward question of morality was never raised.

Of course, wherever there was fabulous wealth to be found, cunning thieves coexisted, and that night was no different. Throughout the genieverse, apart from a certain bandit spider by the name of Flip-Flop Freddy, if one wanted something stolen, it was best to find a Mmicky. And the best Mmickys were a strange little creature of a mongrel species known as two-tailed Slugmen. Standing erect—when not drunk, which was most of the time—they averaged about three feet in height, without their stovepipe hats. They were a blend of two distinct halves. From the belly button up, they were human, but from the belly button down, they were slugs. They had no scruples whatsoever when it came to stealing, and their only true allegiance was to themselves. They would happily double-cross their own families for the price of a tankard of grog. However, as was often said with pride in the brothels and boozers of the criminal underworld, they were without doubt the best stealers in the business.

High above the carnival atmosphere, two thieving rogues peered warily out of two open windows set in one of the loftier levels of a grand-looking palace. Their two little human heads, with their dirty squashed piggy faces, sniffed the air for flying creatures. When happy that all was safe, they allowed their eyes to flow out of their heads on long stalks. With these, they peered around corners and pried under ledges. When they were absolutely sure no one was looking, they made their move.

With bulging bags of booty clutched tightly in their sweaty

hands, the pair slithered silently out of the windows and onto the rough plaster wall. After a cautious, slimy descent, the pair slipped safely into the shadows of a secluded back alley. With their sacks of ill-gotten loot swung over their shoulders, they quickly headed for the protection of the nearby slum town of Mudwollow.

'You know what, Skatt?' remarked the slightly larger slugman as they turned into Split Gut Lane. 'If that their snail, Grooobee, had a bit more up top in his noodle box, our growing-up life might have been right better.'

Skatt slid his sack off his shoulder and swung it around fast, striking his brother in the stomach, knocking the wind from him.

'Ow!' he cried. 'What was that for?'

Skatt groaned despairingly. 'Grooobaa. His name was Grooobaa, you twonka, not Grooobee. How many naffin' times do I have to tell you before it sinks into that thick head of yours? And for your information, our mangy freebooter of a father was a two-tailed Slugman, just like what we is. Not a blooming snail!'

At nearly forty inches high, Skatt's crackbrained brother Nogga was the tallest Mmicky in the neighbourhood. Lofty Nogga they called him—big on stature, short on brains.

'Ma ruined you with all them picture books and whatnot.' Skatt scowled, poking him hard in his podgy, hairy belly. 'Now shut your pie hole and show us what goodies you've pilfered from that fine lady's boudoir.'

Nogga rubbed his belly, mumbling. 'Don't pokes me, bro. You knows I don't like it!' He tried to pull his faded, tatty old waistcoat down over his stomach, but the bottom button pinged off in protest.

'Oh, don't poke me.' Skatt sniggered childishly. 'It makes me tummy sore.' He poked a dirty finger at his own face. 'I don't naffing care what you like.' He prodded his brother again, harder. 'Now shows me the goods, or I'll take a pointy stick to the whole of your fat, sluggish hide!'

Nogga cursed his older brother's bad temper but, sucking in his quivering bottom lip, swung a tatty canvas sack off his shoulder. It fell with a clattering clunk onto the cold, wet cobbles.

'Two naffin' candle sticks and a broken teapot,' grumbled Skatt disappointingly as he sank his sharp, pointed teeth deep into a candlestick. 'Jagdar's teeth,' he cried in disgust, spitting out chewed bits of metal. 'They're not even real! Them's knock-offs, you twonka.'

For the Mmickys, being a thief was not so much of a matter choice but a vocation to which they aspired. They were naturally lazy, and it was considered much easier to steal than to work. Throughout history, some of the most notorious vault robbers, pocket filchers, swag snafflers, and brigand boppers were two-tailed slugmen. And jolly proud of their heritage they were too. Also, tradition amongst these creatures was bickering, bartering, and splitting of the booty after the job. Unfortunately, it was during that moment of heated debate that the pair of hapless villains came well and truly unstuck, falling accidentally foul of the most dreaded figure of authority throughout the genieverse. Fate had them on a collision course with a huge figure wrapped from head to foot in a blood-red hooded cloak.

Split Gut Lane was a narrow, dimly lit, cobblestoned

excuse for a passageway that wound its way between tightly packed, rickety overhanging houses, decrepit shop fronts, and rat-plagued taverns. At one end was the ironically named Paradise Plaza, and at the other, Kelly's Web, which was home to murderers, thieves, cutthroats, and pirates. It was a place where, for the right price, anything could be purchased, and anyone disposed of.

Although of meagre dimensions, there was ample room in the lane for the mysterious cloaked figure to have skirted past the two Mmickys, but it chose instead to continue a direct course. Whether or not the mysterious figure assumed that the lowlife scum before him would naturally acknowledge his superior presence and immediately move out of his way, one would never know.

The figure's flowing pace caught Skatt with a hard glancing blow to the shoulder, knocking him roughly aside. His precious stovepipe hat flew off one way whilst he tumbled the other, bouncing off a grimy wall before falling face down in a muddy puddle, cursing and swearing.

Coughing and spluttering back upright, Skatt looked down angrily at his soggy, muck-splattered waistcoat. Despairingly, he spied his prized hat sitting atop a large pile of steaming shovelhead elephant poo. 'What the...?' he cried, outraged by his sudden ill fortune, splashing about furiously. 'Hey, you! Wilde!' he bellowed angrily, shaking a dirty fist at the back of the cloaked figure.

The tall figure drifted to a stop, the hem of his long cloak swirling the dank evening mist about his boots.

'Yeah, you, you naffing-great-clodhopping-gangly-worm brained toff!' cried Skatt, pointing a finger at the cobbles in front of him. 'Come right back here and try that again!' Skatt's colourful tirade of threats suddenly turned to a choking knot of fear, wedged tightly in his throat. As he watched the ghoulish figure slowly turn, he shivered as its wraithlike presence floated a full fist above the grimy cobbles.

'Are you addressing me?' asked a deep, cold voice from the depths of its crimson hood. The stranger's voice penetrated Skatt's head like spears of ice, sending him squelching backwards into a mud-caked wall.

The figure's scary appearance alone should have made the foolish Mmicky stop and think, but it didn't. The hooded figure watched in astonished silence as the small mud-covered Mmicky hesitantly slithered forward and dragged itself awkwardly out of the murky puddle. In an act of mind-numbing stupidity, Skatt felt his shaking right hand slowly move towards his belt, from which fingers more suited to cracking a safe or lifting a lady's purse rather rashly drew a pathetically small, short sword. 'Naffing toff, you'd better say sorry before I dice your kneecaps!' he demanded in a tone more of a mouse than a lion.

The scarlet figure floated menacingly forward. Its outline loomed up like the billowing clouds of a gargantuan storm, blotting out the lonely pool of smoky yellow light from the one working streetlamp.

Suddenly, Skatt found his courage robbed of its voice.

The stranger raised a sleeve, from which appeared a polished gauntlet of crimson.

Skatt's tiny brain went into meltdown, every cell screaming in terror as he dropped his sword and fell prostrate on the wet, filthy ground. Abject fear flashed through his whole being as he recognized the hand. It was none other than Baldizar, the supreme genie himself.

'My El Supremo, please forgive me,' he cried repeatedly, smothering the hem of Baldizar's cloak with grovelling kisses. In that fleeting moment of horrifying enlightenment, Skatt saw his whole miserable life flash before him. It didn't take long.

'Forgive me, my El Supremo. I didn't realise it was you,' he blubbered. 'Please forgive me. I begs you, please have mercy on your most humble servant, Skatt.' His snivelling request was tainted by the pungent tang of steaming urine. 'And if you could be finding it in your big merciful heart, please don't be turning me humble self into something unnatural.'

A soft light filled the figure's hood, illuminating the supreme genie's huge crimson-metal helmet, its demonic red glow embellishing the angular features of his cold, cruel face. 'Please wipe your tears and nose,' said Baldizar in a calm, soothing voice that wrapped Skatt's terrified mind in a false, honey-soaked kindliness. 'Be not afraid, for I am nothing if not benevolent!'

'Oh cheers, your Royal Holy Supremeness,' blurted a voice from behind Skatt. 'Me brovver and me is really big fans of you and your genie mates.'

Baldizar's gaze shifted to the owner of the second voice, his curiosity spiked by its laughingly barefaced sincerity. 'Why thank you. Nogga, isn't it?'

'You knows me name.' Nogga laughed, doffing his stovepipe hat respectfully with the boldness only a true halfwit could have. 'How about that, bro, our grandiose El Supremo here knows me name.' Then he looked up at

Baldizar with his beady little eyes and asked, 'Er, El Supremo, does that mean we're bezzy mates?'

No single creature of any known species had ever dared talk to El Supremo in such a blatantly candid manner before and lived. Baldizar was simultaneously aghast and intrigued. Leaning slowly forward, he stared down at the two quivering Mmickys through hellish red eyes as round as moons.

'Nogga,' he hissed like a snake about to strike. 'You must be the single most stupid creature in the entire genieverse.' The faintest hint of a smile flickered across his thin, cruel lips. 'But nevertheless, be you either foolhardy or suicidally brave, I like you.' In the same instant, he shot Skatt a withering glance of an intensity that singed his very trembling soul.

'Cheers, mate,' chirped Nogga. 'I likes you too!'

'Tell me, my despicable, filthy, scum-like street urchins...' Skatt smiled lamely, readily accepting the insult. 'If you could have one wish right now, what would it be?'

Skatt's tiny mind was only capable of four working modes: greed, more greed, cowardice, and self-preservation, the last one naturally being the strongest. He spoke immediately. 'W-W-Well, your godliness, I'd really likes some legs, so I could run really fast.' He tried to look as sincere as possible then hastily added, 'I'm really fed up with slivering everywhere.'

'Hmm,' Baldizar replied, his mind quickly deciphering the lowly creature's rudimentary thinking, 'legs for a mongrel two-tailed slugmen. Now, that's an original choice.' Without warning, he reached towards Skatt's shaking head, the mutterings of an ancient incantation spilling from his lips.

Paralysed with fear, Skatt could do nothing but watch, as if hypnotized by the tip of the approaching metal finger. Part of him had already accepted his fate. The other part was nervously peeing himself again. Fearing that his end had finally come, he braced himself for a horribly unnatural death. Yet as every muscle in his trembling body tensed itself to the point of snapping, oddly, nothing happened.

Or so it seemed at first. He hardly noticed the soft, tranquil rhythm rising in his head. It sounded like the tinny clanking harmonics of a cheap wind chime. Then it became louder and faster, like the hammer blows on a blacksmith's anvil. Without warning, Skatt was struck by the most awesomely terrible sensation. It felt as if an angry ogre had sat on his chest and rammed two long icicles up his nostrils. Then things got really freaky.

All the organs and bones in his body suddenly started jiggling about in a frighteningly peculiar, musical extravaganza. His pounding heart bounced about his rib cage as if it were a xylophone, whilst his kidneys used his spine as a washboard. Then a large portion of his lower intestines snaked their way up through his quivering guts and lassoed his stomach. The resulting bizarre strangling motion about his podgy belly induced a smelly trumpet solo of epic proportions from his quaking bottom. And as if all of that wasn't enough to embarrass the flea-ridden britches off any creature, his stubby little piggy nose suddenly chose to join in, blowing streams of snotty purple bubbles in perfect harmony with the beat of his wildly jiving body.

Without warning, Skatt's snout peeled open like a banana, revealing a long, slim new nose with a shiny black blob on the end. With a whimper, his frantic mind surrendered. There was only one thing left for him to do: bawl and blubber hysterically. Sucking in a huge breath, he filled his eight lungs to bursting point then screamed.

Nogga, on the other hand, was finding his big brother's painfully weird predicament very entertaining, especially his loud woofing. He watched in bemused silence as his brother's ripe-yellow skin with its trademark brown splotches exploded into a speedily growing coat of mangy, tan-coloured hair.

'You wish to be able to run fast,' said Baldizar. 'Are four legs enough?'

Skatt, standing dazed and shaking, simply nodded dumbly. What was left of his fragile mind wasn't exactly sure what had just happened.

'Oh, Skatt,' sniggered Nogga, 'what a silly sight you look!'

Skatt's head dropped in dismay, only to see through red, puffy, tearful eyes a scruffy pair of paws where his leathery tubby belly had been.

'Oh, bro, you're a mutt.' Nogga laughed hysterically. 'And you're a flipping ugly mutt too!'

Miserably, Skatt squatted on his new hind legs. His precious, tailor-made waistcoat flapped about his much smaller body, and his stovepipe hat floated in the puddle next to him.

Towering above him, Baldizar's thin lips curled at the edges in a mocking smile. He then turned his attention to the other giggling Mmicky and said, 'Now, Nogga, my newfound friend, what would you like?'

Nogga removed his stovepipe hat respectfully and scratched his big leathery head for a moment. He went to speak, thought better of it, then scratched his bum instead.

'Surely there must be something you need or have always

secretly desired?'

'W-W-Well, methinks there's one thing I'd likes to try, if I may,' he said politely, glancing nervously across at his brother.

'And that is?' hissed Baldizar.

'Well, Boss…'

The supreme genie leeringly smiled. '"Boss." Yes, I rather like the sound of that,' he mused. 'Direct and respectful. Carry on, Nogga.'

'Oh, righto, Boss. Well, me old ma said I have a brain…' For Nogga, the process of stringing words together wasn't easy, and every now and then, he would momentarily phase out.

El Supremo, frowning impatiently at Nogga's blank face, clicked his fingers, the very tips sparking like mini lightning as they touched.

Instantly, Nogga continued as if nothing had happened. 'But no sparks to make it work.' He smiled up at Baldizar with a naive innocence. 'Could you make me brain work, Boss?'

El Supremo, a creature with a heart carved from ice a thousand years old, found himself almost touched by the street urchin's genuinely honest request. Reaching out, he gently tapped the head of the starstruck two-tailed slugman with his metal fingertip.

Skatt didn't understand the evil magic that the supreme genie had just used upon him, but he did know that he was more terrified than he could ever remember. So, whilst El Supremo was busy with his brother, he turned unsteadily on his four new legs and slinked cowardly to a nearby dark corner. There at least he could watch Baldizar's diabolical doings from the safety of the shadows.

'You're on your own now, little bro,' he muttered fearfully. 'And may Jagdar have mercy on you!'

A tidal wave of soapy bubbles whooshed into Nogga's empty head, and when his watery eyes registered full, someone threw in a bag of hyperactive porcupines. The rush of bursting bubbles felt so real that for a moment, he actually thought that he was back at his homey tree stump, sloshing about in the battered tin tub, having his annual bath. It was a lovely sensation, and he even lifted one hand to an ear to wipe away some imaginary soap suds.

However, when the last bubble burst, someone jammed a string of woolly ping-pong balls into one ear then popped them out of the other. Briskly backward and forward, the string moved, picking up speed, the being responsible oblivious to his squeals. The feeling of having one's brain vigorously dried with a chain of lumpy balls of cotton wool was, to say the least, unusual, but it felt weirdly agreeable to Nogga. However, it was over in seconds, and soon he was left with a wonderfully snug feeling of intellectual wellbeing.

'How does that feel, Nogga?' asked Baldizar. 'Nice fit?'

Nogga gingerly touched his head all over, as if feeling it for the very first time. 'Hmmm, nice, very nice indeed, Boss,' he purred smugly. Then he bowed graciously and added, 'An exceptional fit, cut by the master tailor himself!'

Baldizar's eyes narrowed evilly. *Now this zealous spawn of the gutter has a modicum of intelligence, he may well be useful,* he deliberated, whilst wringing his gauntlets together in a shower of sparks. *A new addition to my spy network, perhaps!* Then he glanced disapprovingly at Skatt. 'Now, what shall we do with your brother?'

'Begging your indulgence, my El Supremo, in the matter of my older brother, could you humour me and leave him as a dog?' Nogga asked with a wicked smile. 'It will make a nice change for me to be doing the poking and kicking for once!'

A chill breeze sprang from nowhere, swirling the ground mist and making Skatt shiver.

'This was indeed a fortuitous meeting, my slimy new friends,' hissed Baldizar, 'for I have a *problem* that a cunning pair such as yourselves might be able to help me with.'

'It would be our pleasure, my El Supremo,' said Nogga, bowing graciously.

'Well then, won't you accompany me to the rather seedy-looking alehouse over yonder?' said Baldizar, floating away down the alley. 'We shall seal the deal.'

'Ah, the Duck's Guts,' declared Nogga, smiling. 'Considered by some as the sleaziest den of villainy you'll ever find in Kelly's Web. Mind you, Boss,' he added, licking his lips hungrily, 'on a purely culinary note, the chef in that despicable establishment is renowned for serving a mean hedgehog-and-toadstool pie on a Saturday night!'

'Really?' Baldizar scoffed. 'I must be sure to remember that morsel of gastronomic information, should I ever decide to lower my standards and dine in the sewer!'

The supreme genie turned quickly, his crimson cloak billowing in the cold night air as he floated towards the tavern, beckoning Nogga to follow with a curling metal finger. 'Enough of this puerile chitchat, for I have an important rendezvous within.'

As they approached the tavern, Nogga noticed a group of

ruffians loitering menacingly to one side of the door. They were heavily armed and mean-looking, and they had been carefully watching the hooded figure for some time. His Mmicky nose immediately sensed trouble. With their courage buoyed up by their numbers and too many tankards of ale, the gang viewed the stranger as easy pickings. The nearest creature, a black-hearted cinnamon spider, rose, his battle-scarred face a sneering mask of overconfidence.

Baldizar approached him, and in a move so quick that Nogga barely saw it, the supreme genie decapitated the poor creature with the lightning slash of a hidden blade. As the cinnamon spider's head toppled from its neck, his comrades suddenly lost their nerve and quickly vanished down a murky alleyway. Baldizar neither glanced to the side nor broke step but simply carried on to the tavern door.

At the door, he raised a gauntlet and knocked three times, each impact of his metal hand making the letterbox rattle. A small hatch in the door, no bigger than a hand, slid open. 'Who is it, and what do you want?' rasped a grog-sodden voice.

'I am a stranger in these parts who is looking for the one who goes by the name of Serpentina,' stated Baldizar.

The small hatch slid closed, and for a few moments, they could plainly hear muffed voices talking inside. Then the hatch slid back open, and a sweet feminine voice spoke. 'What is the rhyme of the chosen ones?'

To this question Baldizar replied,

> 'To enter the race, a collar you'll wear,
> a sign of the maggot for those who dare.
> Read me a riddle and still be blind,

not with your eyes. See with your mind.
Buried in legend, a myth lost in age,
a legacy of Merlin, the one true sage.
The fangs are hope. These you must find
to bring all together in freedom kind.
Mark my words. They're true and clear.
Heed them not, and it's dusting you'll fear.'

Before his words had faded, they heard the clunking of heavy iron bolts being withdrawn, allowing the heavy tavern door to creak slowly open. Nogga and Skatt, who were eagerly craning their necks around the supreme genie's legs, were astounded to see a figure clad in emerald-green armour, standing in the doorway and backlit by the smoky yellow lights from within. They could plainly see from the cut of her armour that she was a striking female. The single vivid-blue horizontal stripe that crossed her face was her personal signature, renowned throughout the genieverse, and emphasized her beautiful golden cat's eyes.

Skatt, shaking fearfully, stood with his head bowed and his new tail firmly between his legs. Not only were he and his brother standing alongside the most powerful genie in the whole of the genieverse, but they'd been joined by Serpentina, the most infamous assassin of all.

Chapter 5

EARTH.
SOUTH COAST OF ENGLAND.
OLD McGINTY'S SCRAP YARD.

As the crow flew, from the old oak tree to Archie's secret destination was just over two miles. However, as going through the town centre was out of the question, he chose a more discreet route, skirting around the edge of Drudge on the Marsh. It was a detour of an extra three miles but no problem for his trusty Welbike.

Although the sky was grey and overcast, there was a warm breeze tickling the leaves in the trees, and the rain from last night's storm gave the air a fresh, clean smell. Archie felt more alive at that precise moment, bouncing along through puddles and mud, than he had for months. *If this signals the start of my great adventure, then so be it*, he thought defiantly, a bold smile upon his face. *To hell with the past. Bring on the future.*

Then an uneasy image popped into his mind. It was of Boff, pasty faced, knees trembling, rooted in the mud, and surrounded by angry, armed policemen. He'd deserted his friend, leaving him to face the wrath of the local constabulary for what were basically his crimes.

It should have troubled him greatly. But worryingly, it

didn't. And with a total lack of concern, he cast the ugly thought from his mind and rode on, callously leaving his friend to his fate.

The last leg of his detour took him away from the village and up onto an old hiking track that ran up over the old chalk hills and towards the sea. At its highest point, he stopped to admire the view. He stared in silence, as he had done there many times before the boundary of bushes that bordered the edge of the chalk cliffs grew too thick. Off in the distance was the river Dweeble, and in between lay a geek's paradise, his very own private El Dorado: old McGinty's scrapyard.

Sprawling across the landscape like a mammoth metal scab, the scrapyard covered nearly twelve square miles, making it by far the largest scrap-metal dealership of its type in Europe, even boasting its own rail terminal and river berth. Its motto, formed with a collage of scrapped items welded to a huge sign that was held aloft by four massive fourteen-inch battleship gun barrels over the main gates, simply read: IF IT CAN BE SCRAPPED, WE'LL TAKE IT!

It was a massive jigsaw of rusting cars, vans, buses, lorries, blackened and scorched boilers of all shapes and sizes, diced-up aircraft, boats, and small ships. It even had two decommissioned submarines. Scattered amongst the rusty graveyard and filling the gaps were hundreds of pyramids boasting the wrecked, smashed, and dismantled remains of once-proud machines.

Taking centre stage in the metal mayhem stood the Dragon, a mighty machine that roared like a waking monster, with massive hydraulic iron jaws that could eat a whole ten-ton truck in one mouthful and poop it out three minutes later as a one-metre cube of crushed metal. All around the Dragon, teams of gas cutters and wrecking crews were constantly cutting old wrecks into bite-sized meals, which a crab crane would then feed to the ever-hungry metal-devouring monster. From all sides leaked small rivers of oily water, seeping away from the Dragon as if it were spilling the blood of its victims.

To the odd passer-by who braved the lonely cliff path, the scrapyard was an eyesore, its disagreeable stench of oil, rust, and decay fouling the breeze upon which it was carried, soiling their clothes and souring the nose. It was a miserable place to hurry past with no looking back.

But to Archie, the scrapyard was his sanctuary, his home away from the home. There were no council rules and regulations there, just his limitless imagination and a wealth of unwanted mechanical hardware. It was a place full of technological rubbish, where anything was possible, and a budding genius could thrive in private. It was Archie's own private playground and the hiding place of his special secret.

As far as the eye could see in both directions, the cliff top was edged with an impenetrable weave of thorn bushes, brambles, and the odd weather-worn tree. Even the old coastal footpath itself was overgrown, with a plentiful scattering of rabbit pellets holding testament to its only frequent visitors.

Archie twisted the throttle on his Welbike and chugged slowly alongside the thorny barrier. After a short distance, he found a large oddly shaped rock nestling in the long grass.

He'd just flicked down the bike's side stand and was about

to get off when a familiar voice asked, 'And where exactly do you think you're going?'

'Blimey,' groaned Archie, his head snapping around in surprise. 'How did you get here?'

'Well, as you so accurately pointed out back in the field'— Boff smiled smugly— '*you're* the one the police are looking for, so I merely took a nice stroll through town.'

Archie eyed him suspiciously. 'That might explain how you got here so quickly,' he hissed irritably. 'But just how did you know that I would come here?'

'Archie, if there's a boring centre to the universe, it's Drudge on the Marsh. The only good thing about this place is the road out of it! And that road, my disagreeable friend, leads here!' It was a spur-of-the-moment lie that he hoped Archie would believe. *He may be obnoxious,* thought Boff, *but he's not stupid.*

Archie gave a loud, annoyed snort then turned his attention to the large rock. Bending at the knees, he wrapped his arms about the boulder and heaved.

'And the best of luck moving that.' Boff laughed heartily, but his sarcasm was short-lived. As he watched in utter amazement, the boy effortlessly plucked up the boulder then placed it neatly to the side. Hopping back on his motorbike, Archie rode through the gap, shouting over his shoulder for Boff to close the gate behind him. Striding forward, Boff was amazed to find that the large rock wasn't a rock at all but a plastic imitation. Miffed by the deception, Boff looked up just in time to see Archie ride clear off the cliff's edge.

'Archie!' he screamed, but it was too late. Sprinting in a panic, his trembling legs stopped only inches from the edge.

He stared out into the void in silence, his mind numb with shock. 'Oh, you stupid, idiotic human youngling,' he said, 'Baldizar's going to hang me for this—and on the very last day of my sentence as well!'

'Boff, you're talking to yourself again!' came an amused voice from below. 'Oh, and be careful. The path's not exactly straight.'

Boff stared down at the area at the base of the cliffs, his watery eyes quickly finding the source of the laughter. He was relieved to see the boy alive—no hanging today. However, a tiny part of him would have been deliriously happy to see Archie's very annoying, broken body in a splattered puddle of red. 'How did you get down there so fast?'

'Look just in front of your big clumsy feet, Boff!' shouted Archie. 'What do you see?'

Boff looked confused. 'Nothing. Just the white-chalk ground where you're standing.'

'Do you trust me, Boff?'

'Definitely not!' he retorted loudly.

'Oh well,' Archie sighed, not really caring. 'You can stay up there and enjoy the view, then!'

Chapter 6

Cursing and snarling, Boff exploded in a short but brutal attack on a nearby tuft of grass, which he sent flying over the cliff's edge with great satisfaction. However, to his utter astonishment, it didn't fall—it simply hung in mid-air.

The previous night's storm had made the edge of the chalk cliff damp and crumbly, and Boff being Boff, he rather stupidly leaned forward for a better look.

Screaming, he toppled into the void but immediately smacked onto something invisible and ridiculously hard. He barely had time to whoop for joy at the thought of not falling to a horrible death when he suddenly felt himself start to slide uncontrollably forward and down.

Consumed by fear and out of control, Boff felt his body spiralling earthward in a wildly accelerating drop. Faster and faster, he went, in tighter, torturous circles, until suddenly, like a thrown beanbag, he hit the ground and tumbled.

With a skidding thud, he eventually landed face down on the chalky soil, his battered chest letting out a very loud and painful oomph. Dazed and confused, Boff lay there, sucking in dust and blowing out bubbles.

Archie dropped a bottle of water next to his groaning head. 'Have a drink.' He sniggered. 'I think you need it.'

Boff groaned and rolled onto his back, snatched the bottle, ripped off its top, and took a large gulp. 'What the hell was that?' he demanded groggily.

'Blimey, Boff, where's your backbone?' Archie asked, helping him up. 'It was only my secret entrance, not a flipping torture chamber.'

Gripping Archie's shoulder to steady himself, Boff stared in the direction Archie pointed, but he still couldn't see anything. 'What secret entrance?' he asked, puzzled.

Archie guided him forward until his hands suddenly touched something. 'Feel it?'

'Yes. Yes, I do.' Boff scratched his head. 'But I don't see anything.'

Archie walked him backward several paces. 'Don't look for a solid structure. Look for a faint outline. Use your peripheral vision.'

Boff tilted his head this way and that until he suddenly glimpsed a ghostly image out of the corner of his eye. It was a huge conical structure with a domed top that was easily level with the cliff top. Then it dawned on him. 'It's a helter-skelter'—he gasped in amazement— 'one of those old fairground rides.'

'Correct.' Archie smiled proudly.

'But why paint it white?' asked Boff. 'You can't see it?'

'Of course you can't see it, you galactic plonker.' Archie groaned and threw his hands up in dismay. 'If it were bright red and yellow, it wouldn't be much of a secret entrance now, would it?'

'Flipping dangerous if you ask me,' grumbled Boff.

Boff turned to view the scrapyard. In the centre was a huge

block made up of old, rusting, London double-decker buses, flanked on each side by rows of battered old coaches. Off to one side, there were also two disused road tankers and a tangled heap of curving roller-coaster track. Stored precariously on top of the old buses was more track, but it appeared to be in a straight line, one end of which vanished somewhere within the block of buses.

Taking a deep breath, he found himself coughing throatily. The atmosphere of the place, heavy with used oil and rust, bit at the back of his throat, leaving a bitter tang that he couldn't quite spit out. He didn't like the mechanical graveyard—it made him feel uncomfortable.

He kicked a battered car headlamp and watched it tumble across the road, splashing to a halt in a water filled pothole. 'This place is a dump,' he proclaimed.

'To you, maybe,' replied Archie. 'To me, it's a land of untold possibilities.'

'Possibilities!' He waved his hands about. 'What, this pile of junk?'

Archie picked up an old electric motor and gave it a quick visual examination. 'It's like this. Boff, my retarded wart of an unwanted companion, you see things for what they are, whereas I see things for what they could be! That's because I have two things that you'll never possess.'

Boff glared at him. 'Oh yeah, and just what would they be?'

'Firstly, an imagination!'

'Huh. A fat lot of good that's done you. Most of your inventions have been failures.'

Archie dismissed his comment with a casual laugh, although deep down, the truth hurt.

'So, my cocky young friend, what's number two, then?'

Archie's smile quickly returned as he pulled a sliver of plastic from his wallet. 'This!'

'You've got a credit card?' Boff snorted in disbelief. 'Oh no, no, no—you have to be eighteen and have a job to get one of those.'

Archie flipped the card over. 'Mr Horace B. McGinty. American Express Platinum Card.'

Boff's jaw dropped with a loud pop. 'You've got Old Man McGinty's credit card?'

'Yup. We've been friends, and I use the term loosely, for many years now,' declared Archie, sliding the credit card safely back into his wallet. 'The old fool treats me like the son he never had. He gave me the use of this card four years ago when I needed some *special equipment* for an experiment.' He turned slowly on the spot, gesturing grandly with open arms. 'He gave me full use of this end of the yard.' He nudged Boff sharply in the ribs and winked knowingly. 'He's even ordered his staff to keep out.'

Some distance away, basking in the late-morning sun, a pair of keen eyes watched the boys as they walked over to one of the old double-decker buses. So intent were they with their own business that neither of them noticed the small scruffy dog lying next to the flat front wheel of a wrecked coach.

'Skatt, get out of view,' ordered Nogga.

Skatt rose slowly, yawned, then jumped up into the coach. 'Bro, did you see that skinbag fall down that big twirly thing? What a twonker!'

Nogga laughed in agreement. 'Only having two limbs to walk on is a seriously freakish disability. Even dogs have sense enough to have a limb on each corner!'

No sooner was Skatt back onboard than the leathery tip of one of Nogga's two tails whipped out and stung him on the rump.

'Ouch—what was that for?' yelped Skatt.

'Boss said we were to stay out of sight, observe, and report. Got it?'

Skatt shuffled quickly backward out of whipping range, his precious waistcoat dragging in the dirt. There were only three things of importance to a Mmicky: his credibility as a thief and his precious waistcoat and hat. Made of the finest Truglian bat silk, Skatt's waistcoat had once been the envy of the brotherhood, but it hung like a rag from his new, wretched body. And Jagdar only knew where his precious scarlet-beaver-skinned hat was.

'Okay, okay!' snarled Skatt. 'So how long have we got to stay on this stinking planet, anyway?' he asked, staring anxiously out of a cracked window at all the strange-looking machines that surrounded them. 'I hate machines. Them's the spawn of the ancient black art of technology and no mistake. Ma always warned us to stay clears of them, and I thinks we should heed her words.'

'Jagdar's teeth.' Nogga sighed disapprovingly. 'We work for El Supremo, and he's the meanest, most powerful genie in the entire genieverse, so somehow I don't think a few old rusty machines are going to bother us. Do you?'

Skatt, seeing his brother's two tails start to quiver, quickly changed the subject. 'Aye, bro, as we now work for El Supremo, is we going to get free tickets to the festival of Atunka Gaar?'

Nogga's face lit up. 'Baldizar himself told me that our mission on this grubby little planet would be finished before midnight.'

The fact that his brother was using El Supremo's name filled Skatt with both dread and confidence.

'Furthermore, he assured me that two of the best seats in the great amphitheatre of Garrknock had been reserved just for us.' Nogga licked his lips with hungry anticipation. 'This festival of Atunka Gaar is going to be the best ever and certainly one the genie council will remember for a long, long time.'

'The best ever!' repeated Skatt eagerly.

Nogga laughed. 'The best ever. Apparently, he's got something special organised for the council of the power ten genies. All we have to do is watch out for a signal from that human professor bloke and do as were ordered.'

'Hey, do you think old hollow-legs Squiffy will have a grog bar on the go?'

'Oh, I hope so.' Drool dripped from the corner of Nogga's mouth. 'The last time I had a few tankards of Best Majestic Gutstrangler grog, I was hallucinating for weeks!'

'Ooh, yes, Best Majestic Gutstrangler,' Skatt said fondly, but his smile turned sour. 'Better than the armadillo's spit they call grog here.'

Nogga tossed a big plastic container to him. 'Add some of this stuff, bro. It gives this pig swill a bit of a bite.'

'What is it?' he enquired, marvelling at the shiny blue liquid.

'Something called brake fluid!'

Skatt nodded then looked at the two boys. 'So, what's so irksome about them two, bro?'

'See the one with curly white hair and the eye patch?'

'What, the one what looks like a big bog brush?'

'Yes.' Nogga chuckled at the comparison. 'El Supremo has an extra-special interest in that one.'

'And the other ugly one?'

Nogga lied nonchalantly. 'He's of no importance.'

Skatt eyed his brother suspiciously, his hairy dog brows all crinkly and rough. 'What did you mean' he began warily, 'when you said the genie council won't forget this Atunka Gaar?'

Nogga turned and smiled at his brother. His eyes were wide and scarily glazed, his lips twitching excitedly at the corners. Skatt had never seen his brother like that before. It was well creepy.

'We're Mmickys, right?'

'Yeah,' acknowledged Skatt uneasily.

'What's the ultimate goal of our species?'

'Species?'

'Sorry,' said Nogga sarcastically, 'word too big for you. Try "our kind"!'

'Oh, you means us Mmickys. Well, that's as blooming obvious as a wart on old Jagdar's snout. To be the bestest blooming thieves in the land.'

Nogga smiled from ear to ear. 'And what's the biggest robbery that your tiny pathetic mind can think of that would put us in the history books as the greatest thieves ever?'

Skatt, whilst dislodging several fleas from his ear with a good scratch, pondered this question. 'Er, robbing Sissy Flapjack's Spungold Emporium on Blogger Street!'

'No.'

'I know,' added Skatt excitedly. 'The fabled, jewel-encrusted artificial leg of General Zod Zod Baawonga the Flatulent?'

'Cheeky. I like your thinking, bro, but those would only make us famous.' He slithered over to Skatt, carrying an unusual carpet bag. 'But I don't want us to be famous. I want us to be *infamous!*'

'Well,' said Skatt, somewhat confused, 'what else is there?'

Nogga licked his lips then recited an old poem that their mother used to say when they were grubs:

'Out of sight, but plain to all,
A big square room as round as a ball.
No bolts to slide, no locks to click,
So, saunter in and take your pick.'

'By the curly horns of Jagdar,' gasped Skatt, spilling his grog, 'you're not blooming serious? Please, bro, I begs you, tell me you're not contemplating… *that!*'

Nogga's eyes sparkled like diamonds in the sun. 'Why not?' he snapped, his tone deadly serious. 'It's the ultimate robbery.'

'No, bro, not the waking-dream vault. Not where the council of the power ten genies stow all their treasure!'

'Yesss,' Nogga hissed, sounding rather like a snake. 'And what a treasure it's rumoured to be.'

'But bro, it's not real. That's why it's called the blooming Waking Dream Vault. It's a blooming myth. No one's ever spied it. It would be easier to find a shadow in the noonday sun than that there vault!'

Nogga winked at his brother. 'But I know where it is.'

Skatt's incredulous laughter instantly dried up. 'You do?'

'Yes.' From inside the carpetbag, he withdrew a large scroll then spread it out on the deck of the bus. 'Look at this.'

'Welcome to my inner sanctum,' announced Archie proudly.

Boff stared, unimpressed. 'It's a clapped-out old double-decker bus, Archie!'

Archie beckoned him on board, waving his hands along the seating area. 'Correct but check out the inside.'

Stepping in, Boff glanced into the worn and tatty driver's cab, then at the dirty stairwell that curled up behind it, leading to the upper deck. 'Yeah, well, I'm looking, but all I see is a manky old bus!'

Just behind Archie was a faded poster depicting a family on a day trip to London. He placed his right thumb on the father's head and pushed firmly. With a hiss of air, a cleverly disguised door slid open. Archie grinned at Boff. 'Thumbprint recognition to open the door. Cool, huh? Now, you may enter my personal sanctuary.'

Reaching in, Archie flicked a switch. Boff found himself staring into a room that could have come straight out of a science fiction film—it was a true geek's paradise. But as he gazed in awe, his wondering eyes unexpectedly came face-to-face with a pair of evil, red, glowing eyes housed in a machine man that was obviously designed for death and destruction. Boff screamed.

Archie laughed. 'It's a life-size model, you drongo. It's a T-1000 Terminator—you know, from the film!'

Boff tried to laugh it off, but his fear of technology was deep-rooted.

'Do you like the rest of my little collection?' asked Archie, pointing at the walls.

Boff hurried quickly past the inanimate monster and focused on the many shelves beyond that were cluttered with dozens of miniature models of strange flying machines. He recognized many of them from the TV programmes and films that Archie was always prattling on about. However, on the right side was a more sinister, purposefully built rack containing eight futuristic weapons.

Archie noticed Boff's lumpy Adam's apple bobbing up and down anxiously. Carefully, he plucked one from the rack. 'This is a multi-phase, high-intensity-laser rifle,' said Archie, pressing a small button then watching with pride as it glowed to life. 'Zap!' he cried, laughing as Boff nervously leaped backward in shock. 'It's a toy, you drongo. Egad, you're so pathetic.'

Boff, feeling his temper rising, sucked in a deep breath and pushed past the boy. To his left was a small workshop area, housing two benches covered in a mishmash of electrical and mechanical debris and tools. Farther down were banks of machine control panels, alive with blinking green, red, and amber lights, dials, levers, and switches of all shapes and sizes. In the exact centre of the left wall console was one rectangular panel that stood out from all the others. Six inches square, its backing plate was brightly coloured with diagonal black-and-yellow stripes, like some weird rectangular bumblebee. Standing alone were two big buttons. The left one was large, round, and green, with the word LAUNCH written in large capital letters above it. The other was bright-red and labelled ABORT.

There was also a bank of TV screens, one of which displayed a live video feed of the main gate to the scrapyard.

There was even a radarscope tucked in the corner, its bright-orange screen silently sweeping in circles. At the far end a long table sat on the left, with an architect's angled drawing board on it. To the right stood a bank of computer games and an old Astro Blaster pinball machine. Finally, tucked up in the corner, a food-and-drink vending machine was built into the centre of an overflowing set of floor-to-ceiling bookshelves. The far end of the room was a large semi-circular window with thick black curtains drawn across.

Typical geek, he mused, letting his eyes rove over the mishmash of bookshelves and panels. *Be wary of machines, for they are the product of the ancient ones, born of the evil black art of technology,* whispered the voice of reason in his head. *Tread carefully, for they can never be trusted.* Boff found himself unconsciously nodding in agreement. *What's more,* added the voice as a sinister afterthought, *can you completely trust a teenage boy who draws his curtains during the day?*

Archie had moved to the far end of the room and was standing with his back to the curtains. His arms were folded across his chest, his legs planted firmly apart. Boff strode forward and brushed his defensive posture aside.

'Jagdar's teeth, Archie, you raving lunatic!' Boff shouted, ripping the curtains aside, his eyes wide with horror. 'You've built *another* mechanical monster!'

Archie opened a small door and stepped calmly out into the sunshine. 'This situation reminds me of a passage out of an old horror story,' he said in a scholarly tone, shrugging off Boff's hysterical rant. 'It was that most bezzy of books,

Frankenstein, by Mary Shelly. You are naturally the dim-witted, God-fearing priest who is forever the pessimist and only sees my creations as pure evil. Whereas I, on the other hand, being the well-educated scientist and born optimist, see my machine as a thing of beauty and a true enhancement of mankind's future quest for knowledge.'

'Codswallop!' squawked Boff, thumping his clenched fists down hard on the machine's shiny metal skin.

'Careful, you clod!' shouted Archie, angrily pushing him aside. 'This is a highly technical prototype.' Quickly flipping open his phone and selecting a specific page, he sighed thankfully as he was greeted with a row of green lights. 'There's nine months of design and construction here,' he lectured, his face stern. 'This model is worth over fifty grand, you drongo!'

Boff snorted defiantly, his chest heaving as he hesitantly circled the craft. 'This thing looks nothing like your other rockets,' he said, feigning interest. 'It's not a long tube. It's more'—he stared at its rounded front and broad back, its triangular wings, and its odd, long, fishlike tail— 'like an animal.'

Archie smiled with great pleasure. 'Yes, this design is revolutionary, and yes, its origins are from the animal kingdom. The two-metre triangular wingspan and the rather unusual cockpit are based on a manta ray, whilst the fuselage and its long tail mimic a whale shark.' He touched its smooth aluminium skin lovingly. 'Hence its name, the Skyshark.'

Boff was many things, but aggressive, he was not. So, a hammer blow from him ranked between being annoyed by a fly and struck by a foam mallet. However, to the party of foraging earwigs that had entered Archie's prototype flying machine via a small vent during the night, it was an earthquake.

The titanic shockwaves struck the group as they happily explored a wonderfully weird new world of freaky, shiny flower-like things hidden amongst a jungle of tasteless colourful creepers. Shaken violently off their claws, the fear-struck earwigs lashed out with their miniscule legs and pincers, desperately trying to snag a hold onto anything to save their puny lives.

Unfortunately, Lady Luck was out shopping that day, and the whole party fell screaming through the maze of circuitry that made up the aircraft's computer control box and onto a small but powerful cooling fan. Because of their size in relation to the outside world, no one heard their cries of pain as they were minced into a thousand pieces.

But all creatures, no matter their size, had one unique characteristic in common when faced with such a fate. Fortified by the instinct to survive, they lashed out wildly. So as the intrepid troupe of earwigs plummeted to their doom, they lashed out with their tiny but very sharp pincers, snipping, scratching, and gouging at anything within grasp. More importantly, their tiny bodies bounced off vital components, snapping and dislodging them.

Boff noted the ramp it sat on. It was the hidden end to the roller coaster track he'd noticed outside. 'Not going straight up like all the others, then?'

'No, it'll use a trolley that runs along the ramp to get airborne then return like a normal aeroplane.'

Boff was about to walk away when his eagle eyes spotted

two small but incredibly significant identical manufacturers' labels on the engine-exhaust ports.

'Archie,' he gasped fearfully as he read the inscriptions. 'These are De'vile Thunderstrike missiles! Didn't the United Nations ban these because they're so destructive?'

'And blooming right too,' agreed Archie. 'Those things are lethal!'

Boff stared at the boy, totally gobsmacked. 'But you have two of them?'

'You knucklehead, Boff. You're always jumping to the wrong conclusions.' Archie gestured to the two exhaust ports. 'What you can actually see here, housed safely in the *Skyshark*, are the *rocket motors* from two De'vile Thunderstrike missiles. Although to be precise, they're not actually rocket engines. They're modified MK-3 Phantom propulsion units.'

Boff squared up to him, his face reddening. 'Dare I ask what you've done with the warheads?' He knew full well that Archie's idea of good security was using a chocolate padlock.

'What?' joked Archie.

'The warheads,' he repeated crossly. 'You know, dunderhead, the pointy ends that unleash mass destruction!'

'You really are a cowpat, Boff,' said Archie, shaking his head as he headed back into his control room. 'Do you really think that I could order two prohibited missiles if they still had their warheads attached?' He busied himself at the first panel, flicking switches and noting dials. 'The police would have been all over this place months ago.'

Boff followed him back inside and was about to say something when Archie stuffed a chocolate bar into each of his open hands. 'Eat these, my friend.' He laughed, pulling out a chair and pushing him roughly into it. 'And sit back and enjoy the show.'

'What show?'

Laughing, Archie turned and punched the big green button.

Chapter 7

THE SCRAPYARD.

Honk, honk, honk. An alarm sounded, followed by a soft, pleasant female voice. 'Launch sequence activated. The *Skyshark* will launch in sixty seconds.'

Boff sprung up from his chair like an exploding firework. 'What have you done, you idiot?' he screamed.

Archie ignored him and carried on logically checking dials and adjusting levers.

Honk, honk, honk. 'The *Skyshark* will launch in sixty seconds.'

Archie smiled blissfully as he glanced outside just in time to hear the Skyshark make a satisfying series of quiet but well-defined clicks, whirs, and bleeps before both of its engines growled simultaneously to life.

'Archie, you dunderhead,' snapped Boff, frantically shaking him by the shoulders. 'It's broad daylight out there!' he shouted, gesturing wildly towards the window. 'Blue sky and sunshine! The whole world will see your toy plane take off.'

Honk, honk, honk. An alarm sounded, followed by a soft, pleasant female voice. 'Attention. The Skyshark will launch in forty seconds.'

'Actually,' corrected Archie, 'no one will see it take off.'

'What?!' Boff was stunned by his friend's lack of concern. 'It's

74

broad daylight, you dummy—a blind man will see it take off!'

Honk, honk, honk. 'Attention. The Skyshark will launch in thirty seconds.'

'And can't you shut that irritating voice up?'

'No,' stated Archie bluntly. 'It took me months to create her voice, and I'm rather proud of her.'

Honk, honk, honk. 'Attention. The Skyshark will launch in twenty seconds.'

Archie pointed out the window. 'Notice anything, Boff?'

'No,' he snapped.

'So, you haven't noticed that it's getting darker?' Archie asked, chewing merrily on a liquorice stick. 'And yet there's not a cloud in the sky.'

Boff stomped across to the window, his anger suddenly replaced by bewilderment. 'No clouds,' he said with a frown, 'but it's getting dark. That's impossible.'

Archie pointed to the large wall clock. 'Not if there is a full solar eclipse at precisely eleven thirty-one GMT.'

Outside, high in the sky, the moon slid silently in front of the sun, and day became night.

Honk, honk, honk. 'Attention. The Skyshark will launch in ten, nine, eight, seven, six–'

The Skyshark's two MK-3 Phantom fury engines greedily sucked in fuel, spat out flames, and growled. Whereas Boff, shaken by the sudden loud growling, edged away from the window, Archie stood spellbound, his eyes wide with delight as his creation came to life.

'Five, four, three, two, one... Ignition.'

Both Nogga and Skatt stared in astonishment as, without warning, the two human younglings burst out of the bus, screaming hysterically. It was obvious to Nogga that their irrational behaviour meant something was terribly wrong. The pair tumbled out of the bus, rolled awkwardly, scrambled quickly to their feet, then sprinted across to the nearest coach, behind which they dived face down into the dirt.

Very strange, thought Nogga.

Back inside the control room, two rotating amber warning lights on the ceiling had flashed on, their pulsing beams filling the room with an electrifying sense of panic. In stark contrast, the female computer voice calmly informed all those listening of a slight technical glitch. On the TV screens, the launch message in bold black was swiftly replaced by a new message in bold, flashing red: 'WARNING! ENGINE ONE IGNITION MALFUNCTION. DANGER OF EXPLOSION IMMINENT!'

Inside the Skyshark's main computer, there was a strong smell of burning. Earwig-damaged circuit boards sparked and fizzed, causing the ignition programme to falter.

Engine number two burst into life with a thunderous roar, its thrusting exhaust shooting out like a flamethrower. A fraction of a second later, after a violent cough, engine number one also roared. They were unfortunately out of sync, and instead of a smooth take-off along the launch track, Archie's precious machine shot vertically out of its cradle and into the dark sky like a giant Catherine wheel.

'Jagdar's teeth!' cried Nogga in terror as a twirling mechanical fire-breathing monster with a spiralling tail of thick smoke exploded out from amongst the big red buses and roared away, up into the dark sky.

'Holy thieving toe rags,' whispered Skatt fearfully from

under a seat. 'Do you think those two had anything to do with the day going dark and that thing?'

'Oh, undoubtedly,' croaked Nogga, fighting to regain his composure. 'Apparently, humans are renowned for making those sorts of things!'

They watched the spinning thing disappear into the sky, trailing thick black smoke.

'What do you think it was?' asked Skatt.

'Who knows,' said Nogga. 'And if it's going away from us, who really cares?'

Boff, his face buried in the dirt, could be heard muttering a prayer, but Archie, although scared stiff, just had to see. It was the culmination of nearly two years of work, so he felt compelled to look. Although he couldn't see the Skyshark, he could definitely hear it.

From behind, Boff peaked timidly over his shoulder and whispered, 'Well, I'll be jiggered. It actually worked!'

'Of course, it did!' Archie replied, his mind full of questions. *What the hell had gone wrong with my perfectly planned take-off?* 'It took off more or less exactly as I'd planned.' He stood up, brushed the dirt from his shabby clothes, then walked back to the control room.

Boff followed several nervous paces behind and wafted his arms in a vain attempt to clear the smoke and acrid stench of burning, which stung his throat. The only good thing to have come from the whole mess, as far as he was concerned, was that the irritatingly calm female computer voice had stopped.

'Oh dear, what a mess!' laughed Boff, happy to see so much tech stuff in ruins. The launch area was surrounded by double-decker buses, all of which had been heavily scorched by the Skyshark's fiery engines.

'I don't understand. It was supposed to launch from the ramp,' muttered Archie, casting an empty fire extinguisher aside, 'not spiral upwards.' He strode back into the control room and began furiously stabbing keys. 'What went wrong?'

'Huh,' Boff said. 'You went wrong, as usual.'

Ignoring him, Archie concentrated on the screen. Page after page of schematics of the Phantom propulsion unit flashed on and off, punctuated by huffs, sighs, and the odd profanity. Then after several diagnostic checks, he clapped his hands and whooped with joy. 'Yes!' he cried. 'There's the problem.'

Boff rolled his eyes. 'What's your lame excuse this time?'

Archie chuckled with great satisfaction. 'For some reason, the main computer circuit board failed, which in turn caused the engines to ignite two seconds apart, thus losing synchronicity.'

'Layman's language, please?'

Archie smiled. 'Sorry. For you morons, both engines didn't start together. It should have been propelled along the ramp, but due to a slight technical hitch, it made a vertical lift-off instead.'

'Archie, if it failed, why are you smiling like a stuffed baboon?' Boff asked, dumbfounded by the boy's totally inappropriate reaction. 'Your precious experiment was a calamity!'

'No, it didn't fail.' Archie beamed, pushing the screen of his mobile phone into his friend's smug face. 'Telemetry informs me that after the Skyshark's unorthodox lift-off, the backup computer came online and rebooted the whole system.'

Grinning, he blew a loud raspberry at Boff. 'So, everything is back on the planned schedule.'

Outside, the rare solar eclipse had just finished when a loud boom suddenly rocked the bus.

'Flaming heck, what was that?' cried Boff, his head snapping in all directions, looking for its source.

'No worries,' said Archie, 'it's all part of my plan. The boom you just heard was the Skyshark going supersonic!'

'Should I be worried?'

'The eclipse nicely hid the Skyshark's lift-off, but a sonic boom is different. You see, to get the Skyshark into high Earth orbit, she had to go supersonic immediately after launch!'

'But you can't see a bang,' stated Boff naively.

'True,' agreed Archie, 'but you can hear it if you're listening with the right electronic equipment.'

'Dare I ask if anyone might be listening?'

'Oh, only probably every intelligence-gathering agency in the entire northern hemisphere,' Archie muttered.

Boff's jaw popped open as he flopped into a chair. 'So, Einstein, what are you going to do?'

'Organisations that electrically eavesdrop never do anything without having two or three meetings first, the British government being a prime example. Blimey, they'd have a meeting before they even tied their shoelaces.' He checked his mobile. 'The Skyshark's entire mission has a duration of sixty-one minutes.' He looked up at the big clock on the wall, the one that had FLIGHT TIME written in big letters above it. 'It's been flying for three minutes, so we have fifty-eight minutes left before its return.'

'Then what?' asked Boff nervously.

'Simple. We download its precious data then get the hell out of here before the cops turn up!'

Boff frowned in anger. 'Is this all about some stupid computer information?'

'Listen, if I'm going to fly into—' Archie suddenly went quiet. Quickly, he snatched up a pair of binoculars and chucked them at Boff. 'Get upstairs and make yourself useful,' he growled. 'Keep a look out for the police!'

Chapter 8

EARTH.
UPPER ATMOSPHERE.

High above the world, all was going to plan.

The Skyshark's Phantom jet engines had successfully propelled the flying machine up to the very fringe of space. There, where the air pressure thinned with the extreme altitude, a sequence of valves automatically opened, allowing Archie's special fuel mixture to flow. Once in the Skyshark's air-starved engines, it instantly and flawlessly converted them into powerful rocket motors, boosting the craft into high orbit.

Flying up into space wasn't easy—in fact, with all the junk that orbited Earth, it was a bit like stepping blindfolded out onto the motorway at rush hour. Archie had already hacked into NASA and downloaded their files on all scientific and commercial satellites and orbiting junk. But there were secret satellites, and the Skyshark would need to fly close enough to an orbiting military satellite to hack into its system. It was the Skyshark's sole mission.

Unfortunately, as it rendezvoused with the target satellite and began hacking data, fate conspired to stick its meddlesome oar in. This oar, in the shape of an obsolete Soviet spy satellite that weighed in at a chunky ten tonnes, was at that moment hurtling over the horizon, on a direct collision course with the Skyshark.

Back on Earth, the moment Archie's drone had broken the sound barrier, electronic eyes and listening stations all over the Northern Hemisphere had instantly locked onto it. The RAF and NASA were intrigued, and MI5 was already asking discreet questions, whilst the air traffic controllers at both Heathrow and Gatwick looked to their surprised supervisor for answers that they clearly didn't have.

Meanwhile, many thousands of miles away in a cold, damp military bunker deep in the Ural Mountains of Russia, shrouded in secrecy and stale cigarette smoke, an aging rocket scientist with a sagging beer belly, thinning grey hair, and high blood pressure looked on in utter dismay. Igor 'Gremlins' Bogginski, failed Star City cosmonaut, stared through red rimmed eyes, transfixed at the small blip that had unexpectedly appeared on his radarscope.

'Why me?' he groaned. From that fateful day when he'd made the woefully wrong decision to abort his first planned space flight, thus destroying a multi-million-pound rocket and launchpad, his career, along with his rocket, had crashed. At the age of forty-nine, he had been unceremoniously downgraded to the lowest of the low, janitor for all of Russia's obsolete space junk.

'Damned gremlins.' He scowled in his tiny control room. 'It's all their fault!' He had to do something. For some time, he'd been aware that his masters on the top floor had already pencilled him in for retirement in Siberia. They were simply waiting for his next big blunder.

Shaking off his melancholy mood, he swiftly collected his

thoughts and attempted to reactivate the redundant satellite's onboard computer. If he could somehow fire its manoeuvring jets, he might have a chance to save the day and his own neck, if there was still enough fuel left in its aged, frozen tanks. After the longest ten seconds of his miserable life, a single green light blinked on, indicating the satellite's acknowledgment of his command.

'Yes!' cried Igor, frantically tapping out orders on his keyboard, whilst his tired eyes anxiously flicked between back and forth to the radarscope, watching the two converging blips.

In the cold silence of space, where no one could hear the screech of metal upon metal, Igor's nimble rotation of the ten-ton satellite through one hundred eighty degrees was *almost* the perfect emergency-avoidance manoeuvre. Sadly, the heavy metal tip of one of its derelict solar-panel wings creased the Skyshark's underbelly with a rivet-popping clunk that sliced through its outer skin, severing two major fuel lines.

The Skyshark's two roaring rocket engines, suddenly fuel starved, coughed violently, their brilliant swords of thrusting flame spluttering promptly to extinction. The Skyshark tumbled aimlessly in space for several long seconds.

On all the watching radarscopes across the Northern Hemisphere, the two tiny blips separated. One continued on its merry way, whilst the other slowly started to descend.

Somewhere in Russia, a lonely, downtrodden man jumped for joy.

On board the Skyshark, deep inside its mechanical guts, a large spherical and very technical thingamajig about the size of a football belched, allowing a high-pressure stream of fuel to squirt along a narrow conduit to another cog-like, very technical thingamajig, which promptly snapped off its spindle. Propelled by the expanding gas, it shot like a bullet through the side of the Skyshark's computer, violently assaulting the delicate multiprocessors housed within.

It was at this point that the Skyshark decided to have a full-on electrical heart attack, thus deviating wildly from its programmed mission.

Meanwhile, back in the scrapyard, inside bus control, Boff stared angrily at a perplexed Archie. 'What do you mean, it's not answering?'

'Beats me,' Archie groaned, anxiously running his fingers through his mop of curly white hair. 'For some reason, the Skyshark isn't responding to its pre-programmed mission. Every time I ask it a question, all it says is, "Computer error. Returning to point of origin."'

Boff looked horrified. 'You mean that mechanical disaster is coming right back here, and there's nothing you can do about it?'

Oddly, Archie smiled. 'Unlike you, my pea-brained friend, I plan for emergencies.' From a nearby drawer, he withdrew a small black box. It had two small silver levers on its face and a telescopic antenna, which he extended. 'This is the Skyshark's remote-landing-control unit. I hadn't planned on using it, but it seems I have no choice now. Once it's within a one-mile range, I can manually take control and guide it in for a smooth landing anywhere I wish.'

On board the Skyshark, which became a fiery ball as it re-entered the Earth's atmosphere somewhere over the Atlantic, the highly corrosive propulsion fuel leaking from its twin-pressurized tanks had reached the backup computer. Sizzling merrily, it dissolved its way quickly into an old cake tin labelled SKYSHARK MANUAL REMOTE LANDING UNIT.

Archie's gallant assurance that he could safely land his monstrous contraption did little to comfort Boff's frayed nerves as he leaned back against the control panel, desperately trying to relax his twitching body. 'So, exactly when is your monster due to return?' asked Boff.

Archie consulted his computer then announced confidently, 'It's just approaching the west coast of Ireland. I expect to take control in about'—he glanced at his mobile and grinned— 'thirty minutes.'

Boff's eyes narrowed suspiciously. 'That precise, huh?'

'Of course,' replied Archie proudly.

'Nogga, what exactly was that thing that shot into the sky?'

'Good question.' Nogga toyed wistfully with the rim of his stovepipe hat. 'To be honest, I haven't the foggiest.' Skatt went to speak, but his brother added, 'However, I will be perfectly happy to remain blissfully ignorant of that thing's purpose in life, as long as it doesn't—' Nogga stopped, suddenly aware that his brother wasn't listening but staring out of a window. 'Skatt, what are you looking at?'

'It's them there bushes up there on the cliff top,' he whispered. 'They're moving!'

'Of course, they're moving, you stupid mutt,' said Nogga. 'It's the wind!'

Skatt was grumbling something about not being

appreciated, when suddenly, two other bushes crept three feet to the left. 'There,' he woofed anxiously. 'They did it again!'

Nogga half-heartedly glanced at the cliff top but saw nothing. 'Skatt,' he growled, 'if you continue to annoy me, I'll ask Baldizar to leave you as a dog. Got it?'

Upon the cliff top, one of the bushes that Skatt had seen move whispered into a radio mic, 'Papa Oak Tree, this is Eyeball One, status report twelve-oh-three. Both targets still in bus. No further movement. Over.'

'Eyeball One, this is Papa Oak Tree. Stay put and continue surveillance. Out.'

'Archie, why are we wasting time here? The cops will be banging on the gates any minute.'

'The data the Skyshark has collected is of mega importance to my work. I can't possibly fly—' Archie bit his lip and looked away. 'Boff, I know that my fanatical love of science has always baffled the hell out of you, but—'

'Gadzooks, now there's a gargantuan understatement if I ever heard one,' snapped Boff.

'All of this,' declared Archie, sweeping his arms overdramatically about the control room, 'is my world, the world I love.'

Boff laughed contemptuously.

'Have you never felt so passionately about something that it completely takes over your life, to the point where nothing else matters?'

'Er, no.' Boff concealed the lie.

Honk, honk, honk. 'Attention. Skyshark approaching.

Heading zero nine zero, speed five hundred miles per hour and decelerating. Range ten miles.'

'What?' cried Archie, snatching up his mobile phone. 'No, no, no, that can't be. It's way too soon!'

Boff groaned. 'Oh no, not her again. It's old doom and gloom herself.'

'I don't understand.' Archie gulped, rushing forward and rechecking the control console. 'Why didn't the radar proximity alarm warn—' His words trailed off as he spied the volume dial under Boff's elbow. 'You blithering idiot, Boff,' he cried, shoving him roughly aside. 'You've knocked the speaker off!'

'Huh? Sorry!'

'Sorry?' Archie scowled.

'Yeah, sorry,' said Boff meekly. 'So, what now, Buck Rogers?'

'We bring her in to land, you moron,' snapped Archie, his hands dancing wildly over the console switches. 'But I must get that data downloaded first.'

'I hope your downloading is quicker than that lot!' said Boff, tapping him anxiously on the shoulder and pointing to the monitor showing the main gate.

'Oh, flippin' heck!' cried Archie. 'Coppers! Loads of them!'

Chapter 9

EARTH, THE SCRAPYARD.

'**H**ow did the coppers find me so quickly?' gasped Archie.

'Who cares!' snapped Boff, shaking his head in disbelief. 'The police and the army are going to make the fiasco at the orphanage earlier look like a flippin' tea party! So, what now, Einstein?'

'First things first,' declared Archie, trying to sound decisive, 'we must retrieve the data from the Skyshark.'

'Stuff your flippin' da—'

Honk, honk, honk. 'Skyshark range five miles. Speed four hundred miles per hour, decelerating.'

Archie snatched the remote and dashed upstairs. The bus in which he'd wisely built his control room was an open-top double-decker facing west. Staring at the horizon, he switched the remote on. His throat felt parched, and although his grip on the control unit was tight, his hands were still shaking.

From off in the distance came a loud screeching.

'Yes,' Archie muttered. 'At least the *Skyshark*'s air brakes are still working.'

Honk, honk, honk. 'Skyshark's airbrakes deployed. Speed decreasing. Remote control activated.'

'Where is it?' asked Boff from the top of the stairs.

'There it is!' Archie cried, pointing to the western horizon. 'Over there beyond the river, just passing by Dagget's Hill.'

Suddenly, two huge explosions filled the air, followed by two rapidly expanding balls of rich red, yellow, and white flames. Instantly, two massive billowing mushrooms of thick black smoke blotted out Dagget's Hill.

Boff's jaw dropped with a loud pop. 'Blimey, Archie, what was that?'

Honk, honk, honk. 'Warning: Skyshark jettisoning auxiliary fuel tanks. Landing sequence engaged.'

Boff scowled at the tiny speaker then at Archie. 'You didn't tell me that that thing was carrying bombs!'

'They're not bombs, you cow pat. They were the external fuel pods. And yes, the Skyshark's programmed to drop them before making an emergency landing.'

'Oh well, that's okay then.' Boff laughed hysterically. 'I bet the people underneath them really enjoyed being flash fried!'

Archie swallowed nervously, a pang of guilt stabbing his heart. He hadn't thought of that. 'Well, I'm sure nobody was up there,' he offered feebly, quickly turning his attention back to his approaching drone.

With subtle touches of the remote's control levers, Archie made the Skyshark descend to one hundred feet, dropping its speed to a manageable forty miles per hour before bringing it in. The deep, thunderous roar of its two Phantom jet engines seemed to fill the whole world as it approached the yard. At the main gate, everyone scattered, diving for cover. From behind cars, in dikes, and along the riverbank, incredulous eyes watched nervously as the unidentified craft cruised menacingly overhead.

'You see, Boff?' Archie grinned as he manoeuvred the Skyshark into a tight turn over the yard. 'See how the law and the military quake in fear at my technological marvel?'

Boff gasped at the insane smile on the boy's face, his eye wide and white, his laughing mouth drooling at the corner. 'You're ruddy nuts!'

'Huh, nuts, Boff.' Archie laughed. 'It's a thin line between genius and insanity.'

Honk, honk, honk. 'Warning: remote-control signal lost. Skyshark taking autonomous evasive action.'

'What!' cried Archie, his bubble of triumph popping. 'No, this can't be happening.'

The flying machine had almost finished its pre-landing lap of the scrapyard, when from on top of the cliff, a flash of white with a fiery tail whooshed into the sky. The handheld anti-aircraft missile took but a mere two seconds to lock in and reach its target. The resulting explosion, although small, was a surgical strike that was greeted with loud, echoing cheers from all sides of the scrapyard.

Suddenly, the air was thick with the fumes of burning fuel, which fell upon the scrapyard like fiery rain. Spontaneous fires broke out everywhere, giving the derelict metal wasteland a gruesome, post-apocalyptic look. Archie coughed violently, the acrid stench of the burning fuel biting viciously at the back of his throat. He desperately needed to wretch.

With one of its engines belching thick black smoke and the other desperately trying to compensate, the Skyshark fell from the sky. Fatally wounded, the craft swayed haphazardly from left to right, its damaged flight computer struggling desperately to keep it airborne.

90

'Yippee!' cried Boff joyfully. 'Your metal monster is going to crash!'

'My data!' Archie yelled, snatching his mobile phone from his pocket, his finger frantically tapping the small screen. His head jerked wildly between watching the final death throes of his precious flying machine and his phone's screen. A mini keyboard flashed on the screen, and he quickly typed in a series of code words. Viciously, he jabbed the download icon. The *Skyshark* was barely fifty feet from the ground when it started transmitting. Archie was sweating hard, his neck ached, and he honestly thought his pounding heart was about to burst out of his chest. 'Come on! come on! Just a few more seconds is all I need.'

Then, unable to believe his luck, Archie roared with laughter as miraculously, his ailing Skyshark struck the top of the scrapyard's monster metal crusher at just the right angle and with just enough momentum to bounce it back into the air, smoking but giving him the few extra precious seconds, he needed.

On the road outside the scrapyard's main entrance, waiting lorry drivers, shouting policemen, and squads of newly arrived, heavily armed soldiers sprinted for cover.

Boom!

The Skyshark's burning shell fell from the sky in a nearly vertical kamikaze dive, finally smashing into the middle of all the parked vehicles. The blast from the explosion knocked people off their feet, and the ensuing fireball engulfed all the vehicles, causing several more explosions, one of which blasted the two police cars clean off the ground, their burning shells propelled high into the air.

Archie watched, impassive to the destruction unfolding before him. He should have felt guilty, but strangely, he didn't. In an odd way, he felt detached, as if he weren't kindred to those about him at all.

'You really hate police cars, don't you, Archie?' Boff asked. 'That's four you've destroyed today, and it's only dinner time!' When Archie turned to face him, Boff was shocked to see not a face raked with remorse but a wicked smile.

'I just don't understand you, Archie,' said Boff. 'Your precious machine is destroyed, and you'll be in prison within the hour. What's there to smile about?'

Archie presented the screen of his mobile phone to him. 'Look. Download complete. I've got my data!'

'Looks like you boys have been having a whole heap of fun, huh?'

Startled, the boys spun on their heels, surprised to see the scrapyard's owner grinning at the top of the stairwell.

Mr McGinty was a squat, robust ball of a man, with no neck and a small round head with a thinning patch of greasy, greyish-black hair plastered upon it. If his build was that of a snowman, then his eyes belonged to the devil. People didn't argue with Mr McGinty, and those who were foolish enough to try seemed to have very nasty accidents shortly thereafter. However, he'd been Archie's benefactor for the last ten years, so as far as Archie was concerned, he was totally trustworthy, albeit a little odd.

'Mr McGinty, where did you come from?' asked Archie. The scrapyard owner ignored his question and bowled over to him with a big smile on his face.

'A most spectacular launch,' he laughed, slapping his big

belly. 'To be honest, Archie, I never really thought your invention would get off the ground. By far the ugliest flying machine I've ever seen.' He grabbed the boy's hand and shook it vigorously. 'The lads and me were just taking receipt of an old navy submarine when you launched it. We didn't see a thing because of the eclipse—clever idea—but the noise it made fair scared the poop out of the lot of us.'

Archie chuckled. 'Yes, it was rather spectacular, wasn't it?'

'Mind you, lad, you've stirred up a right old hornets' nest out the front, though,' continued Mr McGinty, waving a fat, oil-smeared finger in the direction of the main entrance. 'The police all have guns, and the fellow in charge, a short, snotty-looking geezer who likes to shout orders'—he jovially nudged Archie in the ribs— 'is right hacked off about his burning patrol cars. Told them army blokes to shoot you on sight.'

Archie swallowed nervously. '*Shoot on sight?*' he repeated.

The scrapyard owner watched the colour drain from the boy's face. 'So, what's your next move, then?'

'I... er... I...' was all that Archie could manage.

'I thought you might say that.' Mr McGinty said with a chuckle. 'Course, if I were in your boots, I'd be speechless too!'

'Mr McGinty,' Boff said through gritted teeth, 'I wondered if you were going to make an appearance.'

The old man shot him a scathing glare, his hairy eyebrows knitting together in a mean scowl. 'This is my scrapyard. Where else would I be, dummy? Now make yourself useful and go below and check Archie's security monitors.'

'Why?' insisted Boff.

'Don't question my orders, boy,' barked the old man

angrily. 'Just obey!'

Archie had never really liked Boff, but he was shocked by Mr McGinty's sudden draconian tone. He was even more shocked by the way Boff meekly scurried down the stairs without even a fight.

'Well, Archie,' continued Mr McGinty, his tone flicking like a switch from hostile to genial, 'what are you going to do, then?'

'I-I-I hadn't really given it much thought, sir,' Archie confessed, suddenly a little scared of the old man. 'I was so wrapped up in my experiment that I couldn't see any further than its culmination and the retrieval of the data I needed.'

The old man glimpsed a subtle twinkle in Archie's one sapphire-blue eye. The boy was obviously hiding something. 'And do you have the information you require?'

'Yes, sir.'

'Well, I admire your spirit. Coming back here to finish what you've started, especially after what happened at the orphanage, shows real guts. However, you're not—'

'The bushes are moving,' blurted Boff as he burst up out of the stairwell, jabbing a finger towards the cliff top. 'There. See? They moved again.'

Squinting at the high wall of bright chalk, Archie saw nothing odd. But to be sure, he plucked from a nearby locker a replica Star Trek laser rifle and used its telescopic sight to scrutinize the bushes.

Amongst the bushes, a calm, mean voice spoke. 'Papa Oaktree, this is Eyeball One. We have a code red. I repeat, we have a code red. Targets are armed with high-tech weapons, and our location has been compromised. Over.'

'Eyeball One, this is Papa Oaktree. You have a green light to attack. The use of unnecessary violence has been authorised. Out.'

'Holy cow!' cried Boff in horror. 'The cliffs are coming alive!'

The three of them watched in amazement as all along the cliff face, dozens of lengths of black rope suddenly uncoiled, snaking their way down to the ground in front of them. Then, as if by magic, all the bushes leaped recklessly over the edge and began abseiling down the ropes.

'Them's Royal Marines,' said Mr McGinty. 'They'll be swarming over this bus within a few minutes.' Archie felt his big, oily hand clamp on his shoulder. 'When they storm this bus, they won't view you as a couple of kids mucking about with fireworks. Oh no, to them, you're terrorists. They'll come in with guns blazing!'

Archie's Adam's apple yo-yoed. If Mr McGinty's aim was to scare him, he'd succeeded. 'But it's just an experiment,' blurted Archie, the consequences of his actions finally dawning on him.

'So, what's it to be young, Archie Wilde?' demanded McGinty, impatiently thumping the side of the bus. 'They're halfway down the cliff face. Surrender like a wimpy kid or escape?'

'Escape,' blurted Archie. No sooner had the words left his mouth than he felt himself being hurled down the stairs.

Seconds later, a barrage of stun grenades shattered every window in the bus, followed by a thick plume of smoke then a hail of murderous gunfire. Smoke billowed, bullets ricocheted, and thunderous bangs filled the air as the bus erupted in a cocktail of violence. However, much to the adrenaline-fuelled Marines' amazement and obvious annoyance when the smoke finally cleared, they found the control room completely deserted.

Chapter 10

For an elderly person who had never shown any obvious inclination towards exercise, old Man McGinty moved with a fluid grace that surprised both boys. His pace was steady, his sense of direction unwavering. More astoundingly, he negotiated the hazardous metal terrain, with all its abrupt twists, turns, tunnels, and climbs with the ease of someone out for a Sunday stroll.

Upon exiting Archie's control centre, the three had weaved their way through six dilapidated buses, two dustbin lorries, and a stinky old horsebox before clambering into the huge drum of a rusting cement mixer. Mr McGinty sidestepped a wide hole that had been cut into its base—unfortunately, the boys, who were not looking where they were going, stepped straight into it. The drop was only about six feet, but it was pitch-black, and the pair fell, sprawling into something wet, sticky, and smelly.

Their screams of panic had the old man roaring with laughter.

Dropping in behind them, the old man, who had landed squarely on his feet, struck a match, its tiny flaring flame illuminating their faces. What he saw only made him laugh louder. They were covered in filth from head to foot and smelt like a fresh dung heap. Hanging to their left were three Tilley lamps, fuelled and ready to use. He lit them all, took one for himself, and handed the other two to the boys.

Boff coughed. 'Yuck, it's a filthy sewer! And it stinks, and it's gone inside my trainers!'

'Whose moon boots are silly now then, huh?' Archie laughed.

Waving his lamp about, Archie quickly recognized where they were.

He caught Mr McGinty staring at him with a suspicious look in his eyes. 'Something wrong, boy?' the man grunted, thrusting his lamp into Archie's face.

'No sir,' he replied, baring his teeth in a distorted smile. 'Well yes, actually. Sir, are there any rats down here?'

The old man leant forwards, his dirty, round, fat, stubble-encrusted face looming up scarily in front of Archie. 'Better nibbling rats down here, boy, than trigger-happy Marines up there, huh?'

'Yes, quite right,' agreed Archie forcing a smile, 'better rats than marines.'

With his free hand, Mr McGinty yanked hard on a long length of rope that dangled nearby.

On the other end of the rope was a wooden chock wedged under a large steel bathtub, which was precariously balanced on top of an old ship's mast. With a twang, the rope went taut, the chock popped out, and the bathtub, screeching against the metal platform, slid clear and plummeted earthwards. On its way down, it struck a precisely positioned steel lever, which in turn rotated the old cement-mixer drum one hundred eighty degrees.

McGinty beamed. 'Don't fret, lads. If a curious marine does peer inside the mixer drum, all he'll see is a hole facing the sky.' Unfortunately, as they moved off, Boff, still whinging, slipped in the muck, crying out in pain.

Archie and Mr McGinty sloshed their way back, only to find Boff sitting in the stinky muck, struggling to free his left foot from broken drain cover.

'I can't get my flippin' foot out,' cried Boff helplessly. 'The cover's broken, and it's clamped tightly about my bloomin' ankle.'

From somewhere in the distance, Archie could hear shouting. 'Those marines are nearly at the cement mixer,' he said, his finger lightly caressing his tingling eye patch. He glanced down at Boff, noting his awkward predicament, then up at the old man. 'Let's go,' he said calmly.

'What about me?' Boff asked.

'*What about you?*' Archie replied coldly. 'I didn't ask you to follow me!'

'Your friends in a right pickle,' added Mr McGinty. 'Do you not think we should help him?' Archie sensed the odd tone in the old man's voice. Just for a second, he felt as if it wasn't so much of a question as a test.

Archie looked the old man straight in the eyes and stated clinically, 'I've got what I need. Leave him!'

For a few seconds, Mr McGinty studied the boy, his stubbly face deep in thought. Then he smiled. 'You're a cold one, Archie Wilde!'

'W-what about me?' stammered Boff, desperately trying to wriggle his foot free. 'It won't budge, and those blooming marines will be here soon.'

Mr McGinty withdrew a hand axe from his belt, it landed with a plop in the muck next to his foot. It was old and well used, but Boff could see his lamplight reflecting in its clean, sharp edge. 'If you keep your big mouth shut, they may not find you.' He glanced at the hand axe. 'But if they do, well, the choice is yours!'

Boff watched the white glow of their lamps fade into the dark. They weren't coming back. He was alone with the rats, and in the light of his own lamp, he suddenly found himself staring at the axe.

Safely hidden underground, the old man walked at a more leisurely pace. They squished through the winding maze of sewers for some ten minutes before emerging into the engine room of an old Royal Navy minesweeper. Three sets of rickety old wooden steps took them up to the bridge, where through grimy windows, they watched the chaos about them. Uniformed figures dashed here and there, helicopters filled the sky, and a cacophony of blaring sirens assaulted their ears.

Archie cautiously used his sleeve to wipe a small clear patch in the dirt. 'Oh my.' He chuckled quietly. 'I've caused a right ruckus, haven't I!'

To his amazement, he realised that they had crossed nearly the whole length of the scrapyard in just under fifteen minutes, finally emerging just behind the main office building.

'Er, Mr McGinty, sir,' he whispered, somewhat confused, 'why are we heading for the yard offices? Won't the coppers look there first?'

'Oh, don't you be worrying yourself about them,' he said

over his shoulder. 'They're too busy trying to put out their burning patrol cars.'

They bent over as they passed behind a long row of old aeroplane wings, stacked on end like the teeth of a giant comb, when a sudden gust of wind blew acrid, choking smoke in their direction. It stung Archie's eyes and throat, and he suddenly found himself desperately coughing.

'Hold it in, boy,' snapped Mr McGinty, 'or they'll hear you.'

From out of nowhere, the heavy whooping sound of rotor blades filled the air. A huge blue helicopter thundered overhead. It was cruising slowly, at a height of no more than a hundred feet, the down draught from its roaring engines blowing up a storm of dust and dirt.

'Shield your eyes,' shouted Mr McGinty over the noise, 'till it's gone.'

No sooner had the old man issued his warning when Archie grabbed him and forcefully shoved his round body into a narrow crevice between two wings. Mr McGinty's face flushed red with anger, but Archie simply pointed up and shouted, 'That helicopter is fitted with heat-sensing equipment. They would easily have picked up our body heat through the dust storm.'

The old man glared at him, mulling his words over, then smiled. 'Good call, young Archie Wilde,' he finally acknowledged, moving off swiftly as the helicopter departed.

At the end of the row of wings, they turned left behind a huge pyramid of old copper boilers and stopped short of an odd-looking shed. *That's funny*, thought Archie. *In all the years I've spent scavenging about this yard, I can't ever remember seeing this shed before.* 'Blimey!' he exclaimed with a beaming smile. 'This is an old British Railways brake van, isn't it?'

'Certainly is, my boy.' Mr McGinty winked. 'I received it as part of a large British Rail job lot about ten years ago. I scrapped its wheels but didn't have the heart to break up the van. So, I decided to use it as a store for a very precious item.'

The words 'precious item' fired Archie's curiosity. He watched in intrigued silence as the old man retrieved a thin loop of string with a key on it from his grubby vest. He dangled the strange key seductively before him. 'Want to see what's inside?'

Archie tottered forward as if hypnotised by the shiny metal object. It wasn't just a plain old iron key—oh no, it was a strange golden one. Its shaft was a tube as thick as a man's thumb, with several grooves of varying depths, along which were set lines of spiked teeth. However, it wasn't the key's rich lustre that captured his imagination. It was the sound it made when he pushed it into the lock. He could have sworn he heard a soft, pixyish voice say, 'welcome, old friend, all is safe.'

The old man proudly pushed the thick wooden door open on well-oiled hinges. A single light automatically flickered on.

Archie's pumped-up sense of expectation suddenly deflated like a popped balloon as he stepped curiously inside. 'It's... *a toilet,*' he muttered dejectedly, staring at the otherwise empty room.

'This is not just any old toilet, lad,' announced Mr McGinty proudly. 'This is an original 1891 Lionel Crapper Montague Mark 1, built especially for Queen Victoria herself. Note the hand-painted blue-floral decoration around the bowl and over the cistern. All the fittings are twenty-four-carat gold, including the down pipe and flush-lever pulley chain.'

Archie's face was a picture of befuddlement. 'Yes, I can see that, Mr McGinty. But it's still just an old toilet!'

The yard owner was about to explain when a lone policeman burst in on them. He wasn't armed but did immediately recognize the pair of them. He'd just grabbed his radio mic and was about to raise the alarm when, out of the blue, a metal bucket struck him on the back of the head. The pair watched the dazed policeman crumple like a wet paper bag and fall with a thud onto the wooden floor.

Boff, still clutching the dented bucket but wearing a smirk of satisfaction, casually stepped over the unconscious policeman.

'Nice of you to join us,' remarked Mr McGinty, eyeing both of his feet. 'Didn't need the axe, then?'

From the far side of the long row of wings, there came the heavy stamping of boots, all heading their way.

'Flipping heck,' Archie whispered. 'We're going to be caught like fish in a barrel in here!'

Mr McGinty heaved the limp body of the policeman out of the wagon then slammed the wooden door shut. Quickly, he slid two heavy iron dead bolts into the locked position, just as several pairs of fists began pummelling the outside of the door.

He smiled. 'There. No one's coming through there now.'

Totally confused, Archie stared in disbelief at him and gasped. 'But now we're trapped!'

Mr McGinty moved to the toilet proudly. 'No, we're not. Let me introduce you to my private hydroportal.'

'A hydro *what?*' asked Archie, scratching his head.

'A hydroportal,' continued Mr McGinty. 'One of the finest and fastest transportation units ever devised.'

Archie frowned at the pair of them. 'Toilet, hydro thingy, transport unit... What are you talking about?'

'Mr McGinty,' said Boff, 'if you show a creature a device that their meagre brain can't comprehend, they generally tend to disbelieve. Maybe a revelation might be in order?'

The old man glared at Boff with hate-filled eyes. 'For once, cretin, I think you may be right.'

Archie was quickly becoming uncomfortable with McGinty's apparent dislike of Boff and felt he needed to defend him when something very gross caught his attention. It was a pulsating black dot, which had suddenly risen on the top of the yard owner's bald head and was rapidly swelling into a large, angry, red spot the size of a walnut.

Archie flinched as the spot burst with the force of a mini volcano. Then, like a scene from a horror movie, hundreds of tiny black jagged lines sprouted from it, racing in all directions, encompassing his head like a spider's web. To Archie's revolted amazement, the lines were actually Mr McGinty's skin splitting, but oddly, it sounded more like tearing baking foil. Within seconds, the tears had raced down his neck and vanished under his clothing.

With a sharp crack, the top of Mr McGinty's head split open, his skin peeling back like segments of a huge rotten fruit, exposing a gruesome red mass within. Archie gagged, desperately fighting to keep his breakfast down, when he suddenly realised that the red mass wasn't bone and blood at all, but metal.

Like soggy autumn leaves, the remnants of Mr McGinty's head fell away, revealing a large red helmet crested with a strikingly vivid red-and-black Mohawk. It had a vague resemblance to an old knight's helmet, only it was more like an upturned bucket with an evil-looking Y-shaped slit in the front. From the neck down, all of Mr McGinty's clothes and skin had also peeled away and fallen into a dishevelled pile about his feet, revealing more red ironwork. As the head rose, so it was followed by a set of broad shoulders, under which came an iron chest that could easily rival a tank's armour plating.

Before Archie's goggling eye, the monstrous crimson thing just kept growing to eight, nine, ten feet tall. Its massive iron physique towered over him, its dominating presence holding him captive in spellbound silence.

Then the strange creature flexed his arms—*all four of them*. It completely blew Archie's mind. Not even the angry pounding of the fists upon the door outside could break the spell.

The tall crimson-iron figure that was, until a few moments ago, old Mr McGinty, casually kicked the remains of his old body aside with the flick of a large metal boot. It was at that point that Archie's scientific curiosity carved its way through the chaos in his mind and slapped his brain back to the real world.

Leaning forward, Archie forced himself to touch the mess on the floor. There was no blood on his fingertips, and it felt sort of rubbery. 'This is a disguise,' he offered, his tone fearful but impressed. 'A very elaborate one but a disguise nevertheless.'

'I apologize for the deception, young Archie Wilde, but it was necessary. My real name is Baldizar. I am a treasure hunter and explorer from another world.' Lied the red giant.

'You're an *alien*?' gasped Archie.

'Yes,' the metal man said resolutely.

'So that suit of armour you're encased in must be your spacesuit?'

'Well, yes. I suppose you could call it that.'

'Do you have a spaceship hidden somewhere in the scrapyard?'

'Not as such,' offered Baldizar, his black eyes sparkling deceitfully. 'I have something much better and faster!'

Archie's imagination rocketed into overdrive. Once again, he noticed the metal giant's arms. 'You have four arms!'

'Being multilimbed makes life so much easier,' said Baldizar. 'You should try it someday. A couple of extra limbs always comes in useful.'

Archie's eye patch started to tingle as the giant reached out with a huge iron hand. It wasn't like the way it was during his nightmares—the tingling bordered on pain. During his short life, he had come to accept his eye patch as a kind of inbuilt warning system, one that had saved his neck many times. But he couldn't do anything about it. His personal alarm was ringing, but he was trapped.

Forcing a smile, he reluctantly shook the massive hand. 'You look like a character out of an old Hollywood Knights of the Round Table film in that getup!'

Baldizar laughed awkwardly. 'Yes, I do rather, don't I? The

similarities are very striking.'

'Your gauntlet,' Archie said, running his fingers curiously over its smooth surface, 'isn't metal at all. It feels more like glass?'

'An astute observation, Archie Wilde,' replied Baldizar. 'You are indeed intelligent.' He flexed all four hands and arms in a display of manoeuvrability that would be impossible for a human shoulder joint. 'On my home world, this material is called Blood Vagga. It is a kind of diamond-infused metal.'

Archie marvelled at his armour. 'Your suit must be worth a king's fortune!'

Baldizar clenched his upper left fist then smashed a hole in the wooden roof as if it were rice paper. 'It is beyond value.'

Boff, who had been watching the goings-on outside the hut through a spy hole, turned and spoke. 'Baldizar, the Marines are here. They're going to shoot the lock off. I think we should be going.'

'Archie Wilde,' said Baldizar, placing two reassuring metal hands on his shoulders, 'it's time to leave.' Through the slit in Baldizar's helmet, Archie glimpsed the iron man's black, red-veined eyes and felt his heart freeze. His eye patch really started to burn.

From his belt, Baldizar unclipped an object that reminded Archie of a Himalayan prayer wheel. It looked to be made of wood and was colourfully decorated, with a short handle and three drums that rotated. Each drum was covered in lines of intricate symbols, which the iron man spun individually, as if setting a code. Then he pointed to the toilet pan and clasped another free hand about the flusher handle.

'We shall use the hydroportal to make our escape,' said Baldizar.

'But it's a toilet!' exclaimed Archie again.

There was a crisp clicking of metal fingers, and Baldizar turned to Boff. 'You, demonstrate the hydroportal.'

Without hesitation, Boff yanked the flush chain hard. At that point, all comparisons with any toilet Archie had ever seen before stopped. Inside the bowl, the flowing water rapidly turned into a maelstrom of breath-taking colours, streaked sporadically with spiralling lightning flashes. Without a word, Boff leaped feetfirst into the bowl.

As he spiralled downward, his image became like mist, his whole body vanishing into the swirling vortex. In the wink of an eye, Boff had vanished.

'But... how... where... what?'

'You, inside the hut!' shouted a stern voice. 'This is your last chance to open the door! If you don't come out right now, we'll be forced to shoot the lock off!'

Baldizar stared down at the trembling youth. 'I do believe that those Marines mean business. If they force their way in, the least they'll do is stomp very aggressively all over your spotty teenage head.' He waved two hands invitingly towards the toilet. 'So, what's it to be? Exceptional pain or my hydroportal? The choice is yours.'

What else could Archie do? He felt trapped and out of control—he had no real choice. If this was meant to be the adventure he'd craved all his life, he didn't like it one bit. His pounding heart was making his confused head spin even more. He looked fearfully at the toilet then up at the scary red iron man.

With no time left, Baldizar made the choice for him. Grasping Archie by the neck, he pulled the chain and dumped him like a bundle of washing into the swirling vortex.

From outside, they heard sharp clicks as several rifle safety catches were flicked off.

'Off you go, Archie Wilde,' said Baldizar. 'Enjoy yourself!'

Chapter 11

Have *blooming fun!* screamed the voice of reason in Archie's head. With his eye clamped shut, he felt every muscle in his body tensed to the point of snapping. 'This must be a dream. No one really gets flushed down a toilet by a giant, red-armoured alien!'

'Oh, this is no dream,' a gruff little voice said with a chuckle. 'This is as real as it gets!'

Archie's eye flicked open in surprise. Standing before him was a small, dusky-brown meerkat with the biggest pink eyes he'd ever seen, who was calmly blowing square bubbles from a round pipe. He was stylishly dressed in a white collar and yellow bowtie. Pristine white spats adorned his feet, whilst a matching yellow bowler hat sat at a jaunty angle on his head. Beneath his spats, his clawed feet gripped tightly to one end of a multicoloured surfboard.

Archie was terrified when he looked down to find himself standing on the other end.

'Welcome to the genieverse, Archie Wilde,' offered the meerkat politely.

'The genieverse?' Archie croaked.

The meerkat waved his tiny arms expressively about him.

'All that surrounds you is the genieverse. It is everywhere and everything.'

Archie squinted; his mind awhirl with thoughts. After everything that had happened to him in the last couple of hours, to suddenly wake up to a talking meerkat on a surfboard in space seemed, well... quite acceptable.

Archie took a breath. 'If I'm not dreaming, then I'm definitely nuts!'

The meerkat's mouth curled into a friendly smile as it reached forward with a tiny paw and brutally yanked a fistful of his hair from his leg.

'Ow!' cried Archie. 'That blooming hurt!'

'Hi, I'm Taggy. Still think you're dreaming?' asked the meerkat. 'I'm a spiv. Your species would regard me as a messenger from God.'

'Einstein's underpants!' cried Archie, dropping to his knees and digging his fingernails into the surfboard's edge. 'W-we're really in space.' His logical mind tried to grasp the fact that all about him was indeed the vast empty vacuum of space.

'Don't fret, youngling,' said the meerkat reassuringly. 'It's impossible to fall off. Think of it as a fairground ride, dangerously thrilling but safe!'

'I don't do fairground rides. They make me sick.'

'Some would-be explorer you are.' The meerkat chuckled. 'At least sit up. It will make our conversation so much easier.'

Reluctantly, Archie slowly loosened his stranglehold on the surfboard and manoeuvred into a sitting position. Suddenly filled with curiosity, he daringly dipped a hand over the board's edge. There was nothing tangible there to either see or touch, yet he was sure that he could feel a subtle sensation in his fingertips, like that of a gentle breeze.

'Careful, youngling,' warned Taggy. 'You may not be able to fall off my surfboard, but the cold, deadly vacuum of space can have a queer effect on some species.'

Archie shuddered, fully aware of the effects of space on a human body. 'So, you're a messenger from God, huh?' he asked, rubbing the sore bald patch on his leg.

The meerkat frowned. 'Yes, from God,' he muttered, shaking his head. 'Your kind always sneer when you ask that question.'

'*My kind?*'

'Yes, your kind,' tutted the meerkat. 'The so-called intelligent ones!'

'The intelligent ones?' repeated Archie.

'Will you stop repeating everything I say?' snapped the meerkat. 'It's so damned annoying! Your sort was gifted a handful of brain cells, and you think you have Jagdar's right to question everything.'

'Huh. Sorry for breathing,' mumbled Archie.

'Enough,' growled the meerkat. 'I digress. You are indeed awake. Your body and mind are at this moment hydroporting through deep space from Earth to the planet Hexx. You are being carried upon the very breath of Zephyar, demigod and lord of the solar winds, engine of the hydroportal transport system.'

Archie tapped the surfboard with his fingers. It felt real enough. Glancing backward, he could see a surge of stars propelling him forward, their motion reminiscent of an ocean wave. 'Does everyone who hydroports get a guide?' asked Archie.

The meerkat smiled. 'Oh no. We are rarely seen and almost never heard.'

'So why me, then?'

'Why you? Because you're the Rainbow child, of course,' answered the meerkat, bowing graciously. '*You,* are the sword of the prophecy.'

'Sword of the prophecy?' echoed Archie, screwing up his face in befuddlement.

'Don't try to understand it, human. You'll only burn out your brain cells,' declared the meerkat. 'Simply accept it but be assured of this: Zephyar himself has taken an interest in your perilous quest and will intervene if he deems it necessary.'

'"Perilous quest,"' muttered Archie anxiously. 'I don't like the sound of that.'

'Think of it as the first of many adventures, then,' the meerkat said, smiling. 'After all, isn't it what you've always wished for?'

Archie went to speak, but the meerkat waved a tiny paw at him.

'The time for questions is over. I have delivered my message, and your destination beckons.'

The spiv's image began to waver and fade. 'Taggy!' shouted Archie. 'Why a surfboard?'

'Why not?' The meerkat laughed as his smirking face faded to nothing.

Archie didn't even have time to laugh. With a loud whooshing pop, he arrived on the planet Hexx.

'Huh.' He chuckled. 'One second you're chatting to a meerkat in space—the next you're standing next to a toilet in a tent!' But it wasn't a tatty old canvas Boy Scouts tent. It was a Bedouin tent fit for a desert sheik.

It was without doubt the most opulent and lavishly decorated tent he'd ever seen. All the fixtures and fittings could have come straight out of Buckingham Palace. Eight thick poles of highly polished ebony held the roof aloft. Suspended from each of these were golden oil lamps of the finest oriental design, bountifully encrusted with precious gems. Their flickering flames, although delightful, gave off the overpowering aroma of fresh camel dung. In one corner, standing alone was an extravagantly embellished cast-iron stove about the size of a wheelie bin. Behind its glass front was a brightly glowing fire and next to it a basket full of logs.

The fabric lining of the tent appeared to be woven silk of Asian design but not very thick. For outside, illuminated by what Archie assumed was bright sunlight, he could see many vague silhouettes of passing people and flying things. All their movements seemed to be in rhythm with the sound of loud, jolly music being played very badly.

In front of him, covering an entire wall panel was a large round circle of thick, braided gold the width of a man's hand. The inner circle was brilliant white with the image of a helmet similar to the red giant's helmet embossed upon it, only it had six fearfully long black horns, three sprouting out on each side. Archie assumed that it was some kind of tribal emblem or logo.

Out of the blue, a curious notion suddenly stormed his brain. Events at the scrapyard had escalated with whirlwind speed, what with the gun-toting Marines and burning police cars and all. He suddenly realised that he'd never actually taken the time to consider the giant red man's claim that he was in fact an alien. In all the haste, he'd simply accepted it. 'Most unscientific,' he said, scolding himself.

A hand slapped Archie hard on his back. 'I see you heeded his advice, then, and kept your eyes closed,' said a grinning Boff.

Archie, startled by Boff and the red giant's sudden appearance, glared up at him. 'How can you tell?' He scowled, rubbing his back. 'And did you have to hit me so flippin' hard?'

'To answer your first question, you're still alive,' said Boff. 'No creature that has opened their eyes during a hydroport has ever survived to tell the tale.' Then his grin turned to a wicked smile. 'And yes, I genuinely enjoyed whacking you on the back.'

Archie frowned at the pair of them. He had no idea what was going on but instinctively knew that he should keep tight-lipped about his encounter with Taggy.

'You look disappointed,' said the red metal giant coldly.

Archie looked at the giant then to Boff. 'Well, I...'

Without warning, Boff cuffed him hard on the side of his head with a small but heavy leather pouch.

'Ow!' cried Archie. 'What was that for?'

'When in the presence of your El Supremo, Baldizar, the supreme genie of the genieverse, address him, not me, dunderhead!'

'What? Sorry,' moaned Archie, rubbing the side of his aching head. 'I was only going to say that, well, it wasn't—'

From nowhere, vice like pains gripped his chest, and he suddenly found himself fighting to breathe. His hands flew to

115

his neck as his words were choked off by frantic gasps for air. Through quickly blurring vision, he saw a pair of hands appear before his face. One forced his jaw open whilst the other roughly jammed something into his mouth. Then his nose was pinched hard, and he was forced to swallow whatever it was.

He gagged at the taste of dirt in his throat, but miraculously, the crushing chest pains swiftly began to ease, and his breathing suddenly became normal.

'Quite a pathetic species, really,' offered Boff, watching the boy on his knees, panting like a dog. Baldizar, who seemed to be studying Archie, simply nodded in agreement. 'There. Feel better?'

'Yes, yes. Much better, thanks,' croaked Archie, nodding gratefully. 'What was that thing?'

'That was a Muzzberry pip,' answered Boff, thrusting the leather pouch at him. 'Here, tie this bag of them to your belt. You'll need them to help you breathe until your body acclimates to being on Hexx. They may taste like a chieftain's underpants after a heavy night on Old Majestic Gutstrangler grog, but without them, you'd be dust within a minute!'

'Much obliged,' said Archie, not really wanting to know what a chieftain might be, let alone the state of his underpants.

'Drink this,' said Baldizar. 'It will ease your throat.'

'Now, what were you going to say before you almost croaked on us?' asked Boff, smiling.

Archie took a big swig of water. 'I was about to say, it wasn't exactly the rocket ride of the century, which I'd always dreamed of.'

Baldizar strode forward, his evil black eyes crisscrossed with jagged, angry red veins.

Suddenly, Archie's eye patch prickled viciously, his right hand automatically shooting up to rub it. 'Although this is without doubt the most spectacular tent I've ever seen,' he added swiftly. 'One truly fit for a king!'

With his pride placated by Archie's quick thinking, Baldizar's pace slowed to a halt. Unfortunately, the evil glow from his helmet remained.

'Archie, the hydroportal was developed simply as an everyday form of transport. It wasn't designed to be a sensory journey of enlightenment or a fairground ride,' said Boff. 'Besides, most of the creatures who use them barely have the intelligence to operate one, let alone understand how it works.'

Archie shook his head and laughed. 'Well, if that machine is real, then it has awesome scientific and financial potential,' he announced. 'We could set up a—'

'*Enough!*' growled the red giant. 'Your childish babbling annoys me.' He then turned to Boff, pointing. 'Reveal yourself, Storm Raider. There's work to be done!'

Archie's mouth fell open, stunned by what happened next.

Boff seemed to be holding his breath, as if he were about to explode. Funnily enough, that was exactly what happened next.

Before Archie's very eyes, his friend's legs and lower body split open, revealing a huge mass of leathery green flesh. There was no blood or stinky yellow fat to be seen, and just like Mr McGinty's disguise, it made the sound of tearing aluminium foil. From his waist down, Boff was now a writhing mass of long, flowing, squid-like tentacles.

'You're not h-h-human either?' stammered Archie. Two, five, eight, ten tentacles in all, he counted. 'And you've got hands on the ends of all of them!'

Boff cheekily waved his hands before Archie's ashen face. 'Well, trounce me trunnions!' the creature roared heartily, causing his head to burst like a balloon. 'Oops! That wasn't supposed to happen!'

Boff's new head was a large bullet-shaped affair with a mouldy green, leathery complexion to it. His mouth was the biggest Archie had ever seen, with thick, rubbery lips running right across the front of his face. From under his multiple chins, two thin metre-long feelers uncoiled themselves. On either side of his head, two huge cone-shaped eyes sprang out. Rather bizarrely, they seemed to be moving independently of each other. Without warning, Boff's whole body shock like a wet dog, flinging bits of skin and ragged clothing in all directions.

Archie wasn't so much frightened as grossly intrigued. 'You're a sea creature of some kind, aren't you?' he asked flatly, staring at the seven-foot creature hovering in front of him.

'Jagdar's teeth!' cried Boff, stretching and flexing all his tentacles in a wide, sweeping circle. 'Am I glad to be out of that thing.' One of his two cone-shaped eyes winked at Archie. 'Ten years stuffed inside a tiny human body disguise is enough to drive you stir crazy. And don't you find that it always itches in the one place you can't reach?'

Archie gasped. 'You're two sea creatures in one.'

'I am Boff of Kromper,' he announced regally, puffing out his leathery chest and holding his reptilian head up high, 'son of Clankfoot, Clan Lord of the Northern Nardowells.'

'The creature you see before you,' declared Baldizar with unbridled revulsion, 'is the infamous "Bilge Rat Boff," a cruel and merciless storm raider, a criminal of the worst kind!' Archie's heart skipped a beat as the shine from Baldizar's fiery red eyes made the front of his helmet glow evilly. He didn't just dislike Boff—he despised him.

'That abomination is the result of illegal mixed breeding. Half chameleon and half squid are a sad combination that's of little use to anyone.'

Archie looked at Boff, and although the creature hovered proudly, he could clearly see the hurt that Baldizar's remarks had caused.

'I don't know,' remarked Boff with a loose tongue. 'I think it's quite a cool combination, myself!'

There was a rasp of steel as Baldizar slowly withdrew his long broadsword from its sheath on his back. Its blade flashed through the air, stopping a hairs width from Boff's neck. With a minuscule flick, the sword tip nicked the skin under one of his chins, causing Archie to flinch uneasily as he watched a thin line of blue liquid trickle down his friend's neck.

Now I really do wish this were all just a dream, thought Archie.

'Perhaps, Storm Raider,' Baldizar began, glaring down the blade of his sword, 'you might care to take the youngling's place in the race?'

'Hornswoggle me giblets, my El Supremo,' croaked Boff fearfully, his Adam's apple bobbing perilously close to the blade's tip. 'I was only joshing. I know my place in the pecking order. Under the heel of the pure breeds, down in the muck with the other mongrels.'

Baldizar's thin lips curled into a cruel smile. 'Careful, Storm Raider, or I might have to rethink the terms of our deal regarding the youngling.'

'*Deal?*' said Archie. 'What do you mean, deal?'

'Gadzooks no, my El Supremo. That would be truly awful,' Boff said, grovelling. 'Is not being trussed in that cramped disguise for ten years and having to endure the incessant whining of that pompous little twerp punishment enough?'

Baldizar took a moment to ponder the truth of his argument. 'Babysitting is a hideous chore, especially to one so'—he glanced across at Archie— 'repugnant!'

'Hey, just who are you calling "repugnant"?' snapped Archie angrily.

Archie felt one of Boff's tentacle hands snake about his neck then draw him close. 'Careful, youngling,' he whispered. 'You're on naffin' Hexx now, and verbal abuse is the least of your problems.'

'Hexx,' blustered Archie. 'Never heard of it.'

'Don't mock your El Supremo's home world,' sniped Boff. 'That sort of talk can get you dusted!'

'Dusted?' repeated Archie curiously.

'*Killed!*' Stated Boff with a dark finality.

'You're now on my home world,' announced Baldizar majestically, 'and here, you're the alien!'

Without warning, Baldizar stood fully erect, his four metal fists clenched. Then, like a boiler under pressure, his whole giant red suit of armour seemed to swell at its riveted seams.

On each side of his big, bucket-shaped helmet, three long horns appeared, seemingly growing out of the metal itself, and single horns sprouted out of his shoulders, elbows, and knees.

All were midnight black, and all were tipped with lethal golden points. Then came the silver haze that enveloped his entire body. Its glare was so bright that Archie had to look away for fear of being blinded. When next he looked, Baldizar's entire crimson suit of armour was adorned with a mosaic of thousands of tiny, shiny silver symbols, giving his whole appearance an eerie, magical quality.

'Wow!' cried Archie in terrified admiration. 'Now, that was the coolest thing I've ever seen. Can I—'

One of Baldizar's four gauntlets swung round, clipping him viciously on the side of his head. The blow sent him sprawling to the ground. 'I am Baldizar, supreme genie of the council of the power ten genies!' he bellowed dictatorially, his eye slits glowing like molten lava, his voice as cold as ice. 'You are my maggot, and you will address me as El Supremo!'

Shaken by Baldizar's unprovoked attack, Archie's spinning mind watched in dizzy silence as the red-metal giant ranted and raved. *'If you're planning to escape, Archie, me boy,'* shouted his subconscious, *'now would be a good time!'*

With the red-metal giant's back to him, Archie jumped up, pulled out his electric cattle prod, and laughing courageously, rammed it into the metal man's side. The thin tip of his cattle prod found and slid into a tiny crevice beneath his chest plate, discharging its full electrical load with a loud sizzling hiss. Baldizar's suit of armour lit up like a lightning strike, fizzing and sparking, sending his giant metal body jigging and jumping, clanking and rattling about the tent like a string of tin cans full of thunder crackers.

Seizing his chance, Archie bolted for the door.

Part 2

THE RACE

Chapter 12

THE PLANET HEXX.

Blimey, this isn't Kansas, cried Archie's logical mind as he stood gawping at the most gobsmackingly amazing fairground he'd ever seen.

Coloured tents, marquees, and gazebos of all shapes and sizes, all bristling with bunting and pennants, fanned out before him in an eclectic muddle, which left him speechless. Weird music, most of it awful, was being played on instruments that simply beggared belief. And the smells, oh, the smells were truly scrumptious. The mouth-watering aroma of roast meats, delicious puddings, succulent sweets, and all manner of drinks scented the air.

The fact that mingling throughout the awesome spectacle were creatures that even his imagination couldn't comprehend didn't seem to matter.

Baldizar's loud, bloodcurdling scream jolted Archie from his stupor just in time for him to see the tip of his huge broadsword slash the side of the tent to ribbons. The red-metal giant burst out of the ragged hole like a rampaging bull. So incensed was he by the boy's audacious attack that in his howling rage, he ran smack into Archie, bowling him over and sending him sprawling to the ground.

Archie tumbled to a halt in the cold sand, the force of the

collision knocking the air from his lungs. But as he rolled onto his back, wheezing for breath, he froze in terror as the red-metal giant suddenly loomed over him. His volcanic red eyes glared down at him, the once-neatly trimmed Mohawk singed and smouldering on his helmet.

'You'll die for that, maggot!' bellowed Baldizar, swinging his broadsword high above his head. 'No one attacks me and lives!' Screaming vengeance, the metal giant plunged his sword down with all his insane strength.

I'm going to die! echoed in Archie's head as he watched, frozen with terror, the sword blade plunging towards him. Darting in from the side, two strong tentacle hands grasped his arms and legs, yanking him swiftly sideways seconds before Baldizar's sword thrust deeply into the ground, mere inches from his neck.

Exhaling with relief, Archie almost fainted.

'No, my El Supremo!' cried Boff, ignoring his own safety. 'Think of the last ten years!'

Baldizar, his huge chest heaving, pulled his sword free of the ground and swung it wildly towards the quaking Boff, roaring, 'You dare defy me, Storm Raider?'

All about them, fearing for their lives, creatures scattered, bringing the jovial atmosphere of the fair to a crashing halt. A huge circle formed quickly around the El Supremo and his would-be victim. Everyone spoke in whispers except the ticktacktoes, who eagerly took bets of spungold, giving odds on just how Baldizar would dispatch the youngling.

'Yes, my El Supremo,' declared Boff humbly, holding out ten empty hands in an open act of submission. 'Not in defiance but to help you with your plan!'

'Plan,' was a small yet pivotal word so powerful that it held both their lives in the balance. The transformation of Baldizar's unhinged mind was miraculous. One second, he was a raging monster and the next, an El Supremo, the calm, rational leader of the genieverse.

Yes, yes, my plan, pondered Baldizar, his pulsing eyes relaxing as he reined in his terrible anger. *I have invested many years and much spungold in this youngling. To dust him now would be futile.* One corner of his mouth curled in a ruthless smile as he glared down upon the hapless youth. *When this pathetic creature has found what I desire, his golden collar will serve as my avenger.*

'You're gasping,' whispered Boff. 'Take another Muzzberry pip, quickly.'

Archie had been so traumatised by his near-death experience that he hadn't even noticed that he was choking. He gulped down a pip, and its effect was quicker than the first ones, steadying his breath immediately.

'He was going to kill me!' Archie muttered, rising shakily to his feet. Then he saw the crowd. 'Flippin' heck, will you get a load of that lot!'

Boff floated up alongside him, draping a tentacle across his shoulders, thankful that the boy was easily distracted. 'Some of these creatures are born dwellers of Hexx, but most are off-worlders like yourself.'

Archie stared slack-jawed at the crawling, flopping, hopping, walking, jumping, floating, and flying mass of bizarre creatures all around him. His eye patch was tingling seriously—something had changed. When he'd first stepped out of the tent, the barrage of noise was overwhelmingly eerie. One could have heard a pin drop. Thousands of eyes stared curiously at him.

'Boff, why are they all looking at me?' asked Archie anxiously.

'Jagdar's teeth, Archie,' Boff said despairingly, 'you've just tried to naffin' dust their El Supremo, dummy. No creature, let alone a lowly maggot, has ever tried that before and lived!' He patted the boy hard on the shoulder. 'I could have been dusted, saving you from his sword,' he snorted, pushing the boy forward. 'You owe me big time!'

'Sorry,' Archie said, suddenly realising the truth of the matter. 'I won't forget.'

'You won't have long enough to forget, boy,' muttered Boff. 'You've only got the next twelve candle marks!'

Archie didn't understand what Boff meant and let it go. He had a more important question. 'Boff, what is Baldizar's plan, and just how do I figure in it?'

Suddenly, the whole crowd sank to their knees or bowed graciously. 'Hey, is this for me?' asked Archie naively.

'Stupid youngling,' spat Boff, pointing over his shoulder. 'That's for him!'

Baldizar, his temper cooled, and his broadsword sheathed, glared menacingly at the crowd. Standing a good three feet taller than most of the other creatures, the sheer evilness of his presence was enough to silence any rebellious thoughts the mob might be harbouring. However, just to be sure, he tensed his armoured body, allowing his black fighting horns to protrude. His threat was enough.

The mob's subservient silence pleased him.

To Baldizar's right were two huge crabs. After a brief

exchange of words, the pair scurried into his tent, returning moments later with rattling chains. Shoving Boff aside, the crabs swiftly shackled Archie's hands and feet. He winced as the manacles snapped shut on his wrists and ankles.

'Take the maggot to the tree!' he ordered Boff. 'He must be prepared.'

Archie felt Boff's grip tighten about his shoulders. Then the mass of strange creatures parted in hushed obedience as Baldizar strode forward, Boff and Archie falling submissively into step behind him, the two crabs scuttling after them.

Archie raised his shackled wrists at Boff. 'Does he treat all his visitors to Hexx like this?'

'Egads no, boy.' Boff chuckled. 'Only the ones who try to kill him!'

As they marched away, Archie heard a soft, pitiful whimpering to his right. It was a kangaroo-like creature, strikingly blue and yellow in colour, with four arms that had human hands on the ends. Unfortunately, one entire side of the creature was covered with a rash of red blisters, some of which had burst and were openly weeping a vile-smelling green pus.

Although Archie couldn't understand its language, his sense of compassion instinctively told him that the creature was ill. To his horror, Baldizar, who had also noticed the creature, struck with lightning speed. Sidestepping slightly but never losing his stride, the metal giant brought the elbow of one of his right arms down across the poor creature's neck. The razor-sharp tip of its black horn cut surgically through bone and muscle, neatly decapitating it. Not once did Baldizar's eyes flinch from the path ahead.

The kangaroo creature's head, complete with shocked expression, toppled sideways, falling with a soft thud onto the sand. A nearby octopus creature glanced up at the supreme genie then back at the fallen body of the kangaroo. Shrugging its shoulders in a blasé manner, it reached across and snipped off the creature's money pouch. A different creature took his boots.

'D-did you see that, Boff? He just killed that poor creature for no reason,' Archie said. 'Isn't anyone going to do anything?'

'Scupper me, boy, there's a lesson well learnt,' whispered Boff, his voice threaded with hatred. 'Baldizar is El Supremo, leader of the council of the power ten genies. He's the most powerful genie in the entire genieverse, and he can do whatever he wants, *especially* on his home world.'

'But where's the justice in that?' Archie whispered. 'Why don't the police do anything?'

One of Boff's tentacle hands twisted Archie's head to the left. 'See that big, hairy fellow with the bull's head and big black horns, standing by the blue-and-white bell tent over there?'

It was hard to miss what Boff was describing. The bull man was huge, both in height and size. His chest armour was vaguely Roman in design, a combination of leather and polished metal. On one arm, he carried a massive round shield with a black bull's head emblazoned upon it. In the other, he held an unsheathed, murderous-looking broadsword, its keen edge glinting in the weak sunshine.

'You mean that minotaur?' Archie asked.

'On Earth, you would call him a minotaur.' He sneered.

'Here, he's called a chieftain, and they are the *Police*.'

'Well, isn't he going to do anything about that poor creature?'

'Oh, I wouldn't worry about him. He was diseased anyway—that's why the chieftain didn't interfere. The Duster brothers already had his name on their collection list, so Baldizar actually did him a favour by ending his suffering.'

Anger flared in Archie's gut. *So much for Earth having the monopoly on callous murder.*

They came to a halt before a large tree. It wasn't a particularly spectacular specimen—in fact, it was quite boring, with no leaves, just huge, rather odd-looking fruit pods. They were teardrop shaped and about the size of a space hopper, with one dangling from the very end of each branch. But somewhat disturbingly, unlike earth fruit, these seemed to be moving.

'Oh, are we having lunch now?' whispered Archie. 'Great. I'm starving.'

'Shush,' hissed Boff. 'Your El Supremo is choosing your Mutmut.'

All this fuss over some food. Archie watched Baldizar moving from one fruit pod to another, carefully inspecting them, sometimes squeezing them. *They all look the same to me. I hope they taste nice.*

'This one!' declared Baldizar in a loud, authoritative voice, snapping the pod from its branch. 'The maggot shall have this Mutmut.'

The crowd cheered enthusiastically, appearing pleased by his choice. *If they make this much noise over one piece of fruit, teatime must be deafening.*

'It's mutmut time.' Boff laughed.

'Okay,' said Archie, 'so get me a plate, and I'll dig in.'

'Hornswoggle me giblets boy, this isn't food you eat,' Boff said, chuckling heartily. 'This is food you *receive*!'

Suddenly trembling, Archie tensed as Baldizar strode towards him with the fruit pod raised high above his head. 'What—hey, what are you going to do with—'

Without warning, two of Boff's tentacles snaked around him and gripped him tightly.

'Hey, what's going on?' cried Archie. 'What are you doing?'

At the very last moment, Baldizar pierced the bottom of the fruit pod with a metal fingertip before slamming it down hard over Archie's head with a loud *splat*. Instantly, he was encased in a world of gloop that oozed into his ears, squirted up his nose, and filled his eye. Fearing suffocation, he instinctively clamped his mouth shut.

Then he felt it, a tiny *something* crawling up his nose. Shaking his head, he desperately tried to snort it out, but it just kept crawling farther up before suddenly, with a sloppy pop, it was inside his skull.

Archie tried to scream, but his throat was choked with goo. Just as he was on the verge of fainting, the pod was suddenly pulled clear of his head. Coughing and spluttering, Archie fell to the ground, his hoarse retching making the crowd laugh and Baldizar smile. He then threw up several times.

'Yuck,' moaned Archie between coughs. 'What happened? What did you do to me?'

'You have received your Hector's gift,' announced Baldizar. 'You should feel proud. Only the privileged few are bestowed with such an honour.'

'Proud... honoured,' croaked Archie, hawking up more gloop. 'It tastes disgusting.'

'Drink this,' said Boff, shoving the spout of a water bag into Archie's mouth and forcing him to drink. 'You're a maggot now, with your very own mutmut.'

Never had plain water tasted so good. It revived him, quickly clearing the foul taste from his mouth and affording him the strength to drag himself up into a wobbly sitting position. 'What the heck's a mutmut?' he asked bleary-eyed.

'I think it's best if the little feller himself explains,' said Boff, throwing a rag at him. 'Wipe your face. You look a mess.'

'Agreed,' said Baldizar, who oddly seemed not to be addressing Archie but the top of his head. 'Declare yourself to me, mutmut, for I am Baldizar, your El Supremo.'

What happened next was without a doubt the most bizarre sensation Archie had ever felt. His jaw and vocal cords started moving of their own accord whilst foreign words flowed from his mouth.

'Well, well, well,' said a scratchy, audaciously arrogant voice, 'if it isn't Mr Pompous himself.'

'*Grizwold,*' groaned Baldizar, folding all four of his arms tightly across his chest. 'I'd prayed to Jagdar that you had been dusted many years past.'

'Now, now, Baldizar, that's no way to greet an old friend, is it?' Grizwold asked sarcastically.

'Boff, what's going on?' asked Archie, confused and afraid. 'My head's talking, but it's not me!'

'Say hello to Grizwold, your very own mutmut,' said Boff.
So, you're the one I've heard so many rumours about, are you?

The so-called Rainbow child! Archie heard the voice in his head and freaked.

'Grizwold, he's only a human youngling,' beseeched Boff. 'You scare us elders. You're terrifying him!'

'If the rumours are true,' replied Grizwold, using Archie's mouth again, 'he's far more than just a human youngling!'

Archie's left hand suddenly rose and slapped himself hard across his face. *Speak, boy. Time is of the essence, and there's a lot to do.*

'Err,' gurgled Archie.

Look, the situation is simple, declared the voice in his head. *I'm your guide and mentor for the race. Without my abilities, you don't stand a chance of surviving.*

Boff felt a little sorry for the boy—he looked so lost and pitiful, sitting there with tears in his eyes, on the cusp of a nervous breakdown.

'Boff,' whimpered Archie, 'there's a voice in my head, talking to me!'

Wiping Archie's eyes with the back of one hand, Boff smiled down at him and explained. 'Grizwold isn't talking to you. He's thalking to you.' Archie's blank expression wasn't helping matters. 'Thalking,' continued Boff, 'is talking with your mind, not your tongue.'

That's weird, Archie thought.

Believe me, thalked Grizwold, *thalking is way beyond weird!*

'You heard me?' Archie was astonished. *I mean, you heard me.*

Of course, I heard you, you dunderhead. You thalked.

At that point, despite his own open-minded logic, Archie gave up. 'This is ridiculous,' he said. 'How can I be think-talking to a tiny creature inside my skull? The idea's just preposterous.'

No it isn't, thalked Grizwold, *because I'm doing it right now.*

Archie thought for a moment. 'Oh no. There's not enough room in a human skull to accommodate both an uninvited creature and a brain.'

Hmmm, hissed Grizwold. *By 'brain,' I presume you're speaking of this shrivelled-up, walnut-sized lump before me?*

I'll have you know that an average human brain weighs—hey, what do you mean, walnut sized? Archie was indignant.

As a controlling organ, it's pretty pathetic, remarked Grizwold, suddenly spying a small, familiar-looking scar. He systematically searched the corresponding inside of Archie's skull and found another scar, identical but bigger. *Interesting,* he thought.

Suddenly, Archie felt a sharp stabbing pain in his head, a bit like ice-cream freeze but more precise. 'Ouch, what was that?'

I just smacked your tiny brain. Now do you believe me.

It was turning out to be a truly horrendous day for Archie. Not only was he wanted by the police and government back on Earth, but he'd been kidnapped by aliens, flushed down a toilet, and transported to another, not very friendly world. To top it off, he had a tiny, annoying bug camping inside his head. Some birthday it was turning out to be.

Okay, Archie thalked, surrendering. *Let's agree, for the moment, that you are inside my head and that I haven't totally lost my mind.*

Which I am, persisted Grizwold.

Why are you there? What do I need you for?

I'm a body controller, thalked Grizwold proudly, *one of the best in the genieverse.*

Hang on there, grubby, sniped Archie crossly. *I control my body, not some gross little bug.*

Oh, you do, do you? Grizwold sensed that a demonstration of authority was necessary.

Without warning, Archie's body suddenly snapped smartly to attention. Then in a loud clear voice, Grizwold, using Archie's mouth, issued the following warning: 'Attention all creatures! This disbelieving maggot is about to be road tested. For your own safety, stand well clear!'

Archie began to shake anxiously as Baldizar, Boff, and the crowd quickly formed a wide circle. Everyone was laughing and pointing at him. He could even see Baldizar cruelly smiling through the slit in his helmet.

'Oh no,' he groaned, 'what no—'

To the crowd's great amusement, Archie sprang up onto his toes, which was virtually impossible, considering he was shackled and wearing moon boots, then began dancing and prancing like a ballerina around the tree. In and out of the hanging fruit, he leaped and spun, jumping and twirling. All that was missing was a pink tutu. With the crowd laughing hysterically and Archie sweating profusely, he went down on all fours for some mooing like a cow.

Had enough, asked Grizwold. *Do you believe me now?*

Yes, yes. Archie gasped. *I believe you. I believe you. Just stop it.* Grizwold released his control, and Archie flopped onto his belly like a jellyfish.

Boff floated across to the boy, grinning at his red, sweaty face. 'You should really try to be friendlier. It's a tough genieverse for a loner, and you need all the help you can get!'

'Enough of this foolishness, Grizwold,' commanded Baldizar. 'You've had your fun. Let's away to the amphitheatre. There's a race to be run.' With that, he strode off along the path formed by the separating crowd.

'Come on, Archie,' said Boff. 'We must follow, or there'll be more trouble.'

'Give us a minute, Boff,' puffed Archie. 'I'm cream crackered after all that exercise!' Out of the blue, a wave of adrenaline surged through him, washing away his fatigue and revitalizing his tired muscles. With little effort, he jumped up and quickly found himself marching sprightly alongside Boff.

See, I'm helping you, Archie Wilde, Grizwold said. *And Boff is right. It's infinitely better to be a team player than a loner.*

After all those years at the children's home, wanting to be alone, Archie began to see the wisdom in their argument. *Okay, you win, partner,* he thalked, *but let's keep the weird dancing stuff to a minimum, huh?*

Grizwold smiled. It was a half-hearted, grumpy sort of smile but a smile, nevertheless. *Oh, and whilst we're on the subject of teamwork,* he added, *you might want to rethink your attitude towards Boff. He's had a stay of execution order from the council of the power ten genies hanging over his head for the past ten years. It was only the task of safeguarding you, whilst in exile on Earth, preventing his official execution. He didn't have to save you back there, but he did.*

Archie stared at Boff as they marched behind Baldizar. He was merrily gabbing on about something or other in the crowd, oblivious to the fact that no one was listening. He wondered whether the strange creature might possibly be a new, real friend and not the encumbrance he'd always viewed him as. Grizwold was right, and suddenly, he felt very guilty. His eyes sank miserably to the ground. Sensing just how bad the boy felt, his mutmut intervened by flexing Archie's neck muscles just enough to raise the boy's eyes and turn his head towards Boff.

You haven't got time to waste feeling wretched, thalked Grizwold. *Apologise and be done with it.*

'And that's why no one eats kippers with chopsticks on the forty-eighth day of each month, shipmate,' declared Boff grinning.

'Boff,' said Archie awkwardly, 'I'm sorry.'

Both of Boff's cone-shaped eyes swivelled towards him. 'Sorry for what?' he asked.

'I've been really nasty to you for years now,' he confessed meekly. 'Haven't I?'

'Scupper me, boy, that's putting it mildly.'

'I'm sorry,' offered Archie again. 'Really, I am. I'm deeply sorry for all the pain I've caused you.'

'And believe me, over the last ten years, Archie Wilde, that's a naffin' great pile of pain.'

Archie's eyebrows crinkled in thought. 'If I've been that bad, why did you save me back there? You could have let old Buckethead run me through, and all your problems would have vanished.'

Boff's rough leathery face took on a warm pinkish glow, and he wrapped Archie up in a ten-tentacle hug so full of emotion that it threatened to snap every bone in his body. 'By the curly horns of Jagdar, Archie Wilde, why do you think I did it?'

Archie's sullen, blank face just made him laugh more.

'It was either babysit you for ten years or be naffin' dusted. In an extremely painful manner, I might add.'

It wasn't quite the answer Archie had hoped for, and his disappointment must have shown, for Boff suddenly laughed so hysterically that his large belly bounced up and down, bashing him repeatedly under the chin.

'Jagdar's teeth, why do you think I did it?' Boff asked, releasing the boy from his grip and locking both of his eyes on him. 'Because I've'—his big leathery face flushed red— 'because I've grown naffin' fond of you, that's why!'

Archie glanced up at Baldizar, then whispered, 'Boff, why am I here, and why do these creatures keep referring to me as the "Rainbow child?"'

'A Rainbow child is a newcomer to Hexx,' lied Boff. 'And you're here because of a certain... er... *competition*.'

Grizwold intervened. 'Well, that's the slushy bits over. Shall we move on to more important things, like formally welcoming Archie to Hexx and the decennial festival of Atunka Gaar. What do you think of your first alien planet, Archie Wilde?'

Archie heard the question, but his mind had flashed back to Baldizar's attack. Something wasn't right. Several times, he'd heard the word 'plan,' and each time, it bore more weight than the last. Whatever the plan was, he must figure somewhere in it. And if the mere mention of it could stop a metal megalomaniac mid kill, then it was no small matter.

He looked over at Boff, his big leathery face now its normal shade of puke green, but interestingly, he was only watching Archie with one eye. The other was rigidly fixed upon Baldizar.

Archie knew a lie when he heard one, but he wondered suspiciously whether Boff was friend or foe. *Did he save my life out of friendship, or was it just another tactical manoeuvre to save his own neck?* Suddenly, Boff's unexpected outpouring of sincerity seemed suspiciously hollow.

Grizwold coughed loudly in his ear, snapping him out of his thoughts. *What do you think of your first alien planet, then?* he repeated assertively.

'I've done it!' Archie laughed, quickly forcing a smile whilst deftly slotting his near-death experience with Baldizar and doubts about Boff into a file in the back of his mind.

'Done what?' asked Grizwold, using Archie's voice.

'I'm actually living the dream. I'm a real intergalactic explorer. Although I must admit, Grizwold, having logically deduced that life in outer space would be obviously more varied than back on Earth, I wasn't prepared for such a fantastic diversity! It's all so stellar bezzy!'

Just then, a long, multijointed, bony arm reached out from the crowd and shook his hand. 'Nice one, youngling,' said an odd throaty voice. 'Anyone fearless enough to try and mug the El Supremo is a pal of mine.'

'Oh, thanks,' acknowledged Archie, scanning the crowd for the arms' owner. 'I really was—hey, wait a minute! I can understand you!'

Of course, you can understand him, Archie, thalked Grizwold. *I'm interpreting for you.*

Archie ran his fingertips over his scalp, gently probing for lumps. *Why can't I feel you scurrying about inside my skull, Grizwold?*

I'm too small for you to feel. And—he snorted huffily—*we*

Mutmuts don't scurry anywhere!

Then Archie had a horrible thought and asked a question he didn't really want to know the answer to. *So... what do you look like?*

In Earth terms, answered Grizwold, *I'm a one-eyed octo-creature about the size of a field mouse.*

A field mouse, thalked an astounded Archie. *In comparison with the tiny gap between my brain and skull, that's huge!*

Not really, thalked Grizwold matter-of-factly. *My body has only one dimension.*

So, you're like a shadow, then? concluded Archie.

After a while, they cleared the crowd and left the fairground and hydroportal arrival tent behind, their little group immediately forming a marching order. Two chieftains with swords and shields at the ready took the lead, then Baldizar, then Boff with Archie cradling his wrist shackles to stop them rubbing, whilst two more chieftains brought up the rear.

Inside Archie's head, Grizwold, purring like a sleeping cat, let his tentacles caress the boy's brain, his sensitive suckers interpreting his every thought. *Forget making a break for it,* he rasped. *It's a waterless desert in all directions. You'd never make it.*

They meandered up a seemingly never-ending hill. With Boff hovering and everyone else being so tall, Archie quickly began to flag, even with the aid of his Muzzberry pips and Grizwold.

For the first time since arriving, having cleared the fringes of the fair, Archie got a proper look at the planet Hexx. For the most part, it was a buff-coloured desert with the odd rocky outcrop. The rough path they seemed to be following had been trodden many times, judging by the deep ruts that had been formed by both feet and wheels. Above them, the sky was clear but tinged with a pinkish red. There was a crisp freshness in the air that reminded him of a late-December day back on Earth.

Boff noticed Archie rubbing his arm vigorously. 'Cold?' he asked.

'Yes.' He nodded, shivering.

'Don't worry,' Boff said. 'The Forbidden Wall isn't far now. We'll sort you out a cape there.'

As they plodded on, Boff pointed out many distractions to keep the boy's mind off the cold, one being the long line of white-capped mountains on the far horizon.

Without warning, just for a few seconds, the world about then became black. 'What just happened?' asked Archie, sunlight suddenly returning. 'Is that black lightning I can see flashing above the mountains? Or is it a trick of the atmosphere?'

'No trick,' scowled Boff. 'That accursed black lightning that turns day into night started some fifteen years ago. No one knows why!'

'Does anyone know where the black lightning comes from?'

A particularly good and scientific question, thalked Grizwold. *A fellow mutmut who had guided his maggot amongst those far mountains told me that he had come across a strange, gigantic limbless tree of iron that, when struck by the lightning, glowed a fiery orange. I don't know where the black lightning comes from, but that's where he said it strikes ground.*

'Sounds to me as if someone is harvesting electricity,' said Archie, nodding towards the red giant in front.

Electrickery is the demon that drives the ancient black art of technology, rasped Grizwold irritably. *Its best left hidden in history and safeguarded from all creatures by myth and legend.*

For an empire as supposedly vast as this genieverse, Archie thought, *they're certainly a backwards lot.* Without warning, the world about them suddenly grew dark, and dust devils sprang up everywhere as the air was filled with the sound of thunderous chopping rotor blades.

A mammoth flying machine passed slowly over the top of them, framed menacingly by the pinkish sky. Archie saw its underbelly—its silhouette was truly colossal in size. It was basically oblong in design, but each corner and its waist had been engineered into long, downward curving horns. Its bridge, projecting out from the front like an armoured beetle's head, also carried two smaller, downward curving horns.

On each side of its thick accentuated spine were four massive propellers, and even though the craft cruised at a thousand feet, the downdraft felt like a hurricane. However, it was the craft's colour that intrigued Archie and terrified Boff. Apart from its shiny golden-tipped horns, everything else was a deep shade of crimson.

It reminded Archie of a giant, blood-soaked claw. 'Wow!' he cried. 'Now that's what I call a flying machine.'

'That is evil personified,' whispered Boff, turning his eyes away in dread. 'That is Baldizar's sky cruiser, the *Crimson Raptor*!'

Archie glanced ahead at Baldizar, who was paying the

mighty flying machine no attention. 'So, old Buckethead's got an air force, has he? How many of those things has he got?'

'Jagdar's teeth,' cursed Boff, sighing. 'Just the one, thankfully.'

'That explains the black lightning, then,' offered Archie. He gestured towards the red giant. 'He doesn't strike me as a mechanical whiz kid!'

He isn't, Grizwold said. *The one who lurks in Baldizar's shadow, the Professor, is the sorcerer of the ancient black art of technology.*

They watched the Crimson Raptor cruise off towards the northern horizon, where for the first time, Archie spied what looked like a dark line.

'What's that up there, that long dark line on top of the hill?' asked Archie.

'That,' said Boff reluctantly, 'is our destination, the forbidden wall that surrounds both the Fortress Hexx and the great amphitheatre of Garrknock.'

As they marched closer, so the wall grew in stature. Constructed of roughly hewn blocks of black volcanic rock with a nasty, sharp, jagged top, it looked to be a frighteningly effective barrier. The portal through the wall was a large, fortified watchtower, manned by several big, ugly chieftains. However, it was the long line of tall glass tubes stretching off to one side that snared Archie's interest.

From high above, a giant creature swooped out of the sky, flying low over the group before arcing gracefully up, circling the watchtower, and landing to the side of the gate. Its long, leathery wings blew up clouds of dust as its talons punctured the ground. Its piercing shriek caused Archie to jump and Boff to ink himself. Longer than a bus, its massive body was that of a yellow-and-black snake with twelve wings, its tail tipped with a scorpion's stinger. Riding upon its thick neck was a chieftain armed with a formidable bow and several quivers of arrows.

'Jagdar's fiery breath,' Boff grumbled. 'I wish they wouldn't do that.'

'What is that?' asked Archie, staring intently.

'That,' said Boff, flushing red with anger, 'is a Thargg. The chieftains use them to patrol the deserts.'

'What a magnificent beast,' announced Archie, smiling in awe. He watched, fascinated as it started to wretch, its strong stomach muscles rippling up its long neck. With a wide yawn, it dislocated its jaws, opened its huge, fang-filled mouth, and regurgitated a glass vial. 'Why, it's just coughed up one of those glass cylinders.'

Two of the chieftains, ignoring the drool dripping from the vial, heaved it onto their massive shoulders then carried it across to a large cart parked next to the other vials. The row seemed to follow the outside of the wall, only to disappear over the far horizon. The thargg, probably intrigued by Archie's off-world scent and the thought of fresh meat, started to slither towards him, but his rider quickly reined him aside, guiding the beast back towards the watchtower.

'What are those things?' asked Archie again, laughing. 'Packed lunch?'

'See for yourself, young Archie Wilde,' said Baldizar, gesturing towards them with an open hand. Archie didn't like his creepy smirk, but his curiosity got the better of him, and he circled widely around Baldizar before walking over to the cylinders.

Boff hovered behind him. 'Take care, Archie. Look closely if you must but guard your tongue. Baldizar relishes the screams of all creatures that cast their eyes upon his *statues*.'

Naively curious, Archie sauntered up to the first statue. It was a humanlike creature kneeling in prayer. All four of his hands were clasped tightly together, and both his heads were bowed. Archie ran his fingertips over the vial's smooth surface. 'Well, that's one way to preserve a statue,' he remarked.

Archie was so engrossed in the statue that he failed to hear Baldizar's heavy iron boots closing upon him. One of his metal gauntlets grasped Archie's head and pushed it right up to the glass. 'Look closely,' Baldizar said. 'See the fine detail of the statue's features.'

Archie pushed against the glass with his hands, but it was no use. Baldizar had him pinned hard. Then a scream came roaring up from the pit of his stomach like an express train, as in horror he saw four wide, crazy, staring eyes of the statue flick open.

Chapter 13

PLANET HEXX.
THE GREAT AMPHITHEATRE OF GARRKNOCK.

Archie felt Baldizar's hot breath on his ear. 'That, my young maggot, is a silent screamer!'

Archie stared in horror, his voice strangled with shock at the sight of the poor wretched creature, suspended in a living nightmare, imprisoned in a tube of glass.

'I-It's alive,' uttered Archie despairingly. 'Why?'

But Baldizar didn't answer. He simply walked away, laughing.

What you see before you is a creature who dared to speak out against Baldizar and the other genies, thalked Grizwold.

Archie tried to turn away but felt somehow compelled to look at the poor creature's beseeching eyes, its miserable face contorted with pain and the stringy spittle at the corners of its open screaming mouth mouldy with age.

In the end, it was Grizwold who forced his hands to grasp at his pouch of Muzzberry pips.

'You're evil,' shouted Archie between laboured breaths, 'to condemn a creature to *that*!'

The small crowd of workers and vendors about the gate reared backwards in shock at the youngling's open defiance of their El Supremo. Boff's instinct for self-preservation kicked in, causing him to float away from the boy.

'What you so glibly call evil,' said Baldizar, 'I call order.' He raised a gauntlet and pointed to the far end of the line of vials. 'Beyond the horizon lies the valley of the silent screamers, where their kind number in the hundreds of thousands. These you see here,' he added, turning on an iron heel, 'are merely a deterrent to others. Here on Hexx, and likewise throughout the genieverse, there is no civil disobedience, just order. My order!'

Archie suddenly felt a strange sort of strength reinforce his will. He instinctively knew that the sensation, whatever it was, welling up from deep inside his very soul, wasn't Grizwold's doing.

Stomping his boots hard into the sand, he countered boldly, 'What you call order, Baldizar, educated, free people call tyranny!'

Inside his head, Grizwold frantically tried to override the boy's speech.

'And you know what they say about dictators, don't you?'

Baldizar hesitated, intrigued by the boy's audacity. 'Please,' he hissed, 'enlighten me.'

'A dictator rules by fear alone.' A winning smile spread across Archie's face as he watched all four of Baldizar's clenched fists start to shake. 'But when the courage of the people overcome that fear, then the days of that dictator are numbered!'

'Jagdar's teeth,' grumbled Boff to a small group of carrot creatures, 'Baldizar is going to dust him for sure now.'

Baldizar glanced back over his shoulder whilst deliberately dropping one hand threateningly onto the hilt of his broadsword. 'I made examples of others who dared to speak as you do.'

If that's the way genies treat people, thalked Archie, swallowing hard, *then I'm surprised there's anyone left.*

Oh, it wasn't always like this, Grizwold replied. *What you see is only recent.*

Let me guess, Archie said knowingly. *It all began when Old Buckethead was elected El Supremo?*

Boff dropped a mangy animal skin at Archie's feet. 'Put that on,' he said. 'It may smell like a boondook's butt, but it will keep you warm.'

Archie said nothing as he swung the manky fur skin about his shoulders. It was a rough fit and long enough to drag in the dust, but he felt its warming effect immediately. It stank horribly.

Marching forward, their group passed through the gates of the watchtower, with Baldizar giving the chieftain guards who snapped smartly to attention but a cursory glance. Archie's eye patch tingled, but the hostility he sensed from the guards wasn't directed towards him but rather oddly at Baldizar. It only took a passing glance at the minotaur's big black eyes to realize that their show of respect was only for his political rank.

As Baldizar passed the winged serpent, it snorted fiercely, small jets of flame erupting from its nostrils, turning the sand about its feet to black glass. *Even the thargg hates old Buckethead*, mused Archie, chuckling. *What good taste they have.*

Once inside the wall, the path divided. To the left, it ascended a long, winding incline towards an impressive-looking fortress. To the right, a path led to the great amphitheatre of Garrknock, a structure so huge it made the Coliseum of Rome look like a garden shed.

Baldizar strode to the right.

The area within the wall was vast and completely empty. 'Why is the crowd kept on the other side of the wall?' asked Archie. 'There's loads of room in here.'

'Oh, they're not kept out,' replied Boff. 'You see, this is the forbidden zone!'

The word 'forbidden' struck him as slight overkill, mainly because the wide-open space, although cold and windswept, seemed quite tranquil in appearance. 'Forbidden, huh?' he repeated mockingly, pulling his smelly cape tightly around him. 'Sounds to me like fearmongering by those minotaur thugs if anything!'

'The chieftains aren't bothered by any creature stupid enough to wander in there,' said Boff. 'They just leave them to the Dreadlies!'

'The Dreadlies?' echoed Archie. 'What are they?'

Boff was about to explain when a flock of large, winged, green rhinoceroses came flapping across the sky.

'See those Grumnucks?' Boff asked, pointing with a tentacle hand. 'Watch that young one on the end, the straggler flying low and slow.'

Even before Boff had stopped speaking, there was a puff of sand to their left and a horrible scream from the young flying rhino bird. A long, sinewy thread with a barbed end shot out, piercing its chest. In the blink of an eye, it was snatched out of the sky. At ground level, a large set of jaws within jaws appeared, gobbling down its squawking victim with one swallow.

'Was that thing a dreadly?' asked Archie, his face pale with shock.

'That thing was just the mouth of a dreadly,' said Boff.

'That's sick,' Archie replied.

'Trounce me trunnions, boy,' said Boff. 'You haven't seen the best part yet.'

There was a sudden sound, like an elephant spitting. Archie's stomach tightened as he watched the severed, skinless head of the young green rhino bird fly through the air and disappear over the boundary wall.

Archie's shoulders dropped as he ran a hand through his thick mop of curly white hair. 'Is there anything nice about this flippin' planet, Boff?'

Boff thought for a moment then sighed heavily. 'No, absolutely nothing!'

Turning towards the great amphitheatre of Garrknock, the group walked along a special path, its sides marked with hand-sized red glassy rocks.

'Red rocks,' offered Archie. 'A warning?'

Boff smirked. 'Oh, yes.'

As the trio marched silently along the path, Archie felt his eye drawn towards the fortress and its murder of noisy crows circling above. 'Is that where old Buckethead lives?' he asked.

'No,' answered Boff, not taking his eyes off the path beneath their feet. 'That's where the chieftains are garrisoned.'

It reminded Archie of an old gothic castle; the scary type he'd seen pictured in horror books. But there was a quirky difference to it—it seemed to have been haphazardly modified over the centuries with new bits and gizmos, the vast majority of which he didn't recognize. 'Those screeching birds would drive me bonkers,' he said. 'Do they keep them as pets or something?'

Look closely at the fortress walls, thalked Grizwold, *near the top of the battlements.*

Adjusting his chains, Archie took a small monocular from a vest pocket and focused it on the walls. Instantly, the reason for the crows became apparent. Iron cages ran along the outsides of all the walls, and from between their rusty bars dangled the limbs of dead and dying prisoners.

Yet another one of Baldizar's grisly warnings to the masses, thalked Grizwold.

Before them, the giant amphitheatre of Garrknock rose imposingly into view. At a stone's throw from its mighty gates, Baldizar stopped. The pair of ancient wooden gates towered dauntingly above them, their massive bulk nestled between two more watchtowers of the same design as the outer wall, only much bigger. Archie marvelled at the hundreds of iron reinforcing bolts that ran through them, each as thick as his arm. On either side of the gates, a bare high stone wall ran off, curving away in the distance. To a newcomer to Hexx, the amphitheatre looked like the base to a manmade mountain.

On a colossal arching beam of wood, spanning between the two watchtowers, was a carved image. Its head was that of a crocodile with a long, open mouth and bleached bones jammed between its rows of vicious pointed teeth. Holding the grisly sight aloft was the body of a mighty eagle, its long yellow talons buried deeply in the beam. From its sides, blotting out the sun like billowing sails were two enormously hideous black bat wings, their edges lined with claws.

Archie shuddered. 'Einstein's underpants, what's that flippin' thing?'

'That is Garrknock the Great,' answered Boff, his tone betraying his clear admiration.

'He's a bit of a Heinz 57, isn't he?' Archie chuckled disrespectfully. 'What was he, anyway?'

'It is believed by many that he was the very first chieftain. It is said that he, upon the orders of the one god, Jagdar himself, etched the very first laws of the genieverse into the living backs of the kalifar.'

Now that story sounds familiar, thought Archie. 'What are kalifar?'

'They are the immortal giant turtles who range across space and time on the winds of Zephyar,' said Boff, who was about to elaborate when he was interrupted by a deep, powerful voice booming out from atop the watchtowers.

'Who approaches the great amphitheatre of Garrknock and falters, quaking before his mighty likeness?'

Baldizar stepped forward with all four arms spread wide, displaying empty hands. His crimson armour shined in the sun, its myriad engraved silver symbols glowing brightly with ancient power.

'I, Baldizar, El Supremo of the council of the power ten genies and elected ruler of the genieverse, stand before you and demand entry to the great amphitheatre of Garrknock, on this third day of the festival of Atunka Gaar.'

For a few tense seconds, no one said a word. Archie, swept up in the magic of the moment, felt his heart pounding as he feverishly licked his dry lips.

'Be you here as ruler or keeper?'

'Both!' Baldizar declared arrogantly.

'Does he have to do that every time he wants to go to the theatre?' whispered Archie.

'No,' said Boff, reaching out with a pair of tentacles and drawing the boy close. 'But during the ceremony of Atunka Gaar, all creatures must declare themselves.'

'Or what?' asked Archie. 'It's only a flippin' wooden statue!'

Looking about the ground, Boff selected a suitable-sized stone then tossed it high into the air, towards crystal eyes set in the head of Garrknock.

Instantly, two brilliant red beams flashed out, disintegrating the stone in a puff of black dust.

'Just a wooden statue, huh?' Boff asked smugly.

As Baldizar's glowing red eyes faded, a loud creak and chorus of monstrous trumpeting announced the opening of the doors.

After loud thudding, slowly, against its will, each door began to open. From behind each came a chorus of deep primordial rumblings. Archie smiled upon hearing the sound of his favourite animal, but his happiness was quickly dashed as he stared in horror at the appalling sight before him. Six heavily chained, eight-legged woolly mammoths, each the size of a double-decker bus, were being forced by lash to bulldoze the huge gates open. Their massive flat skulls, scarred and bleeding, repeatedly butted the heavy wooden gates, whilst their heavy footfalls made the very ground tremble.

It took the mighty beasts nearly ten minutes to open the gates fully before the voice of authority spoke again: 'Baldizar, supreme genie of the council of the power ten, you may enter.'

'Who's the voice?' enquired Archie.

'That was Goldhorn,' replied Boff. 'He's the captain of the chieftains. When he speaks, everyone listens, and when he orders, everyone obeys, even the genies!'

'Wow,' Archie said, reaching for his phone. 'Heavy!' Without warning, the muscles in his right hand twisted, and he involuntarily let his mobile phone slip back into his pocket. *What are you doing, Grizwold?* thalked Archie angrily. *I just wanted to snap a few shots.*

Never ever use earthly gadgets on this planet, Archie Wilde—it's a sign of the ancient black art of technology. If Baldizar doesn't dust you for it, then the crowd will stone you for sure.

Okay, okay, I won't. Archie rubbed his hand. *But really, you only had to tell me, you know.*

The gates were fully open, and from the bottom of each watchtower, two minotaur's appeared, carrying drums and beating out a loud military march. Then a fifth minotaur who seemed to dwarf the others appeared from the shadows, and in a manner used to authority, he marched out to the middle of the gateway. As his huge iron boots came to a stomping halt, so did the drums.

As minotaur's went, Captain Goldhorn was the pinnacle of their species evolution. He stood nine feet tall, with a massive barrel chest and arms and legs like knotted tree trunks. His huge, shaggy, black-haired bull's head with mean-looking golden horns studied the group with unblinking chocolate-brown eyes. His chest armour and leather skirt were adorned with the finest spungold, decorated throughout with silver religious images. Unlike the other minotaur's, he had sheathed his broadsword and slung his shield across his back.

Both Archie and Boff found themselves squirming under his caustic glare but not Baldizar—he stared right back at the captain with an equal if not superior hatred.

It was common knowledge throughout the genieverse that the chieftain legion barely tolerated the genie council and openly despised Baldizar. The tension in the air was electric, but eventually, Goldhorn gave a loud snort and beckoned them in.

Baldizar strode passed Goldhorn, acknowledging him with a dismissive huff. Boff's two independent eyes suddenly found the ground remarkably interesting. It was only Archie who, filled with naive curiosity, dared to look up at the chieftain.

Goldhorn drew from his belt a large horned trumpet and gave a single long blast, causing the spectators within to roar with excitement. Baldizar led them down a long wooden tunnel with rough walls and ceiling. Every few yards, a strange torch burned with a dancing pale-yellow flame. Its odour was rank, and Archie felt himself gagging in the cramped space.

As they neared the light at the end of the tunnel, so the muffled roar of the crowd grew steadily louder. When they finally stepped back into the sunshine, nothing could have prepared Archie for what he saw. The wildly singing crowd and the song they were shouting at the top of their alcohol-fuelled voices made him shudder with fear:

'Maggots away and make it a runner!
Sport for the chieftains
And death for the dusters!
El Supremooooooooo!'

They repeated the simple verse twice, its theme drilling violently into Archie's head.

'Maggots,' he croaked. 'They're all singing about maggots and chieftains and dusting.' He suddenly felt like a one-legged gladiator. It was definitely, a two-Muzzberry-pip moment.

As arenas went, the great amphitheatre of Garrknock was undoubtedly the biggest and noisiest stadium Archie had ever seen, either first-hand or on telly. Turning slowly on the spot, he tried to take in the sheer vastness of it, but it was all too much. Being logically minded, he visually dissected it, assessing one section at a time.

Its overall design was that of a circle, two-thirds of which were ascending rows of seats some hundred tiers deep. These were all chock-a-block with drunken, jeering creatures of all shapes and sizes. To Archie's utter disgust, the arena floor at the base of the first row of seats was awash with empty bottles and tankards, gnawed bones, half-eaten animal carcasses, and worst of all, steaming stinking piles of vomit and excrement. The black cloud of flies swarming all over it buzzed louder than a chainsaw.

From behind the top rows, hundreds of wooden spars jutted out, between which were strung flapping canvas sheets. Considering that Hexx had two suns, neither of which apparently produced much heat, Archie naturally assumed this was a pathetic attempt at shading.

The section of the amphitheatre in which he stood was rough and ready in its construction. Built from wood, its curving benches were flat and purely functional. Although never originally decorated, it had over the centuries become adorned with scratched messages of endearment and foul comments alike.

Before the crowd was a large circular open space marked on the left and right sides by Corinthian columns and ornate arches. Inside each arch stood a mean-looking chieftain with a broadsword in one huge hand and a large round shield in the other. Judging by the numerous bloodstains on the arena's dirt floor, they weren't there purely for aesthetic value.

In the middle of the arena was a large splodge of brown that strangely appeared to be edging its way to the left. Upon closer inspection with his monocular, Archie was amazed to see a dense stream of ants flowing away towards a drainage hole in the far wall. Carried upon their backs were the lifeless remains of two creatures, a short sword, a shield, a trident, and a net. Scuttling away to the right, clicking its vicious, bloodstained claws triumphantly, was a huge crab. Stopping briefly by an open portcullis, it snatched up a leather purse, howled victoriously at the baying crowd, then vanished inside the dark tunnel.

Spartacus the crab, thought Archie nervously. *That's novel!*

The remaining third of the theatre was a large open wooden stage over which were also fitted long wooden spars. However, the awnings there were richly coloured, neatly fitting tapestries. Beneath these were dozens of flagpoles, all flying fluttering colourful flags and banners of all shapes and sizes. Some of the symbols, such as earth, wind, fire, and water, Archie recognised immediately. Others were linked to stars, and the rest baffled him.

Seated quietly upon a pyramid-shaped formation of seats in the right-hand corner of the stage were nine figures of obvious importance. Archie presumed they were the main body of the council of the power ten genies. Uniformed servants served them wine from bejewelled decanters, and each one was more outlandishly dressed than the next. As fashion blunders went, they were a multicar pileup.

In stark contrast to all their outrageous opulence, swaying forlornly in the centre of the stage was a ragtag assortment of stupidly grinning creatures. There were no heavy chains manacling their feet, claws, or hoofs, yet they waited as if rooted to the wooden planks upon which they stood.

To the left of the stage was the ugliest throne Archie had ever seen. Both it and the plinth it stood upon were made of black stone. In a semicircle behind it were four crimson flags, each displaying the same image: a crimson helmet with six black horns. Baldizar marched towards the podium.

Archie sighed forlornly. 'Blimey, this place is like a school Christmas pantomime!'

Baldizar headed directly for the ugly throne. Archie was about to follow when a huge, hairy hand with fingers like bananas grabbed him by the scruff of the neck and hoisted him unceremoniously into the air.

'Where do you think you're going, maggot?' growled a thunderous voice from behind him.

'Hey, what's going on?' cried Archie, his manacled feet rattling. 'Put me down at once!'

The thick, muscular arm held him solidly aloft, bent at the elbow, bringing him face to face with none other than Goldhorn himself. The chieftain captain stared at him with big, unblinking eyes then snorted, covering Archie's face with steaming snot.

'Be you the maggot known as Archie Wilde?' he asked in a rumbling voice.

'Yes, I am!' snapped Archie boldly.

Goldhorn drew Archie's pale face closer and snorted again. 'Do you accept the challenge of the race,' he growled, 'be the consequences good or grisly?'

Say yes. Say yes, thalked Grizwold frantically. *His stinky snot's seeping in everywhere!*

'Yes, I accept,' blurted Archie rashly, not really sure just what he'd accepted. 'Now could you...'

Goldhorn effortlessly threw Archie a full thirty feet onto the wooden stage. 'Then take your place alongside the other maggots.'

Archie struck the hard wood planking with an elbow scraping smack, his head bouncing like a rubber ball as he tumbled painfully across the stage floor. 'Aw, that hurt, you great, hairy, cow-faced clod!' His tirade escaped his lips before Grizwold had chance to censor it.

A loud gasp of shock silenced the drunken crowd instantly. No creature, let alone a lowly maggot, had ever spoken to the mighty Goldhorn like that.

'What did you say?' roared Goldhorn, leaping up onto the stage and stomping towards the panting youth.

Grovel, pleaded Grizwold. *If you want to save both our lives, grovel like you've never grovelled before.*

'Well, sir, when I said "hurt,"' squeaked Archie, 'I... er... I didn't really mean painfully hurt, Captain, sir...'

Standing astride Archie, Goldhorn glared down menacingly. 'Test not my patience, maggot.'

For the second time in one day, Archie gurgled in horror as

a broadsword fell towards him. Archie felt the razor-sharp edge of his mighty blade nick his left ear before stabbing deeply into the wooden stage floor.

'This is your first and last warning, maggot,' snorted Goldhorn, his massive bull's head blotting the sun. 'Once you're collared, your fair game!' The captain of the chieftains dropped to one knee, his hot, rancid breath steaming Archie's face. 'Personally, I neither like nor dislike you, but as the overseer to the race, justice is mine to dispense. And I have an exceptionally long blade!'

Goldhorn wrenched his sword free, and Archie sucked in a deep breath of relief as the giant minotaur raised himself to full height and turned away, leaving Archie's sweaty head bouncing on the planks as his huge ironclad boots clomped across the stage.

You've only been on Hexx for less than a candle mark, thalked Grizwold angrily, *and already you've been threatened by the two most feared creatures in the genieverse!*

'Jagdar's teeth, Archie, you twonka,' cried Boff angrily. 'His mother, if he ever had one, didn't name him Slaughterium because of his stunning good looks, you know!' He roughly hauled the boy onto his feet then threw the filthy animal cape about his shoulders. 'Egads, Archie, your problem with authority is going to get us all naffin' dusted!'

'Well, actually,' injected Grizwold with Archie's voice, 'Goldhorn only ever intended to scare Archie. He has yet to be collared!'

'*Collared?*' repeated Archie. 'Goldhorn said something about being collared.'

'All maggots are given a band of gold to wear about their

necks,' said Grizwold, deftly avoiding the truth. 'It is recognized throughout the genieverse as the symbol of a contestant, announcing your legitimacy to enter the race.'

'A band of gold, huh?' Archie asked. 'That doesn't sound too bad. Is it valuable?'

Boff smirked. 'Oh yes. It's designed like a serpent with three ruby red eyes, biting its own tail. Made from the purest spungold, it has the lustre of a setting sun and the touch of fiery silk. It's considered one of the most precious items in the genieverse.'

'And this collar is mine to keep?'

'For as long as you... *live*,' said Boff reluctantly.

'And I get this just for entering a race? Why?'

'The true purpose of the race is to find the legendary Fangs of Jagdar, an ancient dagger lost in time,' said Grizwold. 'Find this dagger, and your prize will be elevation to the status of an elemental genie, the first level in the council of the power ten genies.'

'Einstein's underpants,' Archie said. 'Fancy me being an apprentice genie!'

Chapter 14

PLANET HEXX.

From his stone throne, Baldizar watched with amusement as Goldhorn toyed with Archie Wilde. During the early part of his rule as El Supremo, he had quickly learnt of the minotaur's volatile nature, a most desirable attribute in a captain of the chieftains. Frustratingly, though, he also cursed the creature's fanatical addiction to law and order. However, that somewhat inconvenient side of the minotaur's nature would serve his needs perfectly.

When the race began, as was laid down in the ancient scrolls by the Kalifar, every maggot could be legally hunted. Their spungold collars, sought after by every pirate, cutthroat, bandit, and robber throughout the genieverse, would be the prize. Therein lay Baldizar's problem.

Every piece of villainous scum alive would do their damnedest to hunt him down and cut his head from his neck to obtain that collar. And that could not be allowed, at least not until the boy had fulfilled his purpose. His cold eyes wandered back to Goldhorn, his clinical mind scheming feverishly. *And that, my brutal captain of the chieftains, is where your doppelganger will come into play*, he thought.

Baldizar sat majestically upon his throne, his four arms at rest, his head held high, his sneering contempt for the lowlife scum in the stands masked by his closed helmet visor.

To his left was a seat of polished teak, its only embellishment a simple yet striking enchantment inscribed in the ancient tongue. Unlike his own, it was adorned with Graffarian sun-silk cushions and was reserved for the wife or concubine of the elected El Supremo. On many ceremonial occasions and to the abhorrence of the council and the masses alike, only one *special* female had ever sat upon this throne. Many speculated in private as to why she, of all creatures, had been chosen, but none dared to question El Supremo.

Surrounding the two thrones stood his bureaucratic infrastructure, the chosen few. They were close allies, paid nobles, and local dignitaries.

A tree adorned with tiny silver bells chimed, filling the air with fairy-like tinkling. All eyes turned expectantly towards the ornate Victorian toilet at the rear of the podium. The toilet flushed, its porcelain handle bobbing and dancing on the end of its long gold chain. A column of glistening-rainbow water droplets erupted from its bowl, and from amidst the mist of its swirling vortex, a vague image appeared.

An uneasy hush rippled out across the amphitheatre as every creature stared uneasily at Baldizar's personal hydroportal. With great theatrical flair, a figure dressed in metallic emerald-green armour stepped clear of the mist and approached El Supremo.

'Serpentina,' said Baldizar in a loud voice laced with a thread of disapproval. '*You're late!*' His cold black eyes never once left hers. 'The collaring is about to begin.'

Clad in her figure-hugging suit, Serpentina turned slowly, allowed her curvaceous form to dazzle the crowd, all the time holding a large leather bag above her head. Timing her twirl perfectly, she finished and faced her El Supremo, and with a flash of her vivid golden-yellow cat eyes, she bowed graciously. The most notorious assassin in the genieverse had made her statement entrance, and the crowd was eager for her to reveal her latest trophy.

All creatures, young and old, near and far, recognized the face of the beautiful woman, who had the charismatic nature of an angel and the sadistic heart of a killer. Whence she came, nobody knew, but some said that Baldizar himself had plucked her from a nightmare, creating his own personal champion of evil.

A mischievous smile lit up the blue horizontal strip across Serpentina's face. Playing the moment well, she teased her El Supremo just enough before falling submissively to one knee and offering him the leather bag with her head bowed.

'For my beloved El Supremo, a present just for you, wrapped in my most humble apologies for not arriving sooner.' Her humble words soothed his bloated ego. 'Once a thorn in your side, I now offer this to you as a trophy and a token of my loyalty to your magnificence.'

Taking the bag carefully in one hand, he weighed its roundness thoughtfully before peering inside. 'Behold!' he cried, triumphantly rising to his feet and thrusting the object into the air. 'The crystal eye of the rebel traitor, Mog Droddle!'

The crowd erupted, shouting and screaming the glories of their El Supremo.

'To the victor go the spoils, my El Supremo,' offered Serpentina, her eyes never leaving the floor. 'It will make a fitting addition to your other trophies.' By his grace, she slowly rose, and once again bowing long and low, willingly accepted his motion for her to sit at the wooden throne to his left.

Before taking her seat, she quickly assessed the rows of court officials lining the back of the podium with the cold eyes of an assassin. Only one had the brazen audacity to lock eyes with her, a tall man dressed in a designer grey suit that exuded authority up close yet faded like a spectre at a distance. Her eyes narrowed scornfully as she tried to focus on the man's vague, almost ghostly facial features, half hidden beneath the brim of his matching grey homburg hat. The professor was both an enigma and an abomination.

Him again. She cursed inwardly. *I might have guessed he wouldn't be far.* From the gutter to the throne room, all whispers had linked him to the ancient black art of technology and other foul atrocities. Like a leech, he seldom left Baldizar's side, his forked tongue and devious manner forever manipulating El Supremo with his own insidious brand of evil.

As they waited for the trumpets to signal the ceremonies to start, Baldizar found himself staring thoughtfully at Serpentina. *Such loyalty, my sweet,* he mused. *If only you knew the truth, the reality of your birth right.* The professor had done an excellent job in fashioning her helmet in the shape of a striking serpent's head. It complemented the blue flash across her vivid golden cat's eyes, the last remaining key to her real identity. It had been an inspired final touch to a faultless disguise.

On the stage, Archie stared across at the fashion disaster to his left. 'That mob in the pantomime outfits—I presume they're the council?' he asked.

'Jagdar's teeth, boy, that they are,' Boff said bitterly. 'Next to Baldizar, the council of the power ten genies are the most powerful and hated creatures in the genieverse.'

'They're a motley-looking bunch, aren't they?' He laughed. 'What do they actually do?'

'Never underestimate that lot, for they see and hear all,' warned Boff. 'Creatures who foolishly provoke genies tend to vanish in the night!'

'Hmm, thanks for the heads-up,' said Archie quietly. 'Who are the two at the front? They don't strike me as scary.'

'Odds bodkins, you're right there, boy,' he agreed. 'The wrinkly old man in the yellow-and-blue stripes with the doughnut hat and feathers is Eccles Nimrod, the genie in charge of order. The six-legged fellow next to him in the awful brown-and-white spots is a cinnamon crab called Archibald Pinchwick. He's the systems genie.' The corners of Boff's thick leathery lips curled down in a nasty scowl. 'That pair's evil. The rest? Well, I wouldn't give them the naffin' barnacles of me bum!'

Grizwold twisted Archie's head to the left. *For the sake of your future health, Archie Wilde, it's the other maggots you should be studying.*

They're a strange bunch too, Archie replied. *Who are they, Grizwold, and did they get volunteered like me?*

No. All these maggots have been declared criminally insane.

What? cried Archie. *So, I'm up against a bunch of crooks?*

The creature at the far end, continued Grizwold, *the one that looks like a sixty-foot-tall, multicoloured exploding feather duster, is a gunnygunny bird called Boondok. They don't talk as we do—they communicate by gestures. That one is particularly stupid and will be of little threat to you. Next is a strewth.*

What, that sausage-shaped thing floating in mid-air? thalked Archie inquisitively.

Yes.

The thing without a mouth?

Well-spotted, Grizwold said. *You're learning fast. The strewth communicate by whistling various tunes out of their bottoms with compressed methane.*

They fart-sing! Archie laughed childishly. *Well, that's original, if not smelly!* The next in line was a small, shaggy-haired, feral-type creature who looked like an extra from *The Hobbit. And the next?*

Grizwold groaned heavily. *That is Spagbot. He's trouble! He's a shape-shifting hobgoblin who relishes mischief and other creatures' misfortunes. Don't be misled by his tiny stature. He can be a wily, ruthless individual when he wishes.*

Archie raised an eyebrow. *Is that a hamster next to him?*

It is, and a ridiculously cute and amiable little fellow he is too. Goes by the name of Ohloo.

He doesn't look criminally insane to me, Archie said.

Oh, he's not, thalked Grizwold. *He's simply misunderstood.*

Misunderstood?

Yes. They're without doubt the most placid race in the genieverse most of the time.

Most of the time, Archie echoed suspiciously.

Unfortunately, they have a trigger word that sends them into a violent murderous frenzy. Most regrettable, but there are reports of whole villages being destroyed by an unsuspecting stranger uttering the wrong word.

So, what's the trigger word, then? asked Archie.

Sadly, thalked Grizwold, *only the hamsters know that.*

How sad, declared Archie, leaning casually against the metal statue next to him. *Sounds like a self-defence mechanism gone terribly wrong.*

And the last one is Boombelly, announced Grizwold.

Archie peered around the statue. *There isn't another one, Grizwold.* The sound of grinding metal made Archie look up, straight into the piercing blue eye of the statue, whose big square head and jaw were directly above him.

Archie Wilde, maggot from Earth, meet Boombelly of Mexx, Grizwold said cordially. *He's a mechanoid, aren't you, Boombelly?*

Actually, thalked a deep metallic voice, *we prefer to be known as Ironiods.*

I humbly apologize, thalked Grizwold graciously. *We haven't met for a while. How are you?*

My stovepipe chimney is puffing merrily, thank you, and my furnace heart is ticking over with a rhythmic boom, boom, boom on a hot bed of nicely roasting phutt phutt nuts. Life couldn't be better.

Flippin' heck, Archie thalked, *you can thalk!*

My kind can do a lot of things, human youngling, said the mechanical man.

But you're a robot, thalked Archie thoughtlessly. *Who made you?*

We Ironiods are a sentient life form. Whereas you humans crawled out of the sea, we crawled out of a volcano. His square eyes in his big square head smiled. *Enough thalk. The race will commence soon, and I must conserve my steam.*

'Well, trounce me trunnions,' Boff said, laughing. 'You weren't expecting old Boombelly Ironsides kind, were you?'

'Er… no,' replied Archie. 'But then, first thing this morning, I wasn't really expecting any of this!'

'In the beginning, the race originally had Olympic status,' declared Boff. 'Only the fittest athletes and adventurers used to enter. Back then, it was deemed an honour to be chosen to search for the fabled Fangs of Jagdar dagger.'

'So, what went wrong, then?' asked Archie.

'Time went wrong,' continued Grizwold, using Archie's voice. 'After one hundred decades, the power ten genie council concluded that either the dagger simply didn't exist, or it was lost forever to history.'

Boff slapped two tentacle hands together, rubbing them greedily. 'But the ceremony of Atunka Gaar was a grand money-maker. And if rumours are to be believed, then over the years, the genie council has made many thousands of chests of spungold out of it.'

'So, it's all down to money,' sighed Archie. 'Who are these poor creatures then?' he asked, nodding at the line.

'Like we said, they're the criminally insane,' answered Boff.

'Criminally insane,' spat Archie, suddenly feeling sick to the core. 'They're going to race those poor sick creatures just for money.'

'Why not?' said a deadpan Boff. 'The crowd gets a free three-day festival, chock full of fun-filled entertainment and the chance to win a few snippets of spungold. The greedy genie council get to fill yet more of their chests with reels of spungold. And thanks to the race, the chieftains neatly dispose of some of its worst criminal elements.'

Archie's jaw popped open, his face pale with shock.

'Jagdar's teeth,' roared Boff, twirling his tentacles like a windmill's sails, 'everyone's a winner. Why change it?'

Archie was about to declare his outrage and speak out for the poor creatures when he was struck by a disturbing thought. 'Hang on a minute. What exactly do you mean by, disposed of?'

Boff flushed a pale grey, and Grizwold went ominously silent.

'I said, what do you mean by, *disposed of*?'

Boff anxiously drummed his forty fingers together. 'Well, I suppose you would have to find out eventually,' he said reluctantly, 'so I might as well tell you now.'

Archie frowned at him; his arms folded tightly across his chest. 'I'm waiting!'

'It's the golden collar you're given.'

'Yes.'

'After twelve candle marks, it...'

Archie's eye patch suddenly flared painfully. Whatever Boff was going to say, he knew he wasn't going to like it. 'Spit it out, Squid Boy,' snapped Archie. 'After twelve candle marks, what happens?'

'After twelve candle marks'—Boff flushed a sickly white but forced himself to continue— 'if you haven't found the dagger, it contracts upon itself, decapitating its wearer.'

Icicles suddenly ran down Archie's spine. '*Decapitates*? As in, my head falls off?'

'Er, yes,' Boff replied awkwardly.

Archie shuddered.

In the outer reaches of the stadium, up in the cheap seats, Nogga hid beneath the hood of an inconspicuous, bright-yellow cape and interpreted the nod from the professor as his signal to act. From within the carpetbag the human scientist had given him, he withdrew an aggressive-looking weapon. Nestling the butt of the gun into his podgy left shoulder, he took aim. Exhaling slowly, he waited for the target to move into the crosshairs of its sight then squeezed the trigger.

A brilliant-green beam of light the thickness of a human hair flashed across the amphitheatre, striking Archie's head like a surgical thunderbolt. Inside his skull, Archie's brain went berserk, as if suddenly wired to a nuclear power station.

He went gaga. Abruptly, Archie stood bolt upright, every muscle in his body rippling like tumultuous waves on a stormy sea.

'Jagdar's teeth, Grizzy,' Boff said, 'what are you doing to the poor boy now?'

Archie threw off his old fur cape then bent down and counted his toes. 'Ha ha, it's a grand day for bog jumping!' He laughed aloud. 'Especially if you're a potato peeler.' Then with a weirdly self-righteous grin, he shoved Boff aside and did a handstand. 'Beat this if you can, Bilge Rat Boff,' he goaded, walking about the stage on his hands.

The crowd loved it. As criminally insane maggots went, the human youngling was the best.

Annoyed, Boff floated back over to the boy. 'Hornswoggle me giblets, Grizzy,' he cried in his ear, 'ease off on the naffin' adrenaline, mutmut! He's only a youngling!'

'Not... me,' stammered Grizwold's scratchy voice. 'Not... me... Help!'

Somersaulting nimbly back onto his feet, Archie then cartwheeled over to the front of the stage, lifted his arms high in triumph, and bellowed, 'Behold! Elvis is in the house!'

Back in the cheap seats, a dozing, double-necked giraffosaurus, roused by the noise of the crowd, lifted both his heads in curiosity. As he stretched to full length, the green beam sliced through both his necks. Both mouths opened in shock, and then fell with a double thud onto the wooden floor.

Next to the giraffosaurus's crumpled body stood an annoyed looking swizzer crab. 'Hey, did you just cut my mate's heads off?' it enquired gruffly.

Nogga released the weapon's trigger and pulled back his hood. Nervously, he eyed the growing pool of yellow blood and the extremely large, rather annoyed front claw that the angry swizzer crab was pointing at him.

'Sorry,' he said uneasily. 'My picture maker seems to have malfunctioned!' It was a lame excuse, but no one cared—it was only a dumb giraffosaurus.

Whereas dolphins were considered the intellectuals of the ocean, so swizzer crabs were deemed the moronic thugs of the crustacean world. They were devoid of any sense of humour and notoriously slow at cottoning onto an outright lie. However, what they lacked in intelligence, they made up for with brutal hostility.

From along its spiny back, one of many long wispy antennas whipped down and snatched the device out of Nogga's sweaty grip. Using all eight of its stalked eyes on the front of its bony head, it curiously studied the object. As it struggled to engage its single brain cell, it snatched a small snail from the head of another crustacean with its second antennae, popping it hungrily between its crunching jaws.

'That isn't no picture maker,' it finally deduced. 'Not likes what I've ever seen!'

'Well spotted, my friend,' said Nogga, snatching the weapon back. 'The device you see before you is in fact the latest word in picture makers.'

The swizzer crab eyed the slugman suspiciously. 'The clod's not buying it, you buffoon,' whispered Skatt.

'Jagdar's teeth,' snapped Nogga, losing his patience. 'No, it's not naffin' picture maker, you excruciatingly stupid excuse for a life form. It's a crazy-ray brain disrupter, loaded with an organically grown cucumber. Okay, there, *happy?* Or is that too much information for that speck of a brain of yours to handle?'

Now, although not the cleverest creature, the swizzer crab did understand verbal abuse. Yanking the device back out of Nogga's hands, it wrenched open the loading chamber and delicately squeezed the cucumber. It seemed genuinely saddened by the squishy green goo.

'Er... that's not nice. Poor, defenceless cucumber!' remarked the swizzer crab.

'Who cares?' yelled Nogga. 'It's only a stupid vegetable!'

The swizzer crab's left claw was large, hard, and covered in barnacles, and it struck Nogga square in the face with the force of a cannonball. Nogga's smile was squashed into the back of his head by its tremendous impact. His blubbery piggy face and leathery, bulbous bulk lifted clean out of his seat and went whirling off into the distance.

'Me half-brother Eric is a cucumber,' remarked the swizzer crab to no one in particular as he turned his attention back to the stage. 'Mmickys shouldn't do things like that, not even to a vegetable. Not nice!' There was a sudden yelp as the crab flicked a small, hairy creature out of the amphitheatre in roughly the same direction as the disappearing slugman. 'And take your scabby mutt with you!'

As the green bean suddenly stopped, so Archie's fleeting insanity cleared, the words of the ranting mob became louder and clearer. 'Murderer! Murderer! Murderer!'

'Archie, Grizwold, snap out of it,' begged Boff, gripping the boy's shoulders and shaking him hard. 'Look what you've done!'

Baldizar, having witnessed the flash of green and then watched in horror as Archie went bananas on stage, exploded with rage, smashing two gauntlets down and chipping the arms of his throne. 'Whoever is responsible for this outrage,' he hissed, glaring at his petrified entourage, 'will pay with their lives!'

To the rear, lurking in the shadows, the professor stifled a knowing laugh.

Chapter 15

PLANET HEXX.

'Listen to me, Archie,' said an anxious voice in the fog. 'Just do exactly what I say, *okay?*'

'Hee hee,' giggled Archie, relishing the sensation of his brain slopping about in his head like a dumpling in a bowl of stew. 'Oookaaay.'

'Slowly lift your right foot,' pleaded Boff anxiously, 'then step carefully backwards.'

Archie took a breath, focused, then did as instructed, only to abruptly stop mid move. 'Boff, why are they all shouting, murderer,' he asked flatly, the last of the fog lifting. 'And why am I holding my foot up?' Archie, his eye patch seriously burning, watched Boff swivel both his eyes at him. 'Oh, fubar. I've done something stupid, haven't I?'

'Scupper me, boy, you going utterly gaga on stage was actually quite entertaining. It had the crowd in hysterics,' said Boff, 'until you dusted one of the other maggots!'

'Oh, blessed Jagdar,' groaned Grizwold, using Archie's voice, 'have mercy upon us all.'

'Jagdar's teeth, Grizzy,' moaned Boff, 'it's worse than that.'

Grizwold's groan sounded like a creaky door slowly closing. 'Oh no. It wasn't—'

'Oh yes, it naffin' was,' said Boff. 'Young Archie here has

only dusted none other than Mugwart the Indigestible, the odds-on favourite to win the race!' He cuffed Archie on the side of his head. 'Thanks to you, dullard, most of that angry mob over there have just lost sizable amounts of spungold!'

Confused, Archie quickly looked up the line of other maggots. 'I'm confused. They all look fine to me!'

Boff tapped his right foot with a tentacle. 'Try looking under your boot!'

An empty tankard sailed across the arena, striking the stage at their feet. Its owner yelled, 'Murder! He's done old Mugwart in!'

'Yeah, and the bloomin' race hasn't even started yet!' bellowed another.

Archie stared at the wooden floor. 'There's nothing there.'

'Check the sole of your boot, laddie!'

Archie grabbed his right boot and pulled it upwards. 'Oh, yuk!' he cried spotting a gooey splodge of orange. 'Oh, that's disgusting.' Without thinking, he scraped the goo off on the edge of the stage. The entire amphitheatre, including the chieftains, gasped in horror at his gross act of disrespect. 'Oh, what now?' he groaned.

'That goo that you have just so callously scrapped off were the remains of the one-hundred-and-tenth Bonsai ruler of the venerable Mugwart dynasty.'

'It was!' whispered Archie.

'Scupper me, boy,' said Boff. 'What possessed you to do it?'

Baldizar watched the crowd surge forward, those at the front spilling out of their seats and onto the dirty, rubbish-strewn arena floor. Sensing the mob's outrage at being swindled out of their anticipated winnings, he quickly realized that the situation was getting out of control.

Goldhorn understood that the murderer needed to be swiftly punished and moved quickly, backed by a squad of his chieftains, but Baldizar moved quicker. With a gravity-defying leap, he launched himself out of his throne and into the air. Using his genie magic, he hurled himself eighty feet, covering half the length of the stage, before crashing boot first onto the wooden planking, making everyone jump in shock.

Archie, awestruck by old Buckethead's attempt at flying, recoiled in horror when he saw him snatch up an open golden collar. 'Einstein's underpants,' he gasped, guessing Baldizar's intentions. With a hostile crowd and the chieftains before him, a collar toting El Supremo to the right, and the council genies to the left, he was left with only one course of action.

'Stuff this,' he muttered. 'I'm off!' Stomping his right foot hard, Archie lurched backward in full getaway mode, instantly slamming into something huge and hairy, which, laughing grotesquely, wrapped him up in six long, hairy, strong arms.

'Let me go!' yelled Archie.

'Going somewhere, *matey*?' growled a throaty voice. Twisting his head around, Archie was shocked to see the face of a one-eyed gorilla.

The council of the power ten genies thought it great sport. They leapt to their feet, clapping and cheering, as they watched Baldizar and Goldhorn race towards the trembling maggot.

'Oh crikey, I'm going to die,' whimpered Archie, fearfully clamping his eyes shut. However, it was not the kiss of cold steel he felt but the firm, surprisingly calm voice of Baldizar.

'Head please, Og,' he requested. In answer to this command, a large, leathery hand plastered itself across Archie's face, yanking his head backwards.

'Me pleasure, gov,' grunted Og.

'*Desist, Baldizar*,' bellowed Goldhorn, 'in the name of the law!'

With Archie's neck exposed and no chance of wiggling free, Baldizar slid the golden collar neatly about it, snapping it shut with a satisfying click.

'As always, a timely intervention, Og,' Baldizar said. 'You can release him now.'

'Okay, gov,' grunted the gorilla.

'Stand fast, Captain Goldhorn!' commanded Baldizar in a tone so deep and powerful that even the advancing crowd suddenly hesitated, unsure what to do next.

'As decreed by the ancient laws,' Baldizar proclaimed, 'the maggot Archie Wilde has now been officially collared, and the chieftains can neither help nor hinder him.' Stretching himself up to full height, he glared menacingly across at the seething crowd, at the line of minotaur's then back at the furious captain. 'Goldhorn, I *order* you to take your chieftains and subdue the mob!'

Goldhorn, his massive chest heaving like a fired-up boiler, glared angrily at the genie. *If the great god Jagdar had given me wings*, he thought bitterly, *then the murderer Archie Wilde would now lie upon the floor, cleaved in two, justice done!* But it was not to be. The maggot was collared, and that was an end to it.

With frustration burning in his eyes, Goldhorn stomped furiously off the stage. But as his iron boots hit the arena's dirt floor, he suddenly stopped and glared back, addressing El Supremo with bold, harsh words. 'You use the ancient laws cunningly, Baldizar, as would a thief in the night.' Raising his sword, he pointed it accusingly at Baldizar's metal heart. 'Heed my warning, *El Supremo*. Dare to challenge the law and my authority again, and you'll find my sword tip waiting!'

Baldizar's red eyes flared, but he stayed his temper and was shrewd in his silence. Then with a calculated leisurely turn, he studied the murmuring crowd, gauging their mood. He could almost taste their desire for rebellion, but it was the time for diplomacy, not bloodshed. He glanced furtively up at the giant image of Garrknock rising majestically above the stage and smiled. That time would come soon enough.

'Still here, Captain?' He sneered mockingly at the minotaur. 'Away with you and be about your work.'

Whilst Goldhorn hated genies, *especially* Baldizar, he was the law and must be seen to uphold it. Fighting the urge to strike the loathsome creature down, the captain of the chieftains sheathed his sword and grudgingly obeyed. Baldizar gloated as the minotaur marched out into the arena floor, bellowing orders and demanding to know where his useless second-in-command, Lieutenant Redhorn, was.

'Take this flipping thing off me,' growled Archie, tugging and pulling at the collar. 'Go and cut someone else's flipping head off.'

Baldizar flicked the collar with a metal fingertip. 'No.'

'Why not?' demanded Archie, his face red and sweaty.

'Because I don't want to,' replied Baldizar, '*yet*.'

Archie stopped tugging and glared at him, his eye patch

really burning. 'You could take this thing off me then if you wanted to?'

'Oh yes, and I fully intend to—'

'Why do I sense a *but* coming?' muttered Archie.

'How perceptive,' continued Baldizar. 'You're turning out better than I'd hoped.'

Archie remembered both Baldizar and Boff speaking about him earlier that day as if he were an item rather than a person. 'Hoped? What do you mean?' he asked.

'Let's just say that for the last ten years, I've been preparing you for this race.'

'Preparing me how?' asked Archie.

'Why do you think I gave you a free run of the scrapyard and my credit card? Why do you think I allowed you to do all those insanely dangerous experiments of yours?'

Archie felt angry, used, and betrayed. 'So, for all of those years, all that time I'd thought I'd finally found some sort of family, it was all a façade. Just a place where you could train your own pet mouse for your stupid race.' Archie was close to tears, but he didn't want Buckethead to see, so he let his head loll forward, sniffing quietly.

Boff, who up until that moment hadn't dared approach the boy, floated tentatively forward and put a reassuring tentacle about his shoulders. Suddenly, he knew the real reason he'd stayed on Earth all those years.

'Find me the Fangs of Jagdar dagger, Archie Wilde,' declared Baldizar magnanimously, 'and I'll release you from that collar. But also remember this: complete this task, and an apprentice genie you will become!'

'Archie, my boy, agree to his offer,' whispered Boff. 'You

have no real choice!'

Boff speaks the truth, thalked Grizwold sadly. *Acceptance of his offer is your only chance.* Then he added optimistically. *And it will give us twelve candle marks to formulate a solution to this problem.*

Archie sniffed back his tears and raised his head, his face set with a dogged determination. 'Okay, Buckethead. You win,' he hissed venomously. 'For the moment, you need me, and I need you. What next?'

'Good,' said Baldizar. 'Your anger will only strengthen your resolve. Better standard of entertainment all round.' From a pouch on his waist belt, Baldizar withdrew a scroll of parchment, which he handed to the boy. 'Take this and read it. It will guide you to the dagger.'

Archie opened the scroll and read it aloud:

'If you be a maggot, then listen ye well.
Seek you a place that's neither Heaven nor Hell.
A cauldron of fury, both fire and ice,
An Eden of monsters that slash and slice.
Dawn till dusk, it's ruled by *him,*
A fearsome creature both violent and dim.
A single feather of blood so red
You must pluck from its clucking head.
But heed the bones cast asunder
Of those poor souls who failed to plunder.
Yet if courage prevails with Jagdar's prize,
Then return to Hexx and join the wise.
Be hero or fool, a warning to muse:
Candle marks twelve, then heads you'll lose.'

He paused for a moment then spoke again. 'Okay, I've read your silly riddle. Now what?'

Baldizar adopted an outrageously pompous stance. 'Once I have collared all the other maggots,' said Baldizar, 'I shall officially begin the race, and the contest will start.'

'*Contest?*' asked Archie. 'What contest?'

Baldizar smiled. 'Oh, did I not mention it. You and the other maggots will cast into the Storming Kaleidoscope Falls, and from that point on, it's every creature for himself!'

'How will I know where to go?' asked Archie.

'You have almost a candle mark before the race starts in earnest,' said Baldizar, walking towards the chest that held the remaining five golden collars. 'Plenty of time for you and Boff to figure it out.'

'*Me?*' Boff asked in surprise. 'I'm not a maggot. I can't enter the race!'

'For this occasion, I've changed the rules,' Baldizar said. 'You will accompany the boy!'

'Jagdar's teeth,' cursed Boff aloud, his whole body flaring a furious red, 'that's a mean trick, even for you.'

'I feel that the boy would benefit from your wisdom,' Baldizar said coldly.

Boff scowled. 'Scupper me. So, the word of the elected El Supremo really does mean nothing these days!'

Baldizar jerked to a halt, spinning on his iron heels. 'Hold your tongue, Storm Raider,' he hissed, 'lest I dust you here and now.' Struggling, Boff checked his anger, his body flushing a vivid red. 'Wise choice, *babysitter!*'

Archie watched Baldizar move away then turned to Boff. 'Looks like your freedom was just a lie, and we're both prisoners.'

Boff's disappointment was obvious. 'Jagdar's teeth, he's a cold-hearted villain for sure. I should have naffin' known better.'

'How long is twelve candle marks, anyway?' asked Archie.

'About twelve Earth hours,' answered Boff quietly.

'When does it start?'

'It already has.'

Archie's jaw popped open. 'What do you mean?'

'Yeah, the moment he clicks the collar shut, your candle starts to burn.'

'*What?!*' cried Archie in dismay. 'That was a whole flippin' five minutes ago.' Fumbling frantically, he opened his mobile phone and quickly set the stopwatch to eleven hours, fifty-five minutes. 'I need to go now!'

The nearly riotous mob, although corralled by the line of burly chieftains, was steadily shunting nearer to the stage. 'Blimey, they've blocked the entrance,' Archie said. Then he remembered his escape from the children's home that morning and grinned mischievously. 'What we need now is a good dose of chaos.' He laughed, pulling out his last remaining smoke grenade. Giving it a good-luck kiss, he yanked the pin out and tossed it into the approaching crowd.

'Hornswoggle me giblets, boy,' cried Boff, 'what are you doing? The race can only officially start when Garrknock's wings fall!'

Popping a couple of Muzzberry pips, Archie declared, 'This collar is around my neck, not yours! If you want to stay and listen to old Buckethead finish his speech, then be my guest, but I'm off now!' From another pocket, he retrieved four large jumping-jack fireworks, lit one, and tossed it towards the leading edge of the crowd. Then using his catapult, he fired the last three in a line towards the exit.

The smoke grenade fell and hissed amongst the angry creatures, who were quickly engulfed in a billowing cloud of purple smoke.

As the first jumping jack began exploding, scattering howling creatures in a frenzied panic, so Archie leaped from the stage. Grizwold, horrified at the boy's actions, tried to overrule his body but once again found himself strangely powerless to intervene.

Boff, praying as he floated off the stage, could do little else but follow.

From the stage, Baldizar watched Archie and Boff disappear into the purple fog. The move was totally unexpected but nevertheless impressive—the youngling's decision to go on the offensive immediately was a sure sign of courage and quick thinking. However, he found himself troubled by a nagging thought. *Had the professor designed the youngling too well?* Archie Wilde was clever, and he might possibly prove himself to be troublesomely so. Baldizar needed to know that the boy wouldn't deviate from his plan.

Acknowledging his commanding gesture, Serpentina quickly joined him upon the stage.

'Yes, my El Supremo,' she purred, 'what is your bidding?'

'The youngling, my dear. See how he has used the black art of technology to clear a path to the exit tunnel?'

'Yes, my El Supremo,' she agreed. 'For his age, he shows much intelligence, audacity, and cunning.'

'Whilst I admire these traits,' hissed Baldizar, placing a masterly hand upon her shoulder, 'I do not entirely trust the boy. You will join their party, ensure his safety, and guide him on his quest.'

'Yes, my El Supremo,' she replied without hesitation. 'As you command, so shall it be.'

Baldizar watched, intrigued as the multiple explosions set the mob panicking. He found their fear and confusion most satisfying. As he smirked at Goldhorn and his minotaur's desperately trying to regain control of the surging crowd, he sensed a creature's stealthy approach from behind. The footsteps were mouse-like—it could be only one person.

'Is sneaking up on other creatures second nature to you?' Baldizar asked mockingly as a tall, shadowy figure in a grey suit neared, hesitating just short.

'My El Supremo, I have good news,' announced Professor Ratchet Madspanner, ignoring the insult. 'The replication went well, and your *special* squad is now ready for deployment.'

Baldizar's cold eyes narrowed as he stared down at the despicable little toad of a man. 'Your doppelgangers of Lieutenant Redhorn and his platoon of chieftains... You're quite sure no one will notice the exchange?'

'I've had them on the fortress's parade ground, drilling for the past two candle marks. None of the other chieftains gave them a second glance, my El Supremo.'

'You have done well, Ratchet,' Baldizar said, his use of the professor's first name a rare compliment. 'Dispatch the duplicates immediately to Bleak to await the youngling's arrival. Order them to keep Archie Wilde safe at all costs until he finds the dagger.'

Madspanner swallowed as Baldizar leant forward, the heat

from his glowing red eyes making him sweat.

'Understood?'

'Until the dagger is found. Yes, my El Supremo,' he repeated, bowing respectfully. 'I will dispatch Redhorn and his platoon to Bleak immediately.'

'Good. Now go!'

The professor backed up several paces before turning and scurrying off the stage. Minutes later, from the safety of a seldom-used passageway, he stopped and peered through a small, barred, cobweb-festooned window. Although at ground level, his view of the stage and the collaring ceremony was clear. 'Baldizar, you're a small-minded, pathetic creature,' he murmured, his long, bony fingers curling tightly about the old iron bars, his daringly loud laugher echoing safely in the deserted tunnel.

'Oh, I'll give Lieutenant Redhorn his orders,' he declared treacherously, 'but they will be *my orders!* Archie Wilde will die at the first opportunity, along with that ridiculous mythological claptrap about a magical dagger.'

'I, Professor Ratchet Madspanner, will usurp you, you sad little tin-pot dictator, and purge this universe of all genies. I will be the rightful dictator of the universe, and my secret technology army will ensure my rule forever!'

Chapter 16

'**G**eronimo!' yelled Archie as he leapt off the stage.

Before Boff could utter a word, Archie had vanished into the billowing purple fog. 'Jagdar's teeth, that boy's hotheaded,' he grumbled, puffing up his hydrogen bags and floating over the bedlam below.

With the jumping jacks exploding everywhere, the smoke-filled arena had become a mass of screaming creatures. From deep within, Boff bellowed a storm raider's battle cry that fired his blood and terrorized those nearby. Electrified by the moment, Bilge Rat Boff charged forward, lashing out with his ten-tentacle fists with combat precision, smacking, punching, and shoving anything that came close, carving a gangway straight through the mob.

Below, submerged in the fog, Archie was dodging and weaving his way through a jungle of panic-stricken aliens. Along with the tang of the smoke grenade, he could also smell the unmistakable aroma of burning wood. Luckily, he was fast and nimble on his feet, and he somehow managed to avoid the groups of fighting creatures and bloodied corpses that peppered the arena floor. Having a brilliant mind was a wonderful thing, but he was no Bruce Lee, so he was astonished when his hands and feet took on lives of their own. Chopping, jabbing, throwing, and thrusting, he fought towards his goal, thankful for his new brain bug's help.

'Yes!' cried Archie, victoriously punching the air. By instinct alone, he'd found the tunnel, and to his delight, it was both open and unguarded. Skidding to a halt behind the cover of the gate, he paused, panting, and glanced back. Archie burst into laughter at the sight of Boff's chamelesquid body flushing a royal red as he fought his way towards him.

'Enjoying yourself, Boff?' shouted Archie over the noise of the crowd.

'Trounce me trunnions, boy!' roared Boff, 'I haven't had this much fun in naffin' years!' Glancing past his friend, Archie thought that just for a moment, he glimpsed a green smudge in the fog. But with so many brightly coloured creatures running about, he could have been mistaken.

'Move your butt, matey!' shouted Boff as he floated into the tunnel. 'That smoke's thinning fast!'

Away from the brightness of the arena, the tunnel leading back to the massive outer gates, although well-lit by dozens of flaming torches, seemed murky and full of shadows. With no cover, they moved cautiously forward, hugging the wall, desperately trying to control their panting breath. Archie did his best to ignore the strange glowing orange spiders that watched them from every crevice with hungry eyes.

Archie stopped, crouching behind a small statue, a mere sixty feet from the gates. He popped a Muzzberry pip, marvelling at its instant calming effect. Surprisingly, given the sound of bedlam coming from the arena, the four giant shovelhead mammoths stood peacefully, swinging their trunks to and fro seemingly oblivious to the ensuing riot.

'What now, Archie?' whispered Boff, still pumped up and raring for action.

'First things first,' Archie replied. *Grizwold, my friend, thanks. I would never have made it through that lot alive if it hadn't been for your skill and expertise. I'm really glad to have you aboard.*

Stunned by his words, Grizwold lost his balance and slipped off Archie's brain. *M-my pleasure* was all he could falteringly thalk. In all his centuries of being a mutmut, none of his maggots had ever referred to him as a friend.

From a vest pocket, Archie produced two of the biggest jumping jacks Boff had ever seen. 'Jagdar's fiery breath, Archie,' he whispered. 'They're not fireworks—they're military weapons!'

Archie smiled devilishly. 'These babies are "Disruptors." They're so powerful that they were taken off the market for safety reasons.' He looked across at the lounging mammoths, his smile fading.

'What's wrong Archie?' asked Boff, aware of the boy's sudden sadness. 'Won't they do the trick?'

'Oh, they're plenty powerful enough to scare them into opening the doors,' replied Archie, 'I just don't like to do it.'

Boff was confused. 'Back there in the arena and this morning at the orphanage, you didn't seem to care.'

'That was different,' said Archie.

'Different?' asked Boff. 'How so?'

'Most people, including those creatures back there, are all the same vile type.' There was a thread of loathing in his voice, one that Boff had never heard before. 'It's always their kind that cruelly mistreat animals who just want to live in peace and get on with their lives.' He waved a hand towards the mammoths. 'They force peaceful creatures like those to do horrible things like that.'

'Scupper me, boy, whilst your words are admirable, we need to get out of here,' said Boff comfortingly. 'After all, one step at a time, huh? Today we escape, and tomorrow we crusade for the naffin' mammoths and all their mates. Okay?'

Archie grabbed the nearest of Boff's tentacle hands and clutched it hard. *You promise?*

'I naffin' promise,' declared Boff, feeling quite good about his declaration. 'If I fail you, you can hornswoggle me giblets on an open fire!'

Archie knew his friend was right—they needed to get going. With a heavy heart, he flicked his lighter, its flame instantly igniting the Disruptors' small blue-paper fuses. As he watched them flare into life, he heard a smooth, honey-sweet voice speak from behind.

'They're just dumb animals bred to serve, human youngling. No one actually cares about them!'

Startled, the pair turned to see Serpentina, her emerald-green armour glowing in the torch light, an arrogant smile on her beautiful face. 'I'd throw those if I were you,' she said, nodding towards the pair of hissing fireworks, 'before you lose your hand!'

'Jagdar's teeth,' cursed Boff, glaring at the assassin, 'what do you want?'

Serpentina stood proudly erect. She had no reason to hide and certainly nothing to fear. 'Baldizar has ordered me to

191

accompany you on the maggot's quest.'

'Why?' growled Boff.

She slowly approached Archie. Being roughly the same height, she had to raise a gauntleted hand to ruffle his thick mop of curly white hair. 'Let's just say that our El Supremo thinks that your endeavours on Bleak might prove far more fruitful with my help.'

'Why? Is there someone there for you to murder?' Boff glared at her.

'Bleak,' stated Archie. 'Is that where we're going?'

'Yes,' replied Boff. 'Although I don't know how, because the nearest hydroportal is back on the stage, and the Storming Kaleidoscope Falls won't arrive for another candle mark.'

'What about Baldizar's tent back in the fairground?' asked Archie. 'Why can't we use that one?'

'And just how do you expect to get past the chieftains at the wall watchtower?' enquired Serpentina. 'You may technically be a collared maggot, but the race hasn't officially started yet. They'll see your golden collar and arrest you on sight.'

'Not necessarily,' Archie said, grinning. 'They might just think the race has started early.'

Serpentina smiled at him as if he were a simple child. 'The giant carved image of Garrknock that towers above the amphitheatre have the outspread wings of a giant bat. These will drop to signal the start of the race. Also, the maggots will leave Hexx via the Storming Kaleidoscope Falls, a natural phenomenon larger than Fortress Hexx and the amphitheatre combined. Somehow, I think even a creature as dumb as a minotaur might just notice that neither of these things has actually happened.'

Archie grimaced at her patronizing tone, quickly appreciating why all creatures loathed her so. It was all the more confusing because when he stared at her inky-blue face and into those beautiful golden-yellow cat's eyes, he found himself rather annoyingly attracted to her.

'You're naffin' enjoying this, aren't you, assassin?' Boff asked.

'The youngling has courage,' said Serpentina, watching him throw the fireworks towards the slumbering mammoths, 'a trait lacking in you, Storm Raider.'

Boff spat angrily onto the dirt then warned Archie: 'Jagdar's teeth, boy, she's as cruel as a knife in the dark, that one!'

The jumping jacks landed between the huge, shackled feet of the four giant mammoths, exploding in a staccato of deafening bangs. All at once, the domed entrance to the great amphitheatre of Garrknock grew full of loud, terrified trumpeting. The mammoths reared up and strained against their thick iron shackles, their fearful cries mixing with the sudden rattling of heavy chains. Desperate to escape the frightening noise, they backed fearfully away, all their tremendous weight suddenly snapping their chains taut and jerking the doors open.

The keepers of the mammoths, large ant-like creatures shocked by the unexpected commotion, poured out of their underground quarters, swarming about the feet of the shackled beasts of burden. In the confusion, no one noticed three figures slip stealthily through the quickly widening gap in the gates and out of the amphitheatre.

Back inside, the Disruptors had lived up to their name, for

all four of the giant shovelhead woolly mammoths trumpeted wildly at their sudden and unexpected liberty. The long lengths of iron chain that had bound them for so long were no match for their fearful strength. As shattered links fell, so their leather bridles and tethers snapped, their bondage finally over. In a mass breakout, sixteen tree-trunk-sized feet trampled their taskmasters into the dirt, pile-driving blows, smashing shells, and breaking bones as they careered through the gates to freedom.

As Archie, Boff, and Serpentina jogged along the ruby-lined path to the watchtower gate, so the giant animals charged out into the open space of the forbidden zone. The very ground shook under their weight, whilst the roosting crows of Fortress Hexx, disturbed by their wailing trumpets, flocked skyward. But as the mammoths stomped and trumpeted wildly, so the Dreadlies began to circle.

Archie couldn't bring himself to watch. He felt tears running down his cheeks as he turned his eye from the slaughter.

Archie and Boff approached the watchtower with a flaky veneer of laid-back calm. Luckily for them, all six chieftains on guard seemed more interested in the gory demise of the rampaging mammoths than watching the gate.

'Those poor beasts might just be your saviours,' whispered Serpentina ghoulishly.

Deliberately moving to the far side of the arch, they were just sauntering past the guards when a deep voice from a dark doorway bellowed, 'Halt!' From the shadows, a grisly old minotaur stepped into the open, his left hand resting ready on his broadsword's pommel. 'And just where do you think you pair are going?'

'Jagdar's teeth,' Boff said dejectedly. 'Of all the chieftains, why did it have to be naffin' Sergeant Rockwolf?'

The other guards, upon hearing their sergeant's voice, spun on their heels, quickly encircling the trio.

Archie stopped before the big, hairy sergeant, and Boff floated nervously beside him. 'Egads, boy,' he whispered, 'I hope you know what you're doing!'

'Greetings, Sergeant Rockwolf. They've run out of ale in the amphitheatre,' said Archie brazenly, 'so we're off down to the fairground for a tankard or two before the race starts.'

The sergeant, flattered that this young stranger should know his name, was about to allow them to pass when Archie's hastily hitched-up sweatshirt sagged, revealing a glimpse of his golden collar.

'Hey, you've been collared! You're a *maggot!*' growled Rockwolf, clocking the upright position of the statue of Garrknock's wings. 'And the race hasn't started yet!'

Suddenly, two chieftains lunged at him with open arms. Insanely, in a situation that would make a grown ogre wet himself instead of running, Archie just stood his ground. Coolly, from a double holster on his belt, he withdrew two small, bright-yellow devices.

'Run, you idiot!' cried Boff, sensing a severe beating in the offing.

'Hmm, this should be interesting,' mused Serpentina, intrigued by the tiny devices.

Gripping the pistols tightly in his trembling hands, Archie pointed at the approaching minotaur's and shouted, 'Stay back, or I'll Taser you!' Disturbingly, his warning went unheeded. '*Honest!* I'll shoot!'

With the lunging chieftains almost upon him, Archie squeezed the triggers. Two little darts spooled out at great speed, pinging off their metal chest plates and embedding themselves in the minotaur's thick, muscular necks. Back on Earth, fifty thousand volts would drop a rampaging rhinoceros. Sadly, a minotaur's skin was almost as dense as his IQ, so apart from a few wisps of smoke rising from singed hair and the tips of their black horns glowing pink, they continued their charge.

Grizwold, sensing the need for action, deftly tapped out a tune on Archie's brain, relaxing his leg muscles and making him flop like a pancake, flat on the ground. Next came a series of arm spasms, causing his body to roll several times beneath the groping, empty arms of the chieftains before making him spring nimbly back onto his feet on the outside of the forbidden wall. The pair of overreaching minotaur's, carried by momentum, careered into the far wall of the watchtower with a loud, painful thud.

Boff, using the confusion, flattened himself against the roof of the arch and hovered over the heads of the stunned guards. 'Run, you dunderhead!' he shouted, floating down next to the boy and shoving him forward. Archie, staggering blindly, fired both Tasers again. One dart bounced harmlessly off the watchtower gate, whilst the other viciously pierced the rump muscle of a sleeping thargg.

The giant dozing creature roared in agony as the tiny dart speared its leathery flesh and unleashed its deadly charge. The livid serpent's rear leg flexed wildly from the electrical charge, kicking its minotaur rider tumbling down the hill. Its scorpion-tail stinger quivered insanely for a split second before flashing down, its needle-sharp point piercing the iron boot of a chasing chieftain, pinning him, yelling, to the ground.

At the ferocious end of the Tharggs long, writhing body, its roaring head belched a thunderous sixty-foot flame.

Although the planet Hexx was permanently cold, it was also very dry, luckily for Archie. As the minotaur guards regrouped, the long, snaking tongue of flame from the furious thargg swiftly turned the dry timbers of the four-story watchtower into a raging inferno.

Sergeant Rockwolf, stunned by the speed of the blaze and the strange weapons used by the escaping maggot, wisely ordered his minotaur's not to fight the fire. He'd witnessed the ancient black art of technology at work before and felt it made sound military sense to keep a blazing fire between himself and his minotaur's and the angry thargg and the strangers.

Since returning recently from a two-year posting in the southern swamplands, he'd felt uncomfortable around some of the other chieftains. The minotaur grunts in his platoon had reported the same uneasiness, along with weird rumours about Professor Madspanner and the strange goings-on in his laboratory. There was something different, something *wrong* at Fortress Hexx, but he couldn't quite nail it down.

The watchtower had become a blazing inferno, the sky above blackened by its massive plume of smoke. *Let it burn*, he mused to himself, shrugging off the thought of the report he would later have to give to Captain Goldhorn. His minotaur's were safe, and that was what mattered. *Stuff the consequences!*

'Well, boil me britches.' Boff laughed as he floated to a halt and admired the fire. 'One of your inventions actually worked!'

'Impressive,' Serpentina, who had slipped through amidst the chaos, said. 'I think I may have underestimated you, young human.'

Boff shoved Archie in the back again. 'Step lively, boy. That sergeant's no dummy, and that fire won't burn forever.'

'It didn't spook him at all,' offered Serpentina, pointing to the fire that was already starting to lose its intensity. 'Look through the gaps in the flames.'

'Semaphore,' said Archie, noting the corresponding flag-wavers atop the Fortress Hexx and the amphitheatre. 'They'll be on the move soon.'

'Wrong again,' said Serpentina. 'As I left the far side of the watchtower, I saw Lieutenant Redhorn and a detachment of chieftains but a few hundred paces away.'

'That's odd,' commented Archie, gently rubbing his stinging eye patch. 'How could the chieftains be almost upon us if the watchtower guards have only just raised the alarm?' He frowned at Boff. 'Methinks old Buckethead's behind this!'

With Grizwold and a couple of Muzzberry pips helping Archie, they covered the two miles back to the fairground at a good pace. Archie and Boff plunged into the noisy throng of happy, carefree creatures milling around the jumble of marquees and attractions, thankful for their instant invisibility. Not waiting to catch his breath, Archie immediately began searching for Baldizar's private hydroportal tent.

Back at the forbidden wall, Lieutenant Redhorn and his

detachment were already rapidly jogging downhill towards the fairground.

Boff groaned. 'Scupper me, boy. Give a feller a break. All this floating has fair whacked me sideways.'

'Suck it in, squid Boy!' shouted Archie over his shoulder. 'We need to find that hydroportal and get to Bleak before the others.' When he stopped and looked back, he saw Boff, wheezing hard, leaning against a tent pole. 'Flippin' heck, Boff,' he snapped callously, 'I've escaped the police, been kidnapped by a giant armoured lunatic, flushed down a toilet, shackled in chains, accused of murder, and threatened by a foul-smelling, malevolent minotaur waving a flippin' great broadsword. Oh, and I've only got eleven and a half hours before my head's cut off!'

Boff flushed an embarrassed shade of pink. 'Jagdar's teeth, Archie, I was only—'

'Squad, halt!' bellowed a harsh voice. 'Form a line abreast, a sword's length apart! Search everyone and everything. Find that maggot!'

The whole fairground heard Lieutenant Redhorn deploy his minotaur's. Those creatures taken by surprise were shoved roughly to the ground, and the rest took to their heels, scampering in all directions.

Boff moaned. 'Jagdar's scaly hide, he must have sprouted naffin' wings. Quick, pick a tent and hide.' Before Archie could say a word, Boff had slipped into a tall, thin, blue-and-pink tent that stank of rank food.

Archie made to move towards the same tent when he felt a gentle tug on the bottom of his left boot.

'Hey, lanky,' said a tiny, scratchy voice, 'down here.'

Glancing down, Archie was astonished to see a large cockroach sitting on a white-and-red-spotted toadstool. It was wearing a yellow bowler hat, a white collar with a matching yellow bow tie, and natty white spats on each of its six feet. Whilst staring knowingly up at Archie, it leisurely blew square bubbles from an absurdly large, round pipe.

'Er... hello,' said Archie, his eyebrows screwing up in vague recognition. 'You're a spiv, aren't you?'

A large chicken with six tentacles instead of wings nudged his mate and laughed as they shuffled past. 'Blimey, he thinks he's talking to a blooming spiv!'

'A few tankards too many of Best Majestic, I do believe,' laughed another.

'Spivs are folklore, mate!' shouted a tall, willowy snake thing as the trio headed for the jungle of tents. 'Best you find a bunk and sleep it off.'

Archie looked up, confused. 'But he's there,' he argued. 'I'm talking to him.'

'Yes, of course he is, mate,' said the clucking chicken as it vanished amongst the tents.

'Most folks can't see us,' the cockroach said. 'Best you ignore them.'

'Oh... okay,' Archie replied.

'Archie Wilde, my name's Maggy,' announced the cockroach. 'I believe you met my brother Taggy whilst hydroporting this morning?'

'The meerkat on the surfboard?'

'That's him.' Maggy laughed. 'Always had a thing for water, that boy. It'll be the dusting of him one day, it will. Silly beggar can't swim!'

'Really?' said Archie awkwardly.

The cockroach withdrew her pipe and pointed towards the crowd. 'Hiding in a tent's not going to get you far. Look over there.'

Archie looked and was horrified to see the slowly approaching line of chieftains slashing every tent before them to ribbons.

'You both need to scram and nifty like.'

'On that point, I wholeheartedly agree,' said Archie. 'But how? I can't find Baldizar's tent!'

'You see that odd-looking little creature over there?'

Archie frowned. 'Er, they all look odd to me!'

'Good point! Well taken! Do you see the creature with four legs, two hedgehog heads, and a body all covered in curly blue feathers?'

Archie scanned the crowd, immediately spotting said creature. 'Yes, I see it.'

'He's got what you need,' the spiv said with a smile.

'And what exactly am I looking for?' he asked dumbly.

'Why, a PEEPS, of course,' replied the cockroach. 'I would get a shufty on, boy, if I were you. You've only eleven hours and twenty-six minutes left!'

'Blimey, you're right,' said Archie, checking his phone.

'Odds bodkins, Archie, stop talking to yourself,' growled Boff, hovering up beside him, 'and naffin' hide.'

'Change of plan,' announced Archie, ignoring all the strange looks he was suddenly attracting. 'You see that creature over there, Boff?' he whispered. 'The two-headed blue thing.'

Boff trained both of his coned eyes at Archie with a puzzled

201

expression. 'What... the strady?'

'Yeah, that thing,' agreed Archie. 'Well, he's got a PEEPS with him, and we could use that to escape in, couldn't we?'

'How do you know what a PEEPS is?' demanded Serpentina in a sharp, interrogational tone.

'The spi—never mind,' said Archie. 'I just do. Can we use it?'

Off to their left, a loud commotion interrupted their discussion. As they listened to argumentative creatures being roughly slapped aside, tents ripped open, and stalls overturned. Above all the hullabaloo, they heard a gruff voice barking commands.

'That's Redhorn and his minotaur's,' Serpentina said, her cat's eyes glowing a lustrous gold. 'The chase is almost over.'

Perplexed, Boff and Serpentina watched Archie frantically searching through the dozens of empty pockets in his combat vest, muttering something about needing a diversion and asking where the hell it was.

'Yes!' cried Archie, cheerfully holding what looked like a small prune. 'Perfect.' With a dozen hurried breaths, he inflated the prune to a football-sized sphere, tapped out a quick sequence on its touch screen, then turned and threw the object in the opposite direction, towards the funny small blue creature. 'There, that should keep them busy for long enough.'

'That things of the black art, isn't it?' asked Boff.

'What exactly is it?' Serpentina added.

'That, my friends, is a Tiny Gigantic,' grinned Archie.

Boff focused on Serpentina with a bemused frown. 'Don't look at me. I've no idea what he's talking about!'

Then they both turned and asked in perfect harmony, 'A what?'

'Wait and see,' replied Archie. 'Now, let's go and get that PEEPS thing.'

'But Redhorn's almost upon you,' uttered the assassin in disbelief. 'His sword is almost within striking range!'

Archie waved a dismissive hand towards the minotaur's. 'Oh, don't worry about them.'

From nowhere, the ears of every creature in the fairground were suddenly violently assaulted by the deafening sound of heavy-metal guitars and drums. Then a loud, deep throaty voice began to sing. It was so vocally aggressive that ripples of shock exploded out through the surrounding crowd. The ensuing chaos of screaming creatures, more terrified of the music than Redhorn, stampeded into the bewildered minotaur's, totally overwhelming them.

'Jagdar's teeth, Archie!' cried Boff. 'What the naffin' hell is that?'

'The masters of mayhem themselves!' Archie laughed. 'Motorhead's "Ace of Spades." It may be a bit dated, but it's still got plenty of punch!'

Serpentina, astounded by the staggering, fear-inducing capability of whatever that thing was the youngling had thrown, smiled at Archie as if seeing him through new eyes.

The strady, who was feasting on a small fried rodent, squawked hysterically as it was abruptly snatched into the air by its legs and shaken violently. The poor, incensed creature's raucous shrieking had no effect on Boff's vicelike grip. For a creature so small, a lot of things fell from its few pockets.

'Aha!' cried Boff, tossing the quaking creature aside and

plucking out what looked to Archie like a small flat-packed cardboard box the size of a postage stamp.

'Is that it?' asked Archie, a little deflated.

Boff unzipped a smile from ear to ear. 'You little ripper!' he sang joyfully. 'This little beauty is going to save our bacon.'

'It is?' enquired Archie.

'Gadzooks, boy!' he roared, yanking a red rip cord. 'Here's a piece of black-art technology that's saved my naffin' leathery hide more than once!'

Archie's brows crinkled then blossomed with delight as he watched the little flat box unfold into a weird sort of full-sized toilet. Stencilled on its side in bright-red letters was PEEPS, Portable Emergency Escape Portal, Singular.

'It's a hydroportal!' Archie exclaimed.

'Well, trounce me trunnions. He's got it in one,' laughed Boff.

'Hate to rain on your parade,' announced Serpentina smugly, 'but that thing is only designed for one creature to escape to the nearest rapidly falling liquid.'

'There they are!' bellowed a gruff voice. 'A barrel of ale to the first one who grabs the youngling!'

'Gadzooks, assassin,' growled Boff, 'you're like a zit that can't be popped!' He scooped up Archie and quickly hovered over the open bowl of the PEEPS. 'Brace ya barnacles, Archie. I'm flushing the pair of us.'

Redhorn and his angry-looking chieftains carved a passage through the thick circle of fearfully gawping creatures. Serpentina, loving every minute of the pandemonium about her, gracefully leaped upon Boff's back, whispering, 'You won't shake me that easily, Storm Raider!'

The trio vanished in a vortex of glistening spray just as the chieftains lunged forward, their encircling sword blades clashing together on the very spot where the fugitives no longer were.

Chapter 17

Quicker than the tick of a clock, the fairground vanished, and Archie suddenly found himself hurtling out of control along a foul-smelling, dark, slippery tube. Covered in slime, he veered wildly back and forth, barrelling around corners at eye-popping speed, whilst tumbling around stomach-churning loops over and over again. He was desperately trying not to vomit when without warning, he exited the tube into total darkness.

Down and down he fell, until with a squelchy splat, he landed in a stinking cesspit of filth.

Boff arrived moments later, and he and Archie both sat knee deep in a vile pool of yellow and brown goo, panting heavily. Serpentina, on the other hand, had handled the landing far better. Having fallen with the grace of a striking panther, she'd landed on her feet, her cold, calculating mind alert, her sharp eyes piercing the gloom. With a stiletto blade in both hands, she stood poised, ready to defend or attack.

Archie cautiously poked the floor with his fingers. It felt weird, a bit like slimy bubble wrap. A voice from a darker part of his mind whispered of flesh and something living, and he shuddered at the thought. And then there was the smell, which was like rotting food, only much worse. Close by, somewhere in the gloom, he could hear Boff complaining. He tried to move, but the goo was like sloppy bubble gum. It fought his every attempt to stand.

Even with Grizwold's help and the Muzzberry pips, the combination of the cold, dry air on Hexx, their escape from the amphitheatre, and the gruelling run to the fairground had left him exhausted.

Be still, thalked Grizwold, sensing the boy's emotional turmoil. *Your muscles are flooded with lactic acid from your escape. Be patient. Your strength will return.*

'Damn,' he cursed, wriggling his phone free from his pocket. 'How can I be patient? I've only got eleven hours and two minutes left!'

'Yuk,' whined Boff, cringing at the sight of long strings of yellowish-brown goo dripping from his tentacle hands. 'What in Jagdar's teeth is this naffin' place? And why does it smell like an abattoir on a hot day?'

'I don't know,' said Serpentina in a snooty tone, 'but I would have thought you would feel right at home here.'

'Egads,' grumbled Boff. 'I was kind of hoping you'd fallen off during the ride!' He tried to no avail to hover, so he sat for a moment, casting his eyes about the gloom. It was then that he spied Serpentina with her daggers drawn. 'Well, trounce me trunnions.' He laughed and flicked a blob of goo at her. 'Here we are, all tentacle-deep in muck, and you're ready to strike.' His laughter was more pitiful than mocking. 'Don't worry, assassin, there must be a poor defenceless creature skulking around here somewhere for you to murder!'

Their strange domain was cast in a curious half-light, but

even this was enough for Archie see Serpentina's clenched white knuckles. It was obvious to him that she wasn't ready to strike—she was just scared, like the rest of them!

Turning to his companions, Archie asked, 'So where exactly are we, and just how the flippin' heck do we get out?'

'Hornswoggle me giblets, Archie, my boy. A fairer pair of questions I couldn't have posed better myself.'

Archie frowned. 'So basically, you haven't got the foggiest idea where—hey, wait a minute. I can see both of you!'

'There must be a window around here somewhere,' said Boff.

'Perhaps it's dawn!' offered Serpentina.

'Luminescent amoebae,' stated Grizwold, using Archie's voice in a scholarly tone. 'They're part of the basic physiological makeup of some of the more robust species of creepies, creatures, and mongrel humans that roam deep space.'

'Well, scupper me,' Boff said. 'Light bugs? Now that's naffin' cool!'

'Light bugs?' queried Serpentina, a hint of uneasiness in her voice. 'I can't see any bugs. Why can't I see the bugs?'

'They won't hurt you,' said Archie reassuringly. 'They're simply too small to be seen by the naked eye.'

'Fear not, oh brave assassin,' scoffed Boff. 'I'll save you from this rampaging horde of miniscule amoebae!'

'Jagdar's teeth,' cried Serpentina as the ground suddenly rippled beneath them. 'What was that?'

Boff ran his tentacle hands over the slimy surface. 'Jagdar's teeth,' he whispered, 'is this place actually moving?'

'Blimey, I think you're right,' agreed Archie. 'Could it have been an earthquake?'

'If this mountain is indeed grumbling,' offered Serpentina, prodding the wall suspiciously with the tip of a gauntlet, 'then I suggest we move before it loses its temper.'

'An excellent idea, assassin, but unfortunately not possible,' announced Grizwold, using Archie's voice, 'for I believe I know where we are, and unfortunately, it's not a mountain.'

'And that would be where?' asked Boff impatiently.

'Well, I am almost certain that we are somewhere in the digestive tract of a blue snozzmoo!'

Boff groaned, his coned eyes dropping miserably. 'Jagdar's teeth, you've got to be naffin' joking.'

'Er, excuse me,' interrupted Archie anxiously. 'A what?'

'No.' Grizwold huffed indignantly, annoyed that anyone would consider that he would joke about a matter so serious. 'I strongly believe that we are in fact somewhere inside the digestive tract of a blue Snozzmoo!'

'A *what?*' Archie repeated loudly.

'A blue snozzmoo,' said Serpentina, 'is a creature that lives in the vast emptiness of space. It's a cross between a giant whale and a two-headed cow, with bits of mutant vegetable here and there.'

An odd silence fell as everyone stared at the assassin. She glared back at them, her cat's eyes glowing a burnished gold. 'I may be a killer,' she hissed, sheathing her daggers, 'but I'm not stupid.'

Boff grunted miserably. 'Scupper me, boy. I've heard horrible naffin' tales of those beasties.'

'This thing must be huge,' said Archie excitedly, oblivious to the fact that they were all slowly being eaten. 'Is it like the blue whales back on Earth?'

'Sort of,' said Grizwold, 'but it's about twice the length of a super tanker.'

'Wow, and these giant space-whale-cow things actually have hydroportal's inside of them?'

'Odds bodkins, no,' said Boff. 'They don't have hydroportal's at all.'

'So how did we end up inside this filthy creature, then?' asked Serpentina.

With some difficulty, Boff squelched around just enough to look Archie in the eye. 'Yes, Grizwold, oh knowledgeable one,' he glared. 'And just how in Jagdar's scaly hide did we get here?'

'Well, actually, it's all Archie Wilde's fault!'

Archie gasped. 'My fault?'

'Yes, your fault,' repeated Grizwold, 'because as we all know, after the official start of the race, all maggots are transported to Bleak via the Storming Kaleidoscope Falls.' He twanged one of Archie's optic nerves, causing the boy to wince with pain. 'A rash move on your behalf, Archie Wilde, landed us all in it!'

'But how did we end up inside a blue snozzmoo?' growled Serpentina.

'One of the more obscure peculiarities of the hydroportal system,' continued Grizwold, 'is the little-known fact that if there's no hydroportal within range, the PEEPS will automatically seek out the nearest fast flowing liquid.'

'Fast flowing liquid?' pondered Archie. 'How do you know if said liquid is water?'

'You don't,' answered Grizwold matter-of-factly.

'Jagdar's teeth,' grumbled Boff, 'you've fair done us in this time, Archie!'

'The PEEPS is a last-ditch escape route,' Grizwold said with a sigh. 'What do you creatures expect from a cardboard box that you can purchase for just one snippet of spungold, an in-flight movie, and meals?'

Serpentina glared at Archie. 'So, this is all your stupid fault.'

'Don't blame me, assassin,' snapped Archie. 'No one asked you along.'

'A brash move by an immature fool.' She huffed.

Archie glared defiantly at her. 'Hey, killer, where's your golden collar?'

'Shiver me giblets, assassin,' Boff said, nodding. 'The boy has you there!'

Grizwold cleared Archie's throat loudly. 'Contrary to common knowledge, when activated, an emergency hydroportal doesn't just search the surrounding planets. It can also search a limited area of space about each planet.'

'You mean the other side of the sky?' queried Serpentina in amazement.

'Yes,' said Grizwold. 'And fortunately, or unfortunately for us'—he tapped the slimy side of the tube with one of Archie's hands— 'this blue snozzmoo just happened to be only a few hundred miles away.'

Grizwold was seemingly about to launch into a detailed scientific explanation when the tube about them shuddered violently.

'What's happening?' cried Serpentina. 'What's this blue snozzmoo doing now?'

'Shush. Listen,' barked Boff. 'Can anyone else hear that soft sort of whistling in the distance?'

Everyone stopped bickering and listened.

'Yes, yes, I can.' Serpentina's voice was laced with alarm.

'Einstein's underpants,' said Archie. 'Listen up, people. It's not rocket science. That sound isn't a soft spring breeze blowing through the trees.' He pointed back along the slimy tube and into the darkness. 'We're in the guts of a flippin' great space cow, people, that's about to do some—'

The tremors and wind struck like a knockout punch. The combination of the convulsing ripples and the sudden wind propelled the brave little band farther through the maze of gloomy guts like a pea in a pipe. On and on they slid, surging up and down and left and right, tumbling and rolling on their backs or upside down, their faces in the goo or dragged on their backs.

Then without warning, for a second time, they sailed off a large muscular lip and shot out into a black void, only to fall once again into a deep abyss. Luckily for them, their descent only lasted a few seconds before they landed with a gloopy splat, deposited in a cave of cathedral-like proportions.

'Well, trounce me trunnions.' Boff coughed, spitting up tennis-ball-sized dollops of goo. 'Will you look at the size of this naffin' place?'

'Oh, great,' moaned Serpentina. 'This place smells even worse!'

All around them, the radiant amoeba hung in long flowing curtains, giving the giant cavern a mystical cast almost like twilight.

On Grizwold's recommendation, Archie took another

Muzzberry pip. Then, after several deep breaths, he proceeded to have a nose about. Quickly surmising that the floor was more or less flat, and that the knee-deep slime hid a multitude of dangerous objects buried in it, he proceeded cautiously, directing his attention to only those objects of interest above the slime line. Mostly, he found rocks of various sizes and on the odd occasion a bone, and then he spied something that sent his scientific mind reeling.

'Wow!' he declared excitedly, churning up the goo with several great lolloping strides. 'It can't be! It simply can't be!'

Boff, who had finally wrenched himself free of the goo, roared angrily as a shower of slime hit him broadside. 'Hey, you scurvy dog,' he snapped, 'what's with all the kicking and splashing?'

Serpentina stood in silence, taken aback by the youngling's sudden ridiculous behaviour. *One moment, he's astounding and cunningly intelligent,* she mused. *The next, he's acting like a silly child!*

Archie slopped to a stop next to a thick metal drum-shaped object, his excitement bubbling over.

Boff floated over, chuckling at the boy's feeble attempts to move the object. 'Can I be of any assistance, Archie?' he enquired casually.

'Yes, please,' he replied. 'I need to get this out of the goo and onto that flat rock over there.'

Boff impulsively obliged but quickly realized the object was far heavier than it looked. Not wanting to show weakness before the assassin, he stifled his stressful grunts and strained with all ten of his tentacles till it popped free of the goo.

Archie leapt at him, giving him a big hug. 'That's blooming

wonderful! Cheers, mate.'

Boff peeled off the appreciative boy and lowered him next to his strange object. 'Odds bodkins, shipmate, what is that thing?'

Intrigued, Serpentina approached. 'Yes. Explain youngling.'

'This is Beagle II,' announced Archie proudly.

'Doesn't look much like a dog,' said Boff.

Archie burst into laughter. 'It's not a dog, you noodle. It's a Martian exploratory probe named after the HMS Beagle.'

Boff and Serpentina stared at him with blank faces.

'You've never heard of this famous Royal Navy's eight-gun Cherokee-class brig-sloop before? Does Charles Darwin's second voyage of discovery ring any bells?' Just for a moment, their slowly moving mouths reminded him of a pair of goldfish.

He took out his phone, which was remarkably free of goo, and started typing.

'What are you up to now?' asked Boff, well aware that anything to do with that contraption usually meant trouble.

'This probe got to Mars by piggybacking on another bigger probe called the Mars Express Orbiter back in 2003. As it approached the red planet, the plan was to detach then coast for six days before descending to the surface and deploying. Judging by the fact that it's still in, in-flight mode, I would say that our friendly space cow here gobbled it up whilst passing.'

'So that thing is a machine?' asked Serpentina, her keen sense of survival automatically causing her to step back.

'Cutting-edge at its time and solely British,' said Archie

patriotically. 'And still in amazingly good condition, considering where it's ended up!'

'Will it help our situation?' she asked.

'No, not in the slightest.'

The probe suddenly made five loud sharp clicks then emitted a deep, cracking sound like a walnut being crushed. A soft mechanical whirring filled the air as the probe began to open.

'There,' he announced proudly. 'I knew I had the trigger code somewhere.'

Boff and Serpentina watched with fascinated apprehension as five circular solar panels opened around the central workbench. From the middle, a small robotic arm popped up and flexed, the tiny camera on its tip immediately surveying its new surroundings. When everything finally stopped moving, two rows of bright-green lights blinked on.

'Why, it's like a strange metal flower,' said Serpentina in surprise.

Archie held out a hand, which, to Boff's great surprise, she took. 'You can come closer,' he offered. 'It won't hurt you. It's just an electro-mechanical information gatherer.' As she tentatively neared, he pointed to a shiny brass plate bolted to its surface: Beagle II, Mars Lander. Launched from Earth back in 2003.

When Serpentina realized that she was holding Archie's hand, she snatched it free, mentally chastising herself for such weakness in front of lesser species. 'This *machine*. I assume it was made using the ancient black art of technology?'

Archie turned and eyed her suspiciously. 'You've seen this sort of thing before, haven't you?'

Moving closer, she boldly tapped a dagger's tip against its smooth metal surface. 'Yes,' she confessed, 'I've seen this sort—'

Suddenly, there was a series of loud beeps. The alarm startled everyone but most of all Archie. He swiftly searched out the beeping speaker and its tiny red flashing light, reading aloud its identity label: McNaulty Mk VI Foreign Object Proximity Alarm.

'That's odd,' he said, gently rubbing his tingling eye patch. 'This means there's another electronic device in here!'

Boff slapped a tentacle across his shoulders. 'Wouldn't be one of them gizmos in your army vest now, would it?'

'No,' replied Archie sadly, 'my vest is all but empty.'

'This thing is dangerous,' declared Serpentina, stepping back. As she did so, the beeping stopped.

'Wow. Calm down, everyone.' Archie chuckled. 'Let's not go all lethal, shall we? It was only a warning alarm.' He smiled reassuringly at Serpentina. 'Nice teeth,' he remarked offhandedly. 'You floss regularly?'

Serpentina was mystified by his strange remark, and her scowl slowly turned into a quirky smile. She'd never been spoken to in such a manner before. Such openhearted honesty and kindness made her feel uncomfortable.

'I... Er, thank you, I think.' Her words were softly spoken, and both of them noticed the fleeting blush of pink enveloping her face.

'I think it may be your dagger, Serpentina,' said Archie. He pointed, holding out an open hand. 'May I?'

Her trained reactions made her grip the dagger even tighter, as if suddenly threatened.

'It's okay. I only want to have a look at it.' Smiling warmly, he again offered an open hand. To his relief, she suddenly relaxed and handed him the dagger. Gingerly he reached across and took it by the handle, grinning. 'I'm rubbish with knives. I'm always cutting myself.'

To Serpentina's amazement, a giggle escaped her lips.

Archie waved the dagger in front of the sensor, and the return of the beeping confirmed its guilt. Moving closer to the probe's spotlights, he examined it as best he could but couldn't see anything suspicious or even unusual. Then whilst mulling over the problem, he unconsciously tapped its hilt on the Beagle's metal surface. Through his sensitive fingertips, he felt a tiny movement.

'Bingo!' he said, quickly unscrewing the dagger's tiny pommel.

Serpentina looked questioningly across at Boff. 'Bingo?'

Boff shrugged his shoulders. 'It's a silly Earth game. Ten years I spent there, and I still can't fathom it.'

'Look,' said Archie, removing the multicoloured gemstone pommel and dropping a small metal disc the size of a fly into the palm of her hand.

'What's this?' she asked curiously.

'A bug,' answered Archie whilst retrieving a small magnifying glass from a pocket and holding it up to the light.

'That's disgusting,' she hissed. 'It's not a spell caster, is it?'

Archie laughed. 'No, it's not an insect.' He beckoned her closer. 'Here, look through the glass. Do you see the three letters?'

Intrigued, she peered through the tiny magnifying glass. 'Yes, I see a C, and I, and an A.' She dropped the bug onto the Beagle. 'It's in your language. What do they mean?'

'The CIA, or Central Intelligence Agency, is a bunch of spies from my home world.' He held up the tiny device and frowned at her. 'This is a tracking device!'

'So,' said Boff, 'it seems like your naffin' boss, old Buckethead, doesn't trust you, either!'

'But that doesn't make sense,' she declared. 'Baldizar knows where I am all the time.'

'He does?' Boff frowned. 'How?'

'My suit of armour, of course! From the very beginning, he assured me that it would keep me safe, advising him of my whereabouts at all times.'

'Hmmm,' mused Archie, 'that seems a—'

'The *professor*,' Serpentina hissed through clenched teeth.

'Madspanner?' Boff scowled.

'This bug thing is of the black art, right?'

'Oh yes,' Archie replied. 'The latest available.'

'Argh!' she screamed with anger. 'Deceiver!' With that, she jammed the dagger's blade deep into a thin crevasse on the Beagle's outer frame and violently snapped the handle from its blade.

Her face was red with rage, her eyes a scary gleaming gold, but still Archie sensed something different about her. He reached forward and gently placed his hand on her shaking arm. 'This professor character... Care to enlighten?'

'Professor Ratchet Madspanner is a human like you. It is said that Baldizar rescued him some fifteen years ago, and he's worked in his service ever since.' Even through her armour, she shook with revulsion. 'He is a slimy creature who lives in the shadows, his silvery tongue laced with lies and deceit.'

'What exactly does the professor do for Baldizar?' asked Archie.

'He is a master of the ancient black art of technology.' She sighed. 'It is he who designed and built the Crimson Raptor!'

'That's one awesome flying machine!' remarked Archie with a touch too much admiration. 'But nevertheless, if he works for old Buckethead, who can track you already, why have a second tracking device doing the same job?'

Boff grinned. 'Baldizar ordered you to watch over Archie, right, to keep to him safe at all times. Perhaps our professor has his own agenda!'

Serpentina gasped. 'You mean he's a traitor?'

'Why not?' added Archie. 'After all, he is the brain behind Baldizar's brawn.'

'But if Baldizar ever found out, he would have him dusted in the most tortuous of ways.'

'Too naffin' true,' agreed Boff. 'But don't forget, old Buckethead's a megalomaniac. In his deluded world, no one would dare betray him!'

Serpentina nodded in agreement then added, 'With that bug, even on a planet as gigantic as Bleak, there would be nowhere to hide.'

'Jagdar's teeth,' growled Boff. 'And with his flying machine, he could easily find this great blue snozzmoo and blast it to bits!'

Serpentina took an object from a small leather waist pouch and held it out. 'Well, I suggest we best be off, then.'

'Scupper me,' said Boff, staring with both eyes, 'you've got a bog spinner?'

'Of course!' She smirked.

'Jagdar's fiery breath, Assassin,' he growled angrily, 'why didn't you use it back on Hexx? We could have hydroported directly to Bleak.'

Serpentina frowned at Archie. 'Someone was in a hurry!'

Archie glanced at his phone. Ten hours and forty-four minutes remained. 'That's enough, the pair of you!' he barked. 'We've been in this flippin' space cow for eighteen minutes. Let's just go, huh?'

'Problem!' stated Grizwold via Archie. 'The only way to escape from a blue snozzmoo is when it urinates, which unfortunately is only once a year!'

'Once a year?' asked Boff and Serpentina in dejected harmony.

'Oh, that's no problem,' Archie said, pulling a slim, shiny silver tin from his vest and tossing it casually in the air. 'Red Rocket is the single finest, most potent energy drink on Earth,' he announced, pouring it all over the floor. 'It only has one drawback.'

'Which is?' asked Serpentina.

'It instantly makes you want to pee!' Archie grinned.

Chapter 18

From its lair of gently swaying weeds, a little blue fish with a big mouth full of nasty, pointed teeth hungrily watched a snack-sized yellow fish swimming his way. *Hmm*, thought the blue fish happily, *lunchtime!* Closer and closer, he watched the little yellow fish swim, carefree and totally oblivious to the ambush that awaited him.

Just a tiny bit closer, thought the blue fish eagerly as he moved silently to the edge of his lair in readiness to pounce, his jaws gnashing with hungry anticipation. 'Wait for it,' he whispered excitedly to himself. 'Come on, my beauty, just a tiny bit closer…'

Suddenly, his tranquil world was shattered as giant things rained down out of the sky. Objects the size of boulders splashed into the river all about him, causing huge waves and sending spouts of water exploding high into the air.

Propelled by a steaming torrent of blue snozzmoo pee, Archie, Boff, and Serpentina exploded out of the crest of a huge waterfall, tumbling though the open air, wildly thrashing and screaming before plummeting into the river below. Boff, curling his tentacles tightly together, pierced the river's surface like a dart, whilst Archie slapped the water in a spectacularly painful belly flop. Neither witnessed Serpentina, encased in heavy armour, hit the water with all the grace of a cannonball and sink immediately out of sight.

The blue fish watched agog as two strange, gangly-looking creatures splashed about crazily at the river's surface. These, he chose to ignore. However, the odd sparkly-green thing that had drifted gently down before him, settling with a soft bump on the riverbed, was far more intriguing. Sensing a feast in the offing, the blue fish finned forward curiously. Sadly, after a tentative inspection and four broken teeth, he thought better of it.

'*Tinned food.* Yuk!' he said grumpily as he swam off into the murky darkness.

A frenzy of silver bubbles encased Archie as the river enveloped him. But instead of panicking and frantically trying to claw his way upwards, he fanned his hands and held his position. He loved everything about the water, from its varying shades of blue and green to the weird and wonderful creatures that lived in it. Then of course, there was its fresh, cleansing feel, especially given that he had just passed through the stinky bits of a giant space cow.

To him, negative buoyancy was near enough to weightlessness and yet another way he could train for his fantasy adventures in space.

He could see Boff nearby, flying through the warm clear water, rolling and twisting before eventually heading back up. *Oh, to be half squid,* thought Archie jealously. With a strong kick of his legs, he followed his friend, broke the surface nearby, and greedily sucked in the fresh air. *Wherever this place is,* he thought, leisurely floating on his back, *I like it!*

'Well, hornswoggle me giblets,' said a voice from behind. 'For a human youngling with all his clobber on and those silly boots, you look fair at home in the water, boy.'

Archie swam around to face his friend. 'I've always loved swimming. The water is like a second home to me.' He looked on in amazement as Boff surged through the water, ducking, diving, then leaping like a dolphin. 'You seem to be enjoying yourself too.'

'I should,' Boff said, squirting a spout of water from between his pursed, rubbery lips. 'I'm half squid, remember.'

The race briefly forgotten, Archie was happily laughing at Boff, watching him jumping and splashing about, when Grizwold spoke up: *Archie, where's Serpentina?*

Splashing in a swift circle, a fizz of fear filled Archie's heart as he suddenly realized that she was nowhere to be seen. He stopped kicking and allowed his big, water-filled moon boots to drag him down the fifteen feet to the riverbed. As he hit bottom in the translucent green world, he quickly realized he wasn't alone. Darting in and out of his peripheral vision were other creatures. He only caught fleeting glimpses that were never quite whole but more substantial than shadows and always watching.

From a vest pocket, he removed a pony, a small device that looked like an old-fashioned egg timer, which he clamped over his mouth. The pony was a miniature mouthpiece-cum-demand valve with two tiny metal bottles attached, a unique miniature breathing apparatus designed by and specifically for the British secret service. He was grateful for the pocket-sized diving set that gave any would-be James Bond a good ten minutes of air.

She was suited in green armour in a green river, so finding Serpentina shouldn't have been easy. But almost immediately, he got lucky—off to his left, he noticed a school of fish circling something lying on the riverbed. Bouncing along the riverbed like an astronaut, he forged forward, and fortunately, his sudden appearance scared away the strange, hungry-looking fish.

Seeing no bubbles escaping her lips, he quickly covered the gap between them in several bounds, landing awkwardly beside her head, his big boots kicking up clouds of sediment. Pulling the pony from his own mouth, he deftly forced its rubber mouthpiece between her lips. Fortunately, she began breathing again almost immediately, her initial panic quickly quelled by his reassuring smile, and although not understanding what the device was, her senses automatically told her it was good. After several deep, calming breaths, she acknowledged Archie's weird thumb signal by pointing to the surface.

Repeatedly, he tried to grab her arms, but his fingers couldn't grip her suit's shiny surface. It almost felt as if the armour itself was trying to repel his grasp. Instead, he scooped up her limp body then tucked his legs beneath her and pushed hard with all his might, propelling them both upwards. But it was no good—together, they were simply too heavy.

Archie groaned. The water's surface was only a mere seven feet away. Dropping her back onto her feet, he signed for her to give him the pony. Reluctantly, with fear in her golden eyes, she handed it to him. Smiling, he took a single deep breath then placed it back in her mouth. Then he pointed to the riverbank.

Having never been underwater before, Serpentina found the whole experience simultaneously exhilarating and terrifying. She mimicked his bizarre bouncy walk, and they slowly worked their way along the riverbed side by side, with her drawing strength from his courage. It wasn't long before she felt the ground beneath her feet start to rise.

Serpentina splashed out of the river, staggered up the grassy bank, then collapsed to the ground, exhausted, her once-shiny suit of armour covered in mud and leaking like an old fish basket. Archie, his curly white hair plastered to his head, fell laughing onto his bum beside her. She watched with childlike pleasure as he pulled his big boots off and emptied them onto the grass.

He pulled his boots back on, stood up, and proudly squished about. 'They're a bit soggy, but they'll be dry in no time.'

'Your eye patch,' she said between slow, controlled breaths. 'Back there in the water, it glowed.' She watched as he gently traced its outline with a finger, as if it were a dressing on a wound. 'Random flashes of light formed a loose circle,' she continued, 'a bit like a crumpled halo!'

'Huh. I never thought of it like that,' mused Archie.

'You saved me,' she said tenderly, her bright-yellow eyes full of admiration and questions. 'Why?'

'Odds bodkins, Archie, me boy, good naffin' question!' Boff, watching from the top of a nearby boulder, cut in acidly. 'I wouldn't have bothered!'

Archie empathised with him—after all, her reputation made Sweeney Todd look like a Sunday school teacher. 'That's not nice, Boff. The poor girl's wearing half a ton of armour,' he jested half-heartedly. 'She could have drowned!'

'She's an assassin, evil to the core,' he growled. 'If she'd drowned, it would have done every creepy creature and mongrel throughout the genieverse a big favour.'

Archie took a deep breath then spoke his mind. 'Well, Boff, when I look at Serpentina, I obviously see something you don't. Call it a gut feeling.'

Boff flushed an angry red, muttered something, then turned away.

'You actually enjoyed being down there under the water, didn't you?' asked Serpentina, her raspy cough much improved.

'Yes,' Archie replied. 'I love the water.'

'You're seriously weird,' she said, a faint smile gracing her lips. To her mind, nothing but fish needed to be in water, let alone under it.

Archie took a long, slow lingering look at the countryside about him. Lush, wild green grass bordered either side of the river right up to the foot of the huge waterfall, which had a distinctly odd appearance to it. Dotted here and there were mature oak and beech trees that changed to pines as they marched up the hillside. Overhead was a stunningly blue, cloudless sky with a single blazing sun. It looked and smelt just like the countryside around the orphanage.

He suddenly thought of the other kids he and Boff had left behind some hours ago, billions of miles away. He felt nothing. His conscience whispered that he should, but he didn't miss them at all.

Off in the distance, a rasping cry filled the air, making his head spin fearfully this way and that. 'Fear not, Archie, me boy,' said Boff. 'Nothin' to worry about. There's some strange winds on this Jagdar-forsaken planet.'

'It's actually rather beautiful here,' said Archie. 'It's reminiscent of Earth in the late summer.'

Don't be fooled by the pleasant weather, thalked Grizwold. *The planet Bleak is definitely not on any sane creature's list of top ten holiday destinations, although it does have two of the most remarkably unique features in the genieverse!*

Oh yeah? enquired Archie. *Please, do tell.*

Firstly, there is the famous Drawkcab River, with its topsy-turvy falls, our arrival point. This unique geological feature is famed for the fact that it is the only known river that flows out of the sea backwards along its entire watercourse then flies up the Topsy-Turvy waterfall, eventually reversing all the way back to its source in the Beginning Mountains. Luckily for us, we fell into the shallows along the river's edge, where the flow is slack.

Is it fast flowing further in, then? Archie asked.

Because of its unusual nature, its centre course runs at more than one hundred miles an hour. Grizwold paused for dramatic effect. *At the top of the falls, it is, as you say on Earth, like being fired from a cannon.*

Its second claim to fame. Archie asked.

Is this planet's darker side. Bleak's weather system is so staggeringly abnormal that it experiences a full year's weather cycle every eight candle marks.

Archie gasped in disbelief. *You have got to be kidding me Grizwold, that's one season every two hours!*

Yes, a very unusual weather pattern indeed. I estimate we have roughly thirty of your Earth minutes of summer left, and within three hours, it will be midwinter. And believe me, Archie

Wilde—his tone was suddenly full of dread—*no creature wants to be on Bleak in the wintertime!*

Archie sighed. 'Blimey, what I'd give for a stick of liquorice right now.'

'What is liquorice?' enquired Serpentina.

'It's a sweet made for children back on Earth,' interrupted Boff before Archie had a chance to answer. 'On Hexx, we call it black twig.'

Archie ignored him and pulled his phone from his soggy pocket.

'Oh yeah, like that's going to work after your dip in the river,' Boff said.

Archie slipped his phone from its waterproof case and switched it on, smirking as he watched Boff's smug smile fade. Sadly, the first thing he read was that he had only nine hours and forty-nine minutes to live.

'Are you okay, Serpentina?' asked Archie, staring at the strange expression on her face.

She made no reply, just stared dumbly off into space. The skin on her hands was cold and white, with odd lines of tiny red dots running down to her fingertips. More worrying still was the fact that she offered no resistance when he touched them.

'Jagdar's fiery breath, will you get a load of those insane eyes?' Boff whispered over his shoulder.

Look, thalked Grizwold, *her gauntlets are glowing!*

'Serpentina, can you hear us?' asked Archie anxiously. 'Tell us what's wrong.'

Without warning, tears suddenly cascaded from her eyes, a look of excruciating pain contorting her face. 'My armour,' she suddenly screamed hysterically, 'is burning my skin!'

Without warning, as if jerked savagely by an invisible wire, she flew off the rock, her screams of agony spooking the pair of them. In the next moment, she was on the ground, her body writhing and thrashing as if she were possessed by a banshee. Such was the force of her jarring movements that her armoured elbows and ironclad boots smashed any rocks that they struck. But it quickly became obvious to Archie that it was in fact the suit of armour that was throwing her limp body wildly about. She was trapped inside, with little strength to resist.

'It's the armour!' shouted Archie, jumping clear seconds before the suit of armour sprang back up onto its iron boots. 'It must be controlling her in some way! Get her back on the ground! We must cut it off her!'

Boff hovered straight in without hesitation. With all ten tentacles spread widely, he rammed into her like a living net and swiftly wrapped her up tightly. Even with his superior strength and multiple limbs, it was a struggle.

'Jagdar's teeth! You mean it's bewitched?' screamed Boff, grappling her to the ground.

'Yes! I'm sure of it!'

'This magical suit's naffin' strong, Archie!' He gasped, his straining muscles already starting to burn. 'Whatever you're going to do, boy, now would be a good time!'

With an unexpected burst of strength, Serpentina's armour kicked free two of his tentacles and lashed out with a free boot. Boff felt its rough iron heel graze his cheek.

Flaring red, angry at being caught off guard, Boff deployed a double whip action, cunningly ensnaring her free leg and binding it tightly to the other. However, even with his renewed aggression, it was obvious that it was going to be a very short-lived fight.

'Archie, I don't think I can hold it much longer!' The strain on his muscles was unbearable—his whole body felt as if it were on fire. His laboured breath was full of tortured grunts and groans, his vicelike grip slipping fast.

Archie's fingers scrabbled for his pocketknife. 'Damn it,' he cursed, 'I must have lost it in the flippin' river.'

'I'm losing her, Archie!' Boff groaned, his whole body flushed red. 'Naffin' do something!'

It was then that Archie noticed the scattered pieces of smashed black rock. 'Flint!' he cried aloud.

He snatched up a razor-sharp slither then recklessly threw himself on top of Serpentina and Boff. With one hand and his legs, he gripped like a rodeo cowboy on a bucking bronco. With the other hand, he deftly slashed joint after joint in her armour whilst nimbly avoiding cutting Boff's straining tentacles. Luckily, the suit was of an old design, so his prehistoric blade sliced through all its leather straps with ease.

Her helmet gave first, its chin stay severing easily, falling away in two parts and releasing a long shock of intensely white hair. Next, he attacked the interlacing web that held her shoulder armour and back plate. Gritting his teeth, he forced his fingers underneath the thin leather thongs and pulled with all his might. Straining against the tight leather lashings, he frantically began cutting. Several times, his brittle blade dashed against the superior metal of the armour, shattering into useless fragments.

Absurdly, though, it was the thrashing motion of the suit

that was helping him by creating more flint blades.

With a twang, the spider's web parted, and her gauntlets, forearm shields, and shoulder protectors slid away, revealing her breastplate and waist-girdle lashings. These, Archie attacked recklessly, ignoring the countless tiny nicks to his fingers and hands as he worked his way through all the leather straps and thongs.

'Let her go!' he yelled as the last buckle parted with a *ping*, and he and the suit parted company in opposite directions.

'*My naffin' pleasure*,' cried Boff relaxing his grip, rolling exhaustedly aside.

In a final, desperate convulsion, the remnants of the suit fell free of Serpentina, pieces scattering in all directions, leaving her fragile, semi-conscious body lying still in the long green grass.

For several minutes, no one moved. Boff lay on his back, his strained tentacles quivering about him as he gasped for breath, sweat oozing from his flushed skin. Archie had been thrown some distance by the thrashing suit of armour, landing with a muddy splat on the riverbank, his feet splashing in the river. There he lay, unable to move, completely shattered.

Serpentina, now devoid of her armour, was motionless and barely breathing.

Boff, having two hearts, was naturally the first to recover. Intrigued by the discarded pieces of armour, he tentatively approached a single shoulder guard. It, like all the other segments, was still, although its emerald glow seemed just as lustrous as before. Then, rather stupidly, he touched its padded inside.

'Ow!' he screamed, snatching his tingling finger away.

Archie, despite a thumping headache and aching limbs, was struggling up the riverbank towards Serpentina's unconscious body when Boff screamed.

'Hornswoggle me giblets, boy!' He sucked on a blistered fingertip. 'It naffin' bit me!'

Archie carefully picked up the shoulder guard for a closer examination. The bright-green metal was of a type he'd never seen before, so he presumed that it was the same material that Baldizar had spoken of earlier. However, when he flipped it over, he recognized the lining immediately. Beneath the thin padding was an intricate latticework of printed circuitry, tiny flashing lights, and thousands of pin-sized electrical receptors, the sharp points of which were just long enough to pass through the padding and prick the skin of its user. Without doubt, it was the most sophisticated neurological control unit he'd ever seen.

From a vest pocket, he took a small screwdriver, the tip of which he placed on various parts of the armour's electrical innards. At each point of contact, a tiny light in its top glowed brightly.

'This thing's still live,' declared Archie in dismay.

'It's metal, boy,' argued Boff. 'How can it be alive?'

'Not *alive*,' Archie said. 'It's *live*. It has electricity running through it.'

'Electrickery is the work of the ancient black art of technology,' Grizwold said in Archie's voice. 'But that foul abomination is far beyond anything Baldizar has ever constructed before.'

Archie turned, hearing Serpentina murmur. 'That suit of

armour can only be the work of the professor,' he said, hurling the shoulder guard aside then kneeling beside her. 'He's the only one with the knowledge to build such a technological monster!'

The shoulder guard landed metal side down at the muddy water's edge, discarded without a second thought. Unfortunately, with both Archie and Boff preoccupied with Serpentina's health, neither of them noticed the piece of armour flinch then start to wriggle itself free of the wet mud.

The thousands of receptors covering its inner lining sparked and flashed, moving like tiny legs kicking haphazardly at first then becoming synchronized, as if suddenly obeying new orders. Within seconds, the inanimate piece of metal flipped itself over and began crawling forward under its own power, probing this way and that, all the time sensing and searching.

Archie gently lifted her shoulders and carefully cradled her head in his lap. 'Serpentina,' he whispered tenderly. 'Serpentina, can you hear me?'

'By the curly horns of Jagdar,' exclaimed Boff, hovering beside him, the pale face suddenly jarring wretched, long-forgotten memories. 'Will you look at her beautiful face?'

Gone was the swirling inky-green mask, save for a dash of royal blue across her eyes from ear to ear, which somehow complemented her fair skin and long locks of soft, snow-white hair. Hers was a lovely face with a captivating smile and eyes that radiated warmth and tranquillity. She looked like an enchanting maiden and immediately instilled trust. The sudden polar shift in her personality left Archie smiling and Boff wary.

Serpentina could see the boy's mouth moving, yet his words were no more than garbled sounds lost in the muddled chaos of her mind. *Where is this strange world? Who are these creatures smiling down at her?* They were questions with no answers.

Her pale-blue lips moved, but her croaky voice was hard to understand.

'Here. Try this.' Archie took Boff's water bag and wet her lips, and the speed of her recovery was startling. After a few sips, a fresh, healthy pinkness swiftly coloured her face so much that her soft sulphur-yellow eyes lit up with a refreshing glow.

Archie smiled. 'A little water really does go a long way.'

Her white brows crinkled slightly. 'Why do you call me Serpentina?' she asked. 'My name is…' She frowned, her mind dithering. 'My name is… *What is my name?*'

So focused were they on calming Serpentina that they failed to notice the danger crawling in the grass behind them. The red crystal eye of Mog Droodle that crowned her helmet burned with an evil brilliance, acting as a beacon to the other scattered parts of armour. The breast and back plates were the first to reunite, making their way to the helmet as one. Next went the shoulder guards, arms, and gauntlets. Fortified by the demonic power of Baldizar and bound together with the magic of electrickery, the suit of armour with sinister stealth slowly reassembled itself.

Taking control of Archie's voice, Grizwold said in a loud, joyful tone, 'I know exactly who you are, my dear, but I think that formal introductions are necessary.'

'Yes,' she agreed, the hint of a smile curling on her lips, 'for

I know not who I am!'

'Firstly, I am Grizwold, a mutmut of senior rank.' He pointed at Archie's face. 'The youngling you see before you, is Archie Wilde, my maggot for the race. You will have to forgive his bland appearance and unusual ways, as he is a human from the planet Earth.'

She smiled up at Archie's sapphire-blue eye. 'He does have a youthfulness about him, but I also see the makings of a man.' Her smile was warm and sincere, her features fresh and beautiful. Archie blushed so quickly that felt his ears flush tomato red.

Grizwold raised Archie's left arm and pointed to Boff. 'This creature is Boff, a chamelesquid from the planet Kromper. He is a *reformed* storm raider and Archie's companion.'

For a moment, her mind phased out, lost in thought, then she blinked and was back in the present. 'Boff and Archie, of you I know nothing, but you, Grizwold, you stir an ancient memory about a warning of evil.' She clutched her head as if merely thinking made it ache. 'A genie, a powerful, evil genie... *Baldizar!*' She spat the name as if it were poison on her tongue.

Boff hovered around Archie, both of his coned eyes focused suspiciously upon her. 'Well, trounce me trunnions,' he said, 'aren't we suckers one and all? A flash of those beautiful eyes and attractive smile, and she's got you! How do we know she's not lying?' He hovered close to her face. 'Just another one of old Buckethead's tricks!'

'This is not one of Baldizar's tricks,' said Grizwold firmly. 'In fact, it's quite the opposite. The reason, I shall explain.'

'Yeah, go on, Grizzy,' cajoled Boff venomously. 'You naffin' tell us all why we should trust this assassin?'

Grizwold turned Archie's head and addressed Serpentina. 'If you feel strong enough, would you please stand, my dear?' Behind him, he heard Boff mockingly mimic his words, but he chose to ignore them.

Serpentina rose unsteadily to her feet, braced her legs, and gently rested one hand on Archie's shoulder. The hot summer sun had dried her clothes, a plain buff-coloured catsuit in a quilted, figure-hugging cotton. Although simple in design, its quality of stitch and fabric were second to none. Archie found her beautiful, but Boff's obvious hatred of her was clearly etched upon his face.

Grizwold, using Archie's hand and with her permission, gently turned back her quilted tunic top on her right shoulder. 'There,' he said joyfully. 'A birthmark I have not seen for many a decade, one that I sadly thought I should never lay eyes upon again.'

Boff nonchalantly hovered closer, examining the birthmark with both coned eyes. 'Huh. It looks like a squashed fly to me!'

'Look again from this angle, Boff of Kromper, and see the majesty of the mark,' Grizwold said, making Archie's face scowl. 'Can you not see the unmistakable mark of the WHITE DWARF STAR, with a unicorn's head at its heart?'

'No!' snapped Boff adamantly. 'All I see is a squashed naffin' fly.'

'Enough!' Archie demanded, snatching back control of his voice. 'Will somebody please tell me just what the heck is going on?'

'By the curly horns of Jagdar,' cried Boff, 'I do believe old

Grizzy is trying to foist a fake princess on us!' Several of his tentacles folded stoically across his chest. 'Well, you'll not sucker me in, mutmut.'

A tear rolled down Serpentina's cheek, her soft yellow eyes glazed with confusion. 'I feel as if I have just awoken from a nightmare. Please tell me—I beg of you—*who am I?*'

'You, young lady,' Grizwold announced respectfully, 'are Ssasky, first daughter to the House of the White Dwarf Star, the original ruling dynasty of the genieverse!'

'Ssasky... What a beautiful name,' said Archie. 'Does it mean something?'

'In her tongue, it means "guiding light,"' answered Grizwold.

'A wrecker's light, more likely,' Boff muttered.

'Ssasky,' she said softly, as if reaching out for a distant memory, a sudden seriousness sweeping across her face. 'Then tell me. If I'm the first daughter, where are my family?'

Boff scrutinized her guardedly, moving his entire head. 'If you are who Grizwold seems to think you are, then I'm sorry, lass, for they're all dusted.' Although every fibre of his being screamed not to trust her, when he saw her sway with grief, he couldn't help himself. Compassion made him reach out and catch her as she fell. He lowered her gently onto the small rock.

'How?' she whispered.

'*Baldizar!*' hissed Boff. 'It was his doing.'

'But why?' she asked, desperate to know but fearing the truth. 'He is the supreme genie of the council of the power ten genies. What greater position of authority can be had?'

'Baldizar wanted more than that,' explained Grizwold. 'He wanted to rule the entire genieverse. After deceiving the council genies with his silky lies, he declared a holy war against the House of the White Dwarf Star. But not content with defeating its army, he summoned up a blizzard of such a titanic magnitude that the planet of Vlan was consumed by snow and ice in a storm that raged for fifty years.'

'He dusted my whole family,' she muttered pitifully.

'Jagdar curse that metal monster,' growled Boff, flushing crimson with rage. 'He dusted every last living creature on your home world!'

Archie wanted to say anything to help ease her pain, but such a tale of horror left him sick and speechless.

Ssasky looked up through red-rimmed, tear-filled eyes. 'Has anyone ventured back to Vlan to search for survivors?'

'I have, lass,' Boff said. 'There were none.'

The overwhelming sadness that suddenly swamped her was too much to bear. 'Why me?' She sobbed. 'Why keep me alive for all this time?'

'The answer to that question is fiendishly simple,' said Grizwold. 'With your father, the king, and his army destroyed, Baldizar suddenly found himself the most hated creature alive. You see, many creepies, creatures, and mongrels throughout the genieverse were and still are fiercely loyal to the House of the White Dwarf Star. Fearing open rebellion, he kept you alive as an insurance policy.'

'*Me*, insurance?'

'Scupper me, that's a wretched thing to do, even for Old Buckethead,' growled Boff. 'Baldizar announces his marriage to you, legally ascends to the throne of the White Dwarf Star, and immediately becomes the legitimate naffin' ruler of the genieverse. What a scoundrel!'

In the rough grass beside the riverbank, a small click went unnoticed. The suit of armour was half rebuilt, its helmet back upon its neck. Sitting up like a ghostly half knight, the helmet's single red eye watched and listened to the small group huddled before it. When enough had been heard, it turned its attention to the pair of metal legs crawling back towards it.

Ssasky's shoulders slumped, her head sinking into her hands. 'So where have I been all this time?'

Sadly, it fell to Grizwold to enlighten her to the character of Serpentina that she had been unwittingly portraying these many years. And even though Archie repeatedly told her that it was the suit of armour that was responsible for all the wicked things that had happened, she still felt the crushing weight of responsibility upon her heart.

'Ever since the professor turned up,' added Grizwold, 'Baldizar has been going from strength to strength. His moves against the council of the power ten genies have become more openly bold and brazen. There are whispers in all corners of the genieverse that he's plotting something, something big, and I'll bet my Mutmuts reputation that this ceremony of Atunka Gaar is the keystone.'

'Jagdar's teeth, that's as plain as a barnacle on old King Neptune's bum,' Boff said. 'He's been training Archie Wilde back on Earth for the last decade, and his latest toy, the Crimson Raptor, is powerful but only as a threat. Baldizar needs the dagger to truly fulfil his dastardly ambitions. What better time to culminate his plan than at this decade's ceremony of Atunka Gaar?'

As the group pondered the thought, the suit of armour

quietly reattached its left leg.

'But that's ridiculous,' sniffed Ssasky. 'The Fangs of Jagdar are myth. The dagger doesn't exist—and if it did, it's just a source of *supposed* magic, not a divine right to rule. That power lies with the council of the power ten genies only.'

'Very true,' said Archie, voicing his thoughts aloud. 'But what if the council genies suddenly became extinct?'

'That's an outrageous notion,' she cried, jumping up, a look of majesty in her flaming yellow eyes and the tone of a leader etched in her voice. 'If Baldizar tried to take the genieverse by force, the chieftains would obliterate him on the orders of the council.'

'Unless the council had all been dusted,' repeated Archie.

'Dusted!' she gasped. 'He wou—' Her angry words caught in her throat as a fractured memory suddenly flashed into her mind.

'What is it?' asked Grizwold. 'What have you remembered?'

'I don't know. I seem to recall a vague conversation with one of Goldhorn's minotaur's, something about a vandalized statue and a murder.'

'That would be the statue of Jagdar in the valley of the one true god, deep in the Great Sand Sea,' offered Boff bitterly, 'about two moons ago. A truly gross act of blasphemy if ever there naffin' was.'

Archie shot him a puzzled glance. 'How did you know about that, Boff? You would have been on Earth then.'

'Trounce me trunnions, boy. Babysitting you wasn't a twenty-four-seven job, you know.'

Whilst everyone laughed at Boff's remark, nearby in the

long grass, the suit of armour reattached its right leg.

'Do we know who the murderer was?' Grizwold asked.

'Meggladar, Baldizar's chief artisan,' answered Ssasky.

'What a coincidence,' said Boff. 'Meggladar also happens to be his master weapons builder.'

'Interesting,' Grizwold replied. 'Has his team been seen since?'

'No, I don't think so,' said Ssasky, 'but I fail to see the connection. I checked with the council work records, and the last task they were contracted to do was to refurbish the image of Garrknock above the stage at the amphitheatre.'

'Of course, the statue!' said Archie, clapping his hands with sudden enlightenment. 'I bet you a stack of Christmas presents that the professor has acquired an Earth weapon and that Meggladar and his team have installed it in the statue.'

'At that range,' Ssasky said, 'you would need a dozen archers to dust the whole council in quick time.'

Archie thought for a moment, the fingers of his right hand unconsciously searching his empty liquorice pocket, then spoke. 'Boff, how was the statue in the desert destroyed?'

'Jagdar's leathery mukluks, that's the strangest naffin' part.' He curled a tentacle about his shoulder. 'My informant said that the once-proud statue now lies in a carpet of jagged bits, as if obliterated by a thousand stabbing swords!'

Slowly, with the cautious moves of a snake, Serpentina's old sword slithered its way through the grass towards the fully rebuilt suit of armour.

'Hmmm,' Archie said. 'Sounds to me as though the professor has acquired a high-powered, heavy-calibre machine gun.'

'What is a machine gun?' asked Ssasky fearfully.

As Archie began describing a machine gun, something pricked at Boff's sixth sense. An odd feeling of foreboding caused him to swivel one eye towards the river.

'Jagdar's teeth!' he yelled. With scant regard for his own safety, he lashed out with a tentacle, knocking Archie aside. At the same time, he curled two others about Ssasky's waist, nimbly snatching her off her rock seat and casting her away just as the reassembled suit of armour bought its sword blade crashing down.

They gasped in horror at the sight of the armour standing before them like an inhuman metal monster, its sword blade having sliced the boulder in two. Its red crystal eye glowed as it pivoted on its heels with lightning speed, brought up its sword, and with a sickening swish, sliced off one of Boff's tentacle hands.

Stifling a scream, Boff yanked all his remaining tentacles clear and hovered swiftly out of the way. Ssasky scrabbled backwards on all fours and disappeared behind a tree stump, whilst Archie leapt for cover behind a large boulder.

Seemingly confused, Ssasky's armour stood its ground for several seconds, its sword poised, eyeing the three of them, unsure what to do next.

'Boff, are you okay?!' yelled Archie, distraught at his friend's injury.

'Gadzooks, boy!' he shouted, his cavalier smile not quite masking his pain. 'I've had worse naffin' scratches!'

Archie peeped over the top of the boulder. 'It's the technology inside! It must be programmed to reconstruct itself!'

'Jagdar's teeth!' shouted Boff. 'How do we destroy it?'

With an idea forming in his mind, Archie sprinted from the safety of his boulder over to where Ssasky was hiding. Roughly grabbing her hand, he yanked her onto her feet, dragging her out from behind the safety of the tree stump. They sprinted down to the riverbank, to where a large piece of driftwood lay.

'Grab the other end,' he said smiling wickedly, 'and do what I do.' Nodding between grunts, she doggedly helped him pick up the ungainly length of wood.

Meanwhile, the suit of armour had quickly surmised that Boff was the main threat and through skilful manoeuvring had boxed the wounded chamelesquid in between three huge boulders, which were impossible for him to hover over.

Archie knew that he had to act fast, or his friend would die before his very eyes. The length of driftwood was their only hope. At about twelve feet long and shaped like a two-pronged fork, it was ideal for the task. Unfortunately, having been in the river for many years, its surface was smooth and covered in slime.

'Wrap your arms around it,' Archie said anxiously. 'Hold on tight and aim for its chest.'

With Archie at the front, the pair staggered forward with their makeshift battering ram, gaining speed as they aligned themselves with their target. Grizwold chipped in with a helpful surge of adrenaline, but as they charged across the open grass, Archie feared that they would be too late.

Although Boff valiantly fought the suit of armour with anything he had, he swiftly ran out of ammunition, so he used whatever was at hand. But his improvised makeshift spears were sliced to pieces, his hurled rocks and stones simply batted aside.

From his position, Boff couldn't see the cavalry coming until they appeared out of nowhere, smashing into the side of the suit of armour with a heavy wooden thud. With their speed enhanced by the weight of the wood, the impact took the suit of armour completely by surprise, sending it reeling sideways, making its evil sword fly from its hand.

'Ha! Yes!' Boff cried in joyous relief. 'The naffin' cavalry to the rescue!'

'Keep pushing as hard as you can!' yelled Archie. 'We must get it into the river!' Archie could feel his legs wobbling in the sand. 'Grizwold, help! My legs are going to jelly!' He needn't have worried—his mutmut was on the ball.

Their heroic advance dramatically stopped inches from the lapping water, as the suit of armour, sensing danger, dug its heels in, bracing its shoulder against the wooden battering ram.

Both Archie and Ssasky squealed in pain at their sudden stop. 'Just a few more inches!' shouted Archie, his aching legs trembling and his quivering muscles on fire.

'I'm trying!' Ssasky yelled, her forearms raw from pushing. 'But the log's wet, and I'm slipping in the mud!'

No sooner had the thought of failure reared its ugly head when, with a heroic Kromper battle cry, a speeding Boff slammed into the end of the makeshift battering ram.

Unable to counter such an act of brute force, the suit of armour toppled helplessly into the river. Tripping on something hidden on the riverbed, it crumpled, vanishing with a big splash beneath the water. As the three of them stood panting on the shoreline, their makeshift battering ram at their feet, there was a massive eruption of bubbles, each one sparking and fizzing with tiny flashes of blue lightning. Suddenly, the river before them exploded with a mighty whoosh, sending a column of water sky high.

Archie and Ssasky staggered in exhaustion, but Boff, smirking like a big kid, hovered swiftly forward, sweeping them standing with four of his strong tentacles.

'Well, hornswoggle me giblets!' he roared, hugging the breath out of them. 'Heroes, one and naffin' all!' Quickly interpreting their red faces and pained squeals as sure signs of asphyxiation, he uncoiled his tentacles, allowing them to drop gasping to the ground. 'Oops, sorry.' He chuckled and flushed an embarrassed shade of pink. 'Got a little naffin' carried away there. No one's ever bothered to save my life before!'

Archie rubbed his sore ribs, smiled at Boff, and said between deep breaths, 'It's all right, Boff. That's what friends are for!'

An expression of sadness suddenly flickered like the passing of a lonely cloud across Boff's face. 'I wouldn't know, Archie,' he confessed. 'You see, I've never had a friend before.'

Archie grabbed one of his tentacle hands and wrapped it around himself and Ssasky like a treasured old scarf. 'Well, now you have two,' he proclaimed, smiling. Ssasky pulled away, tears welling in her eyes.

'You have no right to say that.' She said, her voice quivering. 'Who in their right mind would want me for a friend after what I've done!' Boff said nothing and pulled away, not disagreeing.

A sudden violent fizzing came from the river, as the suit of armour, minus its head, erupted from the surface and attempted to stand, as if making one last desperate effort to escape the clutches of the water. But no matter how much it staggered and thrashed about, lashing out wildly with its metal hands, its fate was sealed. A single last bright-blue flash signalled its demise. The suit suddenly became rigid then slowly sank from sight.

Archie made them both jump as, suddenly, he burst into laughter. 'I think that your mysterious professor has forgot the first basic rule of physics.'

'And that would be?' asked Boff.

'Never ever mix water and electricity!'

Chapter 19

Archie unrolled the scroll of parchment upon which the race riddle was written then read it aloud:

'If you be a maggot, then listen ye well.
Seek you a place that's neither heaven nor hell.
A cauldron of fury, both fire and ice,
An Eden of monsters that slash and slice.
Dawn till dusk, it's ruled by him,
A fearsome creature both violent and dim.
A single feather of blood so red,
You must pluck from its clucking head.
But heed the bones cast asunder
Of those poor souls who failed to plunder.
Yet if courage prevails with Jagdar's prize,
Then return to Hexx and join the wise.
Be hero or fool, a warning to muse:
Candle marks twelve, then heads you'll lose.'

Boff laughed. 'Huh... tradition. A total waste of time, yes, but as old as Atunka Gaar itself!'

'So, you know where we're going, then?' Archie frowned.

'See them dastardly-looking mountains cresting the far-off horizon?'

'Er, yes.' Archie's shoulders sagged in dismay.

'Well, the fearsome beast we're after roosts at their feet.'

Archie swallowed hard. He didn't like the sound of that at all.

The land between the river and the mountains reminded Archie more of England than an alien planet. Once away from the muddy riverbank, it was a combination of open, rolling hills covered with wild, rich, green grass and forested valleys. The air was fresh and warm and heavy with the scent of late summer, and the sky a lovely blue, sprinkled with puffy white scudding clouds. Their unexpected dip in the river had temporarily washed Archie's fatigue away, putting pep in his step as he strode after Boff.

Dotted along the riverbank were clumps of extravagantly coloured wildflowers that didn't seem to be swaying in the breeze but more jittering excitedly. Rather bizarrely, on closer inspection of the plant life directly about him, *everything* seemed to be jittering!

'Is it my imagination or is everything in a hurry to grow here?' he asked curiously. 'Don't get me wrong, this place is both invigorating and beautiful, but I also get this unnerving feeling that it's somehow stuck in fast-forward!'

'Of course, the flowers are growing faster here,' said Ssasky dryly. 'This is Bleak. They have no choice. A year's weather in eight candle marks, remember?'

Archie stopped next to a vivid blue-and-black tulip, his jaw dropping as it grew several inches then faded and withered before his astonished eye. 'B-but that is impossible.'

Archie, thalked Grizwold, coughing to clear his throat, *here in the genieverse, the laws of physics are different on all planets, and Bleak is the quirkiest of them all.*

'That's some bombshell to drop on a geek,' muttered Archie.

Sorry, continued Grizwold, sympathetically massaging the boy's brain for his next bolt of bad news. *Worst still, I got my calculation wrong. It's not late summer. It's mid-autumn. I estimate the first snowfall in roughly one candle mark.*

Archie shivered, as did the long, thick dreadlocks of brooding grey clouds rapidly spreading across the sky, which only minutes before had been clear blue. Bizarrely, they were travelling *against* the prevailing wind. In fact, it seemed to him that all the clouds in the sky were converging upon the mountains in the distance—the same mountains to which, unfortunately, they must travel.

From all about him, the breeze quickly freshened, rustling the leaves in the trees, singing that all-too-familiar song of winter's approach.

'We'd best be moving,' said Ssasky, appearing at his side, 'before the jaws of winter begin to bite.' Her stealthy approach made him flinch. 'If you wish to survive the race, Archie, you must focus on the task ahead.'

Archie flicked his golden collar, huffing sarcastically. '*Sorry.* I was somewhat distracted.'

She smiled at him, her powerful golden eyes mellowing to a soft canary yellow. 'The dagger is the key to opening your collar and to your survival.'

He watched her walk on, suddenly feeling very awkward and embarrassed. He felt his face flush with warmth, in complete contrast to the wintry chill that had begun to tickle his bare knees. Having been so wrapped up in his own fate, he hadn't yet given her a second glance since they rid her of her armour. But he did and looking through the eye of a hormonally charged fifteen-year-old boy, he very much liked what he saw.

Her single-piece garment had obviously been designed specifically to protect her body from the rigors of wearing a suit of armour. It reminded him of an athlete's one-piece training suit. However, what it lost in its dull, efficient design and drab cream colour, it made up for by hugging her figure and accentuating her feminine curves wonderfully. She filled it beautifully, and in conjunction with her shoulder-length snow-white hair, blue stripe, and smouldering golden cat's eyes, Archie's emotions didn't stand a chance. He was hooked.

'Hornswoggle me giblets, you pair are going to be naffin' popsicles soon, dressed like that,' declared Boff in a loud, hearty voice, slapping the mesmerized, almost drooling youth hard across the shoulders to break the feline spell.

'What? Er, no… Yes,' stammered Archie, flushing red when he saw Ssasky coyly smiling at him. 'Oh, this is great,' he said. 'Now, I'm going to freeze to death before I have the chance to watch my own head fall off!'

'Scupper me, boy, you're a defeatist!' snapped Boff.

'I don't see you wearing a collar or suffering from the cold, Storm Raider,' Ssasky said.

They walked on in silence, each deep in their own thoughts. It was only when Archie noticed Boff floating alongside him, cheekily mimicking his waddling walk with his two padded tentacles, that he suddenly cried, 'Hey, wait a blooming minute. Didn't that suit of armour cut that tentacle hand off?'

Boff shrugged. 'Odds bodkins, you're quick.' He laughed.

'A lot of species and mongrels have the ability to regenerate their body parts,' said Ssasky. 'And because we're on Bleak, this ability is significantly sped up.'

'Interesting,' said Archie prodding Boff's regenerated tentacle hand.

'Spit it out, boy,' snapped Boff, focusing both eyes on him. 'Something bothering you?'

'Well, yes. Everyone seems to believe that this dagger doesn't exist, so why has Baldizar taken so much time and trouble to enter me in the race?'

'Now that's a naffin' riddle for sure,' said Boff.

'Baldizar has a cold heart and a devious mind,' said Ssasky, watching the storm raider float off. 'He's a schemer, Archie. If he's invested a lot of time and spungold in getting you, then he'll have had a damn good reason for doing so.'

With that thought niggling Archie's mind, the trio fell silent as they strode along the riverbank. Even the pleasantly babbling song of the river failed to lift their spirits. Up front, Boff rather oddly seemed interested in every tree they came across, whilst Ssasky quietly brought up the rear, never speaking but always watching.

After some time, Archie noticed that Boff was squirting ink on some of the trees they passed. 'What are you doing?' he eventually asked.

'Well, trounce me trunnions, boy,' Boff, said, staggered by his naivety, 'what do you think I'm doing!'

'Well, squirting ink over the trees?'

'Well, just how else am I supposed to scent mark my territory?'

Archie groaned, somewhat appalled. 'You're scent marking?'

'Of course,' replied Boff, bewildered. 'Doesn't every species?'

'I don't!' said Archie, miffed at the thought of it.

'So just what do you call farting, then?' Boff asked haughtily. 'And boy, do you naffin' humans do that a lot!'

Archie was about to challenge his remark when Boff suddenly cried, 'Now there's something special you don't see every day.'

Before them stood a towering piece of rock shaped like a single propeller blade, its bluish-black, weather-worn surface smooth and sparkly. 'Beautiful, quite beautiful,' acknowledged Archie, running his fingers over its glassy exterior. 'What's so special about this particular rock?' he asked.

'Egads, Archie, my boy,' Boff said. 'Why, this is a marker stone, of course!'

Ssasky, who was also curiously stroking the stone with her bare fingers, asked anxiously, 'A marker stone for what?'

'This marks an incredibly special place,' announced Boff, wrapping a tentacle about Archie's shoulders. 'To those who recognize it comes possible salvation!' He slid a tentacle hand across Archie's face, completely obscuring his view.

'Hey, what are you doing?' cried Archie.

'Put a sock in it, boy, or you'll spoil the surprise. To the ill-educated, they call it a waste dump, but to an adventurer, it speaks of untold treasures! To you, young Archie Wilde, I present the best naffin' birthday present you've ever had.'

Archie felt his body being gently marched forward and around the rock markers thin edge.

Then Boff announced in a loud, proud voice, 'Welcome to your very own geek's paradise!'

Boff revealed to Archie a sight so awesome that it nearly made his heart explode with joy. Stretching out before him was a giant crescent-shaped split in the ground, nearly half a mile wide by at least five long. But it wasn't the crack in the ground that made him drool excitedly.

Dominating the centre of the canyon was a colossal metal structure exactly nine hundred feet high. He recognized the HMS *Devastator* immediately from pictures he'd seen in history books at school, although seeing it standing vertically, balanced on the tip of its bow, was an unusual perspective, to say the least.

Built in secret during the Second World War, the monster battleship of sixty thousand tonnes, its six triple turrets each housing twenty-one-inch guns, was the mightiest warship ever to prowl the high seas. Or it would have been, if it hadn't sailed from Portsmouth one foggy November night in 1943, only to vanish on its maiden voyage.

Surrounding it on all sides seemed to be a bit of everything. It was a sprawling jumble of aeroplanes, ships, lorries, cars, trains, cranes, bulldozers, tanks and motorbikes. Strewn amongst these were steel shipping containers, wooden crates of all shapes and sizes, bags, boxes, barrels, and drums. Finally, sprinkled everywhere like square snowflakes, were thousands of fridges, freezers, tumble dryers, and washing machines.

Archie nearly exploded with excitement as he charged down the gentle slope at the neck of the canyon, sliding to a stop at the cusp of the dump. Before him, scattered between the big stuff, was everything from clothes and gold and silver coins to gemstones and jewels, knives and forks, toilet rolls, rubber gloves, and Victorian crockery.

'Einstein's underpants Boff, what is this place?' Archie laughed excitedly, so overwhelmed by it all that he thought he might actually cry with joy.

'This is Kicking Rib Canyon,' answered Boff, 'one of Zephyar's many depositories throughout the genieverse.'

'This Zephyar feller must be one of the richest men in the genieverse.'

Without warning, Grizwold suddenly laughed, which created a peculiar sensation for Archie, a bit like a flock of mechanical woodpeckers hammering on the inside of his skull. Luckily for Archie, Grizwold's spontaneous outburst was short lived.

Zephyar isn't a creature like you or me, thalked Grizwold, chuckling. *He is a demigod. He is the everlasting solar wind that blows eternally throughout the genieverse.*

He's a solar wind, echoed Archie dubiously. *How can wind steal something?*

Oh, he does not steal like a thief in the night, Grizwold said. *One of his many traits is that of the master jester. Tell me, young Archie Wilde, have you ever been working on something and put a pen or a pencil or a tool down for just a moment, only to find it gone when you've gone to pick it up?*

Yes, I have, said Archie, frowning, *on many occasions.*

Well, that was Zephyar.

So, he pinches all of this stuff just for a laugh?

Sometimes, yes, but most of the time, no. You see, he redistributes objects throughout the genieverse, knowing full well that a time will come where its future need will be greater than its present.

And dumps them all here!

Well, not just here, added Grizwold. *There are many of these caches throughout the genieverse, all waiting for a creature such as yourself to find and use them.*

'Wow, awesome,' said Archie, marching into the dump, his exhaustion forgotten. 'Look at all this neat stuff.' He let his hands run over all the boxes and packages. 'This whole place is littered with everything I could ever need.' He ran forward, snatching up objects. 'Look, a Cyber 10,000 dot matrix! And here, a Besco's bath time triple-plastic duck set, and—holy Moses! —a full, unedited collection of Einstein's theories.' He turned and grinned at Boff and Ssasky. 'Hmm, a long, weird, red bendy thing! And I thought the scrapyard back home was a—' He suddenly stopped and scratched his head, a puzzled frown upon his face. 'This stuff's clean,' he offered, somewhat confused, 'but it should be filthy and rusty!'

'Archie, my boy, have you ever heard of Gungaders?' asked Boff.

'Er, no,' confessed Archie.

'Well, they're about the size of a field mouse, and they keep this place and all the stuff within clean.'

'There must be loads of them!' exclaimed Archie.

'More than all the fish in the seas, my boy.' Boff grinned. 'But you'll never see one, that's for sure. Fearsomely timid, they be!'

Ssasky looked puzzled as she watched him prodding, poking, ducking, and diving amongst the crates and vehicles. 'Why is he so happy?' she asked Boff. 'This stuff is Zephyar's junk!'

'To us, yes. To him, this stuff is worth more than the finest spungold.'

'But why?' she persisted. 'It's of no practical use.'

'Ever heard of the term "geek?"'

'No.'

'Thought not. Well, it's a slang term for anyone well versed in the ancient black art of technology.' He waved a tentacle hand towards the dump. 'He can build things of unimaginable power from that lot.'

Ssasky shuddered. '*What?* You mean he's like the professor?'

Boff smiled. 'Fear not, Princess. Archie's one of the good guys.'

Whilst ducking under the extended jib of a massive road crane to reach what looked like a toolbox, Archie tripped and fell alongside a partly smashed-open wooden crate. As he picked himself up, he saw on the ground, lying there next to his boot, a single ingot of gold. He quickly pulled two broken planks away from the crate and watched with goggling eyes as several more fell out.

'There must be a king's ransom here!' he cried aloud. 'Enough for me to—' The word 'gold' ricocheted around his brain like a sniper's bullet. As his left hand resentfully touched the golden collar about his neck, so his right hand dropped the bullion bar. Reaching into his pocket, he pulled out his mobile phone, sighing at the clock.

Noting his sudden silence, Boff called, 'Everything all right, laddie?'

'No,' Archie replied. 'We're wasting time here. We need to find food, water, and winter clothes. I only have eight hours and eleven minutes left!' He went to switch off his phone, and it beeped repeatedly, indicating low battery. 'Great,' he grumbled, 'that's all I need.'

'Avast there, shipmate, would one of these things be of any help?' asked Boff, who had floated quietly up beside him and dropped a big box full of smaller boxes at his feet. 'I know you geeks find them a little old-fashioned, but if I remember rightly, they don't require electrickery?'

'Rolex!' cried Archie admiringly. 'Stellar, my friend, absolutely stellar!' It was an Explorer II, tough in design and mechanical workings, but most importantly of all, it was self-winding. 'Perfect!'

'Now that you have a reliable timepiece,' said Boff, 'you best find winter clothes. The weather's turning nippy already!'

The next ten minutes were a frenzied search for clothes, the canyon reverberating with a constant echo of 'no, no, too small, no, no, wrong colour, no, no, oh definitely not!' Then Archie, searching under a huge pile of wedding dresses, found a large crate marked USAF ARCTIC CLOTHING. Quickly forcing the lid off and dropping it to one side, he reached in and pulled out a large blue thing, which Ssasky assumed was a small tent with arms.

'And that is?' she asked, tilting her head curiously from side to side.

'This,' announced Archie proudly, 'is an Arctic funnel hooded parka. Admittedly it's no fashion statement, but it will keep you warm and dry when the winter hits.'

Ssasky pulled the strange coat on. 'You do realize that with the addition of a couple of poles,' she joked haft-heartedly, 'this could be a tent!' But as her cold body quickly began to warm, she grudgingly accepted that he was right. 'Okay, I suppose it will do.'

She was about to turn away when he threw two woolly balls at her. 'I couldn't find any gloves, so we'll have to use these.'

'They're socks!' she hissed in disgust, cringing as she sniffed them. 'And I don't think they're clean, either.'

'We don't have time to be choosy,' said Archie, pulling two pairs on and wiggling his cold fingers vigorously. 'They will do for now.'

'No,' she stated. 'I just can't do it!'

'It's those or frostbite. You don't really have a choice.'

'The boy's right,' whispered Boff. 'Those pretty hands of yours won't be much use without fingers.'

Although her eyes shone a lovely warm yellow, the look of disappointment on her pale face was easy to read. 'Well, if I have to wear them,' she grumbled in a resigned tone, 'at least give me some new ones!'

Archie grinned. 'After all this is over, I think we should return to this place.'

'Why?' she questioned, reluctantly pulling on the socks.

'Because near here, I found several travelling trunks full of ball gowns that would truly befit a princess, and I would love to see you decked out in all your regal splendour!'

Archie didn't have to see her to feel the warmth of her smile.

Boff, who'd just finished sucking out the innards of a dozen fat, juicy worms he'd found under a nearby rock, floated over purposefully. 'Enough of this lollygagging about,' he barked, eyeing Ssasky in her new, rather unstylish blue uniform. 'It's a three-candle-mark march to the beast's lair, so we'd best be on our way.'

'Three candle marks!' Archie cried in disbelief, quickly checking his brand-new Rolex. 'No, no, that won't do at all. I've only got seven hours and thirty-six minutes left!'

'Jagdar's teeth, boy,' growled Boff, wrapping two tentacles about his legs and hoisting him unceremoniously upside down into the air, 'you're a puny earthling with scrawny legs, not naffin' wings.'

'And what about that bug thing you found back in the blue snozzmoo?' added Ssasky as Boff replaced Archie on the ground. 'That will lead the professor's secret agents right here. We need to move now, and fast.'

'Oh, I wouldn't worry too much about that tracking device,' Archie said casually.

'And why not?' asked Grizwold.

Archie's smile was so wide, it would have made a clown proud. 'Because I slipped it into the Mars probe, so the professor and his cronies are, at this moment, merrily chasing that space cow!'

Boff laughed. 'Well, trounce me trunnions. The boy's learning fast.'

'Yes, I am,' agreed Archie, grinning, 'and I may not have wings, but I do have a brain!'

'Odds bodkins. Please, no, not another one of your cranky inventions.'

'Oh yes, and it's a corker!' Archie began issuing orders—'Get those, move that, open this.' He nominated a large open space near the marker stone to be the construction site. Neither Boff nor Ssasky knew what the things were or just what he intended to do with them, but his infectious enthusiasm filled them with renewed hope. Soon, the clearing at the entrance to the canyon had its very own mound of things.

Eventually, Archie came to a halt beside a huge wooden crate, smiling. It was battered and full of holes, but luckily, it had landed the right way up. 'Bezzy,' he growled happily, 'this will do very nicely.'

Boff appeared with a long wooden stick, which he proudly presented to Archie. 'Right, boy,' announced Boff, thrusting the stick into Archie's hands. 'You'll need a long stick for a long walk.'

Laughing, Archie tossed the stick aside. 'Einstein's underpants, Boff, get with the times, huh? We're not walking to the mountains. We're going in that.'

Boff followed his pointing finger. 'What, a wooden crate?'

'A wooden crate with no wheels?' added Ssasky.

'Not the crate, you pair of noodles,' Archie said with a chuckle. 'We're going to use what's inside.' With that, he produced a large crowbar, jammed it forcefully into a crack, then proceeded to prize off the end of the crate.

For nearly a minute, Archie grunted and groaned, yanking the iron lever back and forth.

'Does he know what he's doing?' asked Ssasky.

'Oh yes,' said Boff. 'On Earth, the ceremony of unwrapping a gift or present is taken very seriously.'

'Most bizarre!' remarked Ssasky.

'It's a human thing,' Boff replied. 'Primitive but effective.'

With a long, protesting creak, the end of the crate suddenly fell with a loud *whoomph* to the ground. Archie quickly squeezed inside. 'Boff!' he shouted. 'Grab the two long wooden horns at the front and pull. I've released the brake, so it should move.'

Ssasky gasped in wonder as the most beautiful carriage she had ever seen slowly rolled out before her. It was truly a vision of opulence, standing at least ten feet tall. The whole carriage, its four huge wheels, and its many adornments had such a lustrous golden sheen to it that at first, she had to shield her eyes from its brilliance.

'Is it real?' she asked, letting her fingertips glide slowly over its lacquered woodwork. 'It's the most beautiful carriage I've ever seen!'

'What you have here is the *actual* coronation carriage of Queen Elizabeth II, the Queen of England,' Archie announced proudly. 'The whole coach is covered in thick gold leaf. It's the only one of its kind in the genieverse. And yes,' he added, reading Boff's mind, 'it's priceless!'

'If this belongs to a queen, why is it here?' Ssasky asked suspiciously.

'Many years ago, there was a big fire at the Tower of London. It was in all the newspapers and on the telly,' said Archie, turning and affectionately stroking the coach. 'This beauty was supposed to have been destroyed in that fire!'

'But it wasn't, was it?' Boff asked, smiling. 'Because old Zephyar naffin' stole it, didn't he?'

'Exactly, my friend! The British government would have

lost all credibility in the eyes of the world if they had had to admit that the Queen's coronation coach had been stolen from under their very noses from a heavily guarded fortress. Lucky break… huh.'

'Jagdar's teeth, this carriage is a beauty indeed,' offered Boff. 'But scupper me, boy, how's it going to help us get to them their mountains?'

Archie laughed aloud. 'The great Zephyar isn't the only one who can make the wind blow, you know.'

Two of Boff's tentacles snaked about his shoulders and pushed him close to one of the carriage wheels. 'That I'm sure of, boy, but these fine wheels won't make it through a swamp.'

'Whether it's swamp, water, or grassland, we won't be needing wheels.' Archie grinned.

Under Archie's guidance, they removed the four huge ornate wheels, only to replace them with a weird-looking rubber skirt. Next, they lashed a large propeller to the rear of the carriage, and Archie jammed several large metal bottles inside. Before long, its regal elegance had given way to a far darker image, that of something spawned by the ancient black art of technology.

Neither Ssasky nor Boff had any idea what Archie was constructing or how it was going to help them.

When all was finished, it had taken far longer than Archie had hoped, but it would still be quicker than walking.

Clambering up onto the driver's seat, he beckoned them both to climb aboard, which they flatly refused to do, eying his creation with major distrust.

'Look, I have six hours and forty-five minutes left,' he announced, checking his fine new watch. 'Either get on or move aside. Either way, this carriage is going to those mountains. Understand?'

Chapter 20

To true adventurers, mountain ranges were not just huge lumps of snow-capped rock to be climbed—they were Mother Nature's tantalizing challenge. They were mammoth sentinels, each with their own distinctive personality. Some were picturesque, others fickle, luring climbers with the promise of blue skies and an easy climb. And finally, there were the real bad boys, the ultimate test for the elite few. However, there was one range that was shunned by all, even the insane.

Standing alone, the Unnamed Mountains appeared like the tips of many broken sword blades. Gnarled and fractured over countless ages by the relentless, rapidly changing seasons of the planet Bleak, they loomed aloft like huge blank tombstones. But it was not the physical attributes of these mountains that kept away the bravest of the brave but the evil that once lurked within them.

Even Mog Droodle, by far the most accredited and intrepid climber of his generation, steered well clear of that particular challenge, and Erazmus Snoop, a renowned and fearless tabloid Jabberjockey who, upon temporarily finding himself marooned upon that insidious planet, coined the phrase, 'Better hell than Bleak!'

The Legend of the Ascaree explained why. The history scrolls told of an ancient people that once flourished long ago on Bleak. They were a species like no other, a species fractured by their fanatical beliefs. On the one hand, their strict devotion to the one true deity, Jagdar, ruled their daily lives. On the other was their draconian conviction that their future lay entwined with the black art of technology. It was they who constructed the most awesomely terrifying celestial wheel of power, a device so breathtakingly colossal that it took two whole mountains to hold it erect.

It was there, upon the threshold of the ruins of this ancient species, with the teeth of winter chattering at their heels, that spying eyes eagerly watched the arrival of the intrepid little band of unlikely heroes.

Tucked deep into a crevice atop a mountain outcrop, two shadowy figures huddled close to a meagre fire, keeping a silent vigil over the empty terrain below. From their hiding hole, they had a clear view of the Unnamed Mountains, the river valley that sliced through them, and the ruins of a giant religious structure, which littered its slopes.

Surrounding them on all horizons, threatening storm clouds rumbled and flashed, their broiling black-and-grey masses building steadily into legions of titanic thunderheads. Winter, with its icy winds howling in from all directions, was already ensnaring all before it in a frozen landscape of thick ice and dazzling drifts of snow.

'What's that place, then?' Skatt asked.

Nogga flicked his brother with the tips of his long, leathery tails, their sharp stings leaving two red welts on Skatt's rump. 'As I said earlier, when you obviously weren't listening, these are the Unnamed Mountains, home to the once-great and much-feared Ascaree.'

Skatt wanted to yelp but bit his tongue. Since his little brother's transformation by Baldizar's magic back on their home world, he had gotten too big for his slime trail. 'The smooth curved bits that go halfway up them mountains, what are they?'

'The remnants of the Ascaree's mysterious celestial wheel of power.' Nogga marvelled—even in its ruined state, it was still a truly remarkable spectacle. 'Whatever the wheel of power was,' he continued in an impressed tone, 'it must have scared the slime out of the council of the power ten genies.'

'Why?' asked Skatt, for once genuinely intrigued. 'It's only a big wheel.'

'Because the newly formed council feared that this single piece of black-art technology could be a direct threat to their absolute authority over the genieverse.'

'Huh, they gave them a sound whipping ah.'

Nogga laughed. 'Oh, they did much better than that. Gathering a mammoth army led by Merlin himself, they stormed Bleak, annihilating the Ascaree and totally destroying their mountain stronghold and all their evil machines of technology in the process.'

'What happened to the Ascaree survivors?'

Leaning close, Nogga's cold eyes drilled into his brother's trembling soul. 'None escaped,' he whispered.

If his brother intended to scare him, it worked. Skatt anxiously gulped some water, clearing his parched throat. 'So,' he continued, swiftly changing the subject, 'was Cluck Chuck some kind of weird pet or something?'

'No one's quite sure,' said Nogga. 'Some say he was an experiment gone wrong, and others say that he's the everlasting embodiment of all the Ascaree's ghostly anger.' A shiver ran along Nogga's spine as he stared at Cluck Chuck's nest of twisted, rusting steel, with its apron of bleached bones. 'Whatever he used to be, he's a maggot-killer now!'

Skatt scoffed. 'But he's just a chicken!'

Nogga laughed. 'Oh yeah, a forty-foot carnivorous chicken that drinks blood, gorges on flesh, and crunches bones and metal with its beak.'

Skatt huddled closer to the fire, warming his paws. 'We're here to just watch, right?'

'Don't worry, my lionhearted brother.' Nogga popped a small, dead, overcooked rodent into his mouth. 'We're just here to observe.'

'Well, in that case,' Skatt said, pointing with a paw at a small cloud of dust rapidly approaching the foot of the mountains, 'it looks as if they've arrived! And for three wingless creatures, them's kicking up a big old dust cloud!'

'Interesting,' mused Nogga as he watched the howling wind quickly clear the dusty shroud. 'What in Jagdar's name is that thing?'

'Blimey, look at it sparkle,' drawled Skatt, goggling at its lustrous golden sheen with a thief's admiration. 'Wait—that's not blooming right,' he growled suspiciously. 'There's no hippos pulling or sails blowing it. How does it move?'

'And there's no smoke either,' added Nogga warily. 'And it hasn't got one of those new-fangled Boombelly engines that old Eccles Nimrod, our fruitcake of a cosmic order genie, has been dabbling with.'

'Er, bro,' added Skatt, 'it hasn't got any flipping wheels, either!'

Nogga gasped. 'Well, dry up my slime trail! It blooming well hasn't.'

The pair watched in stunned amazement as the wheelless carriage seemed to float across several small mounds, some scrub weed, and a stream, all as if they weren't there.

'Did you see that?' exclaimed Nogga in admiration. 'It must be—' His mind stumbled for a comparison.

'It's stopping,' said Skatt. They watched the golden carriage wobble to a gentle stop then settle with a soft *whoomph* at the foot of the mountains. 'The maggot Archie Wilde seems to be driving that thing,' he said. 'There's no mistaking a head as ugly as that. But who's the white-haired woman being sick next to that old storm raider Boff?'

'Well, whoever she is, she isn't dressed from head to foot in green armour with a face like a frostbitten prune,' answered Nogga.

'Definitely not Serpentina, then!' Skatt chuckled.

'How absolutely true,' Nogga said, sniggering. 'Maybe she's suffered a fatal accident on route?'

Whilst scratching out a sand flea, Skatt smirked at his brother. 'We'd be deliriously happy, but your boss wouldn't!'

Nogga suddenly crumpled with pain, as if an invisible icy metal hand had reached across the genieverse and squeezed his heart. Reluctantly, he reached for the talking mirror in the professor's carpet bag. 'Baldizar's favourite assassin,' he croaked.

'Me thinks you need to be telling your boss about that there carriage thing, that moves all by itself.'

With trembling hands, Nogga held the old hand mirror. Its glass face was awash with a vail of sepia mist that scarily parted like a pair of ghostly curtains the moment he grasped its handle.

The crisp image of Baldizar's infamous crimson, black-horned helmet appeared. 'Speak!' demanded the image.

'My El Supremo,' Nogga said, 'they have arrived.'

Although Baldizar's voice was perpetually stern and icy, it was his eyes that clued Nogga into the supreme genie's state of mind. Nogga discreetly breathed a sigh of relief—they were a smouldering red, like simmering lava. He was in a good mood.

'They've made exceptionally good time,' said Baldizar, 'considering their untimely departure from the great amphitheatre of Garrknock. What transport have they used?'

Nogga though for a moment, but a sudden flash of black lightning in his boss's eyes prompted him for an answer. 'They used a carriage, my El Supremo, the likes of which I have never seen before.'

'Interesting,' hissed Baldizar. 'Tell me more.'

'Well, it's an old style and seemingly made of solid spungold, but...'

Baldizar leaned forward. 'But what?'

'But it was pulled neither by bullock nor hippo, and there were no sails or smokestacks to be seen.'

Baldizar's eyes began to ripple like a storm brewing at sea, which was not a good sign. 'So just how does this carriage move, then?'

'W... well,' stammered Nogga anxiously, 'it, er, it sort of floated.'

'Floated?' repeated Baldizar in a menacing growl. 'Show me.'

As commanded, Nogga quickly turned the mirror to face the valley below.

Their journey across the flatlands from the dump had been relatively easy. The dreaded swamp that Boff had warned him about turned out to be no problem at all, especially as he feasted greedily upon all the flying bugs that Archie's machine disturbed. They both quickly tired of Ssasky's constant screaming. It was one trip she would remember for an awfully long time.

As they approached the mountain range, what Archie had taken for thick grass swiftly materialized into a mass of stout, stubby bushes festooned with weird yellow flowers. With subtle movements of his control stick, he glided his machine carefully between two clumps and into a large open area. Throttling back, he felt the coach's forward motion begin to diminish along with the whooping noise of the propeller blades. As the machine's lift began to fade, he slewed the craft around and brought it to a jolting stop at the foot of the mountains.

Archie, who had been scared witless at the start, found the majority of the ride exhilarating once he'd mastered his machine's controls. He jumped down from the driver's seat and turned to help Ssasky out of the coach. Brushing his outstretched hand angrily aside, she fell through the open door, tumbling to the ground. In a quivering heap, she proceeded to be violently sick, muttering such words as 'maniac' and 'idiot' between heaves. Her language was punctuated by a lot of very strange, colourful words that Archie presumed were rude.

'Well, trounce me trunnions, Archie, my boy,' Boff said as he floated out of the coach. 'Last time I had a ride like that was back on Firestorm, when some uppity naffin' Attari skin traders took offence at me stealing their hobgoblins.' He hovered past Archie, smiling mischievously at his machine. 'What do you say this naffin' thing is?'

'It's a hovercraft,' Archie said proudly.

'You took perfectly good wheels off, but you didn't replace them with wings or those new-fangled-gas-bag thingies.' Boff scratched his head with three tentacle hands. 'Yet by Jagdar, it flies. How?'

'Contained air pressure,' Archie said, laughing and pointing to the makeshift rubber skirt. 'It doesn't so much fly as hover.' He pointed to the big fan that he had fixed to the rear of the coach. 'The compressed air from all those cylinders inside the coach drives that big fan around really fast, which both lifts the craft off the ground and gives it forward momentum.'

'Lift?' asked Ssasky inquisitively, a fresh pinkness slowly returning to her pale face.

'A lot of air is directed under the carriage and contained within the rubber skirt, thus allowing my hovercraft to ride smoothly along over any surface on a cushion of air.'

'You call that smooth?' Ssasky shrieked, wiping stringy spittle from the corner of her mouth.

'If you were trying to impress her,' Boff said as he floated past, 'you blew it.'

Archie checked his wristwatch—six hours and one minute

remained. Then he tugged at his unwanted spungold collar. 'I only have one priority,' he declared testily, 'keeping my head on my neck!'

Ssasky, her composure fully regained, wandered over to the fringe of scrubby bushes that formed a raggedy barrier between them and the base of the mountains. The strange bushes were covered with bizarre flowers the colour of burnished metal, with beautiful bright-yellow heads the size of sunflowers.

She reached out to touch one, but Boff snatched her hand away. 'Don't mess with those beauties,' he warned.

'But they're so pretty,' she said, a little surprised at Boff's fearfulness. 'Surely I could pick just one?'

Boff took a heavy metal bar from the carriage and gently placed it across a flower head. Instantly, the plant began to vibrate, not wildly but just enough to make it shimmer. Ssasky stared wide-eyed as the mass of deceptively delicate petals sliced through the bar like tiny, furious saws. Backing cautiously away, she watched in horror as the bar fell in several pieces to the ground.

'The locals,' offered Grizwold in Archie's voice, 'simply refer to it as Nasty Old Yellow. And before you get your hopes up, Archie, sadly, they won't cut through your golden collar.'

'Scupper me, boy,' said Boff, beckoning them. 'What do you make of this?'

He waved a tentacle hand in front of another nasty old yellow, pointing to three petals tipped with green goo. Ssasky prodded it with a twig. It was sticky, with a stench to rival Boff's breath.

Grizwold, who had manoeuvred Archie's head in for a

better view, said, 'If I didn't know better, I would say that is blood of some sort. I've heard of some mongrel having blood that colour but not of that consistency.'

'It looks a bit like tree sap,' offered Archie.

Boff scowled. 'Jagdar's teeth... Chieftains!' He pointed to a big ugly boot print in some mud nearby. 'Now, what do you suppose they're doing here?'

'As the official adjudicators for the race,' said Ssasky, who was still poking the green goo, 'they have the lawful right to be anywhere!'

'By the horns of Jagdar, they certainly do,' agreed Boff, his coned eyes flicking nervously between the muddy print and Ssasky. 'But I only told Archie to bring us to this exact location. Coincidence?'

'Coincidence, possibly,' said Ssasky, 'but more likely they were hunting the owner of the green goo.'

'Or maybe they came here for the same reason we have,' offered Archie.

'Odds bodkins, that's a fair point, boy.' Boff grinned, staring up the mountainside with both eyes. 'Maybe they've heard some scuttlebutt about a secret route too!'

'Impossible,' declared Grizwold, hijacking Archie's vocal cords. 'The Ascaree were very shrewd. They polished the base of the mountains until they were as smooth as glass and too slippery for any creature to climb!'

'So do we go around them?' asked Archie hesitantly.

'Egads, no,' Boff said. 'A frontal assault on old Cluck Chuck would be suicide!'

'Then how?' asked Ssasky, confused.

'Easy,' he said, scooping them both up and hovering

effortlessly over the large swath of the razor-sharp plants before them. But as he rounded a huge boulder that nestled snugly against the cliff face, his chuckling stopped as he gasped in wonder. 'Jagdar's teeth!' he roared, dropping his passengers onto the long, wild grass. 'What the mukluks is that thing?'

'It's black-art technology, that's what it is!' muttered Ssasky, crossly brushing the dirt from her clothes. 'And where's he going?'

Archie sprinted excitedly towards it. 'Oh, it's Earth technology, all right,' he cooed. 'Shame it's a wreck, though!'

The object in question was a squashed tube about twenty feet long, pointed at one end and blunt at the other, with two funny oval-shaped holes in the top. Archie recognized it immediately as the front end of a Cold War fighter plane. The front of the fuselage was nearly intact, but the rear was a jumble of jagged edges, shredded electrical cables, and mangled fuel and hydraulic pipes.

This plane didn't crash, surmised Archie, running a fingertip over a scorched patch. *It was blown out of the sky! But by who or what?*

Ssasky moved closer to the abomination and cautiously brushed her fingertips across its battered surface. 'Why, it's metal!'

'And what exactly was it?' asked Grizwold.

'The wreckage you see before you,' announced Archie, waving his hand, 'is what's left of a specially adapted test version of a TSR 2.'

'A *what?*' asked Ssasky, glancing at Boff.

'Beats me, Princess. I was befuddled as soon as he reached

"specially adapted."'

'A tactical strike and reconnaissance bomber, so technically advanced back in 1958 that it made all other aircraft look like children's toys!'

Grizwold sighed. 'Another war machine. Your kind, Archie Wilde, seem to excel at destruction.'

'Actually, this was an experimental aircraft,' retorted Archie. 'And if I'm not mistaken, it's the answer to an old aviation mystery, to boot.'

'Well, trounce me trunnions, boy,' Boff said, floating closer whilst gleefully rubbing three pairs of hands together, 'tell us more. I like a good naffin' mystery.'

Archie crossed back to a point in the wreck just beneath the first oval hole. Using several gashes in the metal skin for footholds, he started climbing. Near the top, he stopped, then used the sleeve of his parker to vigorously rub at a small patch of dirty paintwork.

'Egads, spit it out, boy,' pressed Boff.

'The pilot of this plane was none other than Henry "Guns" McTavish,' declared Archie proudly, 'a World War Two fighter ace and one of the greatest Cold War test pilots ever. He's a hero of mine!'

Ssasky picked up on the heightened tone of his voice and the sudden reddening around his eye. She was about to speak when a tentacle hand grasped her firmly about the shoulders.

'Best leave the boy with his thoughts for a moment,' whispered Boff, his normally cavalier tone suddenly soft and caring. 'A lot of orphans attach their feelings to creatures of action like old Henry. A hero makes a naffin' good surrogate parent.'

Ssasky's sharp yellow eyes mellowed, and she suddenly a felt a strange yet tender connection in her fluttering heart, an unexpected and profoundly moving response that somehow momentarily and emotionally linked her to the boy. 'What's an orphan?'

'A creepy creature or mongrel with no living mother or father!'

Ssasky felt her jaw drop. 'There are such creatures?'

'Oh yes, Princess,' acknowledged Boff soulfully. 'Sadly, more than the stars in the sky.'

'That's terrible.'

Boff turned to Archie. 'Gadzooks, boy,' he said, tugging at his ankles, 'what's this mystery, then?'

Archie blinked away a tear, smiling down at his friend. 'Well, many decades ago, they fitted this aircraft with two experimental Black Arrow rocket motors and shot Captain McTavish up to the very fringe of space!'

'So how did he end up here?' asked Ssasky.

'I've no idea,' Archie replied, 'but at least we've found poor old Guns McTavish.'

Boff snorted. 'You're joking. You mean he's still in there?'

'No, the plane's empty,' said Archie, pointing back to the base of the mountain and off to the left, 'but I think that might be him over there.' He jumped down and darted between them, quickly leading the way.

Ssasky balked at the sight, automatically crossing her forehead with two fingers whilst muttering a prayer to Jagdar. 'I think it's been a fair few years since the Duster brothers took this poor soul.'

Guns McTavish's skeleton appeared to contemplate the

strange world of Bleak through empty, bleached-white eye sockets. His once-shiny silver spacesuit was faded and mouldy, his flight helmet corroded and broken.

'He must have ejected,' Archie said, 'then crawled here.'

'Crawled?' repeated Ssasky.

Archie pointed to the makeshift splint on McTavish's left leg and the hole in the left side of his suit. 'He must have been gravely injured. His first-aid kit and survival pack are empty.' He lifted the frayed ends of a row of white nylon lines. 'This is parachute string. He must have thought he was on Earth, made a temporary camp, and simply waited to be rescued.'

'By the curly horns of Jagdar, boy, he knew he was on a different naffin' planet, all right,' announced Boff, waving them over. 'Take a gander at this.'

About ten feet away, etched into the smooth rock surface next to the remains of an old campfire, was the pilot's final message: IF YOU HAVE TO CRASH ANYWHERE, BETTER HELL THAN BLEAK!

'How did he know this was Bleak?' Ssasky asked in a hushed tone.

'Thieves or scavengers, perhaps,' Archie replied.

'Certainly, no one decent enough to help him,' Ssasky said.

'That's odd,' declared a puzzled Boff. 'The only thing that'll scratch this rock is a diamond!'

Archie moved back to Henry, checked his bony neck, then kicked the dirt about his body. 'It was thieves,' declared Archie bitterly. 'He was a widower. He always wore his wife's diamond wedding ring on a chain. See? It's gone, along with his revolver, radio, and other bits and pieces.'

'Thieving parasites,' hissed Ssasky, 'robbing a dying man.

They told him where he was, then took anything of value, leaving him here for the Duster brothers!' Ssasky felt a tear rolling down her cheek. 'What an awful, lonely way to go.'

'Well, that's fate for you,' offered Boff bluntly, pointing up the mountainside. 'Let's get cracking!'

Ssasky stared forlornly up the mountain's glassy side. Then her keen cat's eyes glimpsed something just above the wreck, not so much an image, more of a slight distortion suggesting something was etched in the smooth rock surface. Jumping gingerly up onto the wreck in a single bound, she reached out hesitantly, as if about to touch a ghost. Then she smiled in amazement as her fingertips seemingly passed through the solid rock's smooth surface.

'They're steps!' she cried aloud. 'Glass steps are carved into the rock.' She turned to the smiling chamelesquid; her snowy-white brows crinkled in a frown. 'You knew about these all the time, didn't you?'

'Aye, lass, that I did,' confessed Boff, smirking. 'Ready for a climb, Archie?'

But Archie wasn't listening. In fact, he was nowhere to be seen.

'Archie!' cried Boff, alarmed by his disappearance. 'Where in Jagdar's name are you?'

'Over here!' he shouted from the other side of McTavish. 'I've found something really interesting.'

'Archie, the way up is over here,' insisted Ssasky. 'If we're going to climb this thing, we'd better get started.'

Archie popped a couple of Muzzberry pips then began vigorously pulling lumps of turf away from a small mound at the base of the mountain. Within minutes, he had uncovered a small square of greyish metal.

'What's that?' asked Ssasky.

'I think it's a lift,' he declared, pointing to a thick grove running up the mountainside. 'See? There's its running track.'

'But what about the steps?' asked Boff.

'I estimate that climb to be three thousand feet,' said Archie, craning his head, 'and you can't carry the pair of us up there. It would be spring by the time we got to the top if we used the steps. However, if I can get this lift working, we can do it in minutes.' He glanced apprehensively back at the green-goo-tipped petals, which lay withered upon the ground. 'We don't have time to physically climb this mountain,' he said, glancing at his watch, 'especially as I've only got five hours and thirty minutes left! And we don't know who's watching, so we need a faster option.'

Whilst a complaining Boff floated back and forth safely over the razor-sharp plants, unloading all Archie's gear from the hover coach, Ssasky and Archie set about clearing away the remains of the compacted mud and wild grass. When finished, Ssasky wiped the sweat from her brow and sat back, panting heavily. But she was pleased with the small metallic platform she had uncovered.

Archie quickly sorted out all the strange gear that Boff had retrieved from the hover coach. He put aside a reel of string and a large coil of rope then placed everything else into a massive four-handled sack, which he promptly zipped and patted smugly.

Scampering back up onto the wrecked hunk of the fuselage, Archie quickly found and tugged at a small handle next to the glass cockpit. From inside the battered hulk came a crisp click as the rear cockpit dome slid backward squeakily. Before it had stopped moving, Archie dived headfirst into the hole. Frantically, his fingers deftly pulled at various levers and bolts, and he was eternally grateful that decades of weather hadn't penetrated the interior of the cockpit. Within minutes, he had the navigator's seat free of its mountings and was dropping it carefully to the ground.

'Come on, squid boy!' he shouted. 'I need that seat moved onto the lift platform now!'

'Jagdar's teeth,' grumbled Boff, 'it's like the pharaohs have returned!'

'Quit griping,' Archie said, sliding down beside him, 'and let's get this seat moved, huh?'

It wasn't particularly heavy, just awkward. But after a couple of minutes, they had it securely lashed to the small metal platform, and once again, Archie beckoned them both aboard.

Ssasky stared uneasily at the seat, its cold, angular metal design evoking disturbing memories of a torture device. 'I don't trust that thing,' she stated nervously.

'But you do trust me?' Archie smiled as he took her hand and sat her on his lap. 'It's just a rocket seat, that's all.'

Archie could feel Ssasky's whole body trembling, and her soft yellow eyes were full of trepidation. 'This thing is incredibly old, Archie. How do you know it'll work?'

'Military equipment is always the best money can buy. I trust it completely,' Archie lied, more worried about the golden collar about his neck than the sixty-year-old rocket under his bum. 'Once I ignite the seat's ejector rocket, it will propel us up the mountainside in no time. You'll see.'

'*If* it naffin' works,' muttered Boff, wrapping his tentacles about the pair of them.

With a deep breath, Archie yanked down hard on the seat's black-and-bright-yellow-striped ejector handles.

With a jarring jolt, the little platform, ejector seat, and its fearful passengers were violently shot into the air atop a brilliant, white-tipped flame, the little platform's joints and corrugated structure buckling and groaning under the awesome power of the rocket's thrust.

Competing with the screech of metal upon metal were the hysterical screams from the heroic trio as, shaking like jellies, they whistled skyward.

Whereas Archie's newly discovered adventurous side was thoroughly enjoying the ride, his sensible, scientific other half was deeply troubled by the menacing cacophony of pings, whizzes, clunks, and twangs coming from under his bum.

He did his best to ignore the fact that although it was lifting them speedily up the mountainside, it was also rapidly shaking the small, old, rusty metal platform to pieces. As a scientist, he considered all deities and their so-called divine abilities to be hogwash. But after one day in the crazy mixed-up genieverse, where all his precious laws of physics seemed to have been abandoned, he was in favour of any help that would make his rocket seat burn for just a few more precious minutes.

Perched upon Archie's brain, Grizwold silently smiled as the near-death scenario played out. His air of pride in his maggot's newfound abilities came right from the heart. 'Science and deities be damned,' he said, chuckling. 'It's your use of Hector's gift that's holding this obsolete platform together and nothing else!'

'Boff!' cried Archie, squinting through a tear-filled eye. 'Can you see that platform up ahead?!'

'Flobollubob!' cried Boff.

'What?' shouted Archie.

'Flobollubob!' cried Boff again.

Archie forced his head to the left to see what was happening and was amazed to see Boff's big leather lips flapping about in the wind, slapping his face red. Boff was obviously greatly embarrassed by this, and Archie's sudden laughter didn't seem to help.

'Okay!' shouted Archie. 'When I give you the signal, just hover away from the seat!'

Still unable to speak, Boff simply nodded his coned eyes in acknowledgement.

Come on, come on, Archie heard his mind pleading. *Just another few hundred feet should do it.*

With a loud *phut*, the ejector-seat rocket abruptly stopped. Suddenly, all that could be heard was the whistling of the wind and their pounding hearts.

'Archie!' screamed Boff. 'The naffin' rockets stopped!'

'Don't worry,' Archie said. 'Momentum will carry us the rest of the way.'

'Mo who?' Ssasky whispered.

With the platform finally in sight, Archie's jangling nerves were replaced by a sense of impending victory. Unfortunately, at that very moment, he heard a familiar fizzing from beneath his bum.

'What? Oh no!' He gasped in horror. 'Please, no, not reignition!'

Phut, phut, *BANG!*

The sound of the explosion, much larger than the little rocket seemed capable of producing, filled the valley below. So loud was its punch that it startled creatures and triggered avalanches across the snow-covered peaks. It also blasted the fragile old metal platform to pieces, flinging the three heroes off the ejector seat and reeling out into the stormy grey sky.

Boff, as a storm raider who was used to being airborne, flung out his ten tentacles, inflated his internal gasbags, then simply rotated like a helicopter, using the mountain's updraft to hover. Using his eyes independently, he quickly located Archie's wildly thrashing figure careering towards the rock face on the left. To his right, he saw Ssasky. She'd been blown away from the mountainside, her limp body falling fast.

Boff's twin hearts skipped beats as he realised that he could only save one of them.

Nogga groaned. 'Jagdar's teeth,' he said, trying to shake the ringing from his ears, 'that was one hell of a bang. What happened?'

'Blooming bang blown the flipping fire out,' Skatt replied, desperately puffing at the dying embers. 'We're going to freeze!'

Nogga snatched up a nearascope and frantically scanned the mountainside. 'Jagdar's scaly hide,' he said, sweating nervously, 'he's going to hit the mountain!'

'Old Buckethead's not going to like his prize maggot splattered all over a mountain!' Skatt said, smiling as a small flame flickered to life.

In his confused state, Archie's screams of terror turned to screams of joy as the fast-approaching, very big mountain, unexpectedly moved to the right. His face passed so close to the rock that he felt it scratch the tip of his nose. He was so happy not to be squashed against the mountainside that he barely noticed his lung-crushing impact with the concrete platform. Tumbling over and over, bouncing painfully off his elbows and knees, he suddenly felt something grab an ankle, jarring him to a violent stop.

'Trounce me trunnions, boy,' Boff said, huffing and puffing as he hovered down to Archie's side, 'that was naffin' close. Thought you were going to bounce clean off the other side!'

Groaning incoherently, Archie pushed himself up into a sitting position, staring up at Boff's big leering face. 'We made it,' he whimpered, rubbing his scraped knees and elbows. 'We actually made—' He painfully scrambled to his feet. 'What's that weird sound?'

'Jagdar's teeth, it's just the wind.'

'Not the wind, you plonka,' Archie snapped. 'Listen. That soft whistling sound coming from just below the edge, sounds a bit like—'

The pair, having shuffled closer to the edge of the platform, suddenly sprang back in shock as a ball of translucent white light floated up before them. It was the oddest thing they had ever seen. It didn't look solid, for its surface seemed to be undulating like gentle waves on a calm sea. And at its centre, a vaguely human figure.

The ball was a good couple of hundred feet away, and although it swayed erratically, it was heading straight towards them. Boff, never having seen the like before, unsheathed all eight of his zizzers from his bandoleers and swiftly adopted an attack posture.

'*No!*' cried Archie, grabbing his nearest tentacle and yanking it backwards. 'Don't shoot.'

'Why not?' Boff was tense and ready to fight.

'I don't think it's hostile.'

Boff swivelled a curious eye back at the boy. 'Listen ye well, boy. This is Bleak. *Everything's* hostile on this naffin' rock!'

'No, you're wrong,' snapped Archie. 'That thing's friendly. I can sense it.'

Boff directed both eyes at him. 'By the horns of Jagdar,' he snarled, 'you can *sense* it?'

Grizwold, well aware of the storm raider's short and volatile temper, swiftly took over Archie's voice. 'Boff of Kromper, listen to the boy. It's Hector's gift that speaks.'

Boff grumbled a surrendering acknowledgement, then warily lowered all but two of his zizzers.

Archie, intrigued by the fuzzy ball, estimated it to be roughly nine feet in diameter, with a striking resemblance to a dandelion head. Watching its every movement with the keen eye of a scientist, he quickly noted that, although the surrounding storm was gusting viciously from all directions, the ball itself held a steady course towards them. It was also clear that the object was floating gracefully under its own power, rather than gliding on the gusting winds.

After crossing the edge of the platform, the white ball floated to a stop immediately in front of them. To Archie, it seemed as if it was hesitating, unsure of what to do next.

'I could slice it in two with one throw,' whispered Boff.

'No, Boff,' hissed Archie.

'Well, we can't just stand here gawping like a pair of pilchards.'

'Maybe we should we say something?' whispered Archie.

'Jagdar's teeth, boy, how should I naffin' know?'

'Boff, you're an alien, aren't you? This must be normal for you.'

Boff frowned. 'To me, boy, you're the alien!'

Feeling just a bit silly, Archie turned to the fuzzy ball. 'Er, hello,' he said sheepishly.

'Hornswoggle me giblets, boy, that's good.' He smirked. 'I wish I'd thought of that one. Very ET!'

Without warning, the ball split down its centre, and with a sweeping swish, like the sound of a million butterflies taking off, it opened, curved backward and in on itself, then vanished. The pair gasped as a very shaky and bewildered young woman stumbled forward from within.

'*Ssasky!*' cried Archie happily. 'It's you!'

Ssasky stood in silence, her legs rooted to the ground whilst the spinning in her head subsided. Her face was pale and her empty hands trembling, but the vivid yellow glow in her cat's eyes exuded excitement, not fear. 'I can fly,' she said aloud. 'I can really fly!'

'You certainly can,' said Archie, taking her shaking, sock-covered hands in his. 'They weren't wings. What were they?'

'I-I don't know,' she answered, trying to pat her back. 'After your stupid rocket thing exploded, all I remember was falling. Then suddenly, these emerged from my back and I wasn't falling anymore.'

'Egads,' Boff interjected in a proud voice, 'you truly are the firstborn daughter to the House of the White Dwarf Star!'

'She is,' said Archie, his face full of wonder.

'I am?' Ssasky asked in disbelief.

'You most definitely are,' confirmed Grizwold joyfully, using Archie's voice. 'And you possess the hereditary and legendary power of flight known as *Escarlla la Luna*.'

'Escarlla la Luna,' she echoed warily. 'What does that mean?'

'Translated verbatim from the ancient tongue,' continued Grizwold, barely able to hide his glowing pride, 'it means to glide with the grace of the midnight moon.'

'I don't get it,' said Archie, his face a picture of puzzlement. 'How can you fly with round wings? It's not physically possible.'

We're not on earth, Archie, thalked Grizwold, *and your laws of physics don't apply here.*

Sorry, he conceded. *I keep forgetting. But still, how does she fly?*

Put simply, Ssasky's sphere is made up of billions of strands of ultralight, hollow hairs that capture the heat from her body and lift it, thus giving her the power of flight.

So where is this mass of hair?

They're stored inside two long, special muscles, one either side of her spine.

Archie moved curiously to view her back, smiling at two long slits in her parka. 'Those hairs must be bloomin' sharp to cut this neatly.'

'Scupper me, shipmates, congratulations all round upon Ssasky's earning her wings, sort of,' interjected Boff gruffly, 'but shouldn't we be getting back to the task at hand?'

Ssasky turned on the chamelesquid with blazing eyes. 'You

287

deliberately left me to fall,' she snarled, 'knowing full well that I'd be dusted if I wasn't the real princess, didn't you?'

'I could only save one of you,' Boff replied bluntly, focusing one eye on her and the other on the sheer drop to the valley floor. 'I chose Archie!' There was a steely finality in his voice that cut like a knife.

But Ssasky wasn't finished. 'My fall had only one outcome,' she countered sharply. 'Archie had been blown towards the platform and safety. I suppose my previous occupation had a little to do with your choice?'

Boff swivelled both his eyes at her, his whole body flushing an angry red, a mean look on his face. 'When the platform exploded, Archie was my primary concern. He wears the collar, not you.' He placed tentacle hands upon her shoulders, forcefully drawing her near. 'Odds bodkins, girl, I knew that if you were truly the one, then your royal lineage would save you.'

'And what if I hadn't been *the one?*'

He let go of her and turned away, commenting glibly over his shoulder, 'No one mourns the dusting of an assassin!'

Archie moved closer, lacing his fingers in hers. 'He's angry with your old self, the personality that you had no control over. Not you, Princess, not the real you.'

She shrugged his hand away, striding furiously to the far side of the platform and stomping to a halt at its edge. 'I don't need your forgiveness, Storm Raider,' she spat angrily. 'And I don't need anyone's pity!'

'Nice one, Princess Nasty,' growled Boff, glaring across at her. 'You're nearly a centenarian with a head full of worldly experiences to draw upon and a full life ahead of you. He's just a mixed-up teenager with raging naffin' hormones and a few candle marks to live. Jagdar knows just what that boy sees in you.'

Boff turned to Archie, forcing a smile, the conversation already forgotten. 'Right, laddie, now what's your plan for dealing with our feathered friend down there?'

Archie took a deep breath, the cold air stinging his lungs. Filling every horizon around him were devilish storm clouds, which rather worryingly seemed to be gravitating towards the mountain upon which they stood.

Archie, have you noticed the path beneath your feet? asked Grizwold. *It is surely a product of the black art.*

Moving off the platform, Archie knelt next to the tracks that ran down the mountainside, his curiosity spiked by the two raised lines of steel. He winced as his bare knees touched the cold rock. 'Look, these are heavy-duty railway tracks, which should, after all these years, be encrusted in rust. Yet they look as if they've just been laid!' As his scientific eye followed the track down the mountain, his excited voice trailed off, his logical mind suddenly trying to comprehend the sheer enormousness of the monument on which he stood.

He sighed incredulously. 'And I thought the pyramids were an awesome feat of engineering!'

'According to the ancient scrolls, this track, as you call it, was originally a complete loop curving high into the sky,' said Ssasky. 'Both Merlin and Zeplin witnessed first-hand the remarkable destructive power of the Ascaree's celestial wheel of power.' There was a sudden paleness about her soft yellow eyes that hinted of great despair and suffering. She raised both hands as if warding off a great evil. 'Some speak of mountains being levelled, oceans drying up, and even small planets being pulverized. This place and the Ascaree race had to be destroyed, for left unchecked, they would surely either have enslaved or destroyed the genieverse!'

'Unlike Baldizar and the council of the power ten genies, who love us all so much,' Boff said acidly.

Ssasky rounded on him with the speed and venom of a striking serpent. 'The council of the power ten genies were created to bring law and—'

A sudden scream from the valley floor cut off her retort, causing everyone to rush to the mountain's edge.

There in the valley below was a huge, hideous creature the size of a house. Its bloated, round body was a mass of quivering, dirty white feathers, and on its sides were stumpy remains of wings, reduced to angrily flapping muscle and bone. Funnily enough, its head reminded Archie of a chicken, only its white beak was much longer and stained red at its tip.

'That's impossible!' he said loudly. 'I thought you were joking when you spoke of a giant chicken!' Then he remembered his monocular. 'Einstein's underpants,' he declared, focusing on the beast below, 'it *is* a chuffing great chicken!'

'Jagdar's scaly hide, boy, that be the beast,' acknowledged Boff, easing him gently away from the edge. 'That's Cluck Chuck, the meanest naffin' chicken in the genieverse. And do you see that large single red feather sitting proudly on top of his squawking head?'

'Yeah,'

'Well, that's the prize!'

Archie's Adam's apple bobbed in horror as he stared at the ground about Cluck Chuck's nest, a hideous montage of bleached bones and rusting mechanical body parts. These he assumed were the remains of previous maggots who had fallen foul of his vicious beak.

To the right, lying across the river from bank to bank, was a yellowish, fleshy bridge. From the nearest end dripped crimson liquid, which had pooled in the dirt underneath it. At first, he assumed it was a fallen tree. On closer inspection with his monocular, he sickeningly realized that it was the remains of the giant creature Boondocks's single leg.

The surviving maggots had formed a loose alliance—some, like the mechanoid Flexx, were happily throwing large rocks with his powerful mechanical arms from a safe distance, although his actions were having little effect upon the giant beast.

Strewth, the floating sausage creature, was hovering just to the north of the battle and seemed to be doing little more than observing. Only Spaggbot, who had metamorphosed into a large bird of prey, seemed to have a vague plan. He was dive-bombing the wildly thrashing head of the giant chicken with his talons wide open, desperately trying to grab the feather.

Meandering through the carnage, oblivious to all the devastation about it, was the river Drawkcab. Its placid green waters flowed serenely in and around the remains of all those long fallen.

I presume that screeching bird is Spaggbot, thalked Archie quietly, afraid that the creature could hear his very thoughts.

It is indeed, confirmed Grizwold, *a very brave yet foolish*

creature that is failing miserably in its attempts to retrieve the
prize.

'But it's a chicken!' laughed Archie aloud. 'Albeit a monstrous great beastie of a chicken but a chicken nevertheless.'

Ssasky frowned at him. 'That chicken, as you so flippantly call it, has claws of Stagmar titanium that can cut through ten-inch granite like a hot knife through butter, eyes that can penetrate the dark, and a beak that can spit fire over a thousand feet.'

'Enough scary talk!' Boff said. 'Now I've guided you all to this Jagdar-forsaken place, so what's your plan to get that naffin' feather, Archie?'

Archie's face shone with a mischievous glow. 'Oh, I have a plan all right! It's so audacious and technically cunning'—he beamed excitedly— 'that I can assure you of its absolute success!'

Chapter 21

For once, both Boff and Ssasky agreed that Archie's plan sucked. However, as neither of them had a plan, they had no real choice.

On the little platform's outer edge was a small but stocky crane. *It's old and weatherworn*, thought Archie, tugging at the running block shackled to its jib. Carefully gripping the steel block with both hands, he took a deep breath and dangled his full weight from it. It held.

Happy that it would do the task, if probably only once, he untied the string from around his waist and threaded it through the top of the block. On the crane's outer casing was a rusty wheel with a handle on it, which he assumed was the turning mechanism that would rotate the jib out over the platform's edge. As he had feared, the handle refused to move, rusted solid with age. However, after several blows with a hand-sized rock, its mechanism loosened enough to turn.

He grinned at Boff. 'Percussion engineering works every time.'

After a dozen rotations, the small crane was in position, and Archie began reeling in the string. He smiled at Boff and Ssasky, who had been watching in silent curiosity and asked,

293

'Boff, do you think you could roll that big boulder over here?'

The storm raider's brows crinkled with suspicion, but he did as requested, dropping the boulder at the platform's edge.

'Is there a point to this?' asked Ssasky.

'Yes,' Archie said, grinning as the end of the thick rope bobbed up in front of them, neatly tied to the other end of the thin string. He threaded the thick rope through the running block. As tension was brought to bear on its single wheel, it squeaked in protest as it was forced to turn for the first time in centuries.

Archie pulled the rope taut then tied its free end securely around the boulder.

'Fancy knot for a landlubber,' Boff said approvingly. 'Now what?'

Stepping forward, Archie put all his strength behind the big rock and heaved. He could have asked Boff to do it, but it was his idea, and he wanted the satisfaction of seeing it work. Wobbling the boulder back and forth, he quickly built up a rhythm then with a heavy grunt, finally rolled it forward, sending it toppling over the edge.

The instant the boulder vanished from view, far below on the ground, the package of equipment that Archie had so caringly bagged suddenly leaped skyward with a savage jerk. On the platform, all eyes watched the running block's wheel spinning frantically. With little or no lubrication left on its axle, it wasn't long before wisps of smoke appeared.

Considering the bag of equipment had to travel roughly three thousand feet, everyone, including Archie, was a little startled when it abruptly appeared before them. Turning the small crane inboard and lowering the bag onto the platform,

Archie immediately removed a small gas cylinder and a large crinkly mass of opaque plastic. With a turn of the valve knob, Boff and Ssasky heard a rush of air and watched in amazement as the plastic began to swell and take shape.

Archie continued unloading the big bag, chuckling with amusement at their looks of bewilderment.

'A big useless ball,' scoffed Ssasky, circling it several times, prodding its spongy transparent surface. 'This is your glorious plan?' She stopped at a part that seemed to be missing. 'And it's got a big hole in it!'

Archie laughed. 'Of course it's got a hole in it. How else are we all going to get inside?'

Boff's thick rubbery lips made a loud pop as his jaw fell open. 'You want us to get inside that thing?'

Ssasky burst into laughter. 'We're going to attack a fifty-foot, bad-tempered, bloodthirsty chicken... in a big plastic ball?'

'No, we're not going to attack that chicken,' countered Archie, fully understanding their mockery. 'We're going to steal its feather.'

Boff eyed him suspiciously. 'Wait a naffin' minute. How did you know to bring this silly ball?'

Archie smirked. 'Saw the tracks and crane through my monocular back at the canyon.'

Perhaps, thalked Grizwold, *if you were to explain its purpose, they might better understand this... contrivance.*

Archie clapped his hands together excitedly. 'Okay, this is how we're going to steal that feather. Firstly, we all climb into the zorbing ball and roll down the track.' He knelt and reassuringly slapped the thick iron track in front of the sphere with the palm of his hand. 'Our weight inside the ball will give us enough forward momentum to leap from the end of the track on this side of the mountain, over Cluck Chuck's head, across the gap, and onto the track on the far mountain.'

Boff's and Ssasky's heads turned in unison, their eyes fixed on the crumbling ends of the track below and the hundred-foot drop in between. It certainly wasn't confidence Archie could see in their wide eyes.

'Secondly, calculating our weight in conjunction with the distance and our speed, I estimate that the sphere will rotate precisely one hundred six times before reaching the chicken. On the one hundred seventh rotation, the red feather on top of its head will pop through the hole for us to grab. Our momentum will then carry us across the gap and onto the track on the far mountain. Then we make our escape.'

'Just like that?' Boff asked.

'Just like that!' Archie grinned.

Ssasky narrowed her eyes. 'I'm not casting doubts on your ability to count or your seemingly bottomless faith in that silly ball, but what if the feather *doesn't* pop through the hole on the one hundred seventh revolution?'

Asked by anyone else, that question would have made Archie very irritable, but as he stared back into her eyes, he found himself smiling. 'Trust me, it'll work. If there's one thing I really excel at, it's mathematical computations.'

'Jagdar's scaly hide, Archie, that feather is supposed to be the strongest material in the whole naffin' genieverse.' He swivelled both eyes at the boy. 'So just how are we going to cut it off?'

Archie laughed, much to their annoyance. 'That feather

might be strong, but the skin about its root isn't. If we all grip together, I reckon we can simply tear the feather and the skin about it right out of his head!'

Ssasky grimaced. 'So basically, you're asking us to roll down an ancient track at the mercy of violent crosswinds with a bottomless abyss on one side and endless fields of nasty old yellow on the other.' Her pallid face was a picture of utter disbelief. 'Supposing we do manage, by some *miracle*, to pluck the feather from Cluck Chuck. Just how do we escape?'

'Easy,' stated Archie, 'this plastic ball will float. It's basically a spherical boat!'

'Jagdar's teeth, boy, you're nuts!' Boff said. 'This plan is by far the riskiest screwball idea you've ever naffin' had. And boy, have you had some stupendously stupid ideas over the years!'

Archie pointed inside the ball. 'Those straps are for your feet, those for your hands, and those for your stomach.' He gave Boff's many tentacles a long, pondering glance and quickly added, 'Boff, you'll just have to improvise.'

'We strap ourselves down. Then what?' asked Ssasky anxiously.

'Just hold on tight, and momentum will do the rest.'

Archie found himself disappointed by their lack of faith. After all, Boff, a supposed storm raider, was just a nervous twitch away from inking himself. And Ssasky's fearful face was so pale that her soft yellow eyes looked like egg yolks in a snowdrift.

Noting their rising panic, he added reassuringly, 'Look, don't worry. The outside of a zorbing sphere is made from the toughest plastic. It's puncture-proof and slash-proof—in fact, it's virtually everything-proof. The inner and outer spheres' skins are connected by twelve hundred individual flexible ties, which act as shock absorbers and will make for a nice, comfortable ride.'

His bravado didn't fool Boff one bit. 'As long as we don't come off the track,' he muttered sourly.

Grizwold, aghast at the boy's blatant lie, felt he must say something, although he prudently decided to thalk his fears first. *You astound me, young Archie Wilde, for I do believe that you're actually enjoying this, aren't you?*

Archie paused for a moment, suddenly realising that Grizwold was right—he wasn't shaking with fear but with excitement. *Do you know what, Grizwold, old friend? I do believe you're right!*

I've tutored many maggots over the centuries, boy, Grizwold replied irritably, *and they have experienced a whole plethora of emotions, but you're the first who has admitted that he's enjoying danger. Remind me never to visit Earth. Your species is seriously weird!*

Archie chuckled to himself. Grizwold really did remind him of his old headmaster.

'Come on, guys. People will write songs about our adventures one day,' he proclaimed in a loud, proud voice. 'Smile! We'll be heroes.' He patted the zorbing ball tenderly. 'Listen, this ball is made of military-grade plastic. It's virtually bulletproo—'

Without warning, the icy cold wind, which had been stabbing at them relentlessly, suddenly faded.

An eerie silence settled over the mountains.

'What's happening?' asked Ssasky, her cat's eyes suddenly bright and alert for danger. 'Why has the wind stopped?'

Boff's eyes swivelled through three hundred sixty degrees and scanned the eastern horizon. 'Well, hornswoggle me giblets, it must be moonset already!'

'Moonset?' queried Archie.

'Yes, Archie, me boy,' whispered Boff. 'When the autumn moon sets on Bleak, the wind momentarily catches its breath.'

Archie sighed, giving him a knowing glare with his one eye. 'Okay, Squid Boy, spill the beans. What's going to hap—'

From out of nowhere, a blood-curdling wail roared through the valley, and everyone, including Grizwold, instinctively ducked. Like the dying cries of a slain monster, its nightmarish howl shot agonizingly across the cloud-choked sky. Its mournful lament gave every living creature on Bleak, including the mighty Cluck Chuck, a bad case of bladder breach.

'What the flippin' heck was that?' asked Archie, shivering.

'That, my friends, was a wave of fiery hot, dust-choked air, known locally as the devil's gasp,' replied Boff. 'It's nature's way of proclaiming that winter is about to bite.'

Archie raised an eyebrow. '"About to bite" means what, exactly?'

'Odds bodkins,' Boff said, dallying. 'I reckon in roughly half a candle mark; this planet will be shoulder-deep in snow and frozen solid!'

'Wait a minute,' said Archie, suddenly smiling. 'So just how long *exactly* does the windless part last if you please?'

'Oh, about six or seven Earth minutes,' answered Boff. 'Why?'

'Because we can use this still period to our advantage,'

Archie said. 'No buffeting for the ball, and the time left after will be more than enough to escape.' The pair was about to argue when he suddenly shoved both Boff and Ssasky towards the round entrance hole, shouting, 'All aboard the *Skylark*!'

Boff glared at him as he hovered up and squeezed through the hole, grumbling over his shoulder, 'I'm not happy with this.'

Ssasky stood her ground. 'No. No way I'm going in that thing. No way!'

Archie grinned as he watched as a pair of tentacle hands snake out and yank her inside, screaming. He chuckled as he heard Boff's voice bark. 'Strap in, woman, and stop your bleating. We've got a naffin' feather to steal!'

'Nogga, what's that funny round thing they've all just climbed into?'

Nogga put his nearascope down and scratched his head. 'Skatt, dear brother, I haven't the foggiest. Never seen one before.'

'Methinks you should be calling old Buckethead, then,' said Skatt. 'And maybe that professor fella might want to know too!'

Nogga focused his nearascope and studied the strange translucent ball for a moment. From somewhere deep in the back of his mind, a familiar voice was speaking. It was putting together all the strange events of the day, in an unusual order that only a Mmicky would understand.

After a long pause, he finally said, 'I think I'm going to wait a while.'

Skatt repeated him, worried by his brother's hesitation.

'Something tells me that maybe we should let things run their course and see how this odd behaviour pans out.' There was a glint of cunning in his eyes, his big, thick lips curling wickedly at the ends. 'The Mmicky in me smells a profit in the offing!'

Archie tried not to show his trepidation as he checked everyone's straps then stepped over Boff, fell into his seat, and strapped himself in. Lastly, he yanked hard on the length of cord in his left hand.

He had wedged a precisely placed rock beneath the sphere, and it flew into the air, disappearing over the edge of the mountain, snaking the cord behind it.

He glanced forlornly at his watch. Three hours and forty minutes remained. It had taken them over an hour to prepare the zorbing ball.

'If anyone wishes to join me in prayer,' whispered Boff, 'please feel free!'

The zorbing ball moved immediately. Creaking slowly at first, its flexible skin absorbed every pebble and small rock in its path before it started to gather speed, settling into the track and rolling off down the mountainside.

The sphere picked up speed alarmingly quickly. The creaking and scrunching of its plastic skin on the ancient tracks rapidly became a weird whining noise that seemed to be growing in painful intensity the faster they went. With the entrance hole to the ball centred exactly between the tracks, the flashing glimpses of the dark mountainside and stormy sky quickly merged into one nauseating blur of greyish black.

To Boff, at first its slow rotations were acceptable, even

slightly amusing, and somewhat reminiscent of his storm raider days. But the fun factor vanished rapidly as his confused brain quickly began screaming for help whilst his four stomachs suddenly felt the need to vomit violently. 'Jagdar's teeth! Me tentacles are all over the place, and me head's feeling right funny like.'

'Me... too!' shouted Ssasky, whose face had turned a ghastly, seasick green. 'I want out of this infernal thing! Now!'

Archie, ignoring their whinging, focused his mind solely on counting the sphere's revolutions. He even managed, to a degree, to blank out the grotesque image of Cluck Chuck's ungainly, flabby head growing larger and larger. From back on the small platform, the big, stupid chicken had looked quite small and comical. But as they raced towards its furiously pecking beak and thick, stubby, flapping wings, an icicle of doubt pierced his scientific faith.

'We're almost there!' he shouted. 'Get ready to grab the feather!'

'I can't!' shouted Boff. 'Me tentacles won't move! They feel like lead!'

'My arms won't move either!' yelled Ssasky. 'What's happening to us?'

'There's nothing wrong with your limbs! It's the centrifugal force of the sphere's rapid rotations!' cried Archie, forcing his arms up and waving at them. 'It's hard to move them but not impossible!'

The pair of them tried, but no matter how hard they flexed their muscles or screamed, their limbs stayed firmly glued to the sphere's lining.

'By the curly horns of Jagdar, will you look at them go!' Skatt shouted excitedly.

Nogga's attention wasn't on the rolling sphere but on the mayhem in front of the screeching chicken's nests below. In his rage, Cluck Chuck had struck out with one of his stubby wings, catching the robot maggot Mexx with a glancing blow and sending him reeling high into the air, right toward the ball.

'Oh Great God Jagdar, no, no, please no,' whimpered Nogga.

Skatt whirled his nearascope around and quickly appraised the situation. 'Oh my, he's heading for the ball!'

'By all the sacred fluff of Jagdar's seven belly buttons, please don't—'

Both the Mmickys caught their breath as they watched the tiny metal figure tumble high into the sky, arcing ever closer to the mountain track. Seconds later, as a distant clanging of metal signalled the mechanoid's crash landing, Nogga's whole body sagged heavily, his loud groan full of misery.

'Jagdar's teeth!' yelled Nogga angrily. 'Why did that metal idiot have to blooming crash there! He's got the whole of a planet to choose from, and that tin-plated moron has to crash land right in front of them!'

'Oh, that's going ruin their day,' Skatt said to his quaking brother. 'And old Buckethead is going to dust you, for sure.' Skatt shuffled out of tail-lashing range, just in the nick of time. 'Shame, really,' he added. 'Old Mexx is only hanging on by his metal chin.'

'What did you say?' gasped Nogga, snatching up his nearascope, and zooming in on the hapless mechanoid's head.

'Yes, oh thank you, Jagdar.'

'What's the matter, bro?' Skatt asked as he watched Nogga pull a strange weapon from the carpet bag and hoist it upon his shoulder. 'You going to blow your own brains out and save Baldizar the pleasure?'

Nogga, whilst making several adjustments to the weapon, snapped, 'This most beautifully awesome piece of lethally crafted and highly illegal technology is'—he glanced down at the manufacturer's label—'a multipurpose assault cannon, trademark name The Slayer, and it's going to be my salvation! Now watch Mexx's head and prepare to be amazed.'

'That ball thing's getting seriously close, bro,' Skatt said, fidgeting nervously. 'If you're going do something, best do it quickly.'

With the ball perilously close, Nogga flicked a switch on the weapon's side from single shot to automatic scythe and squeezed the trigger. He felt no recoil as, in quick succession, one hundred ultra-thin, diamond-edged discs shot out of the launcher, racing off at an incredible speed towards Mexx's dangling body.

In the tumbling sphere, Archie thought he glimpsed something shiny lying on the outer track, directly in their path.

The stream of discs hit Mexx about his shoulders and neck, instantly scything his head free. With only seconds to spare, Mexx watched a large, strange ball roll past as he and his still-functioning metal body scrabbled wildly down the mountainside.

On a far hilltop, Nogga dropped his head in relief, offering up a nifty prayer of thanks to Jagdar, whilst beside him, his deliriously happy, hairy mutt of a brother barked and yapped himself silly.

Inside the sphere, Archie couldn't believe that stupid giant chicken was so busy fending off the other maggots that he still hadn't seen or heard them coming. He waved his sock-covered hands at Boff and Ssasky.

'One hundred and three—pull your socks on. They'll give you a better grip.'

Ssasky, her face a pasty white, obeyed silently.

'One hundred and four—get ready, everyone!' he cried.

With one final scream of defiance, the pair of them finally managed to heave their aching bodies forward into a grabbing position.

'One hundred and five—one more roll.' Archie flashed a small, evil knife before them and smiled winningly. 'One hundred and six!'

Suddenly, just as Archie had predicted, all bristling four feet of the prized feather popped miraculously through the sphere's entry hole, right between their feet.

'Grab it!' screamed Archie.

Chapter 22

The naffin' feather!' Boff shouted as it slipped from his grasp.

'Ssasky!' cried Archie as both she and the feather vanished before their eyes.

The pair stared bleary eyed, their minds in a whirl as the world seen through the zorbing ball's small round entrance flickered passed.

'There she is!' Archie cried joyously, jabbing his finger towards a speck of blue in the distance.

'And the feather's still in Cluck Chuck's head,' Boff said with a groan. 'A perfect plan, my itchy barnacles!'

Archie slumped as if he'd been kicked in the stomach. After all his boasting, he'd botched it—even worse, he'd put Ssasky in danger. 'I don't understand,' he mumbled. 'Why is she still holding onto the feather?'

'What?' blurted Boff. 'She can fly. Why doesn't she fly?'

Archie frowned. 'How do I know? I'll just nip down and ask her, shall I?'

'Ha naffin' ha. What now, genius?'

Archie was about to answer when he realised that their revolving world was slowing. Tearing off his safety straps, he fell across the sphere, bouncing over to the entrance hole. His head continued to spin for several seconds after the zorbing ball had stopped, his equilibrium fighting to settle. Luckily for them, the entrance hole had ended up on top.

'Einstein's underpants,' declared Archie, peering out of the exit hole, 'we've rolled right over Cluck Chuck's head, across the valley and river, and onto the track on the opposite mountain.'

Boff's brain felt like a dumpling in a tumble dryer. 'Egads, boy, I really don't feel well,' he groaned. 'Can't you stop this infernal thing from rolling!'

Archie grunted. 'We have stopped rolling, but we've got to get going again. We've got to go back for Ssasky!'

'And that naffin' feather! Boff's whole body flushed a putrid green as he fought to keep the contents of his four stomachs down. 'Jagdar's teeth'—he burped— 'I really hate this'—he burped again— 'ball.'

After leaping the valley's gap, the sphere's momentum had taken it five hundred feet up the track on the opposite mountain. From the safety of their little rock ledge, Nogga and Skatt had watched the whole pantomime in stunned silence, their admiration for the maggot's audacious attempt to steal the feather obvious. What they didn't understand was the bizarre behaviour of the white-haired woman who clung insanely to the giant chicken's head.

Archie wriggled quickly out of the escape hole and fell with a thud onto the cold, hard ground. As he gave the sphere a quick once-over for punctures, the howling icy wind snatched his breath away.

All about him, jagged black lightning filled the sky,

flashing day light into darkness. Winter had surrounded them, and what little daylight did manage to penetrate the thick cloud cast ghoulish shadows amongst the rocks.

Do you think we can gain enough speed from this height to reach Cluck Chuck's head, Grizwold? he thalked, but there was no reply.

'You're wasting your time,' bellowed Boff from inside the ball. 'After that ride, he is probably unconscious!'

'A fat lot of help you—' Archie choked on his words as he saw a dark stain running down the inside of the translucent wall of the ball. 'Oh no, please, Boff, don't tell me you've just—'

Boff wiped strings of phlegm from the corners of his mouth. 'What? I challenge any creature not to throw up after that ride!'

Archie, stepping away from the sphere, cringed at the stench, but the foul smell vanished along with his breath as he was suddenly exposed to the biting storm.

Instinctively, he buried his head into his hood, but the freezing wind still found its way in. He stuffed his hands deeply into his coat pockets, clenched his chattering teeth, and stood his ground. It was barely a minute before he found himself shivering violently. Nearby, he could see Jack Frost's handiwork sparkling on the rocks and the track before him. Like a giant blanket of tiny white insects, winter was creeping ominously towards them.

'Crikey,' exclaimed Archie. 'The seasons are moving so fast; it actually looks as if the frost is alive!'

'Gadzooks, you're quick, lad,' Boff replied with a scowl. 'Now get back inside this accursed ball before old Jack Frost rams his icy fingers down your throat and rips your frozen lungs out!'

'Good point,' conceded Archie, climbing back into the sphere and flinging himself wildly at the far wall.

'Come on, squid boy. We need to get this thing rolling. Now do what I do and put your weight behind it.'

Boff grumbled something as he scrambled up and threw himself into step with Archie. Within seconds, the pair were running like hamsters in a wheel, the zorbing ball accelerating quickly back down the track.

'We're going awfully fast, Archie,' offered Boff nervously, his tentacle hands slipping on his own vomit. 'The feather will appear in the hole... Won't it?'

'Of course it will,' lied Archie, busy dodging flying lumps. 'My calculations were spot on the first time. We're simply reversing the process.' Before Boff had chance to challenge his theory, he added, 'When it appears, you grab the feather at its base, and I'll grab Ssasky.'

'Er, Nogga,' said Skatt, 'them dozy twonker's are rolling back towards that big chicken.' He squashed a darting lizard with a paw then wolfed it down hungrily. 'Them's going head on. He'll see them for sure.'

Nogga grinned evilly as he shouldered the weapon again. 'Well, if things take a turn for the worst, bro, we might just have to lend them a hand, huh!'

Faster and faster, the zorbing ball rolled—so quickly, in fact, that both Archie and Boff could barely stay upright. Several times, they hit small rocks and potholes, which made the sphere wobble dangerously. It was only Archie's lightning reactions and throwing his body from side to side that kept them on track.

'Archie, you're not counting,' barked Boff anxiously.

'Shut up!' snapped Archie. 'I'm counting in my head.'

They were quickly approaching the break in the track. The void through which the river ran was littered with nasty, sharp things, the worst of them being Cluck Chuck's evil, thrashing beak.

Even through the thick plastic, Boff could plainly see that they were in deep trouble. 'There's no lip at the end,' he puffed. 'How in Jagdar's gnashing teeth are we going to get this stupid ball off the ground?'

'I'm thinking!' growled Archie.

'Well, think naffin' faster!'

'*Jump!*' shouted Archie in a flash of inspiration. 'Jump up and down, and we'll bounce over the gap!'

Boff didn't have a clue what the boy meant but blindly followed his lead.

At first, the sphere was travelling so fast that all their efforts to make it bounce were useless. Then Archie saw a rock about the size of a football just off to one side. Throwing his body boldly to the right, he managed to alter their course just in time.

The sphere bumped against the rock, momentarily absorbing its mass before reforming its shape and bouncing nearly a foot off the ground.

The sphere bounced again to nearly three feet off the track.

The third bounce took them frighteningly high above the track, the storm's erratic winds threatening to buffet them clean off the mountain.

With renewed optimism, the pair doubled their efforts. Higher and higher the zorbing ball went, the gaps between contact with the mountainside becoming longer and longer. As it neared the break in the track, Archie suddenly began trembling with that awful, gut-wrenching tremble that one only gets when one knows something's terribly wrong, and his eye patch felt as if it was on fire.

Without warning, just as they prepared for the ultimate bounce, Cluck Chuck, still furiously fighting the other remaining maggots, reared up his ugly head and locked them with a killer glare.

'No!' cried Archie in horror.

'Look at the size of that beak!' screamed Boff hysterically. 'We're going to be naffin' shredded!'

At that very moment, the zorbing ball took its final bounce inches from the track's shattered end, launching itself into the abyss.

'Oh, mighty Jagdar,' prayed Boff meekly, his big lips quivering in terror. 'Please receive me humble soul into your naffin' care.' Then he twitched fearfully as if suddenly hit by a thunderbolt. 'Oh, and please be forgiving of some of me past indiscretions, if you've a mind to!'

Archie's jaw popped open as he watched, spellbound in terror at the sight of Cluck Chuck's razor-sharp beak snapping viciously right in front of him. Then, from somewhere in the darkest recess of his mind, his nemesis, the ever-present obnoxious voice of doubt, whispered spitefully in his ear. *You've failed, Archie Wilde,* again, *just like you always do. Only this time, there's no escape. This time, you're going to die!*

As the zorbing ball leapt from the track's end, every creepy creature and mongrel human within gasping distance, even the few remaining battling maggots, stopped mid-fight, staring up as it spun silently across the sky. The whole of Bleak held its breath, enthralled by the insanely brave rescue attempt, which could only ever end in an inevitable bloodbath.

Curving perfectly through the air, the sphere and its two pasty-faced occupants came to within a few yards of its target before they were blotted out by Cluck Chuck's fearsome beak and beady, blood-red eyes. The mad chicken's beak was ten feet long and as hard as metal, and the squishy zorbing ball was made of plastic. Their luck had finally run out.

'Argh!' screamed Archie and Boff.

'Boo!' the crowd yelled and hissed as out of nowhere, a bolt of bright-white light-struck Cluck Chuck's massive beak.

In the valley below, the ragtag maggot survivors cheered and shouted as the giant chicken's beak was sliced in two, its tip falling with a splash into the river.

All the creatures of Bleak, disappointed at not getting to see a bloodbath, turned and scuttled away to hide from the winter. High above, the zorbing ball and its two grinning occupants hit the befuddled Cluck Chuck plumb between the eyes then rolled up and over his two long, prickly brows before coming to rest on top of his feathery head.

They heard Ssasky's screams a second before she popped through the ball's entrance hole, still clutching the feather. Her cherry-red face was swollen with anger and her red-rimmed, bright-yellow eyes streamed with tears.

'Get me off this stupid creature!' she yelled hysterically. 'I hate this stinking feather, and I hate this horrible chicken!'

Archie lunged forward, grabbing Ssasky tightly about the waist whilst Boff encircled the base of the feather with all eight of his tentacle hands. Leaning back, they heaved with every ounce of strength that their trembling muscles could muster.

For a few second, the ball was filled with heaving grunts. Then came the sickly sound of tearing flesh.

With a loud, squelching pop, the feather tore free of Cluck Chuck's head, along with a ragged lump of flapping flesh. As they fell back in a tangled heap, laughing with joy, droplets of blue blood sprayed out, speckling the interior of the zorbing ball.

Ssasky fell into Archie's arms. 'Thank you, thank you,' she said repeatedly through her sobs. 'I thought my end had come. I could hear the Duster brothers calling my name.'

Archie smiled, a warm, genuine, straight-from-the-heart kind of smile. 'Well, you didn't really think we'd would leave you there, did you?'

He means every word of what he says, she thought, panting hard whilst gazing deep into his one sapphire-blue eye. Such adoration made her feel a little uncomfortable, yet it also reignited a fire in her heart that had been lost. *Could this be love?* she dared to hope.

Her face suddenly blushed. 'Thank you, Archie Wilde. Thank you for saving me.'

'Rig for collision, me hearties!' bellowed Boff, pointing to a big feathery blob outside the sphere. 'That naffin' chickens not finished with us yet!'

Cluck Chuck's furious screeches of revenge at having lost

313

both his beak and his prized head feather instantly scattered the remaining maggots below.

The combined actions of grabbing the feather and Ssasky had brought the zorbing ball to an abrupt stop, leaving it perched on the angry chicken's head like a silly hat. To have been attacked and partly dismembered was bad enough, but for the attackers to sit gloating on top of his head was just too much for Cluck Chuck to bear. Exploding with rage, the giant chicken flapped its stubby wings angrily then kicked himself off his nest, launching his fat round body upwards. Wildly swishing his head from side to side, he swiftly dislodged the ball, flicking it straight up into the air. But with his main weapon just a stub, all his manic swipes at the returning ball missed, save for the last one.

Catching the sphere on its side with a punishing whack, the barmy chicken sent the zorbing ball flying up the valley.

From the jumble of arms and legs inside the ball, a voice shouted, 'We're falling!'

Forcing himself round, Archie used the sleeve of his coat to frantically rub an area of the plastic clear. 'Ha! Would you believe it?' he roared excitedly. 'That looney chicken has only batted us clear away from the mountain track!'

Boff shoved Archie aside and peered through the mucky plastic. 'Jagdar's teeth, you're right, boy!' He grinned, wrapping his tentacles about them both in a bone-breaking victory hug. 'We're falling towards the river! We're back in the race!'

Cluck Chuck's whack had stabilized the zorbing ball, so with no gut-wrenching spin, Archie found it easy to stand and pop his head out of its tiny entrance hole. He didn't like what he saw. All about them, the storm was raging, growing in intensity. Every horizon was a curtain of mottled, dirty grey, riddled with jagged streaks of black lightning. The winter blizzards were in full howling advance, and tongues of hoar frost licked across the valley. The quickly flowing waters of the river looked more like slowly moving porridge.

Below and to the left, the vast swathes of nasty old yellow seemed just a little too close for comfort, but he kept that knowledge to himself. He was about to duck back inside when he suddenly felt his eye patch tingle, which seemed a little odd, because Cluck Chuck, who was being harried once again by the remaining maggots, was some distance back, and they would soon be bobbing safely on the river. *Surely the danger was past,* he thought.

Suddenly and seemingly from nowhere, a vicious, metal-tipped, black-shafted arrow whizzed perilously close to the back of Archie's head, but the sound of his close encounter with death masked by the howling wind.

Nogga rocked nervously from side to side, his nearascope pressed hard to one eye. 'They're going to fall into the river!' he suddenly shouted, waving his arms in the air, his fat slugman body rippling with elation. 'They've bloomin' well done it, bro!'

'No one's going to catch them now,' Skatt said, laughing and cocking his leg happily. 'Once they're in the river's flow, they'll be pushed to the waterfall in minutes. Then it's hydroport time.'

'Then can we get off this Jagdar-forsaken rock,' added Nogga hopefully.

'Er, that's not right, bro,' interrupted Skatt, peering intently down into the valley. 'Someone's shooting arrows at them!'

His brother took up his nearascope, quickly scanning the river's edge.

'Jagdar's teeth!' yelped a shocked Skatt. 'It's the blooming chieftains!'

'Don't be stupid,' Nogga replied. 'They're the official judges in the race. They're here to make sure there's no funny business.'

'Oh, yeah?' growled Skatt. 'Well, look down at them rocks by the riverbank, near the bend. It seems to me that those chieftains are now judge, jury, and *executioner!*'

'By the curly horns of Jagdar,' wheezed Nogga, his stress levels erupting. 'What are those Neanderthal minotaur's doing?'

In the valley below, he could clearly see the huge figure of Lieutenant Redhorn ordering his chieftains, a whole detachment of fifty, to shoot at the falling zorbing ball. Luckily, minotaur's were better sword and fist warriors than archers. At that range, hindered by the howling winds, they would be lucky to get close to it, let alone hit it. But that wasn't the point. The real question was why in Jagdar's name a bunch of law-abiding chieftains, the supposed guardians of the race, were trying to murder a maggot.

'Methinks maybe you should call the boss, huh?' Skatt said mischievously, moving safely out of whipping range.

Nogga seemed to physically deflate. He hated to admit it, but his brother was right.

The punishing whack caused the zorbing ball not to fall into the river with a splash but to strike its surface at an angle, followed by a series of gloopy bouncing splats. Each impact caused the ball to spin until eventually, it came to a shuddering stop. Luckily, it had landed in the centre of the icy river and was quickly captured by the fast-moving current.

Inside, unable to believe their luck, the three heroes lay panting in happy silence.

'Well, trounce me trunnions, we've done it,' Boff said. 'We're all alive, we've got the feather, and we're on our way to the naffin' Topsy-Turvy Falls.'

Flushed with triumph, Archie checked his watch. '*No!*' he cried aloud. 'That can't be right!'

'What's the matter?' asked Ssasky, shocked by his pale face.

'That's impossible,' cried Archie, staring through red-rimmed eyes. 'According to my watch, getting the feather has taken two whole hours. I only have an hour and nine minutes left!'

Archie's panic was cut short as from outside came the sound of a mighty splash, followed by the clamour of wildly churning water.

'Oh no!' he cried, poking his head back out of the zorbing ball's entrance. 'Cluck Chuck's in the flipping river! He's chasing—' A hand gripped his ankle and yanked him back inside, sending him sprawling in a heap between Boff and Ssasky. 'Hey, what's the big idea?'

Ssasky pointed to the thin black lines whizzing past the entrance hole. 'Someone's shooting arrows at us.'

'*What?* Oh, great,' Archie replied glumly. 'Enemy archers

to the front, a loony giant chicken gaining to the rear... what else could possibly go wrong! Oh, I know, my head will fall off!'

Chapter 23

Utterly exhausted, Archie fell back, overwhelmed by despair. His left hand automatically opened his little leather bag, and he eagerly swallowed a couple of Muzzberry pips. As they took effect and his mind cleared, he suddenly realised just how light the bag felt. Emptying its contents, he was shocked to see only nine pips left.

'Egads, we're slowing,' said Boff, unravelling himself. 'I can sense it.'

Reenergized by the pips, Archie pushed the clawing fingers of depression from his mind and unsteadily scrambled onto his feet. Grabbing the sides of the zorbing ball's entry port, he warily poked his head through. Instantly, the harsh cold air stung his lungs, as waves of snowflakes assaulted his face.

Even with the snorkel hood pulled tightly across his mouth, he still had to grit his teeth against the bitter cold. With his free hand, he shaded his good eye and blinked out into the storm. He immediately wished he hadn't.

All about him, Bleak's winter storm raged. He could no longer see the storm clouds, just the hazy blur of the blizzard, punctuated now and then by titanic claps of thunder that

319

shook his bones and jagged forks of black lightning that dazzled his eye. *If hell's real*—he shuddered—*it's got to be this place.*

'Blimey it's bitterly cold out there,' he gasped, dropping back into the sphere. 'It's snowing heavily, and the river is just a sluggish current of oozing slush.'

'Odds bodkins,' grumbled Boff, 'and we're barely moving!'

'That's not good,' remarked Ssasky.

'Actually, it is,' countered Archie, forcing a smile.

'Scupper me, boy,' blurted Boff, 'explain yourself!'

'Because we're floating on the surface of the river, the ice forming on the banks is continually forcing us out into the mainstream, where the current is faster.'

'What about Cluck Chuck?' asked Ssasky.

'That giant chicken is going nowhere.' Archie beamed. 'The last time I saw him, he was frantically struggling against the rapidly hardening slush. His claws will anchor him into the ice until spring comes!'

Boff scowled. 'What about those treacherous chieftains?'

'The blizzard is too dense. I could barely make out Cluck Chuck, let alone the chieftains on the riverbank,' offered Archie.

'This river's not that wide, and minotaur's are very loud creatures,' Ssasky said. 'You must have heard something?'

'Above the howling wind, not a chance,' stated Archie.

'What about arrows?' asked Boff.

'I didn't see any,' answered Archie, 'but then if I couldn't see them, they can't see us. Surely, they wouldn't waste arrows by firing blindly.'

'Strange,' said Ssasky, her head tilted in thought. 'The chieftains are the official adjudicators of the race. They have been for centuries. They're meant to protect competing maggots, not dust them!'

Archie checked his watch. 'Well, according to my calculations, it should be spring in five minutes, so we'd better have a look at our prize, huh?'

Nogga let the small mirror fall from his hand. It landed with a soft thump, edge on in the powdery dry snow. Skatt, expecting the worst, was shocked to see a broad smile blossom on his brother's big ugly leather face.

'You're smiling!' exclaimed Skatt excitedly. 'Come on, what did old Buckethead say?'

'Huh, well, I'll be jiggered,' Nogga said with relief.

'Well?' Skatt shivered, his mangy fur offering no protection against the biting cold. 'We need to be off this rock before we become popsicles!'

'He wasn't angry about the chieftains' odd behaviour at all,' said Nogga, bemused. 'He was so delighted that the maggot had snatched the feather that he actually sounded happy, *if that's possible!*'

'Wonderful news,' snarled Skatt through chattering teeth. 'Can we go now?'

'Our mission's over,' announced Nogga, turning to the military hydroportal sitting at the rear of the cave. 'By order of Baldizar himself, we're to return to Hexx and enjoy the grand finale of Atunka Gaar!'

'Great,' howled Skatt in delight. 'Let's go.'

Nogga lashed out with his two long slugman tails, grabbing his brother midleap, choking his cries of joy. 'Let's not be too hasty, huh?'

'But Buckethead said to leave,' croaked Skatt, 'and he's the boss.'

'No, there's something wrong,' insisted Nogga. 'The hairs on the back of me neck are itching something wicked!'

'They're not itchy, you plonker. They're naffin' cold,' growled Skatt. 'Everyone's nice and toasty back at the amphitheatre, bro. Come on! Let's go and join them!'

'Oh, we're going back,' Nogga said with a mischievous smile, 'but not to the amphitheatre.'

'*We're not?*' exclaimed Skatt, suddenly more puzzled than cold.

'You said it yourself, bro. Everyone will be at the great amphitheatre of Garrknock to witness the end ceremonies of Atunka Gaar. Baldizar, his cronies, the mysterious Professor Madspanner, and the whole of the power ten genie council, along with, more importantly, virtually the whole of the chieftain regiment.'

Skatt watched incredulously as the corners of his brother's mouth curled into a roguish smile, his flapping ears twitching with irrepressible excitement. It was his thief's face, only Skatt had never seen it so devilishly aflame before.

Then, like a hammer blow to his brain, the penny dropped.

'Jagdar's teeth,' whimpered Skatt, 'you're not blooming serious about that, are you?'

'Oh, yes,' Nogga said, his mischievous tone laced with insanity. 'We're not going to the ceremony. We're going to rob the Waking Dream Vault!'

The blood-red feather they'd plucked from Cluck Chuck's head was roughly six feet in length. Its spine ran exactly up its centre, with perfectly symmetrical fronds on each side. Etched on the spine, rather unexpectedly in English, was the much sought-after clue:

Climb tealeaf, the apple and pears of
The budding flower in the granite parcel.
But to reap the string bean's life of
Leisure, on the way be ready to outfox
The sweaty palms.
Presuming firstly, you've heeded the old moo
In the stripy sock. Lest, of course, you wish
To be hailed a red-nosed boozer for all to
Mock.

'What a load of ludicrous twoddle!' said Ssasky.

Archie fell back, chuckling.

'Some call it a secret code,' offered Boff. 'I've heard tales of learned scholars going to their dusting, tormented by this ancient riddle.' He tutted loudly. 'Personally, I agree with you, Princess—it's a load of gibberish!'

'Boff, have you heard these words before?' asked Grizwold, interrupting Archie's quiet amusement.

'Odds bodkins, yes,' declared Boff. 'Over the decades, nay, centuries, many a maggot got a glimpse of this riddle shortly before they met their grisly demise!'

'Yet, after all this time,' Ssasky said, 'it still remains a mystery.'

'Well, old Buckethead must know some—' Boff stopped his theorizing and frowned at Archie. 'Just what in Jagdar's leathery mukluks is so naffin' funny, boy?'

'I'm sorry,' Archie said, chuckling and shaking his head. 'It's just so hilarious listening to the way you lot speak about that riddle.'

'Oh, and I suppose you know the answer, do you?' Ssasky asked, scoffing. 'More learned are we than all the greatest sages throughout the genieverse, huh?'

'Come on, boy,' hissed Boff. 'Enlighten us poor souls!'

'This riddle wasn't written in some ancient secret text,' Archie said. 'It's cockney rhyming slang!'

'What's that?' Ssasky asked.

'It's an old language from the East End of London, back on Earth.'

'Can you decipher it?' asked Grizwold, suitably impressed that a lowly maggot should be in possession of such wondrous knowledge.

'Certainly,' Archie said, picking up the feather and pointing to the riddle. 'It's a simple, short poem.'

Boff flushed a brilliant blue with excitement. 'Well, trounce me trunnions, boy! Read on!'

Archie pointed to the first sentence. 'Right, a tealeaf is a thief, apple and pears are stairs, and a granite parcel is a castle.'

Boff gawped at its sheer simplicity.

'A string bean is a queen,' he continued, 'and sweaty palms are men at arms.'

'So, we have to go up a staircase in a castle whilst avoiding the guards,' offered Ssasky.

'Correct,' Archie said. 'Now, the second verse. An old moo is a clue, and a stripy sock is a stick of rock.'

'So, the cue is in a stick of rock?' Boff scratched his head.

'What's a stick of rock?'

'The poem is speaking metaphorically,' Archie replied.

'Metawhatically?' asked Ssasky.

'It's a phrase meaning that one thing can resemble something entirely different.' He explained. 'And as the feather is so light, I would guess that the poem is speaking as if the feather is our stick of rock.'

Boff huffed. 'Gadzooks. Why didn't they just say that?'

While Boff examined the feather from top to bottom, Ssasky asked, 'What's a red-nosed boozer?'

'A loser,' answered Archie.

'Oh.'

'There's no hole or way into this feather,' said Boff. 'Are you sure you read it right?'

Archie took the feather and, holding one end with each hand, braced its middle against a knee. The cracking sound was crisp, then he pointed at one of the broken ends.

Boff's big shoulders sagged in astonishment. 'Well, hornswoggle me giblets, there be writing.'

'What does it say?' asked Archie smiling.

'It says "Tower of London"!'

Archie roared with laughter, the simplicity of the whole thing overwhelming him. 'Of course!' he cried triumphantly. 'What better place to hide a treasure than in a room full of treasure!'

Whilst Archie and Boff whooped and hollered in triumph, Ssasky looked on, bemused. 'And what exactly is a Tower of London?' she asked.

'It's the treasure vault to the kings and queens of England,' answered Archie, still staring at the broken feather.

'Is there much treasure there?'

'Rumour has it,' whispered Boff, suddenly becoming profoundly serious, 'that it makes the Waking Dream Vault look like a kiddie's naffin' piggy bank!'

'That I find hard to believe,' countered Ssasky. 'The waking dream vault is the treasure house of the council of the power ten genies. Two thirds of the entire wealth of the known genieverse is stored there.'

'Yeah,' said Boff, 'and most of its stolen!'

As they excitedly discussed the tower's treasure, no one noticed a tiny dot, about the size of a pea, whiz in through the round portal and impact the inner liner of the zorbing ball with a soft splat. So engrossed were they that even when the small dollop of vivid pink goo began to bubble and fizz, it still went unnoticed.

Outside, spring had finally arrived. But whilst the ferocious white blizzard was already abating, a new, more dangerous blizzard—a blizzard of tiny buzzing black creatures—was gathering.

Archie wriggled his nose in disgust at the tangy smell. 'Blimey, what's that horrible pong?' Unconsciously, he was rubbing his eye patch.

'SPITTERS!' cried Boff, recognising the bubbling pink spot as he launched himself through the zorbing ball's entrance hole like a rocket.

Swivelling his eyes frantically in all directions, he quickly realised that the fading eye of the storm was right over the Topsy-Turvy Waterfall... right over them. Unfortunately, directly astern, crunching and smashing its way through the rapidly thawing river but a mere hundred feet away, was

Cluck Chuck. His stubby wings flapped angrily, and his beady eyes were full of fury.

But it was the grisly scene of carnage on the far riverbank that sickeningly gripped his attention. Lieutenant Redhorn and his chieftains were in a tight defensive circle, shields to the front, slashing wildly at the air with their broadswords.

The spitters were attacking them from every direction. The minotaur's didn't stand a chance. Their defensive formation was so close-knit that several times, they inadvertently struck one another with their swords. But to his consternation, he saw no spurting red blood, just fountains of green goo. More amazing still was the fact that the injured chieftains made no sound, seemingly oblivious to their gaping wounds.

In fighting terms, it was a valiant act of defiance but a futile military manoeuvre. The swarm of attacking spitters numbered in the millions, against which swinging broadswords were useless. Boff found himself ghoulishly fascinated, not because his enemies were being slaughtered but because of the weird green goo.

Like a heaving swollen cloud, the dark mass of the spitters blotted out the sky, their incessant humming piercing the victims' heads like the whine of a chain saw. With a ceaseless spitting bombardment of corrosive phlegm, the small kamikaze wasps simply overwhelmed their enemy. The fight, no matter how brave, would only last minutes before the spitters would settle down to a gorging feast of liquefied flesh.

'What's going on out there?' asked Archie. 'What are those things?'

Without warning, the zorbing ball suddenly lurched upwards, throwing them all together on one side, screaming.

'Keep quiet,' hissed Boff, 'or they'll hear us.'

'Einstein's underpants,' whispered Archie, suddenly realising that the walls of the zorbing ball were soft and squidgy to the touch. 'The zorbing ball's deflating!'

Ssasky shoved Archie's left arm aside, awkwardly retrieving her bog spinner from its pouch. 'We're in the grip of the waterfall and ascending fast.' Considering the jostling effects of being snatched violently upwards in the rushing torrent of water, her slim fingers deftly began twisting the spinner's reels into an ordered pattern of address. 'Where was that place we're going to on Earth, again?'

'The Tower of London, England,' said Archie anxiously. 'Boff, what the flipping heck is going on outside?'

'Jagdar's teeth,' Boff said, his body flushing a fearful white. 'They've heard us.'

'Who's heard us?!' snapped Archie, fed up with being ignored.

'Spitters,' growled Boff, twisting one eye back at the boy. 'Vile little wasps that puke acid to putrefy their victim's bodies.'

Archie pulled a face, shuddering in disgust as he fully understood why the ball was rapidly deflating.

'They dust a creature with such efficiency that they don't even leave its soul for the Duster brothers to collect!'

Their journey up to the turbulent crest of the waterfall had begun to feel like a ride in a rocket-powered tumble dryer. Over and over, they were tossed one way then the other. One minute, they were locked together then thrown violently apart. Bucketloads of freezing water sloshed in through the entrance hole, whilst outside, the spitters swarmed in ever-increasing numbers, readying to attack.

'Get out!' screamed Ssasky. 'We need to physically be in the rushing water to hydroport!'

Boff slid out of the entrance hole and fully inflated his internal gasbags. Hovering close, he grabbed Archie's arms tightly then yanked him out of the sphere. Ssasky had started to move when the floppy, half-deflated ball wall collapsed against her, smacking her backward. Her mind swam momentarily as stars exploded in her head, but she was still conscious enough to understand that something had grabbed her legs and was pulling her out of the ball.

Suddenly, the air was full of rushing water and buzzing insects. The sound was deafening, and although they were immersed in freezing water, their skins felt on fire. Boff, in a mid-air pirouette, pulled both Ssasky and Archie in close and prayed. Below, he could see Cluck Chuck's squawking body being propelled up the waterfall towards them, whilst all about them, the buzzing hungry spitting swarm attacked.

As Ssasky, her bog spinner clutched tightly to her chest, locked in the final destination wheel with a soft click, with the speed of a flash of lightning, their world changed. Gone were the violent horror of the spitters, the freezing, swirling mayhem of the falls, and the imminent prospect of being pecked to death by a giant chicken. All swept away by a totally engulfing rainbow of silence.

Chapter 24

It was a big room, dark and quiet.

Each wall was exactly one hundred feet in length. Three of them had huge glass panels set in robust steel frames, and the fourth had four evenly spaced doors. Ceiling-to-floor Venetian blinds neatly covered each window, although some light did manage to sneak between the odd crack in the closed slats.

Hidden in the shadows of a dark corner, a cluster of stalked eyes suddenly became alert, spooked by an unexpected noise from behind one of the doors. The first was a large set of double doors with wire re-enforced glass panels, which were secured by a heavy-duty padlock and chain. The next two, adorned with the symbols of the male and female of the human species, hadn't moved since his arrival. The last one was labelled 'Janitor,' badly scuffed along its dull metal kicking strip, and appeared to be of less importance than the others.

That one, mused the owner of the eyes, spying a growing puddle of water leaking out from beneath it, *is where the—*

'I've found it,' said a muffled voice from within.

'Well, hurry up. We're drowning in here,' gurgled another. 'I'll give it a yank and...'

The small wooden door burst open, releasing a five-foot torrent of water containing Archie, Boff, and Ssasky. Along with them came several shrivelled chunks of plastic, mops, buckets, and a pair of grubby overhauls. All came spilling out onto the carpeted floor in a tangled jumble of wildly splashing arms, legs, and tentacles.

'Jagdar's teeth, that was a close call.' Boff coughed, hovered up, and flexed his ten tentacles to full length, showering water droplets in all directions. 'We must have hydroported half the waterfall with us.'

'Where are we?' croaked Ssasky between coughs and on her knees.

'That's the smallest treasure room I've ever been in.' Boff snorted, grossly emptying his flaring nostrils of river water and snot.

'That's not the treasure room, you idiot,' Archie said, staggering to his feet and ridding himself of his heavy, water-soaked parka. 'Can't you smell the bleach and carbolic soap? We arrived in the janitor's flipping cleaning cupboard!'

'*Cleaning cupboard*,' echoed Ssasky, copying Archie's lead and shedding her sodden winter coat. 'But I dialled the Tower of London into my bog spinner.'

'Shush, listen,' ordered Archie, cocking an ear towards the cupboard. 'The janitor must have left the cold-water tap running, Ssasky, and as no one's using the public toilets next door, your bog spinner must have locked onto that instead.'

'Egad.' Boff vigorously rubbed a bruised tentacle. 'We're here now, and that's all that matters!'

Archie checked his watch. 'Yes, and with only forty-three minutes left to find the dagger and get it to Baldizar, so I suggest we move.'

Ssasky, understanding his eagerness, was about to make for the nearest door when she noticed Archie's face. The vague halo about his eye patch she'd noticed earlier was glowing again—only this time, it seemed to pulsate in time with his breathing. She'd only known him for a short time, but she'd learnt quickly that when it glowed, trouble was close at hand.

'I agree,' added Ssasky. 'Let's find the dagger and get back to Hexx.'

'Fine by me.' Boff floated over to a nearby switch panel.

'Don't Boff!' cried Archie.

It was too late. Forty long strip lights blinked into life, flooding the large room with blinding white light.

Archie crossed the room quickly and smacked Boff's hand aside, flicking all the switches off.

'What the?' snapped Boff.

'You blithering twonker,' whispered Archie as the safety of darkness returned. 'We're in the flipping Tower of London!'

Boff swivelled both eyes angrily at him. 'Yeah, and?'

'This is one of the most heavily guarded fortresses in England,' growled Archie. 'There's a whole garrison of armed soldiers down there!'

Boff suddenly felt very stupid.

'When you boys have quite finished,' whispered Ssasky harshly, 'we should look for the dagger. Except this room seems to be rather devoid of treasure.'

Archie pulled out a small windup torch from a vest pocket and shone it about the huge room, which to his utter despair, was indeed empty. Feverishly, he flicked the tiny beam of light from wall to floor and corner-to-corner, picking out tell-tale signs such as display cases draped in white dustsheets, paint pots, papering tables, lots of black plastic bags full of rubbish, and bizarrely, a single red flip-flop.

'This room's being decorated,' declared Ssasky.

'Archie, shine your torch on the floor again,' Grizwold said, using his voice.

'Oh, you're awake, then,' chided Archie. 'Nice of you to join us.'

'Guard your tongue, maggot,' snipped Grizwold. 'After what you did to me in that infernal ball, I should rake your minuscule brain with pain and make the rest of your life a torturous misery!'

Archie tugged at his irremovable golden collar. 'What, all forty minutes of it?'

Mutmuts weren't supposed to become emotionally attached to their maggots—they were simply their overseers for the race. The rule was to help the maggot as much as possible then move on when they were inevitably dusted. But Grizwold couldn't help it—for some inexplicable reason, he actually felt sorry for the human youngling.

Archie illuminated the odd object.

'There,' said Grizwold, 'a single red flip-flop!'

All eyes stared at the oddly out-of-place rubber footwear.

Boff, who had been gazing out of a window at the strange grey storm clouds circling above the tower, snapped around at the mention of a flip-flop. Hovering past Archie, he picked up the solitary item of footwear, sniffed it, then gave a long, hearty laugh.

'Flip-Flop Freddy!' he cried aloud. 'Come out, you old rogue. Show yourself.'

From a far corner came the soft sound of scratching. Archie spun around and aimed his torch towards it but could see no one. All his instincts told him that something was creeping towards him.

'Argh!' he screamed as a large, hairy, multi-eyed face attached to a football-sized black-and-red body dropped to the floor in front of him.

'You must be Archie Wilde, the much-prophesised Rainbow child,' it said, its mouth full of gnashing fangs. Then it held out a single long, spiny leg, which, much to Archie's consternation, had a human hand on the end. 'Hi. I'm Freddy.'

At that point, the single red flip-flop came sailing through the air, striking the spider on his flat, round nose.

'Well, hornswoggle me giblets,' Boff said, hovering into view, 'you're still leaving that same silly calling card, huh?'

'By the curly horns of Jagdar,' Freddy said laughing, 'if it isn't that notorious scourge of the skies, Bilge Rat Boff himself!' Then he hesitated for a moment. 'Hang on. I'd heard whispers on the gutter vine that you'd been captured by Baldizar a decade ago. Some even spoke of you parting company with that big fat head of yours.'

Boff grinned. 'Yes, to the first, and thankfully, no to the second, as you can plainly see!' He swivelled both eyes calculatingly upon the spider. 'I take it you're here for the treasure too?'

'Of course,' declared Freddy proudly. 'This place has been on my top-ten-to-do list for some time.'

'This rogue a friend of yours?' interjected Archie.

'Scupper me, boy,' Boff said, turning to Archie and Ssasky. 'This hairy little rascal before you is the most notorious jewel thief in the whole genieverse. My friends, I am proud to introduce to you none other than the genuine Flip-Flop Freddy.'

Archie and Ssasky glanced sceptically at each other, but neither said a word, wounding Freddy's so-called villainous reputation. 'Not heard of me huh.' He stared up at Ssasky and asked gruffly. 'Who's she?'

'Archie is Baldizar's maggot in the Atunka Gaar race.' Boff turned to Ssasky and bowed respectfully. 'And this beautiful creature is Ssasky, firstborn daughter to the House of the White Dwarf Star.' He motioned to her shoulder. 'Show him your birthmark.'

As Freddy clocked the mark, a thousand questions sprung to his lips.

'Before you ask, yes, she is the sole survivor of the planet Vlan,' Boff said.

Freddy hauled himself up his spider's thread, stopping before her face. She stood firm as he stared, seemingly probing deep into her very soul. Then he rubbed a small leathery finger across her skin. The blue band across her face, a hereditary mark of the White Dwarf family, seemed genuine. And then there were her eyes, cat's eyes of the purest sulphur yellow, eyes that could supposedly captivate a man's heart with a single glance.

'Hmm,' he mused, slowly stroking his small, ginger Van Dyke beard, 'I think—'

Everyone froze at the sound of a pair of heavy boots

clomping towards the double doors. Freddy vanished upwards, and everyone else dived for cover behind the nearest table.

The boots came to a halt outside the double doors, and with them came the sound of a radio crackling to life.

'Alpha two zero, this is control, over. Are you there yet, Sid? What's taking you so long?'

'Flaming heck, Bob, give me a chance,' said the voice. 'I'm almost a pensioner, and I've just climbed six flights of stairs, me corns are killing me.'

'Alpha two zero, this is control. What's going on up there, Sid?'

The guard unlocked the padlock, dragged the thick chain free, then dropped it to the floor. Pushing one door slightly ajar, he poked a torch through the gap, lazily shining the beam about the room.

'Naff all,' mumbled Sid into his radio. 'Absolutely naff all!' He turned and stomped back towards the stairs, moaning. 'About time they got them blooming lifts working.'

'Alpha two zero, this is control. Hurry up, Sid. The kettles just boiled.' Then the young voice added pretentiously, 'And use proper radio procedures next time, you old beggar. Control out.'

'Flippin' kids,' muttered the guard, vanishing down the stairwell. 'Out of school for two minutes and thinks he knows blooming everything!'

Everyone exhaled with relief as the sound of boots faded. Archie waited a few more seconds then said, 'That's a bit of luck. He's left the doors unlocked.'

'Archie are you familiar with the layout of this fortress?' enquired Ssasky.

'A little, why?'

'You'd better read this, then,' she said, handing him a crumpled piece of paper that read: DURING THE RESTORATION OF THE WHITE TOWER, THE CROWN JEWELS WILL BE HOUSED IN A TEMPORARY DISPLAY ROOM IN THE VICTORIA HALL, WELLINGTON BARRACKS.

'Is this Wellington Barracks place far?'

'I'm not sure,' he answered, dropping the flyer. 'Oh, what I'd give for access to Google Maps right now.'

Ssasky's brow crinkled. 'Google?'

'Trounce me trunnions, boy, this time we don't need your black-art technology.' Boff grinned, pointing out of a window to his left. 'It's that big building over there.'

'It is?' queried Archie 'Are you sure?'

'Who needs Google? It says Wellington Barracks on the wall over there!'

'Nice one,' Freddy said, swinging alongside Archie's face.

'Hey, boy, when you say barracks, do you mean *barracks*, as in a place full of soldiers?' Boff asked.

'Yes, I do,' he confirmed. 'It's where all the soldiers live who are here to guard the crown jewels.'

The word 'soldiers' made Freddy's stalked eyes bristle anxiously. 'You mean violent creatures who love to flail your skin and smash your bones like chieftains?'

'Blimey, no,' Archie said. 'They're far worse than chieftains. They're Royal Marines—you remember those tough, ruthlessly efficient bad arses who attacked us back at the scrapyard, eh, Boff?'

Everyone froze as two plumes of light burst out from under

the toilet doors, casting mesh rainbows across the floor. Then came the unmistakable sound of multiple toilets being flushed.

'Someone's hydroporting,' whispered Archie over his pounding heart.

'No, really?' Boff asked.

'Correction,' stated Freddy, hopping nervously about on all eight of his legs. 'Lots of somebodies are hydroporting!'

'How could anyone know that we're here?' asked Ssasky. 'I alone dialled in this location.'

'Coincidence?' offered Archie meekly.

With a dull thud, the gleaming, razor-sharp blade of a battle axe burst through the wooden door of the men's toilet. It was immediately wrenched free, leaving a splintered gash a foot long, through which glared the big, round, coal-black eye of a chieftain.

'Jagdar's teeth,' growled Boff. 'Coincidence, my naffin' mukluks!' Reacting swiftly, he wrapped himself around a long, large display case and, with a monumental heave, sent it skidding across the polished floor towards the toilet doors. It slammed home hard, completely blocking both doors just as the blades of three more axes began furiously chopping.

'Run!' yelled Ssasky, pivoting lightly on her toes. 'It's those lunatic chieftains! They've found us!'

Archie groaned. 'Einstein's underpants. Thirty-six minutes left, and these morons have to flipping turn up!'

Everyone piled out through the double doors, Freddy halting just long enough to replace the lock and chain. Archie, Boff, and Ssasky had already reached the stairs when the bandit spider shot a thread up at the ceiling and swung past them, out into the void of the stairwell.

'Hey, maggot!' he shouted, staring down at the lower levels. 'Those soldiers who act like chieftains, do they dress like bushes?'

'Yes, why?'

'Because there's a whole naffin' forest of them running up the stairs!'

Archie peered over the banister, and sure enough, the lower levels were chock full of charging marines. 'Damn,' he cursed, checking his watch for the hundredth time. 'It's one flipping problem after another.' He thumped the banister rail angrily with both fists. 'This birthday really sucks!'

Boff stared forlornly at the whole heap of trouble rushing to meet them. 'All this hassle,' he grumbled, 'for one stupid make-believe dag—' Suddenly, and he wasn't sure why, he swivelled an eye over his shoulder. 'Jagdar's teeth!' He snorted in disbelief as, to his horror, a reincarnated Lieutenant Redhorn appeared on the other side of the double doors. 'Avast, you scoundrel, what naffin' sorcery is this?' he cried in alarm. 'I saw you dusted, good and proper. Those spitters turned you into a puddle of pea's pudding back on bleak.'

The spectre of Lieutenant Redhorn said nothing. It just stared at Boff with dull, lifeless eyes. Then without hesitation, it raised a fist and punched the glass, its badly cut knuckles smashing through the glass and reinforcing wire, leaving a fist-sized hole. With a face devoid of reaction to his injuries, the minotaur reached through the hole, grasped the padlock and chain, and with a single tremendous yank, wrenched the door handles clean off.

Above him, Archie heard the sound of violent chopping,

hacking, and kicking. *Those chieftains' great iron boots will make matchwood of those doors,* he thought anxiously. *We need to escape, pronto.* Then he noticed the wide stairwell. It was a large-scale military design, easily forty feet square. The steps could comfortably accommodate five soldiers abreast, with a clear hoisting space in the middle for a small cannon and ammunition.

'Hey, maggot, looks like you're about to be dusted by two angry mobs,' Freddy said. 'Some Rainbow child you turned out to be!'

Archie grinned. 'Freddy, how strong is that silky thread of yours?'

'Bandit-spider thread is renowned throughout the genieverse for its strength,' he bragged, suspiciously cocking all his eyes at Archie. 'Why?'

The officer in charge of the ascending flood of Marines blinked in utter disbelief, abruptly signalling his men to halt. Dumbfounded, the whole platoon just stood in shocked silence, their wide eyes fixed not on the young boy and woman or the weirdo in the octopus costume, but on the surging group of sword- and axe-wielding minotaur's that had just appeared on the top landing.

'Safety catches off!' bellowed the major. 'Charge!'

'Follow me!' shouted Archie, launching himself over the banister and onto Freddy's back. 'It's Tarzan time!'

Ssasky and Boff didn't ask questions—they just blindly followed his lead. The screaming soldiers paid them no heed as the grinning trio zipped past them on the back of a big red-and-black, angrily complaining spider.

Freddy's idea of a controlled descent made Space Mountain

look like a tricycle ride in the park. It was a stomach-churning, heart-stopping, white-knuckle ride, as all six floors zipped past in a sickening blur. Archie thought his pounding heart was going to burst before they hit the concrete floor racing up to meet them. But at the last moment, a grinning Freddy clenched his butt cheeks hard and brought then to a springy stop inches from the concrete floor.

The bandit spider chuckled as the three of them fell dizzily from his back. 'Hey, Boff, what's a Tarzan anyway?'

Archie wobbled over to the stairwell door, which the Marines had obligingly left open, and gripped its frame tightly, waiting for his head to stop spinning.

'You did that on purpose!' snapped Ssasky, cradling her aching head.

'Yeah, you have a real sick sense of humour, Freddy,' added Archie.

'Some thanks, huh?' rasped Freddy bitterly. 'I just saved your scrawny necks back there!'

The humid summer air hit them like a warm, wet rag. Even the royal flag, the Standard, hung limply at the top of its pole, barely fluttering. From their position in the shadows, Archie cautiously peered outside into the courtyard.

Overhead, ragged, thick grey clouds filled the early evening sky, blotting out the autumn sun. And although the clouds looked normal enough to him, those directly above the Tower seemed oddly different. And then there was that low thrumming in the distance, just snatches of sound, too vague to be an aeroplane yet more substantial than a mechanical ghost carried on the breeze. It was almost as if there was something lurking up there.

That niggling thought along with his itchy eye patch and a knotted stomach gave him a bad feeling about the place.

Somewhere in the Tower, a clock chimed five times, its heavy metallic booms echoing about the still courtyard.

Archie groaned. 'Crikey,' he said solemnly, 'that can't be right, surely!' Just thinking about it made his already dizzy head spin even more. The orphanage, meeting Baldizar in the scrapyard, being flushed to Hexx, being collared in the great amphitheatre of Garrknock, and then attacked by a giant chicken and a gang of minotaur's all seemed so surreal. *And now, back here on Earth,* he pondered, rubbing his eye patch. *Is it possible that all of that had happened in just eight and a half hours?*

'Come on, Archie,' prompted Ssasky, appearing at his side. 'Stop muttering to yourself. We need to get that dagger, remember?'

But he didn't answer. He just continued staring outside.

'Archie,' she hissed, jabbing him in the back, 'you've only got thirty-odd minutes left!'

'This place is a fortress,' he whispered sombrely. 'Doesn't it strike you as somewhat poorly lit and suspiciously... *unguarded?*'

Ssasky stared outside, her vivid-yellow cat's eyes taking in every little detail. 'I get your point,' she agreed. 'Even the birds aren't singing!'

From the upper levels of the Tower came the sounds of shouting, screaming, roaring and growling, peppered with the clanging of metal and sporadic gunfire. Then, in a fluke of synchronicity, from somewhere outside the walls, a band began playing a rousing tune, much to the pleasure of the cheering crowd on the streets outside the fortress.

'What's all that hullabaloo?' asked Boff, hovering up behind the pair of them. 'Sounds like a good old shindig to me.'

Archie forced a smile. 'Apart from being my birthday, it's Trafalgar Day today!'

What's worrying you, Archie? thalked Grizwold, sensing his agitation.

It's the courtyard, Grizwold, Archie replied, nervously drumming his fingers on the doorframe. *It stinks of an ambush.*

I understand your fears, Archie, thalked Grizwold, slowly upping his adrenaline level, *but you need that dagger, which is over there.*

Agreed, said Archie, smiling at the far gate, *but a diversion would be helpful.* From the other side of the Tower walls, the sound of people badly singing 'Rule Britannia' was growing in intensity. 'That's what we need,' he said, '*people!*'

Grizwold had heard enough—the boy was stalling. He was about to take control and get him moving when the boy's skull lit up like a 70's disco. In an instant, Archie's brain was bulging and pulsating, awash with a brilliant glow, but it was the deep, rich thrum that really made him smile. *Finally,* thought Grizwold, *the boy is using his Hector's gift.*

Archie found himself concentrating with ease, funnelling his mind through narrower and narrower conduits, filtering out the world's distractions—mainly Boff and Ssasky—whilst all the time tightening his beam of thought.

And then it happened, as easily as peeling a banana. Everything flickered to a halt, as if he had slipped between the frames of an old black-and-white movie. Then, without warning, the world about him stopped.

Although he was sure that he was alone in his peculiar state of physical and mental limbo, he nevertheless approached the Byward Tower gates warily. He removed, with some effort, the long, thick wooden beam that braced the two huge old gates then turned the big iron key that sat in the bigger iron lock. With a loud click, the lock opened, and Archie pulled them apart. On well-greased hinges of wrought iron, the large gates easily swung open, revealing a throng of drunken revellers frozen in time.

That should do the trick. He smiled, nipping back to the doorway and his statue-like companions.

'Archie, did you just use your Hector's gift?' asked Ssasky, staring at the huge wooden gates that had seemingly opened by themselves.

'I do believe I did,' he said smugly.

Her eyes softened with admiration. 'How did you know how to do that?'

He grinned. 'I've no idea. I just did what felt right.'

Boff wrapped him in a tentacle and squeezed him enthusiastically. 'Well, trounce me trunnions, boy,' he offered proudly. 'Good on you, mate.'

Archie glanced at his watch. There were twenty-nine minutes left. As the drunken crowd surged in, he, Boff, and Ssasky leaped out of the shadows and sprinted across the courtyard, covering the gap in seconds. On the far side, they flattened themselves against the weatherworn brickwork of the barracks next to the main entrance door, praying that no one had seen them.

'Jagdar be blessed,' whispered Freddy, appearing on the brick wall above Archie. 'The main doors unlocked.'

'*Wait!*' Archie snapped, grabbing the spider by a bony shoulder. 'Doesn't this strike anyone else as just a bit too easy?'

'Easy?' exclaimed Freddy. 'What are you raving about, skinbag?'

Archie scowled at the bandit spider. 'Freddy, you keep telling us how you're the greatest jewel thief in the genieverse. Well, in your professional opinion, doesn't it seem odd that in this high-security area, there's little lighting, and all the doors that should be locked... *aren't?*'

Freddy tutted despairingly then clamped a pair of hairy hands condescendingly on the boy's face. 'Skinbag, I've been a great thief for more years than you've had birthdays,' he proclaimed egotistically, 'so when the blessing of the almighty Jagdar shines down upon you, don't abuse it. *Use it!*'

Archie despaired as the master thief nonchalantly opened the door and slipped inside, quickly followed by Ssasky and Boff. 'Damn fools,' muttered Archie.

Don't be angry with them, thalked Grizwold. *The strangeness that afflicts their judgment is not of their doing.*

What strangeness? Archie asked.

The Wardvarks of the jungle planet Wingo Wingo first termed the phrase 'sparkle fever' many centuries ago.

Archie blinked. *What the heck's that?*

Most species, when confronted by a vast amount of unguarded wealth, are suddenly consumed by a form of temporary madness. Logic and common sense are instantly replaced by greed, and their actions become bizarre to the point of insane recklessness. A similar thing happened right here on Earth over a century ago, only you humans called it 'gold fever'!

Using his cuff, Archie wiped clean a spot-on a nearby window and peered inside. Even in the half light, the hall was impressively grand. All the walls were panelled in dark oak, upon which hung huge displays of swords, pikestaffs, shields, and shining armoured breastplates. Like ghostly knights of old, complete suits of armour flanked each doorway, window, and a myriad of murky recesses. Above, from the rafters, hung row upon row of battle flags and pennants, the Royal Standard taking pride of place at the head of the room.

Archie gently rubbed his eye patch, attempting to soothe the pain. That hall screamed of a trap, but with—he glanced at his shiny new Rolex—only twenty-six minutes left, all he could do was follow.

Reaching inside his vest, his fingers quickly found and retrieved his slingshot, which he loaded with a marble-sized steel ball bearing. It wasn't much of a weapon, but it sure felt good in his hands. It might not have been lethal, but he knew it would sure as hell rattle someone's brain.

With great trepidation, Archie edged forward, easing himself slowly through the half-open doorway. The hall smelled old. The wooden floor, layered with decades of polish, reminded him of school.

Dominating the centre of the huge hall was the most fabulous treasure trove he'd ever seen, not that he'd ever seen one before. It was a single display case at least thirty feet square, constructed in the form of a four-sided pyramid. At its base was a profusion of beautiful gifts and ornaments, presents from all around the commonwealth. On the first tier were orbs, sceptres, and other ceremonial paraphernalia that marked the power and majesty of a royal household. The second tier housed official crowns, tiaras, regal broaches and pendants. Atop of this was a mind-blowing collection of swords, daggers and bodkins.

On the penultimate tier came the crown jewels themselves, displayed in all their lustrous glory. At the very summit, overlooking all, sat the Queen's imperial state crown, a diadem trimmed in white mink and purple velvet, encrusted throughout with precious gems and of course bearing the Second Star of Africa, a diamond of three hundred seventeen carats that was dazzling even in the half-light of the hall.

He could sense the grip of sparkle fever creeping into his brain, but the thought of his evil collar and knotted stomach fought back, his mind still screaming that it was a trap.

He was savvy enough to know that a collection of such magnitude would be protected by the best alarm systems known to man. Yet strangely, the room was worryingly quiet.

As he moved slowly about the hall, waiting for the inevitable cacophony of alarm bells, his eye eventually fell upon his three companions all standing like statues, their mouths open, their hands stuck to the display glass.

Sparkle fever, thalked Archie.

Aye, that it is, thalked Grizwold. *It has them all spellbound.*

A fat lot of use they are, muttered Archie. *Still, someone will trip an alarm soon, and I'm sure the noise will snap them out of their greedy trance.*

'Hey… skinbag, up here,' called a scratchy voice from a far corner.

'My name's Archie,' he stated, not even bothering to look up, 'not Skinbag!'

'Whatever you say, Skinbag.' Freddy chuckled as he swung across the hall on multiple threads. 'The alarms won't wake them,' he offered haughtily. 'Infrared, temperature, floor mats, tremblers, and laser beams are all disabled, courtesy of yours truly, so you can put your silly toy away.'

One ball bearing between those smug little eyes, thought Archie, *just one!* However tempted he was, it was a sad fact that he might just need that despicable creature's help again, so he grudgingly holstered his slingshot. As he did, he caught sight of his watch. He had twenty-five minutes left.

Freddy's technical confidence concerning the alarms alleviated his fears about the hall being a trap just a little, but he still didn't fully trust that cocky little arachnid.

He walked to the nearest suit of armour and relieved it of its helmet and brutal-looking mace. The helmet was a one-piece affair and a little on the large side, and it stank. Nevertheless, he popped it on, raised the weighty mace up high, took a deep breath, then swung at the display case with all his strength.

'Blimey, not even a flippin' scratch!' Archie muttered, suddenly unleashing a volley of angry blows that would have pulverised any normal glass to dust.

'Feel better, Skinbag?' asked Freddy, taken aback by the ferocity of the youth's attack.

'*Yes!*' snapped Archie, breathing heavily.

'That puny lump of metal is no good. That's armoured glass, and you need something much hea—look out!' yelled Freddy a split second before the huge Victorian skylight above them imploded in a storm of shattered wood, broken glass, and one huge body.

For a few panic-stricken seconds, debris of all kinds rained down all around them, blinding everyone with billowing dust. Then with a loud and very sickly, squishy whoomph, a large object splatted onto the floor before them.

As the calamity faded, three dirty, dust-covered heads with quizzical faces appeared.

'Flippin' heck!' cried Archie from behind a fallen heap of armour. 'What happened?'

'Are we under attack?' croaked Ssasky, spitting dust and rubbing her head. 'I remember entering the hall and staring at all the treasure, then everything went bang.'

From under a pile of smashed ceiling boards came a protracted moan. 'Oh, who naffin' hit me?' groaned Boff, shaking himself free of smashed plaster and glass.

'More to the point,' said Freddy, shaking a mini cloud of dust from his fur, '*what* hit us?'

Archie chuckled. 'Well, it's nice to have you all back to normal. Anyone hurt? No cuts or broken bones?'

'What do you mean, normal?' asked Ssasky. 'My memory is all fuzzy.'

'According to Grizwold, you were struck with sparkle fever.'

'Gadzooks, will you take a look at that?' Boff pointed to where the treasure pyramid used to be. 'A Chieftain.'

'It's a *dusted* chieftain,' corrected Ssasky.

'Well, that's the display case open,' rasped Freddy. 'Although some of the jewels'—he held up a flattened crown with several stones missing as an example— 'seem to have lost their lustre.'

'Well, hornswoggle me giblets,' said Boff, floating forward and poking the body. 'It's one of them weird green ones. See? It's oozing green goo, not red blood.'

Ssasky picked up a small, jewelled sceptre, prodded a vicious-looking gash several times, then held it up and carefully sniffed the goo. 'Oh, that's disgusting!' she cried, throwing the sceptre aside. 'It smells of rotten vegetables.'

'Hmm, a veggie chieftain,' offered Boff thoughtfully. 'I'll wager ten reels of spungold that that cretin Professor Madspanner is behind this naffin' abomination.'

'That treacherous scumbag. They're doppelgangers,' hissed Ssasky. 'I wonder if Baldizar knows that Madspanner's double-crossing him?'

'That explains the chieftains' attack on Bleak,' said Boff.

'Interesting though this revelation is,' announced Grizwold via Archie's voice, 'our main concern right now is to find that dagger!' He raised Archie's right wrist. 'We only have nineteen minutes left!'

Freddy, his twelve eyes brimming with tears, had already started carefully picking his way through the wreckage. To anyone else, the destruction of such a fabulous treasure was a tragedy, but to the most notorious and greedy jewel thief in the genieverse, it was heart-breaking. With four of his free hands, he plucked up two squashed crowns, a broken sceptre, and a very flat orb.

'Such beauty, such craftsmanship'—he sniffed—'all wasted.'

Ssasky, touched by his show of emotion, reached out and stroked the back of his neck comfortingly. 'Don't worry, Freddy. These fine pieces still have their history. No amount of damage can change that.'

Freddy casually tossed the broken jewels to one side. 'Stuff history,' he snapped, frowning at her. 'I had a buyer lined up for this little lot. Ten thousand reels of the finest spungold,' he declared, sniffing back a tear. 'Now, I doubt if I could sell them for one reel.'

Ssasky pinched his ear hard and watched him wriggle with pain.

'Aww, what was that for?'

'That's for being a greedy, selfish pig—or spider, in your case. We're not here for profit. We're here to find a lost dagger and to save Archie's life!'

'Well, hornswoggle me giblets, I've found it,' cried Boff, holding aloft a magnificent, bejewelled dagger. 'This has to be the fabled Fangs of Jagdar!'

Chapter 25

Archie glanced at the dagger Boff held. 'Nope, that's not it!'

'Scupper me, boy, how do you know?' Boff snorted, a little miffed by his rather casual rejection. 'You only glanced at it.'

'Well,' continued Archie, 'it's a bezzy dagger all right, but I just *know* it's not the Fangs of Jagdar.'

'How can you be so certain?' asked Ssasky. 'After all, up until a few candle marks ago, you had never even heard of the dagger!'

'Do you remember the spiv I told you about, Boff, the one I saw whilst hydroporting from the scrapyard to Hexx?'

'Yeah,' acknowledged Boff curiously, 'the little meerkat with the pipe.'

'That's the one,' smirked Archie. 'Well, I saw him again when I hydroported here.'

'You've seen a spiv?' asked Ssasky sceptically.

'Oh, he sees them all the time,' interrupted Boff. 'Don't you, laddie?'

'Yes, I do. And the last one—Gilwaggy, he called himself— gave me a message from Zephyar.'

Ssasky's mouth popped open in shock. 'Now you're saying that you see spivs *and* get messages from a demigod?'

'Ah, yes,' offered Archie hesitantly. 'Doesn't everyone?'

'No, actually, they don't.' She frowned. Her blue strip crinkled, and her eyes filled with concern. 'Creatures who boast of these things generally wind up in a padded cell or, more often these days, burnt at the stake!'

'Yes,' said Archie knowingly, 'we have that problem on Earth, too, although burning at the stake is frowned upon by the police now.'

'Egads, boy,' Boff said. 'It's no laughing matter. She's right. The only reason I believe you is because you're the naffin' Rainbow child!'

Archie scowled at the pair of them. 'Does it really matter who or what I am, as long as I know how to recognize that stupid dagger?'

'Well, to Baldizar, it obviously does,' said Boff glibly. 'After all, he went to all the trouble of creating you!' The words slipped out before his brain engaged.

Archie's face hardened as Ssasky moved up behind him and placed her arms comfortingly about him. 'Archie, what our blabbermouthed friend here is trying to say is—'

Archie reached up and grasped her hands. As he turned, she was astonished to see him smiling. 'Don't worry about me,' he lied bravely. 'I've always known that I was a round peg in a world full of square holes.'

Boff's mouth popped open in surprise. 'You did!'

'Yes, I did,' he stated boldly but not boldly enough to hide the shadow of sorrow that clouded his eye. 'I arrived at the orphanage on my fifth birthday,' he continued, coughing to clear his throat, 'with no documentation at all, not even a birth certificate. The next day, Mr Brewster, the orphanage manager, being a low-paid civil servant, mysteriously had a one-off payment of two hundred and fifty thousand pounds transferred into his bank account. Sort of fires your suspicion, huh?'

'How do you know all of this?' asked Ssasky.

He grinned. 'I've always known that I was different. In small ways, at first, but later, when I began to fully understand the differences, a void quickly appeared in my life. Then, as if by magic, my so-called saviour and guardian angel appeared. Didn't he, *Boff?*'

'Guardian angel?' questioned Ssasky.

Boff restlessly fumbled with all forty of his fingers. 'Er, that would be Mr McGinty,' he confessed weakly, 'the owner of the scrapyard near the orphanage.' The corners of his big rubber mouth sagged heavily, and his lips quivered as he gathered the strength to finish his confession. 'Or Baldizar, to you and me.'

'Now it all makes sense,' offered Ssasky. 'For years, whilst I was spellbound by Baldizar'—her voice trailed off a touch, her sorrow painfully clear— 'he was always fussing over his rainbow plan, confirming and double-checking every little detail.' Then she smiled, as if winning a tiny victory, and added, 'Oh, he always worked alone. Paranoid about security, he was. But there was one problem that confounded him so much that he had to ask Eccles Nimrod for help. That really niggled him. Angry for weeks, he was.' She shot the chamelesquid a searing glare. 'Your name was mentioned several times.'

'Hornswoggle me britches,' growled Boff. 'Okay, so I made a mistake. I was only trying to do what any self-respecting storm raider would do in that situation: save his flippin' neck.' He swivelled one eye at Archie and the other at Ssasky. 'How was I supposed to know I'd grow to like Archie?'

'Now don't go all mushy on me, Boff.' Archie laughed. 'It'll ruin your storm raider reputation.'

'Tell anyone, boy, and I'll splice your gizzards to a rock and deep-six you,' Boff growled with a smile. Then he swivelled both his eyes at him. 'How did you know all of this, anyway?'

'Easy. I hacked into Brewster's computer, then the local council, the bank, and the police!'

'You devious little beggar,' congratulated Boff, who turned and winked at Ssasky. 'Jagdar's teeth, he'll make a rum storm raider yet.'

'Enough about me,' declared Archie, secretly glad to be changing the subject and checking his watch. 'We've only fifteen minutes left. There're some toilets over there we can use to hydroport, so let's find old Buckethead's trophy, huh?'

'Good idea,' agreed Ssasky, her bright-yellow eyes lighting up her smile. 'There can't be that many daggers in here.'

'Oh, we're not looking for a dagger,' added Archie, stopping them dead in their tracks.

'We're not?' they both chirped in surprise.

'Oh, no. We're looking for a walking stick!'

Ssasky shot him a disgruntled look. 'I thought we we're looking for a dagger?'

'We are,' said Archie apologetically. 'A dagger cleverly disguised as a walking stick.'

'Scupper me, boy,' snipped Boff, 'that's a little ditty that you should have mentioned a tad sooner!'

'Let me guess,' said Ssasky, raising an eyebrow. 'Your little friendly spiv told you, didn't he?'

Archie flushed pink. 'Yes!'

'When you two lovebirds have finished,' teased Boff, 'I found this over there. I was using it to flick bits of rubbish aside.'

'What's the bag on the handle?' asked Archie.

'No idea,' Boff replied. 'It snagged on the handle as I picked it up.'

The walking stick was the wrong type. To this, Archie paid scant attention, but the bag was different. It intrigued him so much that as soon as he touched it, his eye patch tingled. Not with the normal burning that preceded danger but a mild, pleasant tingling that shouted of something good.

It was a small black bag of smooth crushed velvet, roughly eight inches square, with embroidered writing in gold-and-silver thread on one side. As he held it close, he felt his heart skip several beats and had to forcefully stifle an ecstatic gasp. Even through the thick material, he could clearly feel the objects inside, and yes, there were sixteen.

Archie are you alright? thalked Grizwold, alarmed by the boy's suddenly erratic heartbeat.

Einstein's underpants, what luck, thought Archie, his mind on the cusp of exploding with excitement. *Oh, I'm fine,* he thalked, casually declaring it to be rubbish then turning away from the others and deftly slipping the bag deep inside his top.

For the next few minutes, the chaos outside was forgotten as hands frantically sifted through the debris and boots kicked aside anything considered rubbish.

'How about this?' asked Boff.

'No, sorry.' Archie shrugged, staring past the chamelesquid towards Ssasky with curious eyes. 'What's that you're using, Ssasky?'

She held it aloft for all to see. 'I think it's a sceptre of some kind, or perhaps a walking stick for child, or an elf, or a small queen,' she joked.

'Yes, I saw that one earlier,' said Freddy, who was deftly prizing gemstones out of a crown with his needle-sharp teeth then swallowing them. 'It struck me as odd, because here we are knee-deep in treasure, and what do I find? An old wooden walking stick. It didn't make sense, so I threw it away.'

Archie let his fingers lightly caress the wooden shaft. He felt no edges, cracks, or unevenness through his fingertips. He was about to discard it when Ssasky gasped. 'Archie, your eye patch... It's glowing!'

'It glows all the time today,' Boff grumbled.

'Jagdar's scaly hide,' said Freddy, ogling with all of his eyes, 'it's not glowing. It's on fire!'

'Boff's right,' said Archie, strolling over to the window. 'My eye patch has been on and off more times today than a flipping traffic light in Trafalgar Square.' After a few seconds, the scudding clouds cleared, illuminating the stick in the warm evening sun. Suddenly smiling victoriously, he grasped its opal handle and, with a debonair flick of the wrist, watched the plain wooden shaft disengage from the handle, sliding off to reveal a quadruple-bladed dagger.

'Well, trounce me trunnions,' gasped Boff in stunned amazement. *'It exists.* The fabled, Fangs of Jagdar dagger actually naffin' exists!'

Archie held his prize up in the sunlight, its rays striking the blades with such intensity that their brilliance was almost blinding to the eye.

'Is that actually it?' gasped Ssasky, almost too scared to believe her own eyes.

'After all these centuries,' uttered Boff, his voice both hushed and humbled, 'myth finally becomes reality.'

'Yahoo!' yelled Archie at the top of his voice, jumping up and down and jigging about like an electrified kangaroo. 'I've found it! I've found it! No more collar! No more Buckethead!'

Boff and Ssasky beamed with pride, she with tears in her eyes and he with a smile so wide it almost cut his face in half.

Freddy, on the other hand, furiously kicked a battered crown across the hall. 'Curses,' he moaned, clenching his shaking fists angrily. 'The one true treasure of the genieverse, and I threw it away. Look at those blades! That thing must be worth a genie's ransom!'

'Four blades in one,' murmured Archie solemnly.

Deliriously happy, Archie exploded in a frenzied kicking spree. Whooping and hollering, he merrily booted anything within reach at all the silently watching suits of armour, creating quite a commotion.

Some of the empty knights wobbled like drunken puppets, and others clattered to the floor in heaps. Except for Freddy, who was on the verge of tears, everyone laughed loudly and heartily.

Unfortunately, everyone was so swept up in the heat of the moment that no one noticed something disturbingly amiss. One unusually tall suit of armour, standing in a darkened corner, moved ever so slightly. It should have been just another impact induced wobble, but it wasn't. With a slight and barely noticeable adjustment to the angle of its shield, the suit neatly deflected the missile.

Archie, calm down, thalked an exasperated Grizwold, chemically soothing his boisterous emotions. *We don't have time for this nonsense.*

Under his Mutmuts control, Archie could do nothing but respond to his wishes. *You grumpy old devil,* he thalked. *Is this not a moment for celebration?*

Mutmuts don't celebrate, Grizwold informed him sombrely. *Occasionally, we might become mildly happy, but that's our limit. Now stop giggling like a schoolgirl and hold the blade up closer. There's an inscription on it that I wish to read.*

Archie glanced at his watch as it neared his nose. Eleven minutes left. He mentally scolded himself for wasting valuable time.

'What do you see, Archie?' asked Ssasky.

Using Archie's voice, Grizwold replied, 'A text in the ancient tongue, but its message is clear: "Behold the key to a key that bridges the void betwixt flesh and steel."'

'What does it mean, Grizwold, a key to a key?' asked Ssasky. 'It makes no sense.'

'But by the horns of Jagdar,' declared Boff, his face white with fearful awe, 'you are holding the most powerful weapon in the known genieverse!'

Ssasky sensed a striking change in the chamelesquid's persona. 'What knowledge do you have of this blade and its purpose?'

Boff swivelled both of his coned eyes knowingly at the three of them. They may not have been able to see his eyeballs directly, but his calculating manner was all too obvious. 'I've been told,' he continued with a menacing growl, 'that in the right hands, that dagger could be the ultimate weapon to defeat Baldizar, finally bringing an end to his reign of tyranny.'

'Why Boff, my old mucker,' Freddy said, his face a picture of disbelief, 'do my ears deceive me, or are you actually preaching rebellion?'

'Jagdar's teeth, you bet your furry little butt I am,' he growled. 'I say we use this golden opportunity to destroy Baldizar once and for all!'

'He's right,' added Freddy. 'Many moons ago, when a certain heist of mine went horribly pear shaped, I was fortunate enough to meet the leader of Merlin's marauders face to face. He is a powerful genie, and he told me what to do if I should ever come across the dagger.'

'And that is?' asked Ssasky, scarcely believing what she was hearing.

'Plunge the Fangs of Jagdar into the heart of the devil, and his evil will be dusted forever!'

'But that's impossible,' said Archie. 'You said Baldizar is never without his impenetrable suit of armour.'

'There is a way,' announced Ssasky, dramatically gaining everyone's attention. 'It's a slim chance, but a chance nevertheless.'

'Tell us, Princess, quickly,' said Grizwold.

'On the final eve of the ceremony of Atunka Gaar, all of the power ten genies must observe a secret ritual. It's an old ceremony, steeped in tradition and religious law, which goes back to the very beginnings of the genie empire. Its rules must be obeyed by all, without exception.'

Boff, Archie, and Freddy unconsciously moved forward, captivated by her beguiling words.

'All the genies must be seated on the stage of the great amphitheatre of Garrknock to witness the setting of the second sun and the rising of the traitor's moon, which signals the end of the race and the end of Atunka Gaar. This is a period of festivity and peace, and to demonstrate this fact before all the creepies, creatures, and mongrels of the genieverse, none of the power ten genies, *including* El Supremo, are allowed to wear their armour!'

'One chance every ten years,' Freddy said wistfully. 'Oh, what I'd give to watch old Buckethead get dusted!'

'But what about Archie's collar?' asked Ssasky, her bright-yellow eyes full of pain. 'If we dust Baldizar, who will remove the collar?'

'There's another who has the power to remove Archie's collar, you know,' announced Boff unexpectedly.

'*There is?*' exclaimed both Archie and Ssasky in wide-eyed harmony. 'Who?'

'Why, the leader of the Merlin's marauders, of course,' declared Boff, smiling. 'The great and powerful genie of order, Eccles Nimrod himself!'

'*Eccles Nimrod*,' gasped Ssasky. 'But in the genie hierarchy, he's second only to Baldizar himself. Can we trust him?'

Boff placed a tentacle hand patriotically over both of his hearts. 'Yes, because he's the leader of the Merlin's marauders, who fight against injustice and oppression. And I trust him with my life!'

Suddenly, a slow metal-on-metal handclap echoed about

the hall, its measured, heavy rhythm silencing everyone. Frantically, all eyes searched the hall, and with creepy shadows cloaking every nook and cranny, they suddenly feared the worst.

Somewhere in the shadows, something stirred.

'Who's there?' demanded Ssasky, brandishing a discarded sword. 'Show yourself.'

'So the nest of vipers I see before me has thrown their lot in with Merlin's marauders, huh?' The voice in the dark had a familiarly menacing tone that reached out and grasped their hearts with its icy fingers. 'And your brave leader is none other than Eccles Nimrod? I never thought that pompous little twerp had it in him. But then my spies had warned me some time ago that his loyalties might lie with the rebels.'

In a far corner of the hall, a tall suit of armour stepped forward, revealing itself. With long strides, it quickly covered the gap between them, its tall iron image appearing like a crimson nightmare in the late afternoon sun.

'Well, well, well,' sneered Boff. 'If it isn't old Buckethead himself. I should have known you'd be skulking in the shadows somewhere!'

Baldizar ignored the insult, throwing aside his camouflage of earthly sword and shield. Boldly, he marched towards the group, his metal boots crunching glass and splintering wood, oblivious to the treasures he crushed under foot. So confident was he of his own majesty that his own sword remained sheathed, although as he flexed all four of his arms, the vicious horns erupted from his metal suit and helmet.

Stomping to a halt before them, he flicked open his helmet visor, revealing a sallow face with burning eyes of volcanic red.

'You will all address me as El Supremo,' he hissed, his evil glare moving slowly between each of them, 'for as I am your elected leader today, so I will be your ruling king tomorrow!'

Boff's loud, defiant laughter struck Baldizar like a hammer blow. 'The only thing you'll be tomorrow, *my El Supremo*,' he mocked openly, 'is naffin' dusted!'

'You would do well to hold your flapping tongue, Boff of Kromper,' hissed Baldizar, his temper remaining spookily calm. 'The only reason I kept you alive'—he glanced coldly at Archie— 'is because I needed a reliable clod to babysit him.' Black veins pulsed in his red eyes as he watched with glee the chamelesquid's fingers nervously twitching on either side of his bandoleers. 'Think you're quick enough, Storm Raider?' he goaded. 'You're no more a dangerous rebel than I'm a fluffy pink kitten!'

Baldizar's cruel thin lips creased, causing one side of his long, thin moustache to twitch as Boff boldly went for his zizzers.

'Audacious to the end,' he mused, hurling Boff across the hall with the wave of a single gauntlet. So fast was his attack that Boff barely had chance to ink himself before crashing headfirst into a huge Chinese urn and smashing it to bits.

Archie's jaw dropped in awe.

With the use of his Hector's gift, the supreme genie had flung a half-ton creature the length of the hall. Although his action appeared effortless, the explosion of power he produced ruffled all the banners and flags and rattled several suits of armour.

Sensing his momentary distraction, Ssasky seized her chance and lunged at Baldizar. Her aim was swift and sure, her sword striking Baldizar with a resounding clank on his left shoulder. It was a blow that would have felled any mortal creature in an instant, but Baldizar just laughed and flicked it away.

Raising one gauntlet, he sneered down at her whilst his metal fingers wiggled as if tying an invisible knot. Ssasky, shaken to the core by the uselessness of her attack, watched in horror as the blade of her own sword folded back upon itself and snaked like flowing metal about her wrists, binding them securely together. From behind a curtain, a red sash flew up and wound itself about her arms and body, finishing with a flourishing double bow.

'There.' Baldizar laughed with a theatrical flourish. 'We wouldn't want you flying away on your newfound wings now, would we?' He stepped back, admiring his handiwork. 'I had hoped one day to conquer your true spirit with matrimony. The uniting of our two great families would have blessed the genieverse with a lineage of truly magnificent kings and queens to rule over and dominate the lesser species.'

Ssasky's face contorted in disgust, the mere thought of being his bride and the mother of his devilish progeny making her want to vomit.

'Such a shame,' he remarked nonchalantly, 'but then I always knew that one day you would betray me.'

'You can't betray someone you've always despised!' snapped Archie venomously. 'She was your prisoner and nothing else. We set her free to be the strong, compassionate, beautiful woman she was always destined to be.'

'Why, I do believe the maggot has feelings for you?' Baldizar sniggered, winking repugnantly at Ssasky.

'Chew on this, Baldizar!' cried Freddy, scooping up a spider's web full of broken glass and flinging it at him. Incensed by the attack on his friend, the bandit spider's reactions were quick and his aim true. However, his act of brave defiance was rash at best. Like so many mini spears, the glass shards flew at their target, only to stop as if frozen in space just before Baldizar's scornful face.

With a second wave of his hand, he casually threw them aside. 'Is that the best the infamous Flip-Flop Freddy can do? I thought you bandit spiders were supposed to be resourceful.'

Freddy, who was hanging by a single thread from the ceiling, did his best to glare ferociously at Baldizar with all his eyes. 'Let's see how you like this,' he laughed, turning a second thread into a spinning lasso. 'I'm going to—'

For a ten-foot man in a heavy suit of armour, Baldizar's lightning steps left everyone blinking. One moment, he was standing on the far side of the hall. The next, his helmet was right in front of Freddy's upside-down face. One gauntlet grasped the lasso hoop, whilst another niftily grabbed Freddy by his eyestalks and squeezed hard. His face grinned with sadistic pleasure as they started to bulge under the pressure. The spider, although in agonizing pain, refused to scream, even when Baldizar clenched his finger so tightly that two of Freddy's eyes burst with a squishy pop.

Spinning Freddy on the end of his own thread like a child's toy, Baldizar worked the spider's own yarn up and down his furry body, completely cocooning him. When he'd finished, Freddy, outraged by the indignity of it, could barely wriggle as he was thrown across the hall, falling with a sliding thump amongst the debris at Ssasky's feet.

'I'll deal with you two on my return to Hexx,' Baldizar said, flexing all his arms in delightful anticipation.

'You monster,' snarled Freddy as he fought to wriggle free of his own trap. 'You're the vile spawn of the devil,' he spat furiously. 'One day, you'll get your well-earned comeuppance, and I only hope that I'm there to witness it!'

Baldizar huffed contemptuously at the spider's silly threats, turning his full attention upon Archie. Clamping one gauntlet about his throat, he lifted the youngling off his feet and snatched the dagger from his hand. 'I see you've found my treasure!'

'Yes, I've found your stupid dagger,' croaked Archie, trying for macho but coming over wimpy. 'Now take this flipping collar off me!'

'Yes, so I can see.'

His slithery, hypnotic voice reminded Archie of the snake from Rudyard Kipling's *The Jungle Book*, and he didn't like him either.

'You are indeed cleverer than I had foreseen.'

Ssasky noted a barely audible uneasiness in his tone. *I wonder,* she thought, looking on helplessly, *if Archie were to survive this ordeal, he would become a serious threat to Baldizar and the council of the power ten genies.* It was a delicious thought but sadly one that could never be.

'However,' continued Baldizar, dropping him, 'your usefulness has come to an end, and neither I nor the genieverse have any need of you. Such a shame.' He smirked. 'And with a whole eight minutes of life left too.'

'What about my collar?!' yelled Archie, tugging vainly at

the golden ring. 'You said that if I got you the dagger, you'd release me from this lethal contraption.'

Baldizar, who was examining the defunct body of the veggie chieftain, paid him no attention. Archie snatched up a large, bejewelled mace and threw it at him. It struck him on his back with a clank then fell to the floor. Still, he paid no attention. Then Archie changed tactics. Sucking in all his sudden rage and violence, he tuned in his mind and concentrated his Hector's gift upon El Supremo.

Baldizar instantly felt the boy unleash his new power. Its effect caused him to chuckle callously, as Archie's heroic effort washed over him with all the aggression of a gentle summer's breeze. 'Pathetic youngling,' he hissed. 'I must have words with the professor about you and your unpredictable behaviour. He assured me that during your bio-construction, he could alter your DNA to rule out these *undesirable* characteristics you humans are flawed with.' He poked none too gently at Archie's eye patch with a metal fingertip. 'Although this does add an air of sinister respectability to you.' He thought for a moment, stroking the long strands of his moustache. 'Perhaps I should rip it off, just to see what lurks beneath?'

Even before Archie could react, Grizwold jerked his body backward.

'No matter,' declared Baldizar. 'When the golden serpent collar glows red, your wretched life will be over in a few choking seconds.'

From outside in the courtyard, something very heavy violently assaulted the main entrance door to the hall. As one would expect in a fortress, the big door was designed to withstand punishment. Standing ten feet tall by five feet wide, the solid lump of four-inch-thick oak wasn't going to give in easily. Its outer side was liberally sprinkled with iron studs, and on the inside, it was held firmly in place by three massive wrought-iron hinges.

Again, something struck the door, only that time, the blow rattled its hinges. There was a brief respite before the third and final assault on the ancient door. It yielded with a wave of two hands. Bursting inward, the thick wood shattered whilst the wrought-iron brackets that held it buckled.

Archie dived for cover, hoping beyond all hope that it was the Royal Marines come to save them. Curiously, Baldizar knowingly stood his ground. When the dust finally settled, illuminated in the shattered doorway by the sunlight was a huge, horned figure. It was no Marine, but Captain Goldhorn himself.

The mighty minotaur, broadsword in one hand and massive shield in the other, stood in silence, his coal-black eyes surveying the scene of carnage before him. Then, with military, measured strides, he stomped across the debris-strewn floor and straight to Baldizar.

Ssasky, beaming with adulation, looked up at their saviour from where she lay on the floor. He wasn't exactly in the form she'd hoped for, but when in a tight spot, even the leader of the chieftains was better than nothing.

'What are you going to do now, Baldizar?' She laughed bravely. 'When Captain Goldhorn arrests you and presents you to the council of the power ten genies, it will be your head that will fall!'

'Yeah!' cried Freddy, his sharp, pointy teeth having chewed

through his gag. 'It's dusting time for you, Buckethead!'

Ssasky wriggled into an awkward sitting position. 'Goldhorn, captain of the chieftains, I am Ssasky, firstborn daughter to the house of the White Dwarf Star, and I order you, as the lawful guardian of justice and overseers to the race, to arrest Baldizar for acts of treason against the council and all creatures, creepies, and mongrels of the genieverse.'

'Yeah, big boy,' Freddy said, 'do something nasty to him.'

Goldhorn flexed his sword arm then turned his scowling glare upon Baldizar. With two huge, crunching steps, he closed in on the supreme genie, his round black eyes as blank as a starless night. Then, to their heart-stopping horror, the big minotaur dropped onto one knee and lowered his sword.

'My El Supremo,' he growled obediently, 'the area has been secured, and your ship awaits.'

The corners of Baldizar's slash of a mouth curled into a devious smile. 'Not quite the outcome you were hoping for, perchance?' Using the Fangs of Jagdar dagger, he nicked the minotaur's arm. The creature remained impassive as green goo oozed from the tiny wound and trickled down his arm.

'He's a veggie chieftain,' growled Ssasky bitterly.

'Professor Madspanner refers to them as hybrid plant mutations,' offered Baldizar, prodding the dead minotaur in the eye with the dagger. 'But I like your interpretation,' he said, bowing graciously before Ssasky. 'Veggie chieftain sounds much better than HPM, huh?' Turning on a heel, he thrust the dagger tip up under Archie's open jaw, just nicking the skin. 'What do you think, boy, doesn't "veggie chieftain" sort of roll neatly off the tongue?'

'Yeah, like a rancid brussels sprout!'

Baldizar cuffed him on the side of the head with the back of a gauntlet, sending him sprawling to the ground. 'But then, who really cares what you think.'

'You monster!' screamed Ssasky. 'He's only a boy.'

Baldizar noted the flash in her vivid yellow eyes, one that he had hoped she might have had for him one day. 'So a bond of love has formed between you and the boy. How touching!' He beckoned the minotaur to rise. 'Take the woman and the spider back to my ship. They will be executed at the rise of the traitor's moon.'

The veggie Goldhorn rose, strode to the large hole that used to be the door, and bellowed an order. Two more veggie chieftains entered the hall, bundled up the spider and the handcuffed woman, saluted, then marched out of the hall with them over their shoulders.

'My new chieftains are very obedient,' Baldizar said, laughing. 'Professor Madspanner assures me that he can replicate the entire regiment by the onset of winter.' There was a devilish wildness to his red volcanic eyes, and he was rambling crazily, swept along by his own insane delusions of grandeur. 'With the coming of spring,' he announced to the many empty suits of armour, 'my army will march on the genieverse, and there will be a new order in the heavens.'

Archie dared a peek at his watch. Four minutes left. He had to act now, or it would be too late.

Archie glanced over at Boff's unconscious body.

'I wouldn't bank on your friend helping you. He'll soon have problems of his own. Big problems!'

Scrambling to his feet, Archie launched himself at Baldizar, wrapping his arms in a life-or-death grip about his metal waist, screaming and crying. 'You can't leave this collar on me,' he begged, tears streaming down his face. 'You promised. You promised you'd release me if I found the dagger.'

Baldizar, disgusted by his weak show of sentiment, grasped him roughly by the neck then cast him down on top of an old shield, laughing. Baldizar's eyes flared with revulsion as he glared down at the boy cowering amongst the scattered treasure. 'Your weakness betrays you, human youngling. Even if I spared your puny life, you'd never survive in my genieverse.'

Something inside of Archie snapped, and he jumped onto his feet, fists clenched. 'You're nothing but a tin-plated, cold-hearted murderer,' he cried, angrily pointing a wagging finger at him. 'If I can't trust you to keep your word, how do you expect all the different species throughout the genieverse to ever trust you as their leader?'

Baldizar roared with an insane, thunderous kind of laughter that could only be found in hell itself. 'I don't want them to trust me, boy. I want them to *fear* me!'

Then, as Archie watched, trembling in horror while Baldizar, in a flurry of arms, turned on a heel and marched out of the hall, he felt something wriggle against his skin. His eye darted anxiously to a nearby darkened window, where he was shocked to see the three eyes of his serpent collar suddenly glow into life, its golden body snaking around his neck.

Archie watched Baldizar march away, his heavy steps unfaltering. 'Dad, please don't leave me.' He sobbed. 'I don't want to die!'

Part 3

Rescue

Chapter 26

'Scupper me, boy, that made my stomach churn!' hissed a scornful voice off to the side. 'You crying like a baby on your knees, it's enough to make a seasoned storm raider puke. When are you going to learn, Archie, that you can't plead with the devil?'

'You're alive!' cried Archie joyfully.

'Yes, I am. I'm just as much alive as Old Buckethead is a naffin' psychopath with a chunk of ice for a heart.' Boff floated unsteadily, shaking the fog from his head. He swivelled both eyes at the boy and frowned disapprovingly. 'He's power crazy, and he kills just for the fun of it! What did you think that gushingly sick act of grovelling would achieve?' Boff suddenly felt guilty as he watched the boy check his watch. 'How long?'

'Sixty glorious seconds,' chirped Archie cheerily.

Boff could feel a volatile mix of rage and sadness building deep within. For the last ten years, he'd had mixed feelings about the boy, his emotions swinging wildly between loathing and love. But at the very end, it was the crushing clench of bitter sadness that gripped both his hearts.

'Jagdar's teeth, boy'—he scowled furiously— 'how can you

be so damned happy?' He pointed to Archie's golden collar with a shaking hand. 'The eyes of your serpent collar are blazing bright, and the Duster brothers are surfing in as we speak!'

Boff's trembling body flushed angry red, tiny droplets of water forming on the rims of his coned eyes.

Then something insanely fantastic happened. Plunging both hands inside his vest, Archie quickly produced the black velvet bag in one hand and a small glass bottle in the other.

'Hornswoggle me giblets, boy,' beseeched Boff tearfully, 'this is no time for party tricks. You're about to be naffin' dusted!'

He gasped in utter astonishment as Archie suddenly smiled and said, 'If it's a party trick you want, then watch this!' With a pop, he removed the cork top and took a swift nip from the bottle.

What happened next hit Boff like a whack in the face from a concrete cricket bat, causing him to hover backward in disbelief. Quicker than a beat of a butterfly's wing, a wide, sparkly glass collar appeared around the boy's neck, nestled snugly between his skin and Baldizar's accursed golden collar. Even more bizarre was the fact that the eyes of his golden serpent collar were no longer glowing, and miraculously, Archie's head was still firmly attached to his neck.

'What... how... but... huh?' stammered Boff, rushing forward for a closer look.

Archie's smile was brighter than a sunrise on a clear frosty morning, his laughter filling the ruined hall. 'What do you think, huh?' He smirked, flicking his mysterious new neckwear.

'Odds bodkins, boy, what in Jagdar's teeth is that?' he asked, his whole body flushing a happy swamp green.

'Behold,' declared Archie, looking ultra-chuffed with himself, 'the crown of Avalon.'

'The crown of naffin' who?' repeated Boff. 'What the in the name of Jagdar is that?'

Archie pointed to an ornate crown lying on the floor. 'That is the Queen's Imperial State crown. The diamond set in it comes from the biggest known diamond ever found, and that was the size of a large apple.' With a flourish, he gestured towards his new neck attire. 'This little beauty comes from a diamond the size of a *football!*'

Boff hovered right in close, four of his hands touching it, making sure it was real and that he wasn't hallucinating. 'This collar is made from one single diamond, you say?'

'It's not a collar. It's a crown! It was cut into fifteen banana-shaped segments that slot together to form a crown.' He waved the black velvet bag at him. 'When I saw it hooked on the end of Ssasky's stick, I could hardly contain myself. I knew instantly that I had a defence against Old Buckethead's golden collar. Because I knew that if instead of putting it on my head, I slipped it, segment by segment, between his golden collar and my precious neck, I keep my head.'

Boff gestured to the ruined hall about them. 'So, you knew that this was a trap all along?'

'Old Buckethead couldn't have made it more obvious if he'd advertised it in neon lighting! But with you lot delirious with sparkle fever and spouting gibberish, I decided to keep it a secret.'

Sensible and cunning, mused Grizwold a touch proudly.

Maybe this maggot is the one.

Boff's gaze fell regretfully to the ground. 'By the horns of Jagdar, I'll give you that one for sure. You said it was a trap all along, and you were right.' He flicked the tip of the crown with a fingernail, and even against the boy's sweating skin, its crystal *ting* was like the crisp ring of a spring morning. 'But you only had a minute left. How did you get it on so quickly?' he asked, eyeing the boy suspiciously. 'I mean, one moment it wasn't there, and the next, it was!'

Grinning, Archie held up the little glass bottle. 'Essence of hydroport!'

'Essence of what?'

From nowhere, a deep, piercing boom penetrated their heads, its violent tone clubbing their brains. A split second later, as their hands flew to cover their ears, the floor beneath them began to shake violently. Archie watched as the ground physically rippled and waves of destruction rolled under the walls and across the hall, pulling up splintering floorboards and knocking him off his feet.

All about them, suits of armour, shields, and swords clattered to the ground. Overhead, shaking rafters dislodged decades of dust, banners, and flags, whilst snaking cracks raced up the plastered walls.

'It must be an earthquake!' shouted Archie. 'We need to get out of here!'

'Jagdar's teeth, you don't—'

Suddenly, a second, slightly higher-pitched demonic note struck, its deadly voice attacking all the wood and glass. Oak panels burst off the walls like falling slates, whilst to the left, the robust wooden staircase, which had survived the bombing of two world wars, shook itself to pieces in a matter of seconds. All about them, glass panels began to vibrate, tiny vicious circles erupting in their centres and rippling out with such force that they exploded like glass hand grenades.

With several tentacles wound into a makeshift shield to protect himself from all the flying debris, Boff hovered over to Archie, grabbed the wobbly youth roughly by an arm, and dragged him out of the shaking building. They had no sooner cleared the doorway when with a deafening whoosh, the great hall collapsed in upon itself, billowing dust and debris.

'Jagdar's fiery breath!' screamed Boff, pointing up. 'Look!'

Completely blotting out the sky, the massive hull of the Crimson Raptor hovered menacingly overhead. Apart from the giant image of Baldizar's horned helmet emblazoned upon a huge white circle, all that could be seen in every direction was the sleek, glossy crimson underbelly of Baldizar's mammoth sky cruiser.

Archie stood spellbound, instinctively acknowledging just what the giant claw was. He fully understood that the gargantuan flying machine was evil, but the geek in him couldn't help but appreciate, even marvel at, such an awesome piece of technology. Though he could barely see through the swirling clouds of dust and stand against its powerful downdraft, he still could clearly make out the six massive golden-tipped horns of the Crimson Raptor, reaching down to imprison them and the whole of the Tower of London. 'Is that Baldizar's sky cruiser?'

'Oh yes, that's old Buckethead's very own naffin' metal monster, all right,' spat Boff, 'and its belly's open. Move it!'

Diving for cover behind a collapsed wall, Archie watched

in dread fascination as a large, shiny metal object attached to a steel cable fell from one end of what appeared to be a long, open bomb bay. As the object fell, so beyond it, he could see another, bigger object being hauled back up inside.

'They look like huge bells,' he said quizzically, 'like church bells, only the size of houses.'

'Down, boy!' cried Boff. 'He's dropping another one!'

The third bell swallowed a lamppost whole before slamming into the tarmac with devastating effect. Its eighteen-inch-thick rim dug deeply into the road, its lethal tone penetrating the ground like a harmonic spear. As if suddenly punched by an invisible fist, the Tower of London quivered as the blow sent a thousand cracks racing up its aged walls. Instantly, the centuries-old fort, a bastion of strength that had defiantly defeated countless foes, felt its foundations crumble and its mighty walls collapse like a pack of cards.

Almost immediately, the bell's thick metal cable snapped taut as it was snatched up off the ground, casting clods of dirt and lumps of smashed tarmac in all directions. Archie couldn't help himself—brushing aside Boff's fussing, protective tentacle hands, he stared up in gruesome fascination as it was retracted.

'Keep your naffin' head down, you drongo,' barked Boff angrily. 'Do you want him to see you?' But as he slapped a tentacle hand on top of Archie's head and began to push, the hellish bells suddenly fell silent.

Slowly, as the ghostly image of the Crimson Raptor glided away, the brutally buffeting downdraft from its four mighty electric motors began to ease. A cool autumn breeze carrying a light drizzle quickly blew in, dampening the billowing dust clouds as the bright warmth of the evening slowly returned.

Archie watched Baldizar's massive sky cruiser vanish in a shimmering cloud of rainbow droplets as it hydroported away, leaving alone the two unrecognisable figures caked in dust and dirt amongst the rubble of the once-great Tower of London.

'He's done a rum job with your old castle, boy,' commented Boff, casually flicking a brick aside.

'That he did, for sure,' said Archie, barely listening, his mind already two steps ahead.

'Odds bodkins, boy, you don't seem terribly upset,' Boff said. 'I thought this place was special to you humans.'

'It was old,' said Archie casually. 'Some greedy, money-grabbing entrepreneur would have torn it down to build flats sooner or later, anyway.'

Boff watched as the faraway look on Archie's face slowly changed to a smile. 'In my hatchling tree, Shadoo, back on my home world of Kromper, we have an incredibly old and wise proverb etched in its trunk: "He who strikes hard and fast wins the day!"'

'So you think we should go after Baldizar and rescue Ssasky and Freddy?' asked Archie.

The old storm raider's face lit up with a roguish smile. 'Jagdar's teeth, boy, I think we should rescue your girlfriend and that rascally thief, Flip-Flop Freddy first, then dust old Buckethead, naffin' proper like!'

Archie flushed pink at his reference to Ssasky but fully agreed with his plan of action. 'How can we dust Baldizar?' asked Archie. 'He's got the dagger.'

'The dagger is a magical weapon,' replied Boff. 'It's the only thing that will rid us of old Buckethead, for sure. So we'd best steal it back off him, huh?'

'You don't sound very positive,' said Archie, looking at his friend's suddenly frowning face.

'Oh, I be sure it will do him in,' continued Boff, scratching his rubbery chins. 'But how are we going to get back to Hexx?'

'Ah, well, on that score,' said Archie, 'I may just have the answer.'

Intrigued, Boff floated behind Archie as he picked his way through the ruined courtyard and back to the entrance of the great hall, stopping where its doorway used to be. The roof of the building had collapsed inward, along with most of the walls. Luckily, most of the rubble had piled up roughly in the centre, leaving the edges near enough clear. He made a beeline towards the far-left edge of the room. He seemed to know what he was looking for, and within a few minutes, he had found it. 'Here we are,' he declared, kicking two bricks off a battered shield.

'Scupper me, boy.' Boff glared, baffled. 'That's a fat lot of help!'

Archie smirked, pushing the shield aside. 'No, but this is.'

Boff's face lit up like a handful of sparklers. 'Well, trounce me trunnions, boy, where did you get that from?' He picked up the bog spinner from the floor and blew the dust off.

'Well, you didn't think all that grovelling and pleading with old Buckethead was real'—he laughed— '*did you?*'

Boff's jaw popped open in amazement. 'You stole Baldizar's own personal naffin' bog spinner?'

'Of course,' answered Archie smugly. 'How else are we

going to get back to Hexx?'

For a moment, the awful, desolate sounds surrounding them were washed away by Boff's side-splitting laughter. 'Why, you sneaky, lowdown, barnacle-swoggling, thieving sea dog, you.' He spun the three reels of the spinner, listening to the delightful sound of their soft clicking. 'You were planning a rescue all the time.'

'Yup!'

'Jagdar's teeth!' exclaimed Boff, his joyful mood suddenly vanishing. 'What use is a bog spinner here? Baldizar has pulverised all the local toilets to dust! How are we going to hydroport?'

'Oh, that's easy,' remarked Archie, pointing to a broken water main that was gushing high-pressure water. 'I think that will do us nicely for a quick trip back to the scrapyard.'

'The scrapyard!' Boff asked. 'But old Buckethead's taken Ssasky and Freddy to Hexx.'

'Yes, I know,' acknowledged Archie. 'But if we're going to pull this rescue off and live to gloat about it, then we're going to have to get past the Crimson Raptor first.'

Boff's bubble of happiness suddenly burst. 'Oh yeah, I'd forgotten about that,' he grumbled.

Archie turned and started walking towards the impromptu fountain. 'Well, come on, then, grumpy,' he badgered. 'We can't sit here all day. That traitor's moon's not going to wait for us.'

Boff swivelled his eyes contemptuously at the boy. 'And just how are we going to destroy that naffin' great sky cruiser of his, huh? Certainly not with my zizzers and your slingshot!'

'Come, on Squid Boy, this is no time to be a defeatist.'

'Hornswoggle me giblets, Archie,' he groaned, floating after him. 'I don't know what's brewing in that geeky head of yours, but if you really are loony enough to be going up against the Crimson Raptor, then you'll need some awesome firepower!'

'If it's an advantage you want,' Archie said, 'then it's back to the scrapyard we go!'

Boff hovered quickly to him, grabbing a shoulder with a tentacle hand. 'Gadzooks, you've got something stashed there, haven't you?'

Boff felt both of his hearts skip a beat as Archie winked mischievously at him. 'Do you remember my remote-controlled model Skyshark?'

'Yes,' Boff said quietly, fearing the worst. 'How could I possibly forget? That infernal flying machine nearly dusted us and half the flipping town!'

Archie grinned proudly. 'Well, how would you like to meet its big brother?'

Chapter 27

EARTH.
OLD MCGINTY'S SCRAPYARD.

Archie popped out of the hydroportal into darkness.

Although disorientated, he remembered that Boff was hot on his heels and quickly stepped away from the old Victorian toilet.

Feeling nauseous and lightheaded, he found his fingers automatically reaching for his bag of Muzzberry pips. 'Don't be stupid,' he chided himself. 'You're back on Earth. It's food you need!'

Behind him in the darkness, he heard the familiar sound of swirling water, saw a brief bright flash of rainbow, then chuckled at the sound of something large and floppy landing with a loud squish on the hardwood floor.

'Jagdar's teeth!' spat Boff, gathering his bearings. 'That—'

'Shush!' hissed Archie harshly. 'Let's check outside first, huh?'

A dim rectangle of light from a nearby lamppost fell upon the floor where the smashed wagon door lay. Its thick metal hinges were buckled, and only a ragged hole formed by a hail of bullets remained where the lock used to be.

'Oh boy,' muttered Archie, with a shiver, 'those Royal Marines certainly know how to make an entrance!' Then a dreadful notion struck him about his precious control room. That double-decker bus was the nerve centre of his whole operation, and the assault on it would have been a zillion times more furious. Then he smiled smugly to himself in the darkness, lovingly patting the SIM card nestled in his vest pocket. *To hell with the control room. I've got all I need right here!*

A tentacle hand tapped him on the shoulder, followed by Boff's big, ugly chameleon head whispering in his ear, 'Well, are we alone?'

'Of course we're alone, Boff,' huffed Archie. 'No one guards a toilet!'

'Aye, but it's a hydroportal, isn't it?' retorted Boff sharply.

'Yes, but only you and I know that!'

Archie peeped around the door frame, and all seemed quite enough. If they were going to save Ssasky and Freddy before the rise of the traitor's moon, they needed to move quickly.

Fearing an ambush at every corner, or shouts of alarm from every shadow, the pair stealthily retraced their steps back to the rusting minesweeper and the safety of the secret tunnel beneath. The air was hot and stale in the tunnel, but Boff was happy to follow the boy, as he seemed to know exactly where he was going. At the junction where they had fallen through the bottom of the cement mixer, Archie suddenly veered sharply right and unexpectedly opened a well-disguised door in what Boff had thought was a solid wall.

Beyond was a new tunnel that he'd never seen before. It was clean and tidy, its walls lined with thick, armoured plastic pipes, through which he could clearly hear the gurgling of moving liquid. *What have you been up to?* he mused as one of his probing tentacle hands skilfully snatched up a skulking rat, which he consumed in one gulp. Sniffing a nearby joint in the pipes, his big leather nostrils suddenly flapped like a pair of fish out of water.

'Jigger me,' he said quietly, chuckling, 'if I didn't know better, I'd swear an oath to Jagdar that's alcohol I can smell.'

In total, McGinty's scrapyard covered nearly four-square miles, its metal contents neatly stacked in four separate, well-organised areas. Cars and motorcycles were in one, with vans and lorries in another. Next to those, alongside the creek, was a marine and military section, whilst the fourth area, which housed buses and coaches and other large miscellaneous stuff, was tucked away at the far end of the yard, beneath the cliffs.

It was to this last section that Archie's mystery new tunnel led an intrigued Boff.

Climbing up a small ladder, Archie emerged into the darkened boot of an old car. He turned the well-oiled catch and silently released the lid, lifting it barely an inch. They both took a long, deep breath as fresh, rust-tinged night air blew in.

The old car was parked on a corner at the north end of the yard, making it an ideal secret-tunnel entrance and observation post. The pools of light from the sporadically positioned lampposts were few enough to keep people away after dark, yet more than enough to satisfy his security needs.

Archie pushed the boot lid fully open and stepped out. 'This is where I keep my big secret!'

Boff floated out of the hole behind him. '*Big secret*,' he echoed nervously. 'Scupper me sideways, boy, your big secrets always mean naffin' trouble!'

Archie jogged excitedly over to a nearby battered old pick-up truck, reached up, and yanked down hard on its tall rusty exhaust stack. 'I'd move over here if I were you, Boff.'

The chamelesquid had just reached him when, with a loud twang, a thick steel cable snapped out of the road's dirt surface. Somewhere in the dark, two electric motors hummed into life, their soft whining quickly turning to a laboured groan as the slack cable became taut.

Boff frowned as he heard the double-decker buses groaning mysteriously, then gasped as they silently started moving. Rolling on heavily greased wheels, the front of two buses to the left silently yawned open—unfortunately, their opposite numbers on the right seemed to suddenly judder violently, as if gripped by a mechanical seizure.

'Damn,' groaned Archie, 'not again.' Snatching up a metal pipe, Archie calmly began battering the side of another old truck until a second cable sprang up out of the dirt. The fronts of the four nearest buses began to slide open, the labouring electric motor purring softly.

With all four of the bus fronts fully open, Boff was amazed to see that their insides had been completely removed, creating a cavernous workshop. He gasped. 'Well, hornswoggle me giblets, boy. Why, it's a—'

'Giant metal cave,' finished Grizwold, using Archie's voice.

Not only were the first four double-decker buses hollowed out but also the four behind them. Archie had created a massive safe place to work, hidden right under the nose of a totally oblivious world. Flicking a small switch to his left, Archie smiled as the sound of a small petrol engine putted into life. Then, flipping several more switches, he illuminated the whole interior of the workshop in a soft, red light.

'Argh!' screamed Boff in horror, for staring out from its blood-red den was a wild, fearsome face with devilish eyes and a giant mouth full of bloodstained, jagged white teeth. Its sheer ferociousness sent Boff reeling backward in terror, gasping for breath. 'Jagdar's merciful benevolence, protect us,' he muttered in a revered tone. 'I-it looks like something from a Duster brother's nightmare!'

Archie wasn't surprised by Boff's reaction—the old storm raider had a natural aversion to technology and made no bones about it. However, Grizwold, from whom he'd expected a more intelligent comment, seemed unnaturally quiet, and he found it a little unnerving. Over the last twelve hours, he had grown to like and even rely on Grizwold's bold confidence and seemingly endless knowledge as a booster to his own fledgling courage.

Archie, his stomach growling, headed over to a row of cupboards positioned above a long wooden workbench. From one, he took out a box of Mars bars and two bottles of water. As he closed the door, he glimpsed his reflexion in its shiny surface. A haggard, dirty face stared back at him though red, sore-looking eyes. A deep sigh escaped his gritted teeth as he despaired at the state of his usually pristine mop of curly white hair. It was lank and messy, and there was a large, angry-looking bruise on his left cheek. The skin surrounding the lump was an ugly black-and-blue mess, and it was very painful to touch.

Then, smirking at the Crown of Avalon sitting about his neck, a loud, mocking laugh burst from his lips. His sullen frown was suddenly wiped away by a beaming smile. 'Who cares about a silly bruise,' he muttered, 'at least my head is still firmly attached to my neck!' He playfully flicked the serpent's head of his golden collar, noting how its three red eyes sparked with anger. He chuckled. 'Old Buckethead's going to be livid when he realises that his little plot has failed!' Smiling, Archie turned away and pitched a bottle of water and a bar of chocolate to Boff.

He's not the only one unnerved by that thing, thalked Grizwold squeamishly, but Archie ignored him.

'If we're going to rescue Ssasky and Freddy,' said Archie, stopping midsentence to bite off half the bar in one mouthful. 'Oh, that's good,' he said with a sigh. 'At one point today,' he continued between gulping chews, 'I thought I'd never eat chocolate again!' He wagged the remaining half at Boff. 'If we're going to rescue them, then we're going to need the Skyshark to get there.'

'Why?' asked Grizwold, 'You have Baldizar's bog spinner. You can use that to get back to Hexx.'

Archie emptied his bottle of water in six long, thirsty gulps then belched loudly. 'And just how do you suppose that Boff and I fight our way through the whole garrison of veggie chieftains to get into the amphitheatre?'

'And there's the Crimson Raptor to deal with to boot,' added Boff, who had finished his bar of chocolate, wrapper and all, and was floating towards the cupboard for more. 'Don't forget that. If old Buckethead has set a trap to massacre the whole of the council of the power ten genies, then you can bet your mukluks there will be bloodshed aplenty!'

Grizwold was silent for a moment. 'So be it,' he finally

conceded. 'We'll use that *thing* to get us back to Hexx. But I still don't like it!'

Archie opened two tins and emptied their contents into a large dish, which he then placed in a grubby old microwave oven. He set the timer to two minutes at max power. Then he walked over to the flying machine and affectionately patted its nearest metal wingtip as if greeting an old friend.

'I wish I could take credit for this beauty,' he declared wistfully, 'but I can't, because this, my technophobic friends, is Project Skyshark, the Royal Navy's one and only attempt at building a flying submarine. From wingtip to wingtip, it's fifty feet, and from nose to tail fin, it's sixty. For its size, this creation is amazingly light.' For a moment, he considered demonstrating the principles of aerodynamics then thought better of it. 'It's manta-ray design allows it to glide perfectly under the sea, but also fly like a bird in the sky, but sadly, its ability to cross smoothly between the two was to be its ultimate downfall.'

'So basically, it doesn't work,' Boff said bluntly. 'It's just another weird machine that has no real use?'

'To the military who designed it and the government who footed the bill, yes, it was an expensive flop.'

The microwave's door pinged open with a ting.

Boff, who understood Archie's wacky way of thinking better than anyone, began slowly clapping with three pairs of hands. 'Of course, it's not a failure to you, though, is it, Archie?' he injected cynically. 'You're the boy genius. You *always* know exactly where everyone else went wrong, am I right? To you, that naffin' heap is perfection!'

'Oh, it's far more than that,' countered Archie, retrieving

the hot dish with a delightful smile. 'It's super-lightweight, ultra-strong Kevlar aerodynamic construction was the perfect shape and years ahead of other designs. Combine that with not one but two of the then-revolutionary Rolls-Royce Red Dragon vortex engines'—his smile became impossibly wide — 'you have an aircraft with two hundred thousand pounds of thrust!'

His was virtually drooling with technological delight. 'This baby is sharper than a surgeon's scalpel and slicker than oil.' He winked at Boff's stony-faced expression. 'There's more than enough power packed inside this craft to do what I've got planned!'

'Yeah, that's nice,' acknowledged Boff indifferently, both of his eyes glued on the bowl in his hands rather than on the technological marvel before them. 'Trounce me trunnions, boy, that smells dammed yummy!'

'Oh, it is,' grinned Archie. 'Syrup-steamed pudding and custard, my favourite.'

'There looks to be enough for two?' added Boff hopefully, licking his lips.

'There's enough for four,' answered Archie, 'but this is all mine. You want some, there's plenty more in the cupboard. Get your own.'

Grizwold watched the boy's hormone levels spiking. The more he talked about his beloved machine, the more excited he became. The more excited he became, the more his brain pulsated like a fairground ride. *Archie, if this machine is, as you say here on Earth, all singing and dancing, then why didn't it work?*

Simple, thalked Archie. *It needed a fast-thinking, powerful computer to make it fly, which didn't exist at the time.*

But does now? thalked Grizwold.

It certainly does. The Maverick Proton Plus is perfect for the job. That's why I installed it six months ago.

The microwave tinged for a second time, and a grinning Boff snatched out his own piping-hot syrup-steam pudding and custard, at the same time scowling. 'It's a product of the black art—it's evil. I mean, just look at its face!'

'Oh, that? That's nothing to worry about,' Archie said as he climbed onto the top of the Skyshark. 'I was bored one day, so I had some fun with a load of old paint tins.'

Grizwold's head was full of nagging questions when the air was suddenly filled with the sound of hissing, angry serpents. Archie watched Boff jerk with fright, almost spilling his food.

'It's okay,' said Archie, spinning a large wheel handle. 'I keep the Skyshark pressurised. It's just air escaping.' Turning the wheel three hundred sixty degrees, he fully released the hatch locking mechanism. With a gentle tug, he lifted the spring-loaded hatch open.

Boff tossed his empty bowl aside and belched loudly. 'Scupper me, boy, how exactly is this heap of junk going help us?'

Archie gestured towards the hatch. 'Get in and I'll show you.'

Hovering up and over the Skyshark, Boff stopped just short of the round hatch. 'You actually want me to get inside the belly of this evil mechanical beast?'

'Oh for Pete's sake, Captain Courageous, stop dithering and get inside,' snapped Archie. 'The infamous Bilge Rat Boff indeed. You're acting more like a seasick sissy!'

Archie watched him flush an embarrassed pale green, his pride obviously dented. But he also noted that as he slid nearer, two of his hands were clutching at two holstered zizzers, his trigger fingers at the ready.

With a deep breath, Boff grasped the sides of the hatch and slid in. Much to his surprise, although the inside of the machine seemed totally alien, it felt more snug than scary.

'There,' said Archie climbing through the hatch after him. 'See? It doesn't bite!'

'That's a maybe, boy,' muttered Boff grudgingly, 'but the barnacles on the back of my neck are itching something wicked. I still think this machine is naffin' trouble!'

Considering the circumference of the hatch, he had to admit that he was impressed by the size of the compartment within. Its design was very deceptive. From the outside, seeing only the oblong window, he had assumed quite naturally that the space within would be cramped. However, although the deckhead was low, maybe just a hand's width above his head, the space that Archie kept referring to as the cockpit easily matched that of his old sky cruiser.

Grizwold wrinkled his tiny reptilian face in disgust then, using Archie's voice, asked, 'What was that foul smell?'

'Oh, that,' said Archie nonchalantly. 'It's the fuel for the engines. It's a bit whiffy, mainly because it's an experimental formula.' Then he compounded the lie. 'Nothing to be alarmed about, though—you'll get used to it.'

Boff swivelled both eyes up at him. 'This new mixture of yours shipmate,' he said with a grin, 'wouldn't happen to contain alcohol, now would it?'

'As a matter of fact, it does,' Archie replied.

'Well, hornswoggle me giblets,' roared Boff with a wide smile. 'This old hooter of mine has never failed me yet, where there be grog to be had!'

Grizwold coughed violently as the smell bit the back of his throat. *Archie Wilde*, he thalked, *there's more than alcohol here. I've been around the galaxy more times than you've wiped your snotty nose, and I would recognize that evil stench anywhere. It's the worst form of black-art magic there is. I smell electrickery!*

Electrickery? Archie repeated. *Oh, you mean electricity!*

Don't patronise me, rasped Grizwold aggressively. *I know what I mean, and I speak what I—*

Calm down, Grizwold, thalked Archie. *This machine won't work without it, so you'd better get used to it or get out of the* Skyshark.

Huh, very funny, grunted Grizwold. *You know I can't do that!*

I know you can't, my friend, agreed Archie, his stern tone softening, *and to be quite honest, I like having you in my head.*

Grizwold's mouth popped open in surprise. *You... you honestly want me to stay?*

Yes, Grizwold, I do. You can stay for as long you wish.

I can? stammered Grizwold, flushing tomato red. *Thank you.*

Settling himself into the pilot's seat, Archie smiled as he let his eyes wander lovingly over the flight controls. *Finally,* he thought excitedly, *I get to fly this beast for real!*

From inside his combat vest, he retrieved his phone SIM card and excitedly inserted it into a computer interface. As the precious data began downloading, Archie cast his eyes about the console and quickly realised that he had an unforeseen problem. Whilst the crown of Avalon had indeed saved his life, it constricted his head movement. To his frustration, looking at some of the lower dials and controls was almost impossible. And to boot, although the edges of the crown segments weren't sharp, they did rub his chin. 'Most annoying!' he huffed to himself.

But being a flexible sort of guy, Archie quickly resolved the problem by lowering his seat a few turns then moving it two notches backwards. As for the chin rub, stuffing a clean polishing rag over the top of the crown temporarily solved that. Not the most stylish, but it worked.

Catching his reflection in a glass dial cover, he studied the golden collar for a moment, thinking to himself, *that's one problem that will have to wait!*

Whilst a soft beeping signal indicated that the data transfer was fifty percent complete, Archie found himself watching Boff squeeze his huge rubbery body into the small co-pilot's seat next to him with the fluidity of an octopus. His eight tentacle hands and both coned eyes hungrily investigated everything.

'Boff, can you do something with all your tentacles?' asked Archie. 'They're getting in my way.'

'What exactly would you like me to do with them, shipmate? We can't all be imperfect and only have two hands.'

'Well, this craft is designed for people with only two hands, so choose a pair and tie a knot in the rest, okay?'

Boff sniggered under his breath. It was nice to see the old, geeky Archie back. Then he coiled his redundant tentacles around his body and contented himself with studying the strange interior of the Skyshark.

It was obvious from the start that Archie had cobbled together bits and bobs from all over the scrapyard to make the thing work. He recognized a gear stick from an old Ford Cortina, two toilet-roll holders filled with coils of copper wire, a vegetable colander, a set of pink-piggy salt-and-pepper shakers, and what looked like an array of Christmas tree lights. That was just the dashboard. All around him, riveted to the interior bulkheads, was a colourful patchwork of old road and advertising signs, no doubt hiding holes and rust patches. For a supposed technological marvel, it contained more household and garden items than a hardware store.

But what really grabbed his attention was the row of spirit-bottle labels stuck to the bottom of the windscreen glass, including whisky, rum, vodka, gin, and at least a dozen others that he'd never heard of. However, the odd thing about this line of labels, was the small model ship sitting proudly out of place in the centre.

'Archie, what's with the spirit labels,' asked Boff curiously, 'and the little boat?'

Archie looked up from his pre-flight checklist and smiled. 'Do you remember me telling you that the fuel I used in the model Skyshark was a mixture of my own creation?'

'Yes,' said Boff.

'Ever wonder where I get the ingredients from?'

'No,' stated Boff thoughtfully. 'I just assumed you got them all off that web thing you're always droning on about.'

Archie laughed. 'Oh no, not this time. This time, all the ingredients were freely donated by Her Majesty's government.'

'Odds bodkins, boy, do you really expect me to believe that the naffin' government gave it to you?'

'Well, they *indirectly* gave it to me.' He grinned.

'You're sailing circles around me, boy,' huffed Boff, 'explain yourself.'

'Okay, to be precise, it was HM Revenue and Customs that supplied it.'

Boff scratched his three blubbery chins for a moment then said, 'Jagdar's teeth, boy, those lunatics actually gave you rocket fuel?'

'Not gave,' corrected Archie, 'unwittingly supplied. They don't even know that I have it.'

'Jigger me giblets, boy, now I am naffin' confused.'

'Allow me to explain. A couple of miles up the road is Dangdon Court. It's a large, heavily secured dumping facility for customs and excise. All the illegal spirits they seize from all the ports along the south coast are brought here for destruction. Any ideas as to their chosen method?' He looked into his friend's blank, staring eyes and carried on. 'They simply pour it down a big drain and flush it out to sea.'

'Scupper me, boy,' said Boff forlornly, 'all that lovely grog, just flushed away for the fish? It's enough to break an old storm raider's heart!'

'Their main drain runs right underneath this scrapyard,' Archie said. 'All I did was redirect some of the flow into my private storage tanks.'

'Jagdar's scaly hide,' said Boff, grinning from ear to ear, 'so you're a mad scientist *and* a thief now, and your fancy new fuel is nothing more than stolen alcohol.'

'Well, there's a little more to it than that,' added Archie modestly. 'It has to be blended in a special way, and of course there is my own secret additive!'

'Trounce me trunnions, boy, that's a fine-looking vessel!' offered Boff, quickly steering the conversation away from experimental, explosive cocktails.

Archie smiled at the tiny model, announcing proudly. 'That's HMS Victory, a one-hundred-forty-four cannons first-liner, the most powerful warship of her age.'

Such a statement made the storm raider bristle with pride. 'Jagdar's teeth, now that sounds like a ship fit for Bilge Rat Boff to command. I would have willingly severed a tentacle for a chance to take her into battle.'

'Well, it's funny you should say that'—Archie grinned—'because you will soon get your chance.'

Boff watched him flex his hands over the vast flight-control console like a conductor about to strike up a symphony. It was odd because to Boff, the whole thing looked bereft of life. The paintwork was scratched and worn, several switchy things were badly glued back together, and rust had eaten completely through the metal in some places. His whole machine seemed to be held together with nothing more than duct tape, spite, and prayers.

One by one, Archie flicked six switches on, their indicator lights glowing green. At the end of the row, his index finger hovered over a big red button labelled APU. As the last light flashed green, he stabbed the button with an eager finger. From somewhere deep inside the Skyshark, a low thrumming sound wound into life. Almost immediately, two electrical power gauges spiked, announcing that the auxiliary power unit was online.

'What's that noise?' asked Boff, his coned eyes twitching in all directions, hunting for its source.

'That's the electrical generator starting up.' He pointed to the main console, and the numerous coloured lights and rows of waving dials indicated that the Skyshark was stirring. 'It makes electricity to power all of this and the main engines.'

'And just what was that tiny square thing you popped into there?' he asked, pointing to the computer interface.

'That was a mobile-phone SIM card containing all the data gathered from the flight of my model Skyshark this morning. Once downloaded into the Skyshark's computer, it will enable us to safely fly the real Skyshark!'

'*Safely?*' questioned Boff anxiously.

'Yes, safely,' Archie said. 'You see, the Skyshark needs a computer to make it fly. It's just too complex for a pilot to fly manually.'

With a tap of a finger, a brightly coloured large-scale map of southeast England flashed on one of the computer screens. There were two red datum flags on it.

'This little flag here'—he pointed to the one marked A— 'is us in the scrapyard. The one marked B is the Portsmouth naval dockyard, just along the coast. That's where they keep HMS Victory, the flagship of the Royal Navy.'

'Archie, the Crimson Raptor is the most formidable sky cruiser with the most awesome firepower in the whole of the genieverse,' stated Grizwold. 'He has the best archers on Hexx, the most powerful crossbows, catapults that launch the scariest fireballs you've ever seen, and of course his latest acquisition, the Wrath of Jagdar, his new harmonics-bell weapon!'

Boff's body suddenly became like a set of traffic lights,

flushing rapidly between an angry red, a seething amber, and a frightened green.

'Hornswoggle me giblets, boy, Grizzy's right. This thing may fly in the sky and swim in the oceans, but without weapons, just how do you expect to fight Old Buckethead? Or are you planning to just waltz up to him, tell him that he's a very naughty boy, and hope he'll let Ssasky, and Freddy go?'

'On the contrary, Boff,' said Archie calmly. 'When we burst out of the Storming Kaleidoscope Falls aboard HMS Victory, with all guns blazing, he'll immediately realise he's lost. Because if I can outsmart his golden collar, then I sure as hell can annihilate him in a fight!'

Boff's big mouth fell open, his lower jaw smacking the top of the console with a leathery thwack. 'And we're just going to borrow the flagship of the Royal Navy?'

Archie grinned. 'No. We're going to steal it!'

'But—'

'But what, Bilge Rat Boff, self-proclaimed infamous storm raider?' mocked Archie. 'Not up to it, are we?'

'Don't mock me, boy,' roared Boff. 'I have you—'

'Excuse me for interrupting,' said Grizwold, hijacking Archie's vocal cords, 'but am I the only one who can smell something burning?'

Grumbling, Boff sniffed the air, his healthy green colour quickly fading to a pallid white. 'Jagdar's teeth, Archie,' he whimpered. 'What foolishness is this?'

Archie's rascally grin was not the answer he'd hoped for. 'That is the wonderful smell of burning cordite.' Then with a clenched fist and an excitedly beating heart, he thumped down a big red button marked Launch Ramp.

The warm night air was suddenly filled with a rapid staccato of small bangs. Eerily, the huge, tangled mess of old roller-coaster track on the opposite side of the road began to lurch and quake, untangling itself like an awakening giant octopus.

'Shiver me giblets, boy,' croaked Boff, 'what have you done?'

'Each small bang was an explosive trigger that has released a large, heavy metal weight.' He pointed excitedly to the mountain of track on the other side of the road. 'See? It's moving.'

To his amazement, Boff watched in awe as a network of blocks and tackles seemingly pulled the huge heap of roller-coaster track apart. In fact, they were removing debris from a well-camouflaged, long, straight section of track.

'See how that last section of track is now being dragged across the road? That one crucial section will connect the track upon which the Skyshark sits to the rest of the main launching ramp over there.'

The head-splitting cacophony of metal-on-metal tortured Boff's ears whilst filling Archie's watering eyes with sheer delight.

With a heavy, definite clunk, the last piece of track locked into place. Boff, resembling a large, quivering snowman, goggled in terrified amazement at the dirty, rusty, somewhat dilapidated, four-hundred-foot-long roller-coaster launch ramp before them.

'Archie,' squeaked Boff, desperately trying not to ink himself, 'dare I ask what that fuse is attached too?'

'Attention. Attention. Rocket-sled ignition has been activated. Sixty seconds to launch.'

'Hornswoggle me giblets!' He groaned at the sound of the calm, informative robotic voice. 'That naffin' woman's trouble!'

'*No!* That's not right!' cried Archie, suddenly leaning forward and frantically flicking switches. 'It's supposed to be a five-minute countdown, you stupid woman. I'm not ready yet!'

Archie, just what is that fuse connected to? thalked Grizwold.

Archie swallowed hard. *Two tonnes of solid rocket fuel stored in the sled that the Skyshark is sitting on top of!*

To the rear of the cockpit came a loud whoosh, followed by a deep, throaty growling, its powerful reverberations shaking their feet, legs, and tentacles.

'Well,' Archie said triumphantly, 'that's main engine one, up and running.' With no time to gloat, he swiftly turned his attention to cold starting engine number two. For a split second, he glanced at a tall metal locker on his left. There was a cartoon of a spaceman stuck to it. Stencilled beneath were the words Astronaut Spacesuit. For five years, he'd dreamt of that moment—his every working hour had been leading up to that one flight. The time had come to act, but his long-awaited trip into space wasn't going to happen.

The calm female voice spoke again: 'Sled ignition in thirty seconds and counting.'

'Navigation lights on, radar burning and turning.' Archie poked Boff in the belly, flicking his belt buckle, his face an insane blend of terror and euphoria. 'I'd strap yourself in tight if I were you. We're going vertical in a few seconds, and at the speed we're going to leave the ramp, I don't want your big butt squashed against the rear bulkhead, okay?'

Boff wanted to scream, but his panicking brain had tied his throat in a knot.

Five loud honks sounded, and the pair of them jumped at the sound of the alarm, but it was the unexpected, gut-strangling, gurgling noise that made Boff ink himself. 'Jagdar's teeth, Archie,' he cried, shaking with fear, 'what the mukluks is that?'

'Oh hell.' Archie scowled, flicked off his seat belt, and leaped out of his chair, ignoring Boff's baffled look. 'I knew that cheap pump sounded too good to be true.' Then he hesitated just long enough to place one of Boff's shaking hands on a switch labelled Engine Starter. 'When I shout "now," flick this switch. Okay?'

'Okay,' repeated Boff dumbly, his stewed mind simmering with panic. Craning his head around as far as possible, Boff could just make out Archie lifting a hatch cover at the back of the cockpit deck. Immediately, the sounds of the *Skyshark's* engines grew in intensity, along with an odd hammering noise.

'Now!' shouted Archie. Boff obediently flicked the switch.

With a soft plop, Archie landed back in his seat two seconds later.

'Do I want to know?' Boff asked anxiously.

'Oh, don't fret over that,' Archie said. 'The fuel-feed pump to the number-two engine can be a little temperamental sometimes.'

'And you fixed it by hitting it with a hammer?' Boff asked incredulously.

Archie frowned. 'Of course not. That would be stupid. I used a wooden chock!'

'Sled ignition in five, four, three…'

Archie suddenly realised that his hands were sweaty and shaking. *Blimey,* he thought fretfully, *what if Boff's right, and the Skyshark does blow up?* His chest felt as if it was clamped in a vice, and the lump in his throat made breathing virtually impossible. Then, from the basement of his brain, which was reserved for lack of confidence, failure, and cowardice, he heard the nasty voice of doubt shouting. *What if your calculations are wrong, boy? Is your experimental fuel powerful enough? You don't really believe that this heap of junk will hold together in a ten-G turn?* The voice's laughter had a vicious, razor-sharp edge that slashed at Archie's already shaky confidence. *You've failed, Archie Wilde. You're going to crash and burn!*

'…Two… One…'

Archie suddenly felt himself shaking uncontrollably, and it had nothing to do with the rocket sled.

'Ignition, all rockets burning.'

With a deafening, explosive whoosh, eight thrusting tongues of white-hot flame burst from the rear of the sled as two tonnes of solid rocket fuel ignited, shaking the Skyshark like a jelly on a washing machine.

'We're not naffin' moving!' shouted Boff, his voice barely audible.

Archie pointed shakily to a dial on his left. 'When that little needle reaches the red marker, the automatic brake will release!'

The glass fronts of three dials suddenly cracked then exploded, sending shards of glass whizzing through the air.

'Jagdar's fiery breath, boy,' cried Boff in despair, 'this metal monstrosity is tearing itself apart! Release the brake before we all naffin' die!'

'We can't! We're not at the marker yet!' shouted Archie, who was silently praying that the Skyshark would hold together for just a few more seconds. 'Anything less than fifty thousand pounds of thrust, and we'll crash on the town!'

'Stuff the naffin' town!' screamed Boff.

Somewhere behind them, as the tiny needle finally touched the red marker line, something snapped.

Instantly, Archie and Boff were slammed deep into their seats, knocking the air from their lungs and squishing their eyeballs into the backs of their sockets. The unleashed rocket sled propelled the *Skyshark* violently forward from zero to sixty in two seconds. Blasting out of the workshop, it hurtled along the rickety old roller-coaster track so fast that Grizwold was flung off Archie's brain, splatting hard against the back of his skull.

Sergeant Tuppin waited for the taillights of Superintendent Hardman's car to vanish around the corner before heaving a sigh of relief.

'What a day!' he groaned aloud to the empty scrapyard. 'I hate flippin' kids!'

He lit an illicit cigarette then took a long, leisurely, and very rewarding drag. His wife would go bananas if she saw what he was doing, but after the day's events, he honestly didn't care. He stared vaguely at the two burnt-out police cars, one balancing perfectly on top of the other, roof to roof. He pondered how two teenage boys could cause so much damage in such a short time. It confounded him, but it completely bamboozled the superintendent.

His mind wondered back to the wrecked patrol cars at the orphanage and the boy with that strange eye patch. 'He's the key to this whole ruddy mess,' he muttered, 'and the reason why I'm stuck out here in the middle of the night, guarding an empty scrapyard.' He blew a series of smoke rings and watched them fade into the darkness. 'Thank the blooming Lord, I've only got six months left until I retire,' he announced cheerfully.

A loud roaring suddenly shattered Sergeant Tuppin's moment of tranquillity, sending roosting birds flapping and squawking into the night, whilst nocturnal vermin scattered, panicking, back to their burrows.

'What now?' he groaned, jumping to his feet just in time to see, rising out of the darkness, a single bright-white light. It was the weirdest thing he'd ever seen. It seemed to be going straight up but very slowly.

'Hell's bells!' he cried in horror. 'That bloomin' thing's coming straight for me!'

Then something weird happened. The mysterious flying object seemed to split into two parts. Whereas the white light seemed to be ascending, so the glowing bit underneath was...

'Oh God, no,' he whimpered, 'not again!'

For a portly man of fifty-nine, Sergeant Tuppin quickly raced across the open road, jumping feetfirst into a nearby dyke. He splashed into two feet of muddy, weed-choked water seconds before the world about him exploded. Out on the road, the only remaining drudge-on-the-marsh police car, *his* patrol car, exploded in a blinding fireball.

Covered in weeds, Sergeant Tuppin's muddy face glared up

at the night sky as a huge silver flying machine with two fiery, white tails roared overhead, quickly disappearing into the dark.

Chapter 28

THE GREAT AMPHITHEATRE OF GARRKNOCK. ON THE PLANET HEXX.

O n Hexx, the last night of Atunka Gaar was cold and clear. Its second sun had set, and the rise of the traitor's moon was still a full candle mark away. And although the stars in the heavens shone brightly above, and a thousand burning torches illuminated the great amphitheatre of Garrknock, nothing could penetrate the cold darkness beyond its wooden walls.

Yet out in the inky void, something stirred, thankful for the cover of night.

Hidden amongst the ghostly mist of the Forbidden Lake, close to the northwest wall of the amphitheatre, stood a small island of scrub and tangle weed, no bigger than a shovelhead elephant's footprint. And it was there, shrouded in eerie silence, that a large clump of weed mysteriously began to move.

The earth surrounding the small wooden trapdoor gurgled in protest as it was shouldered open. On creaky hinges, the hatch fell with a soggy plop into the sodden, stinky mud.

'Blimey, bro, that place pongs something horrible,' grumbled Skatt.

'It's a smugglers' tunnel, you plonka,' groaned Nogga,

rolling his eyes in disbelief. 'What do you expect, scented candles?'

Nogga followed his complaining brother through the hatch and closed it quietly behind them. For several tense breaths, they crouched uneasily in the squishy mud, studying a large stone face set in the amphitheatre wall on the far side of a small stream.

'How did you know about this tunnel?' asked Skatt.

'I heard Pa mention it once,' whispered Nogga.

Skatt shuddered at the sight of the stone face. 'Blimey, bro, I knows we've used stinky tunnels before to do blags, but none were ever this bad!'

'*Skatt*,' snapped Nogga, 'that's the great amphitheatre of Garrknock before us. Contained within is over two thousand different species of revelling creatures, creepies, and mongrel humans. For the last three days and nights, they've gluttonously swilled back an ocean of ale whilst stuffing their faces with enough food to feed a small planet. Remember what Pa said on Christmas? Nice vittles' may go in one end, but a pongy wind always erupts from the other.'

'Jagdar's curly horns, yeah.' Skatt chuckled. 'Pa could blow Ma's three-headed canary clean off its perch from the other side of the cave.'

'Yes,' agreed Nogga, remembering affectionately the look of horror on the poor bird's face as it tried in vain to escape the smell. 'And there are some creatures in the theatre that have digestive tracts the size of an ogre hippo.'

Nogga slithered cautiously out from the cover of the weeds only to hesitate at the edge of the swirling mist of the forbidden lake. It was merely a minor tributary whose sole purpose was to wash away the sewage and rotting carcasses from the killing arena of the amphitheatre above. But nevertheless, it was connected to the main lake. And that was what worried him.

In stark contrast to its vile odour, ghastly location, and grisly reputation, the mist that clung to the lake's fathomless black surface was bizarrely beautiful. Whilst its lustrous sparkle enticed the eye, its leisurely swirls of trapped silver moonlight tempted the hand. All his thieving senses told him that the coast was clear, but Nogga was no fool. He'd heard the rumours. Although the gap between them and the outfall was a measly ten feet, he knew that lurking inside the honey trap were the Dreadlies.

'Do we have to cross here?' whispered Skatt from behind. 'I've heard tales of them there Dreadlies.'

'Jagdar, give me strength,' moaned Nogga. 'There's a path of secret stepping-stones right in front of us, hidden just beneath the surface. We'll slither across it in seconds. Okay?'

'I can't see them!' growled Skatt.

'They wouldn't be secret if you could see them, you dope!' snapped Nogga. He beckoned his brother to climb up onto his back, which he promptly did. After adjusting his stovepipe hat, Nogga gritted his teeth and slithered forward, praying that the legendary steps were still there.

What he had always assumed to be water felt oddly firm under his belly. It wasn't rock-hard but felt more like tough jelly. And he wasn't so much slithering from stone to stone but sort of gliding as if on wet ice. This sensation he could cope with, but the strange mist that washed against him like a ghostly cloak made his thick skin tingle as if awash with acid. Also, once or twice he felt something ungodly brush against his underbelly. If it was the dreadlies, they weren't attacking yet, just testing. But each nerve-racking bump made him slither a little faster.

Upon reaching the far side, a thankful Skatt was just about to jump down onto firm, mist-free ground when a sinewy tongue flashed out of the mist, its barbed end snagging his furry butt, snatching him backward. All Nogga heard was a yelp and a splash as his brother vanished into the misty lake.

The silvery waters enveloped Skatt in an instant. Down and down, he was dragged, deeper and deeper into the murky depths of the Forbidden Lake. Even with his terrified eyes wide open, all he could see was an impenetrable, inky blackness.

Nogga's heart hammered like a crazy drummer. He couldn't see anything, but he knew that they were about to dine on his big brother.

Skatt knew his time was up.

Suddenly, streaks of bright-blue lightning speared the lake, each sizzling the water about him with its concentrated heat. The intense flashes illuminated hundreds of malevolent glowing red eyes and rows and rows of vicious, spiky teeth. Skatt, his lungs starting to burn, watched in amazement as the lightning storm sliced several of the scary monsters in half, their mates fleeing back into the dark. Not understanding what had just happened but seizing a chance to escape, he kicked with all four paws and frantically clawed his way up to the surface.

Skatt's head exploded out of the lake, and he coughed and spluttered, but even before he had chance to bark his thanks to Jagdar, he felt something slither around his waist and scoop him out of the mist. Deftly using his two long tails, Nogga reeled in his brother, dumping him on the squishy mud next to the sewer outfall gate.

'Jagdar's teeth, those dreadlies are mean beggars,' he said, wiping the slime off his brother's gasping face. 'I thought I'd lost you for good, bro!'

'Dreadlies everywhere,' spluttered Skatt in between snatched breaths. 'Then the blue lighting came and scared them all away.' He spied the strange object his brother was brandishing proudly. 'It was you, weren't it?'

Nogga flipped the device over and whispered. 'It was my Belstead Military Combat Laser.'

'Jagdar's teeth, bro,' said Skatt, coughing up more lake water, 'what's one of them, then?'

Nogga scratched his head. 'I haven't got the foggiest, bro,' he admitted, 'but that lunatic Professor Ratchet Madspanner demonstrated its power by cutting through a big old chunk of metal the size of my waist as if it were chocolate cake.' He turned and faced the sewer entrance. 'So, I think this gizmo will make a fine key to open this big old iron grill barring our way, huh, bro?'

With his near-death experience with the dreadlies instantly forgotten, Skatt grinned. 'Sounds blooming good to me. Waking Dream Vault, here we come.' Then he prudently moved aside, giving his brother room to play with his new toy.

Chapter 29

THE GREAT AMPHITHEATRE OF GARRKNOCK. ON THE PLANET HEXX.

The drunken crowd whooped and cheered wildly as Baldizar, with his crimson armour glowing with power and his heavy stride oozing authority, marched majestically out onto the stage of the great amphitheatre of Garrknock. With his helmeted head held high, his gold-tipped black spikes extended, triumphantly holding the fabled Fangs of Jagdar dagger.

From all around the theatre's highest walls, a fanfare of trumpets heralded his glorious return whilst the packed stands, a writhing sea of waving flags and banners, cried out in awe as clouds of brightly shimmering Valorium rose petals fluttered down out of the dark night sky.

Baldizar drank in the heady atmosphere, relishing the historic moment, for it wasn't just a victory: it was his destiny. In his mind, nothing could stop him now. It was the day that he would finally become the true king of kings.

Flanked by heavily armed minotaur's, the supreme genie came to a stomping halt in the centre of the stage. Standing godlike, he beckoned Goldhorn, the chieftain captain, forward with a commanding wave of a gauntlet. A rousing boom of spiteful, mocking laughter filled the air as Goldhorn hauled his two manacled prisoners into view, dragging them across the stage before throwing them both roughly to the boot caps of their El Supremo.

Baldizar glanced sideways at the gathered council of the power ten genies. He fleetingly acknowledged their existence, his withering sneer of contempt lingering just a moment on their leader.

Eccles Nimrod, the genie of Order, second only to the supreme genie himself, scowled in condemnation of Baldizar, who dared to break the sacred law and appear on the final eve of Atunka Gaar dressed in full armour. Seething with rage, he was quick to rise, only to fall back in stunned horror.

However, it wasn't Baldizar's draconian, malevolent red eyes that suddenly weakened his resolve but the sight of green blood oozing from a fresh wound upon Captain Goldhorn's left shoulder. *Whatever that horned abomination is,* he thought, shuddering with disgust, *it isn't a real chieftain!*

A bunch of flamboyant, worthless dandies thought Baldizar cynically as he turned his eyes upwards and smiled at the ever-watchful carved image of the Great Garrknock. If only they knew just how their final night was going to end.

The rise of the traitor's moon was but a candle mark away, and the baying crowd, relishing the notion of a double execution, sang out their excitement with renewed vigour.

Baldizar stepped forward, the wooden stage groaning under his weight. Then slowly, he raised aloft all four of his long arms, all palms empty, save for one. That metal fist he held the highest, displaying the ultimate weapon.

His gesture was immediately understood, as a wave of hushed obedience washed across the mob.

Baldizar, pleased by the scum's respectful submission, glared out upon the irksome mass of spellbound creepies, creatures, and mongrels.

His calculating gaze wandered across the length and breadth of the theatre, his cold, volcanic eyes scrutinizing every shady nook or fleeting shadow. With the second sun of Hexx having long since dropped beyond the horizon, the theatre before him was ablaze with thousands of brightly burning torches and glowing lanterns. The threat of assassination was ever in his mind. Baldizar left nothing to chance. During the time of darkness, the great amphitheatre of Garrknock always burned brighter than a midday sun.

'Creepies, creatures, and mongrels, one and all,' he announced in a deep, booming voice that echoed around the theatre, 'I bring you greetings upon this, the third and final eve of Atunka Gaar.' A thunderous storm of whooping and hollering shattered the silence, bringing a cold, heartless smile to his thin cruel lips. 'I bring you the fabled Fangs of Jagdar dagger!'

The whole of the amphitheatre seemed to catch its breath as even the dumbest creature suddenly realised that they were in the presence of the most powerful genie in the genieverse.

'Unfortunately,' continued Baldizar, 'none of the maggots in this decennial race have survived to tell their tales.' He glanced down with an evil delight at the shiny new Rolex on his right lower wrist. 'I can also confirm that the jabber jockeys' odds-on favourite for winning the race, one Archie Wilde of Earth'—the crowd cheered enthusiastically at the mentioned of Archie's name—'lost his head precisely one candle mark ago.'

Daringly, the crowd sighed bitterly, causing Baldizar's volcanic eyes to flash red with fury. Although dusted, it needled him that one youngling who heralded from the planet of the ancients had given the fickle mob gathered on Hexx so much hope. Not only did he have the arrogance to dust that despicable Mugwart the indigestible, but he also had the barefaced courage to stand up to the supreme genie himself.

However, a single glorious thought tempered his simmering anger, causing him to smile with evil pleasure. *Be warned, scum of the genieverse. Under my reign, heroes will have a short life span!*

'However,' he cried aloud, 'I do have, for your entertainment, two prisoners awaiting the rise of the traitor's moon!'

The unexpected gift of guaranteed bloodshed, although an obvious bribe, brought vigour back to the voice of the mob. As Baldizar listened, a cruel chuckle escaped his pursed lips. *The scum never ceased to amaze him.* Then, in a rare moment of geniality, he raised his arms high once again and asked, 'And just how shall we deal with these traitors?'

Executions were commonplace throughout the genieverse but only for the most serious of crimes. However, since Baldizar was elected the supreme genie, he had turned it from a resolute punishment to a profitable spectator sport. With the crowd back in full voice, it soon became clear to Baldizar exactly what their chosen instrument of torture was to be.

'Butcher them! Butcher them! Butcher them!' yelled the mob.

Smiling, Baldizar raised his hands high. 'The will of Atunka Gaar has spoken. The traitors will meet the Devil's Butcher!'

Chapter 30

The Skyshark's acceleration along the rickety old launch ramp was so aggressive that instead of screaming with terror, all Boff could manage was a strangled whimper.

Shooting clear off the roller-coaster track, the rocket sled fell away, its fuel spent. The Skyshark's two Red Dragon engines roared with unleashed power, propelling the little craft high into the dark night sky.

As the Skyshark and its rocket sled parted company, the violent shaking and head-splitting noise ceased. For Boff, it was like stepping out of a tumble dryer full of ball bearings, accompanied by his own screaming and dribbling, but for Archie, it was a moment to truly savour, the climax of five years' hard work and a lifetime of dreams. With the Skyshark flying on autopilot, things became weirdly tranquil inside the cockpit, and Archie wasn't sure whether he should be relieved or worried.

In his small library, all the books relating to space flight were well thumbed. He'd read and reread all there was to know about launch procedures, including the inevitable emotional dread and exhilaration of lift-off, the crushing effects of g-force on the body, and the violence of booster separation. All of that and a thousand other random thoughts whirled about in his mind as he tried to focus on the control panel before him.

They were climbing smoothly, at a smidge over 350 mph, the small red needle of the altimeter already past five thousand feet. He checked the engine dials—all the needles were steady and nowhere near their red warning marks. *She's not even trying,* he thought, grinning smugly to himself. Both throttles were only at fifty percent, and all the other readouts were green. Coupled with the soft, reassuring hum of the Red Dragon engines behind him, it went some way to allaying the panic attack that was lurking in the darker recesses of his mind.

Now for the moment of truth, he thought fearfully. *Come on,* he goaded himself harshly, *you've waited all your life for this. You can do it.* With a drumming heart and a choking lump in his throat, he flexed his shaking fingers then tentatively reached forward, grasping the flight-control column gently with both hands.

It felt good. It felt natural. His mind ran through the basics for the hundredth time. *Keep the foot pedals level so the tail rudder remains straight then pull back on the control yoke halfway, all the time remembering not to dip your hands to the left or right.* He'd recited the words so many times, he felt that they should be etched onto his brain.

Taking a deep breath, he reached out with a shaky finger, its tip hovering over the autopilot switch. Then, with a mini explosion of courage, he flicked it off.

He wasn't sure whether it was instinct or fear that made him grip the column so hard that his knuckles went white.

Either way, the expected jolt from taking manual control of an aircraft he'd read about never materialized. All those nagging doubts about wild turbulence, engine failure, structural fatigue, and the inevitable newspaper headline, 'Greenhorn Pilot Crashes Plane,' vanished. Now he was flying the Skyshark for real. From somewhere in the back of his head, he heard his self-doubt give a loud, peeved huff.

'Yes, I can fly the Skyshark,' he said to himself, laughing.

Boff, who was still trembling, his leathery skin a ghastly shade of white, swivelled an eye at him and said between snatched breaths, 'Archie Wilde, you best not be laughing at me, boy!'

'I'm not laughing at you, Boff.' He smiled. 'I'm laughing at myself.'

'Egads, you scare the barnacles off me sometimes, boy.'

One at a time, Archie gently released his sweating hands from the flight column, happily watching his fingers turn pink again. He glanced at the horizon bar, which was nice and level as the tiny craft continued its nearly vertical climb. 'I'll take her up to fifty thousand feet then level out,' he announced confidently. 'That should put us well above any commercial flights. Let's just hope that the RAF's not lurking about tonight!' He tried to relax into his seat, but his body was tense with excitement. He had never ached so much.

'Hornswoggle me giblets, boy,' said Boff, suddenly relaxing, his skin flushing a lovely ripe-apple green. 'Chill. We're up amongst the clouds now.'

'That's rich coming from you, oh fearless storm raider,' Archie said with a snort.

Boff smiled with his big, rubbery lips. 'Flying great,' he

added cheerfully. 'It was your take-off that sucked!' He uncurled two tentacle hands and massaged the boy's shoulders vigorously. 'Your muscles are tenser than a chieftain's bow string!'

'Yeah, no kidding. I'm just realising that there's more to flying this lark than I'd realised.'

'How many times have you actually flown this here garbage scow?'

'She's not a garbage scow,' snapped Archie resentfully, 'and I've flown her several times if you must know.' His indignant glare was to be short lived.

'Several times, huh, laddie?' Boff smirked.

Archie couldn't help his eye glancing nervously at the centre computer screen.

'On the telly-box thing doesn't count. How many times for real?'

Archie knew he'd been rumbled. 'Okay, never.'

'Permission to take the helm, Skipper?' Boff said, grabbing the co-pilot's control column and slipping a pair of tentacle hands into the rudder pedals.

'What are you doing, Boff?' cried Archie in a panic. 'Give her back to me! I need to fly the Sky—' His words dried in his throat as Boff nimbly barrel-rolled the craft to the left and right, followed by a perfect loop, before bringing it neatly back onto their original course.

That crazy chamelesquid can fly your metal monster, thalked Grizwold with unabashed awe.

Yes he flippin' well can, thalked Archie, rather annoyed at someone stealing his thunder, *and he seems quite good at it too!*

'Well trounce me trunnions,' Boff said. 'This here crate's a lot more fun than flying my old cloud-cutter, the Nifty Nipper. A little light on the stick maybe, but a good-weather helm nonetheless.'

'You can fly!' said Archie.

'Jagdar's scaly hide, boy, of course I can fly.' He laughed aloud. 'Unlike some!'

Archie looked confused. 'But I thought that your flying was that twirly thing you do with outspread tentacles.'

'Odds bodkins, Archie, I used to spend weeks hiding in the clouds, waiting for my next victim. Methinks me tentacles may have ached a bit, huh?'

Archie laughed at the stupidity of his own statement. 'So, what was this Nifty Nipper you mentioned?'

'Shiver me giblets, boy, she was a naffin' joy to behold.' His smile was big. 'Most feared little cloud glider in all the genieverse! I had bow and stern catapults, midship slingshots, and two of the biggest triple-barrelled rock droppers ever made. But best of all, she was as swift as the wind itself. With all sheets billowing, she could slice through thunderheads whilst dancing circles about the lightning bolts.' A rascally smile lit up his face. 'The chieftains sky cutters never stood a naffin' chance.'

'You must have been immensely proud of her,' said Archie.

'Jagdar's scaly hide, that I was, boy. And whilst we're broaching the subject of firepower,' he continued, swivelling both eyes at Archie, 'you never did enlighten me as to your plans for arming the Skyshark!'

Archie didn't answer immediately. Instead, he leaned forward and peered over the control console. 'Good, that's Dover ahead, and I can see the coast of France over to our right. We're lined up nicely.' Then he placed his hands firmly back on the control yoke. 'Okay, Boff, I'll have her now.'

'Are you sure, boy?' he asked nervously. 'Cloud gliders can be a tad unpredictable.'

'You've got your wings.' Archie laughed, trying to hide his excited terror. 'And up here is the best place for me to practise, huh?'

Boff grinned. 'Trounce me trunnions, boy, you remind me of when I was a squidling.' With that, he released the control yoke. 'Remember, boy, tiny, smooth adjustments. Jerky will get you dusted quicker than ink from a scared squid's bum.'

Bearing that gem in mind, Archie gently dropped his right hand ever so slightly. The Skyshark banked to starboard, gliding in a slow curve with all the grace of a soaring albatross. At an altitude of fifty thousand feet, in the cold clear air, its smooth metallic skin glowed with a soft, fiery bronze as it was bathed in the last rays of sunset.

With great satisfaction, Archie watched the compass readout slowly move around to two hundred forty-two degrees as they as they did a complete one-eighty, bringing them out over the Dover Strait.

'There,' he said, proud of his first real aerial manoeuvre. 'We'll soon be at Portsmouth.' He smiled at Boff. 'Einstein's underpants, this flying lark's even more fun than I had hoped it would be.' A little more relaxed, Archie settled back and enjoyed the flight. Down below, twinkling in the dark, the bright lights of the southern coast cities and towns made navigation a doddle. *Just keep the sea to my left and the land to my right*, he thought, *and we'll be over Bournemouth before you know it.*

Archie had never believed in luck. After all, he'd spent the last ten years of his life in an orphanage, and the five before that appeared to be bureaucratically non-existent. It was not a shining example of good fortune, yet there he was, gliding through the night sky, the happiest he'd ever been.

'Archie.' Boff's voice had a spoiling, sombre tone to it. 'Have you actually given any thought to just how we're going to rescue your girlfriend and Freddy?'

'It's a simple smash-and-grab operation,' said Archie, his eye never leaving the flight console.

'As easy as that, huh?' acknowledged Boff cynically. 'We simply snatch the pair of them out of the great amphitheatre of Garrknock, from under the very nose of Baldizar, the council genies, and a hundred violent veggie chieftains?'

'Think lightning,' insisted Archie. 'In, out, *gone!*' It was his night, and stuff Boff's whinging. For once, he felt Lady Luck smiling down upon him, and nothing he said was going to spoil it.

He was right. Lady Luck was smiling because she had conspired that on that fine summer's night to make the entire security team keeping watch over the Royal Navy's most historically precious warship consist of precisely one sailor, Able Seaman Spike Hughes.

Affectionately referred to as Tail-End Charlie by his shipmates, Hughes had an unprecedented knack for always being five minutes late for everything. So as penance, whilst his shipmates sang and drank their way around Portsmouth, having a wonderful time, Able Seaman Hughes was saddled with the unenviable duty of being the sole protector of the

HMS Victory.

Hughes sat on his stool with all the military precision of a deflated balloon. Slumped over the quartermaster's desk, he idly slurped his coffee, whilst his sullen eyes wondered forlornly about the empty wooden deck and the deserted harbour about him.

The flash storm that had hit Portsmouth in the late afternoon had blown itself out, leaving the evening air warm and humid. Above him, the miles of damp rigging annoyingly squeaking as it dried wasn't helping his mood one bit.

'What the heck am I doing here?' he moaned, looking up the road to the floodlit grounds of the wardroom. 'Let's have a cocktail party, shall we?' he whinged aloud, mimicking old Admiral Barkalot's shrill, haughty voice. 'And let's have some junior rating stand all night long in full dress uniform, just in case some drunken officer wants to impress his young lady with a stroll and a smooch on a clapped-out old sailing ship.'

Chucking the remains of his cold coffee over the side, he smiled mutinously as he threw the mug as well. It made a lovely smashing sound when it hit the bottom of the concrete dry dock. Sighing despondently at the gangway clock, he set off for yet another pointless lap of the upper gun deck. So deep was his pit of misery that he barely noticed the bright-green-and-white aircraft lights racing west through the night sky.

Being an avid lover of maps and charts, Archie immediately recognized the shape of Portsmouth harbour and The Solent to the west of it. Flying between them and the Isle of White, he aligned the Skyshark perfectly for an approach to Bournemouth.

'Here we are,' he announced one minute later, banking the Skyshark to starboard over the sprawling mass of bright lights below. 'Bournemouth is our next turning point,' he said, bringing the Skyshark around in a leisurely curve, onto a new heading of forty-five degrees.

'Portsmouth dead ahead, just beyond the New Forest,' he declared happily. His broad, confident smile hid the fact that his next manoeuvre could best be described as sheer lunacy.

Stopping on the poop deck above Admiral Nelson's cabin, Hughes leaned on the thick wooden gunwale, gazing indifferently across the harbour. The small Gosport ferry had just tied up and was disgorging its few passengers, whilst beyond, a large cruise liner, the size of a horizontal block of flats, its decks ablaze with lights, slowly headed towards the mouth of The Solent. But it was a tiny set of lights high in the sky over the New Forest to the west that pricked his curiosity.

He could plainly see its red-and-green navigation lights and its bright-white headlight. Having been trained in aircraft recognition, he was well versed in the movements of aircraft. And it quickly dawned on him that whatever that was, it was dropping vertically out of the western sky, which meant that it was both descending and approaching.

He was in a yawn when a horrible thought suddenly struck him. The week had seen the start of a large naval exercise involving several different nations, so Portsmouth Harbour was virtually empty, so whatever that craft was, it wasn't a helicopter returning to a ship. But Commodore Haven had a nasty habit of inviting foreign top brass exercising at sea to pop over for a quick beer and a bite to eat. He looked down dubiously at the empty drill square next to the *Victory*, which doubled as a helipad.

'No, that can't be right,' Hughes said aloud as the cogs in his lethargic mind slowly started to turn. 'If that helicopter is bringing visitors, then there would surely be a ground crew waiting in the drill square.' He shrugged and headed toward the galley to scavenge some food. 'No, can't be,' he huffed dismissively. 'Whoever they are, they're obviously destined for somewhere in the New Forest.'

With Bournemouth behind them, Archie approached the New Forest in a rapid descent whilst maintaining a scary speed of 300 mph.

'Jagdar's teeth, boy,' said Boff, his coned eyes fixed nervously upon the speedometer. 'If you're intending to heave to and pick up some weapons, you'd better put the brakes on… *drastically.*'

Archie laughed. 'Einstein's underpants, Boff, haven't you figured it out yet? We're not going to purchase a weapon from the Royal Navy. We're going to *steal* one!'

Lights flashed frighteningly quickly beneath them as they roared towards the Solent, the stretch of water that separated the New Forest from Gosport. Much to Boff's relief, Archie finally activated the air brakes and throttled back. He felt the Skyshark shudder as two large flaps housed in the aircraft's wings were thrust out to ninety degrees, causing immense drag and making the craft's air speed drop off rapidly.

With a fresh, steaming mug of coffee in one hand and a

plate of toasted bacon sandwiches in the other, Hughes clomped his way up the old wooden stairs from the galley back to the main gun deck. He was about to return to the quartermaster desk when the strange approaching lights caught his attention. He could plainly hear the engines of the aircraft, and priding himself on his knowledge of aircraft recognition, was a little miffed that he couldn't place it. At first, he thought, by the gruff roaring tone of its engines, that it might be a vintage aircraft of some kind, but its speed was far too fast.

Suddenly, his brain screamed as it acknowledged just what was happening. 'Blimey… *Terrorists!*'

He dropped his half-eaten bacon sandwich as his greasy fingers frantically punched in the number for the dockyard emergency services.

'This is the dockyard emergency line,' said an electronic voice.

'This is the Quartermaster HMS Victory,' he blurted anxiously, 'I can see an unidentified aircraft heading straight for me. It appears to be on a collisi—'

'Please press three for the harbourmaster, four for dockyard security, or five for any other enquiries.'

'Argh, bloomin' answering machines!' Stupid flippin' things!' Hughes watched dumbstruck as the mysterious aircraft continued on its collision course with the Victory. 'Ruddy hell,' he mumbled in disbelief, 'they're going to ram us!'

Paralysed with indecision, the gibbering sailor suddenly found his feet rooted to the wooden deck. However, the Royal Navy, being masters of dealing with a crisis, had already prepared Able Seaman Hughes for just such a situation.

Like a still from an old horror film, the image of his stone-faced drill instructor, the dreaded Chief Petty Officer Blocker, suddenly swamped his freaked-out mind. With his shiny black boots, polished peak cap, and brass-tipped wooden pace stick, his loud, thunderous words of wisdom filled his head, stomping all over his panicking brain: 'What the hell are you waiting for, Hughes? Run, you idiot!'

Before he knew it, his legs were off and running. Not daring to look back, he descended the sixty-foot-long gangway in seconds, clearing the last three steps in a single bound. Hitting the tarmacked drill square hard, his wobbly legs buckled, sending him rolling one way, his cap flying the other. With Blocker's tyrannical voice still shouting in his head, he was back on his feet instantly, sprinting towards the nearest cover. Darting to the left, he raced away from the navy's flagship and across the top end of the drill square before diving behind an old iron cannon.

'Ease up, laddie,' said Boff anxiously as the stern of the Victory loomed large in front of them, 'or we'll hit that old ship there!'

'Hit it?' Archie smirked with a wild gleam in his eye. 'We're going to ram it!'

The two-hundred-year-old wooden-framed glass windows of Admiral Nelson's cabin exploded inward as ten tonnes of Skyshark smashed into the stern of the HMS Victory at fifty miles per hour. The blunt face of the flying submarine bulldozed its way through the cabin, crushing the captain's table and chairs and pulverising the ornate writing desk before ramming through two twelve-inch oak supporting beams.

As the Skyshark exploded out of the front door to Nelson's cabin, the thick, immovable bulk of the rear mast presented itself directly in front of them. With a split second to act, Archie pressed a small button on his control column with his left thumb. From beneath them came a sharp hiss of air, followed instantaneously by two loud thwacks.

The Skyshark lurched to an abrupt stop, the pair of them being mercilessly catapulted forward against their restraining safety belts.

Positioned precisely on top of two massive wooden grates, two half-metre-long metal harpoons had been fired. Passing through the holes in the grating, each harpoon punched its way through the middle gun deck and buried its sharp point deep into the planking of the lower gun deck.

'Jagdar's teeth,' squeaked Boff, gasping for breath, 'what have you done, boy?'

'That's the Skyshark's compressed-air harpoon-anchoring system,' groaned Archie as two wire drums whined into life and began slowly reeling them down. With a quick glance both ways, Archie niftily swung the little flying sub like a pendulum then, at the last moment, jammed the port and starboard wing tips into the scuppers running all along the bottom of gunwales on both sides of the quarterdeck.

As the Skyshark hit the deck with a heavy, resounding clunk, the harpoon anchor wires snapped taut with a sharp twang.

'Jagdar's scaly butt,' Boff grumbled, glaring at Archie. 'You call that a landing?'

'That was the easy bit,' croaked Archie nervously. 'The long slits at deck level in the bulwarks act as drains to spill away seawater during storms. They'll also make perfect extra anchor points for the Skyshark.'

From outside came the agonizing groans of ancient timbers and the sharp popping of metal rivets as the old wooden ship shuddered under the extra weight of the Skyshark.

'Jagdar's teeth, boy,' growled Boff, 'what are you doing? What are you playing at?'

'We're going to steal this ship, cannons and all,' he said, smiling roguishly.

Happy that the Skyshark was safely secured, Archie slowly pushed the throttles forward, powering up the two Red Dragon engines. As he felt his flying machine start to lift, they suddenly became aware of a strangled creaking sound coming from all around the old wooden warship.

'Hornswoggle me giblets, boy,' croaked Boff, his eyes frantically searching for the source of the noise, 'what the mukluks is that?'

'The only thing that's holding this ship upright in this dry dock are the thirty-six, eighteen-inch-thick wooden beams,' announced Archie cheekily. 'My delicate landing has dislodged some, and our take-off will shed the rest.'

'Beams be damned,' Boff replied. 'If we're spliced together, then let's get the hell out of here, huh?'

From outside came the sound of a timber scraping against the ship's hull, its juddering motion lasting but a few seconds before it crashed into the bottom of the dry dock. Moments later came the sound of other beams falling.

'That doesn't sound good,' agreed Archie. 'Definitely time to go!'

Outside, several more beams twisted and fell, the mighty

old ship creaking as her wooden keel groaned under the stress. Archie knew she wasn't going to stay upright much longer—there were only two quivering beams balancing a hull weighing three and a half thousand tonnes.

'Jagdar's teeth, boy,' snapped Boff, 'whatever you're going to do, do it now!'

'We need to ease this old ship out of the dry dock,' offered Archie, gently nudging the throttles forward, smiling at the sound of the two responding Rolls-Royce engines. 'We came here to get firepower, not match wood!'

'Hello? Hello? Is that the office of the day?' shouted Able Seaman Hughes into the telephone he was strangling.

From his new hiding place, an old-fashioned red telephone box up on the high-rise tourist walkway on the far side of the square, Hughes could see it all, both the strange aircraft and the destruction it had caused. For some unknown reason, the weird-looking aircraft had deliberately rammed Nelson's cabin, passing completely through before coming to rest on the Victory's stern.

'Hello, this is the wardroom HMS Nelson duty steward speaking,' came a bored female voice. 'How can I help you?'

'Get the officer of the day, at the rush. HMS Victory is being attacked!'

The voice on the other end of the phone went silent for a few seconds then tentatively asked, 'Is this Sub-lieutenant Granger playing one of his silly pranks again?'

'No it flipping isn't!' Hughes shouted into the receiver. 'It's the duty quartermaster on board HMS Victory. Now damn well get me the duty officer of the day.'

The phone went quiet, but in the background, he could hear the stewardess talking to someone else. 'He says the Victory's being attacked, sir!'

'Piffle!' declared an old, male voice. 'Must be drunk or mad.' With that, the line went dead.

Hughes, more angry than terrified, jabbed at the keypad again.

'Hello, this is the wardroom HMS Nelson duty steward speaking. How may I help you?'

'I am not flipping drunk or mad!' shouted Hughes, spitting on the receiver. 'Now get me the blooming duty officer of the day, immediately!'

A very annoyed man with a shrill voice snatched the phone off the stewardess and growled into the receiver, 'Admiral Barkalot here. What the blazes is going on?'

'Sir,' blurted Hughes, 'an unidentified aircraft has crashed through Admiral Nelson's cabin and landed on the quarterdeck of the Victory.' From the far side of the drill square came the scraping sound of the last two heavy wooden beams crashing to the bottom of the dry dock. This was followed by a long, loud, tortuous creaking sound. 'Blimey, all the supporting beams have gone,' he cried. 'She's listing to port!'

'Beams dropping, listing to port...' The admiral scowled. 'Are you stark staring mad?'

'Holy cow,' gasped Hughes. 'I-I-It's rising into the air!'

'What's rising into the air?' snapped the admiral. 'Explain yourself, man!'

'It's the Victory, sir. It's floating out of its dry dock,' said Hughes numbly. '*It's flying!*'

'Don't be ridiculous, man,' huffed the admiral. 'That's a three-and-a-half-thousand-tonne warship. There's no way it could possibly fly.'

'But it is, sir!'

Slowly, with her aged timbers creaking and groaning in protest, HMS Victory, the flagship of the Royal Navy rose up and out of the dry dock that had been her home for over a century. Swinging majestically to starboard, the tip of her bowsprit mast pierced, like a giant tin opener, then shattered a row of windows in the office building on the opposite side of the square.

'Able Seaman Hughes!' shouted the admiral furiously. 'What the hell's going on, man?'

'Blimey, sir,' muttered Hughes in stunned disbelief. 'It's *gone!*'

'Gone? What do you mean, it's gone?'

Gobsmacked and wide-eyed, Hughes stared in silence as the flying wooden warship with its two thrusting white tails of flame roared away into the dark night sky.

'Like I just said, sir,' he uttered matter-of-factly. 'HMS Victory's gone, as in, it's not blooming here anymore!'

Chapter 31

The Planet Hexx.
In the Shadow of the Great
Amphitheatre of Garrknock.

Standing forty feet tall, the sewer outlet had been deliberately designed to look like the head of a hideously ugly gargoyle, with three large, yellow, venom-filled eyes and a huge open mouth full of pointed fangs that spewed a four-foot-wide tongue of foul-smelling black filth. It was rumoured that just one glimpse could send even the bravest of warriors scrabbling for clean trousers.

Originally carved from interlocking blocks of pristine granite, decades later, its once-crisp surface was weather-scarred and dirty, its large, round eyes dull with age. Its once-smooth, sparkling stone skin had become a living latticework of creeping vines.

A huge, round grille bolted to the sewer front barred their way. Because it had been made of two-inch-thick, bewitched genie iron, it was renowned throughout the genieverse as being virtually unbreakable. Its gaps were big enough to let the sewage, garbage, and odd bodily part out but small enough to prevent even the tiniest of criminals from getting in.

Each of the three massive hinges that held the grill in place was as thick as a man's arm, and the lock on its opposite side was the width of a bull's head and undoubtedly bewitched. Nogga pointed his new toy at the three huge hinges.

'Them's beefy-looking hinges, bro,' offered Skatt.

Nogga flipped the weapon over and turned the operation-mode-selector switch to Cutter. He hoisted it up on one shoulder, aimed at the top hinge, and took a deep breath. When he pulled the trigger, an aggressive red beam shot out with a kick like a mule. For a few worrying seconds, Skatt watched the hissing beam burn deep grooves all over the top of the tunnel entrance before his brother wrestled the beam onto his desired target.

Sweating heavily and with aching arms, Nogga eventually brought the beam to bear on the top hinge. In one downward motion, he sliced through the thick metal hinges so quickly that he'd barely reached the bottom one before the top one creaked apart. The glowing red wounds dripped tiny globs of white-hot molten metal, which fell onto the damp soil, briefly spitting and fizzing before turning cold and black.

The heavy iron grille seemed to teeter just for a moment, held only by creepers and decades of encrusted dirt. Then, after a few seconds, it fell as if in slow motion, landing with a splash onto the wet embankment, splattering the pair of them with dollops of smelly mud.

As the pair stood quietly congratulating themselves, neither noticed the mammoth keystone at the top of the gaping mouth skew precariously sideways.

Skatt wrinkled his nose as he peered into the gloomy hole. 'Blimey, this place stinks.'

Nogga's nose wrinkled—it was awful. 'We're Mmickys,' he

announced proudly. 'Suck it in and relish the tang. After all, to city dwellers, it's just a sewer system, but to us, it's a highway to illicit treasure!'

'It still stinks,' grumbled Skatt, 'and I can't see a thing.' He looked down at his four paws. 'And just how am I supposed to hold a torch with these useless things, let alone light it?' From behind, he heard a soft click, and suddenly the whole sewer was lit up as bright as day.

'That nutty professor calls this thing a "lamp." It doesn't burn like a normal fat torch.' He pushed the lamp's bright lens right in front of Skatt's shocked face. 'See? No flames!'

'Huh. That's weird!' muttered Skatt as he edged away from the strange light.

From his bag of goodies, Nogga pulled out a map of the sewer system. After a few seconds, he pointed the light down the tunnel. 'Straight down there,' he announced firmly. 'About two hundred yards in, there should be a junction.'

Stepping forward warily, Skatt reluctantly entered the steadily flowing stream of liquid filth, immediately sinking to his armpits. 'Argh, this stuff's gross!' he whimpered.

'Oh Baldizar, my mighty wondrous El Supremo,' teased Nogga, who had slithered up the tunnel wall and was now hanging upside down, 'give me some legs so I can run fast.' He shook his head glibly at his brother. 'What a stupid thing to wish for.'

Skatt snarled angrily at his smirking brother. 'Okay, so maybe legs weren't the best idea I've ever had. But what am I going do about getting through this lot?'

'Try holding your breath,' Nogga said, laughing as he slithered deeper into the tunnel. 'Or if you can't manage that, you could always try walking along that small ledge to your left!'

'What? Where?' spluttered Skatt, his chin dangerously close to the waste.

Nogga ignored his brother, but as he slithered forward, he sneakily glanced back nevertheless, just to be sure he'd made it onto the narrow path.

Although there was a steady breeze blowing through the tunnel, the stench was truly stomach churning—and when a thieving Mmicky admits to that, then it really does smell. But nevertheless, they forged on, and after about ten minutes, they came to the junction in the tunnel.

'Jagdar, save us,' moaned Skatt. 'There's three blooming tunnels. Which one?'

Nogga took a moment to examine each tunnel in turn then declared, 'We take the one on the right.'

Skatt scratched his head with a mucky paw, his brow crinkling with questions. 'How can you be sure it's that one?'

Nogga slithered to the entrance of the left tunnel. For a few seconds, he scanned the bubbling surface of the flowing filth then reached in and plucked something out. It was a long, bony limb with a shattered claw on the end. 'This,' he remarked, shoving the decaying arm under his brother's nose, 'used to belong to a doughnut crab. Note the end of the arm.'

Skatt dully studied the arm. 'It's a scratched bone. So what?'

'Those scratches indicate that it was gauged out of its owner's shoulder, no doubt whilst it was still alive, probably with a blunt knife. Very painful!'

Skatt shivered with disgust.

438

'I would say that that tunnel comes from the torture chambers under Fortress Hexx.' He casually tossed the limb back into the river of filth, turning his attention to the middle tunnel.

'Note the distinct aroma of this tunnel, brother,' said Nogga.

'I know that horrible stink.' Skatt cringed, wrinkling his nose. 'Yuk, smells like a—'

'Exactly. A toilet smells the same no matter which planet you're on,' declared Nogga, moving swiftly to the last tunnel. 'So, I think we can safely say that this one leads to a certain area under the great amphitheatre of Garrknock!'

Skatt jumped into the third tunnel, landing with a squelchy splat next to his brother. 'So, what's so special about this one?'

Nogga sighed heavily. 'If you were a mighty genie, Skatt, would you walk through sewage to get to your treasure trove?'

'Nah, course not. Blooming stupid if they did.'

'Look at the floor,' said Nogga.

Skatt studied the bare stone floor then looked back at his brother's expectant face. 'It's a floor,' he offered. 'So what?'

'Jagdar, give me strength,' muttered Nogga. 'It's dry and clean, you dummy!'

'Oh yeah!' Skatt chuckled dumbly. 'This must lead to—'

A sudden sharp crack echoed out of the tunnel from which they had just come, stifling his words. Both Mmickys gave each other a puzzled look then turned and stared into the darkness.

Seconds later, off in the distance, they heard a soft whisper, which rapidly became a deep rumbling. Moments after that, a single smelly gust of air blew out of the tunnel.

'Er, bro, what do you think that was?' asked Skatt, prudently placing his brother between himself and whatever his vivid imagination told him was lurking in the dark tunnel.

'Well,' pondered Nogga, rubbing one of his chins, 'I can smell soil and the cold night air, so if I had to hazard a guess—'

'Huh,' interrupted Skatt huffily. 'All I can smell is—'.

'Well, that's to be expected, isn't it?' Nogga asked, laughing. 'After all, you're a lot closer to the ground than I am!'

'Ha naffin' ha,' barked Skatt sarcastically. But when he looked over to his brother, he wasn't laughing anymore but staring at the ground. 'What's up, bro?'

Slithering forward, he pointed at something on the floor of the tunnel junction. 'You can forget that strange noise. It seems we're not the only ones down here!'

'Really?' said Skatt.

Nogga said nothing. He just pointed to an ogre-sized footprint in the dust. 'Jagdar's teeth,' he spat, 'them's blooming chieftain boot marks.'

'They sure is bro, but why are they down here?'

'Why not?'

'Because when we arrived back from Bleak, and you went off to stuff your face, I made some discrete enquiries about the deployment of the chieftains in the theatre.' He gave his brother a knowing look. 'Apparently, Baldizar has ordered the entire regiment to the amphitheatre. Even the ones from the watchtowers guarding the forbidden wall are there.'

'What about them strange ones, old Redhorn and his bunch of minotaur's? Them that bleed green, that attacked the maggot and his mates back on Bleak?'

Nogga didn't have an answer for that one. He just stared at Skatt, buttoned up his waistcoat, adjusted his stovepipe hat, then slithered into the dry tunnel.

Skatt nervously followed his brother, his tiny mind full of grisly images of evil, nasty things lurking in the dark and bad-tempered chieftains.

Outside in the moonlight, glimpsed through the swirling mist covering the surface of the Forbidden Lake, a trail of bubbles slowly snaked its way up the tributary towards the sewer entrance. It came to an abrupt halt before the gargoyle's face. Slowly, a pair of eyes the size of hairy toffee apples rose curiously out of the rank dark water.

Something was wrong.

The face that had stood for countless moons, disgorging its banquet of tasty morsels into the lake, was no more. With a screaming snort, the angry dreadly belched its fury, frothing the surrounding water with yucky green bubbles that popped with small flashes of fire in the cold night air as it hurried away to tell the others. Inside the gargoyle's fallen head, the foul blackness was pooling, its murky depths flowing back up the tunnel, its acidic bite eating ravenously away at the centuries-old foundations of the amphitheatre.

Chapter 32

'It's Merlin's mark. It had to be,' muttered Grizwold. 'Every creature knows that the sign of the rippling cross is the symbol of Merlin's marauders and their fight for freedom.'

One was high on the left side of the boy's inner skull and the other, low on the left lobe of his brain. In themselves, they were a rarity, but they remained synchronized, even whilst Archie's brain cavorted insanely. It was uncanny. And then there was the fact that Archie's brain had almost quadrupled in size, its swollen veins pulsating with oxygen-enriched blood, its whole mass flashing brighter and faster than a hummingbird's wing.

Grizwold wondered if he could really be the one. The signs were right, as was the timing. Could the fact that I'm still in the boy's head, be an indicator that my mission is not yet over. He felt his heart quiver as a sudden flush of goose pimples rushed his body. After so many centuries of tyrannical rule under Baldizar and the council of the power ten genies, maybe Archie really was the rainbow child who would lead the rebellion.

As a mentor, he had nothing to offer the boy, so surely his work was done. Yet instead of being discharged back to the fruit tree with all the other Mutmuts, he was still in the boy's head. Even more inconceivable was that instead of being glad to be rid of him, the youngling wanted him to stay.

The last twelve candle marks had been a roller coaster of a ride, and none of it made any sense. But something cried out to him from the depths of history, telling him that he must stay with the boy, for the youngling was on the cusp of something monumental.

Sliding forward, he grasped Archie's optic nerves, eager to see what was going on in the outside world.

Archie was staring past the deck of the *Victory* at another, much bigger, weird-looking flying machine just off to their right.

Archie, he thalked, *why does that human in the other flying machine look so worried?*

Archie laughed. He knew he shouldn't—he'd placed that poor man in a terrible predicament. But it wasn't his fault. *Well, that man's in a bit of a pickle now,* thalked Archie. *You see, if he tells anyone about seeing an unidentified flying object, then he risks being ridiculed by his boss and all the other pilots. However, if he officially reports seeing a two-hundred-year-old sailing ship flying through the skies, they will probably revoke his pilot's licence and definitely lock him away in a padded cell!*

And either of these things wouldn't be good? ventured Grizwold naively.

Oh no, very bad indeed. His best option is to ignore us and hope that none of his three hundred passengers have seen us, either.

Can we help the poor man? asked Grizwold.

Doing that now, thalked Archie, pushing his control

column gently forward. *We're starting our descent towards the falls now. In a few seconds, we will simply vanish into the clouds and out of his life forever.*

Arnold Plunkett wiped the sweat from his brow, glaring up at the overcast sky. The oppressive, ugly grey blanket of cloud that smothered the Niagara Falls, blocked out the sun, and locked in the oppressive humidity hadn't changed all week. Add to that the billowing spray from millions of tonnes of plunging water, and there was the reason why he turned sprightly on his heels and headed back to the sanctuary of the souvenir stockroom.

He stoically weaved his way through the meandering mass of gawping sightseers, deftly avoiding eye contact. Sidestepping boisterous youngsters was easy—it was ignoring the constant barrage of questions that was the tricky bit. He chuckled to himself as he watched the younger official wardens frantically pulling selfie-seeking adolescents from the wrong side of the safety barriers.

But even a self-confessed freeloader like himself had the occasional attack of conscience, especially when it happened to be a child's voice.

'Look, Mommy!' shouted a whiny, irritating little girl. 'It's a sailing ship!'

'Now don't be silly, Prudence,' snapped her mother haughtily, not even bothering to look up from her magazine. 'Ships sail on the sea, not in the clouds.'

'But Mommy,' persisted the girl, 'that one does. *Look!*'

The child's mother gave a frustrated sigh, half-heartedly glancing over the safety rail at the tourist boats bobbing about on the water below. She scoffed. 'Oh, you silly child, those are the sightseeing boats.'

'No, not down there, silly Mommy,' nagged the child, tugging on the woman's coat sleeve. 'Up there, in the sky!'

With a loud, judgmental huff, the women slapped her magazine down and looked up, gasping in surprise. 'Oh my, it *is* a sailing ship!'

The irksome child sneered. '*See?* Told you, Mommy!'

At five-foot-four, all Arnold could see was the backs of heads. As the child's voice tugged at his heartstrings—they always did—he grudgingly turned and plunged back into the chattering throng. 'Make way, please,' he announced sternly. 'Warden coming through!'

It wasn't the parting of the Red Sea, but with a few well-aimed elbow jabs, it didn't take long to reach the little girl and her mother, especially since they had become surrounded by a large circle of people, all pointing at the sky and making inane comments.

He was about to assert his meagre authority when a loud, demanding voice beside him said, 'Hey you there, Mr Warden Man.' A woman wearing a garish orange dress and a ghastly matching hat stood with her arms crossed. 'Is there a film being shot here today?'

'No, ma'am, there isn't,' he said loudly enough for the whole crowd to hear. 'Those are just the normal sightseeing boats.'

A large man with a round head topped with a smattering of thinning grey hair grabbed him by the shoulder and declared in a loud Texas drawl, 'Do all your tourist boats sail in the sky, sonny?'

Arnold rubbed his aching head and pointed to the two ferryboats at the base of the falls. 'The "Maid of the Mist" on the right sir, and the "Maid of the Falls" is on the left. Neither of them are sailing ships.'

'Sonny, I'm not referring to your pair of tin tubs bobbing around down there,' continued the Texan, fixing him with a steely-eyed, wintry glare. 'I'm talking about that sailing ship up there!'

Arnold's mocking sigh was perhaps a little too coarse, drawing resentful tuts from those about him. 'I can assure you, sir,' he said, following the line of the gentleman's arm, 'that there is no such thing as a—' For a small man, he suddenly had large round eyes, almost as large as his gaping mouth. 'Saints preserve us, would you look at that. A flying ship!'

Even from ten miles away, the Niagara Falls were a truly spectacular sight.

'Jagdar's scaly hide, boy,' Boff said as Archie dropped down through the Skyshark's hatch, 'you took your time.'

Plopping back into the pilot's seat, Archie pinched his eyebrows together and frowned. 'Listen, Squid Boy,' he said between gulps of water, 'HMS Victory has a hundred forty-four cannons. You try loading them all by yourself!' He didn't let on that he'd stopped to admire the view several times.

'Fair point, shipmate,' Boff conceded, handing control of the Skyshark back to him but also noticing the faraway look in his eye. 'Egads, boy, you're tickling your eye patch again. What's troubling you?'

Archie's smile faded, replaced with a look of concern. 'We

will get there in time to save her,' he asked almost pleadingly, 'won't we?'

'Hornswoggle me giblets, boy, I won't lie to you.' He smiled weakly, the corners of his huge mouth quivering slightly. 'For a rescue, we're sailing close to the wind!'

It wasn't the answer Archie had hoped to hear, but then Boff was always brutally honest. 'You could have sugar coated it a bit, for my sake,' muttered Archie.

'That was sugar coated!' offered Boff, fixing both coned eyes on him. 'The truth's better than false hopes any day.'

As Archie gently eased back on the throttles, so the aggressive roar of the twin engines started to calm. He looked up at the middle computer screen, its coloured radar image of the ground below, bright and clear. The blue of the Atlantic was far behind them, leaving the screen predominantly green and grey with flecks of white as they flew over the Catskill Mountains at the northern end of the Appalachian range.

He had decided upon a slightly erratic flight path that would keep the Skyshark away from centres of population and prying eyes. They had crossed the coast between New York and Boston, and leaving Albany, Syracuse, and Rochester to the north, played dodgems with mountain peaks in a vague hope of not being spotted on either civilian or military radars.

Frankly, it astounded Archie, considering the size of the U.S. Air Force and the speed at which they could scramble interceptors, that they hadn't already been joined by a gaggle of fighter planes.

'Okay, we're ten miles from the falls,' said Archie, handing

Boff the bog spinner he'd stolen from Baldizar. 'The stall speed of this craft is sixty-five miles per hour, so I'll keep us at a steady seventy. Best you do your stuff and open the hydroportal.'

Whilst he watched his friend aligning the bog spinner, a horrible thought struck him. 'Boff, on the other side of that thin curtain of rushing water is solid rock!'

'Yeah,' replied Boff, not looking up.

'What if that bog spinner doesn't work?'

Boff gave him a cavalier grin then shrugged. 'Imagine a melon hitting a wall at great speed!'

Archie suddenly felt the icy hand of fate grasp his drumming heart.

'Don't worry,' added Boff. 'I'm sure old Jagdar's on the ball, and if he isn't, well, the Duster brothers will tell you what happened!' Smiling, Boff returned his attention to the bog spinner. He'd used many in his lifetime, but none were as richly sophisticated as that beauty. It really was a thing of beauty, a travel device truly befitting a supreme genie. Its handle was cast from a weighty chunk of the finest spungold, its grip formed by a swath of tiny gemstones, their combined brilliance easily matching a noonday sun. The pictograms on each reel were constructed from tiny slivers of polished stone, each forming a location icon that was instantly recognisable on any planet throughout the genieverse.

Skilfully he turned each of the three reels in sequence to their required positions. Reel one, entry time, he set for plus eight minutes. Reel two, entry location, he set for the Niagara Falls, Earth. The last reel, exit location, he wound round until it aligned with an icon representing the Storming Kaleidoscope Falls on the planet Hexx.

As the last reel locked into place with a soft, reassuring click, so the hydroportal began to work its magic.

'Look!' shouted an excited, young voice. 'Look at the water! It's going all shiny!'

Arnold Plunkett, the large Texan, and all those about them simultaneously turned to where the little girl was pointing and gasped in wonder.

There, materializing as if by magic in the exact centre of the falls, was what could only be described as a giant arched rainbow door filled with shimmering crystals. Confusion reigned as voices cried in awe, 'Look at the pretty rainbow forming in the water,' whilst others yelled hysterically, 'It's the end of the world!' and 'The aliens are coming!'

'Calm down, everybody. Calm down,' said Warden Plunkett, eager to quash the growing panic. 'What you're witnessing is simply a trick of the light. It happens all the time. There's nothing to worry about.'

'And I suppose that old wooden sailing ship heading towards it is just a trick of the light too?' demanded the frowning Texan.

Plunkett sighed heavily as he watched the rapidly approaching ship, which seemed to fill the entire sky before him. From a pocket, he calmly removed a small, well-thumbed, red book. The Niagara Falls Warden's Application Instructions was his definitive guide to the rules and regulations covering any possible occurrence.

After thumbing through its index, Plunkett casually tossed the book into the falls, spun on a heel, and shouted over his shoulder, 'RUN AWAY!'

Archie glanced at the radar. Three miles to run. His eye glided across the Skyshark's controls, reading and assimilating every ounce of data he could. His old Cold War flying machine, against all odds, was performing flawlessly, so he had to wonder what that weird vibration in his boots was.

'Right, Archie, me boy,' said Boff in an unusually serious tone, 'there's something I'd better tell you.'

Two miles to run. 'Boff, I haven't got time for this now,' snapped Archie, ignoring the hysterical voice in his head and pushing the flight column forward, sending the Skyshark and Victory into a shallow dive. 'I need to score a bull's-eye in that shining rainbow in front of us, or we're squashed flies!'

One mile to run.

'Jagdar's teeth boy, you better naffin' listen,' Boff said, forcefully grabbing his shoulder. 'We may be entering the hydroport at fifty feet above the water, but our exit on Hexx will be at ground level!'

Archie's head jerked sideways. 'What?!'

'Yes, ground level! Well, they are designed primarily for creatures that walk and crawl,' shot Boff defensively.

It was far too late to adjust their flight path, and the spray from the falling water had filled the Skyshark's windscreen. Impact was but seconds away. Suddenly, Archie felt very scared. He automatically pushed his body back into his seat, trying to escape the rock-hard death that was rushing towards him.

With sweaty, trembling hands, Archie gripped the flight column until his knuckles turned white. His chest felt as if it was in a vice crushing his pounding heart. Breathing was nearly impossible as he braced himself for impact. They covered the last hundred feet in a single heartbeat, the falling water's glassy, smooth surface blending with the spray and mist, turning reality into a hazy dream as they were instantly swallowed by the falls.

'You know, you would be able to see better,' said a scratchy female voice with a distinct Irish lilt, 'if you opened that eye of yours!'

Other than the strange voice and the pounding of his heart in his head, Archie could hear nothing. Either the hydroportal had worked, or they were dead. He forced his eye open. Everything looked normal. He relaxed his grip on the flight control column, and his fingers turned pink again. 'It worked.' He smiled. 'We're still alive!'

'My, my, but aren't you the clever one?' said the voice sarcastically.

Archie flicked his head about, looking for the owner of the voice.

'Up here, Archie Wilde, by this here moving-picture box.'

'Picture box?' repeated Archie, looking up and spying the meerkat casually leaning against the far computer screen. 'Blimey, not another spiv!'

'The name's O'Shornacy, but you can call me Maggy,' said the meerkat. 'You could also try being a tad more pleased to see me!'

Just like the other spivs who had appeared to him whilst hydroporting, she sported a bright-yellow bowler hat, a white collar with a yellow bow tie, and spats. However, as a feminine touch, the pipe in her claw was electric pink.

Archie eyed the little meerkat with suspicion. 'Let's have it,' he said bluntly. 'What's the bad news this time?'

'To be sure, we're not always the bearer of bad tidings, you know,' she replied, hurt by his cold insinuation.

'So, it's good news then?' asked Archie hopefully.

'Er, *no*,' replied Maggy after blowing a long line of square bubbles from her round, pink pipe.

Archie frowned glumly.

'Oh, by the way, Zephyar sends his congratulations on outwitting Baldizar's golden collar,' she offered, smiling. 'That Crown of Avalon, now that was a nice touch!' Before Archie could answer, she added, 'So, are we all ready to do battle with Old Buckethead's monstrous sky cruiser?'

'Oh, yes,' said Archie confidently. 'I've loaded and primed all of the cannons, and their fuses are ready.' He pulled out a Zippo lighter from a vest pocket, brandishing it like Excalibur. 'All I need to do is light them.'

'Hmmm,' said Maggy, pointing the stem of her pipe at him. 'There lies your problem, laddie.'

'Problem? What problem?' retorted Archie. 'A hundred forty-four cannons will make mincemeat of the Crimson Raptor.'

'Oh, I quite agree,' acknowledged Maggy, tipping her bowler hat to the back of her head. 'It's an awesome amount of firepower for anyone who has them at their disposal.'

Archie burst into laughter, which didn't intimidate the little meerkat at all. It merely made her frown. 'Of course I have cannons,' he said, gesturing with his hands. 'This ship is bristling with them.'

'A valid point, to be sure,' she conceded, using the corner of the screen to empty the bowl of her pipe, splattering it with disgusting yellowy-brown droplets. 'Perhaps I should clarify.

You don't have any *working* cannons!'

'Yes, I do,' he blurted adamantly. 'Every cannon is loaded with a powder bag, cannon ball, and wadding. I did them all myself.'

Maggy's hairy eyebrows knitted together like an angry caterpillar. 'Of course, you did check the powder bags before you loaded your precious cannons, didn't you?'

Archie's heart skipped a beat. 'Er, no,' he admitted hesitantly. 'Why should I? They are all from the powder room.'

Maggy shook her head disappointedly. 'Well, I'm sorry, me boy, but all your hard work's been in vain. You see, if the self-proclaimed genius before me had only checked a bag first, he would have found it full of sand, not black powder!'

'Sand?' Archie was confused.

'Yes, sand,' she repeated insensitively. 'This magnificent battleship of yours is a floating museum piece—you didn't really expect to find real gunpowder, did you?' Archie sagged into his seat as if suddenly side swiped by an angry ogre.

'B-but the cannon balls are real,' he offered pathetically. 'I just assumed—'

'Well, laddie, you assumed wrongly, didn't you?'

'Einstein's underpants,' he groaned despairingly, 'how could I have been so stupid? What do I flippin' do now?'

'Good question,' said Maggy, sliding her pipe into a tiny pocket. 'And when you think of something'—she winked at him mischievously— 'I'd do it really fast if I were you.'

'*Fast,*' echoed Archie. 'Why?'

The little meerkat stood, brushed herself down, then grinned. 'Because you're about to leap out of the hydroport any second now.'

The spiv winked out of existence right before Archie's wide, terror-filled eye, then instantly winked back in again.

'Oh, one other thing,' she added. 'How many Muzzberry pips do you have left?'

Archie didn't need to check. 'Four, why?'

'Best you be taking all of them now,' she advised, her roguish smile revealing two rows of crooked, smoke-stained teeth. 'Because you're going to need them!'

Chapter 33

THE TUNNELS BENEATH
THE AMPHITHEATRE OF GARRKNOCK

Sergeant Rockwolf was a veteran chieftain with twenty-five years of service, but that wasn't the only reason why everyone in his platoon held him in great esteem. The grizzled minotaur had the physique of an oak tree, immense strength, and skill at arms second to none. It was rumoured that he could clip the whiskers off a mouse with a battle axe from forty yards. But his true uniqueness lay with his uncanny sixth sense for danger.

'They're just like the others back in the fortress,' he growled to Corporal Mudgutts, stabbing the corpse with his broadsword. 'They have the skin of chieftains but are filled with putrid green goo.' Turning his massive bull's head, he surveyed the other bodies with disgust. 'Jagdar's teeth, I don't like this. It stinks of genie work!'

'Genie work, Sarge, or someone else?' asked Mudgutts.

'Grogg!' yelled Rockwolf. 'To me, now!' From further up the tunnel, a minotaur who had been examining one of the bodies snapped to attention then hurried forward. 'You're the medical orderly. What are these things, and why do they stink like a sewer?'

The minotaur was about to speak when a deep rumble

shook the tunnel. It wasn't a violent shaking, just enough to dislodge decades of old dust, crack the odd brick, and rattle their heavy iron boots.

'What the—' cried Mudgutts in alarm, steadying himself against the wall.

Sergeant Rockwolf didn't flinch. 'Easy, lads,' he said calmly. 'It's not a ground quake.' He rolled his eyes upwards, a roguish smile on his face. 'Methinks more that the drunken mob upstairs are indulging in a jig or two.'

Laughing at his sergeant's explanation, the medical orderly delivered his report. 'Sarge, I've never seen their likes before on any of the planets I've served on,' he offered, scratching a scraggly patch of thick hair under his large square jaw, 'and there's no mention of them or anything akin to them in the ancient healing scrolls.' He knelt next to the body, which had been neatly sliced in two. 'See here'—he poked the tip of a small dagger into the body's exposed midriff— 'no organs. Just this foul, fleshy green stuff.'

'In your educated opinion, Grogg, what are they?' Rockwolf asked.

'Well, this densely fibrous pale-green section has a definite fleshy texture to it, and this'—he pointed to the end of a small tube weeping a blackish green slime— 'has almost the same consistency as blood.' Then he tapped the hard skin with the blade tip. 'However, strange as it may seem, its skin has the texture of tree bark.' He wiped the goo from the blade, sheathed his dagger, stood, and looked Rockwolf in the eyes. 'In my opinion, Sarge, that thing, along with all the others, is more vegetable than creature!' He watched his sergeant's mouth open. 'And as for where they came from,'

Grogg continued, raising his thick, hairy brows in acknowledgement of the next obvious question, 'nobody seems to know. But the mess-deck scuttlebutt these days is rife with only one particular name!'

'A single name, huh?' muttered Rockwolf, his frowning brows forming hairy crescents over his big black eyes. 'Spit it out then, laddie.'

'Professor Ratchet Madspanner,' offered Grogg.

'Jagdar's fiery breath,' Rockwolf said with an angry snort. 'I might have guessed.' His right hand fell wishfully upon the pommel of his sheathed broadsword. 'That mangy human's been trouble ever since Baldizar first brought him to Hexx.'

'What now?' asked Mudgutts, lifting his torch high, its yellow flames licking the tunnel's curved brick ceiling. 'The traitor's moon is rising. Everyone, including Madspanner, will be at the amphitheatre right now.'

'Then that's where we're going,' snarled Rockwolf, viciously kicking one of the dead veggie chieftains out of his way. His platoon watched him stomp off down the tunnel, his heavy iron boots clattering on the stone floor. 'Follow me, minotaur's,' he bellowed over his shoulder. 'Weapons at the ready!'

'Hey, Sarge!' shouted a confused Mudgutts. 'Isn't the amphitheatre the other way?'

Rockwolf huffed brusquely, crunching to a halt. 'Jagdar's teeth, Mudgutts, I must have been really drunk the day I promoted you to corporal. Take a smell behind you.'

His corporal turned, shuddering at the tang of the rising tide of foul-smelling sewage lapping at their heels. 'Jagdar's teeth,' conceded Mudgutts, his loud, cheery laughter snapping Rockwolf out of his grim mood. 'Naffin' good point, Sarge.'

'Follow me. I know a short cut past the waking dream vault,' announced Rockwolf nonchalantly. 'Be there in under a quarter of a candle mark.'

'The waking dream vault?' spluttered Grogg, running up alongside him. 'But no one knows where that is, Sarge.'

'*I do!*' Rockwolf grinned roguishly, increasing his pace to a jog.

'By the curly horns of Jagdar, Sarge,' cried an impressed Mudgutts, 'where did you come upon such a secret?'

His question was quickly followed by a chorus from the rest of the truly astonished and overly excited platoon: 'C'mon, Sarge, spill the beans.'

Rockwolf stopped so suddenly that three of his minotaur's crashed into him. 'Let's just put it this way, lads,' he said with a grin, puffing out his enormous chest proudly. 'After a heavy night on some of the finest Best Majestic Gutstrangler ale I've ever swilled down my throat, I rather foolishly accepted a challenge from a very dubious character I'd met in the Pig Stickers Arms.'

'And?' cried the whole platoon in feverish harmony.

'Well…' Rockwolf smirked, slapping his corporal hard enough on the back to rattle his teeth. 'Let's just say that I sort of ended up somewhere I shouldn't have been!'

The subterranean passage erupted with deep, bellowing laughter. 'Is it easy to find this vault, then, Sarge?' asked a naïve young minotaur.

Rockwolf winked knowingly at his fresh face. 'Jagdar's teeth, laddie, the Waking Dream Vault is so well hidden and cunningly camouflaged that even the genies need a map to find it!'

'*I've found it!*' cried Skatt, eagerly wagging his tail. 'Look, here it is!'

Nogga slithered forward, pressing so close to the tunnel wall that he could have licked the mould off. 'Where?' he asked, removing his stovepipe hat and scratching his bald, befuddled head. 'I can't see anything!'

'Not up there, dummy,' Skatt said, pawing at the floor. 'Down here!'

'Jagdar's teeth.' Nogga huffed disappointedly, dropping flat on his huge belly. 'That's not a door—that's a brick with a hole in it.'

'Blind and stupid,' muttered Skatt. 'Look, it's a door, I can see a tiny handle and a blooming keyhole too!'

'Blimey, you're right, bro,' he agreed, cringing as he heard his waistcoat's shiny buttons scraping along the rough stone floor. 'But why would a genie who is as tall as a horse build a door fit only for a mouse? It makes no sense. I mean, it's not mentioned in the rhyme.'

'What rhyme?'

'Blimey, bro.' Nogga flicked Skatt's ear. 'Ma recited it enough blooming times!

'Out of sight but plain to all,
The door to open, just quote the scrawl.
No bolts to slide, no locks to click,
Then saunter in and take your pick.'

'What a load of twoddle!' sniped Skatt.

'Large or small,' said Nogga, thoughtfully stroking his chins, 'it's not the size of the door that matters but the spell cast upon it!'

'What about these ancient words above the door?' added Skatt. 'Could they be a clue?'

Shoving his brother aside, Nogga squashed his piggy snout hard against the tiny door. There was indeed a single line of ancient words chiselled into the stone.

To Skatt's astonishment, instead of his brother cursing his bad luck and tail-whipping him, he simply shuffled backwards, laughing. 'The ancient tongue isn't a problem, then?' asked Skatt quizzically.

Rolling aside, Nogga yanked open the professor's carpetbag. 'No problem at all, bro,' he announced, brandishing a shiny, flat, black glass thing in front of his brother's bewildered eyes. 'Because I have this!'

Skatt watched, enthralled as his mumbling brother began eagerly jabbing the slice of black glass with a podgy finger.

'Push the flat button on its top,' he heard him say, 'then lightly touch the flat glass with a fingertip.' He almost dropped the gadget as a bunch of funny-looking little pictures suddenly appeared on its glass front. Skatt watched Nogga's chubby little index finger hover over them as if hunting for one particular sign. Then with a squeak of joy, he aimed the object at the tiny door and lightly touched one that looked like a funny little box with a single round eye.

Without warning, a flash of light from the mobile phone's camera lit up the tunnel, startling the pair of them.

'Jagdar's teeth!' cried Skatt. 'What the blooming heck was that?'

Nogga unzipped a big toothy smile. 'This small glass box thing has just taken a picture of the writing above the door,' he announced smugly. 'Now, if I touch this little picture that looks like a tiny head, it will—' Before his incredulous eyes, the ancient words suddenly became readable.

'Well?' barked Skatt impatiently. 'What does it say?'

'Hmm. Apparently,' Nogga answered with a shrug, 'all we have to do to open the door is *ask!*'

'Well, go on, then.' Skatt panted eagerly. 'Ask it!'

'Er... okay, I will,' said Nogga, dusting himself down and puffing out his chest before commanding in a loud, pretentious voice, 'Door open!'

Nothing happened.

'*Door open!*' he commanded with more gusto.

Rather annoyingly, nothing happened.

'You sure them words is right?' asked Skatt.

'Yes,' snapped Nogga. 'I followed the instruction told to me by the little picture, so why hasn't it opened?'

'Oh, begs yours pardon, sir,' scoffed Skatt, 'I was only asking.'

'Sir,' said Nogga, mulling the word over in his mind. 'Those humans always use silly words when they ask for something. But what was it?'

'Give,' offered Skatt.

'No, no, that's not it,' said Nogga, stroking his chins.

'Gizzit?'

'No, it's more, well, pleasant sounding.'

'Gizzit me!' yapped Skatt proudly.

Nogga tail whipped him smartly on his rump. 'Will you please be quiet,' he snapped. 'I'm trying to... it's please,' he suddenly shouted, excitedly bouncing on his huge belly. 'The secret word is please.'

Skatt, rubbing his stinging butt, crawled up alongside him just as he said, 'Open please!'

The speed at which the spell reacted startled them both.

From deep within the tunnel wall came a crisp click, followed by a heavy metallic clunk. Then came the sound of gears meshing, pistons pumping, and heavy stones being dragged both to the left and the right. Suddenly, the ground beneath them began to tremble. Fearing trouble, Nogga dropped his torch and slithered backwards and up the far tunnel wall at great speed, whilst Skatt vanished into a dark recess.

Like the tiles of a giant Chinese jigsaw puzzle, the small stones surrounding the tiny door slowly started to move. One by one, they began to rearrange themselves in a pattern that doubled the size of the door each time. Every movement was neat and snappy with no juddering or faltering, and within seconds, the tiny door had grown to a hole ten feet in height. Lastly, with a resounding swish, the crown stone slid into place, finishing the arch above the fully opened portal.

The pair stared slack jawed then excitedly slithered closer to the newly formed door in the tunnel wall. They could hardly believe their luck—two lowly, gutter-born Mmickys had finally found and opened the Waking Dream Vault!

'Skatt, Skatt, look. We've done it!' Cried Nogga, excitedly spitting drool. 'We've actually found the council of the power ten genies' treasure trove. We're rich!' Proudly replacing his dented stovepipe hat on his head, he turned and frowned. 'Skatt!' he shouted impatiently. 'Where in Jagdar's name are you?'

'You sure it's safe to go in there?' came his frightened voice from the dark.

Nogga laughed. 'Jagdar's teeth, you're a wimpy mutt. Come here and relish the fact that we're the most famous Mmickys in the genieverse!'

'Ah, bro?' said Skatt, trotting out of the gloom. 'There's a horrible pong coming from down there and a sort of clippy-clopping com—'

Grabbing his brother by the scruff of the neck, Nogga had an evil glint in his eyes and was set to hurl him through the stone doorway, when—

'Well, well, well,' boomed a gruff voice. 'And just what do we have here, then?'

Nogga froze, holding a panicking Skatt dangling in mid-air.

Sergeant Rockwolf stomped out of the darkness, his heavy metal boots sparking on the flagstones. 'I know you. You're that thieving little Mmicky they call Nogga, the dumb one of the two.' He glanced inquisitively about the tunnel then snorted in Nogga's face. 'Where's that scheming, toe-rag brother of yours?'

The whole platoon roared with laughter as Nogga meekly looked down at the quaking mutt in his hands.

'Methinks someone has fallen foul of a genie spell, huh, Sarge,' Corporal Mudgutts said, laughing as he loomed over the quivering pair.

'I-I-It was Baldizar who did this to me,' offered Skatt, both embarrassed and annoyed at the minotaur's' relentless laughter.

'Oh, Baldizar himself, huh?' Rockwolf smirked, leaned forward, and snorted in Skatt's face. 'Your past indiscretions finally caught up with you, ah?'

'No, actually, it was self-defence,' blurted Nogga, his tongue speaking before his tiny brain could think. 'El Supremo knocked him down in the street, and Skatt drew his sword on him.'

Instantly, the chieftains stopped laughing. All looks of amusement suddenly changed to that of mild admiration.

'You wouldn't be lying to me, thief, would you?' growled Rockwolf menacingly.

'May Jagdar dine on my roasted guts if I am,' grovelled Nogga.

Sergeant Rockwolf knelt on one knee, his massive frame dwarfing Skatt, and said, 'You're a thieving little beggar, Skatt, but make no mistake. Any creature brave or suicidal enough to pull his blade on Baldizar is a hero in my book.'

With those bold, unexpected words of praise, Skatt suddenly felt his little body stop shaking, although his heart continued to beat like a drum.

'So, what brings a couple of rapscallions like you two down here, then?' he asked, glancing sideways at his smirking troop. 'As if we didn't know!'

Skatt's reprieve was brief, and he did his best to crush the rising dread he felt inside. He knew full well that if he told Rockwolf the truth, the pair of them would be headless within seconds, so he lied as best he could. 'We were looking for a way to help the two prisoners up there,' he said hesitantly, pointing upwards with a podgy, shaking finger.

'A Mmicky helping someone else?' growled Mudgutts. 'Now there's a lie if I've ever heard one.'

'No, no it's true. It's the woman,' he cried aloud. 'Don't you recognize her?'

'You mean the young woman with the long white hair and the blue swath across her eyes?' asked Grogg, pushing forward.

'Yes, yes, that's her. She's the lost one!' declared Nogga eagerly.

Rockwolf gave his medic a shrewd look. 'Do you know that creature?'

'I believe I do, Sarge,' said Grogg. 'I caught a glimpse of her when they first brought her and the bandit spider in, and her likeness does bear a striking resemblance to the description of the lost one in the history scrolls.'

'And just who do you think she is?'

'She's—'

'Silence!' roared Rockwolf, his command so icy cold that it froze Nogga's word in his throat.

'I would need a closer look to be perfectly sure, Sarge'— Grogg licked his thick black lips with excitement— 'but I think she might be the legendary Ssasky, the firstborn daughter to the House of the White Dwarf Star, whose home world, Vlan, was destroyed in the blizzard. It—'

'Sarge, some say that blizzard was magically induced by Baldizar himself,' interrupted Mudgutts, a knowing smile creeping across his scheming face. 'At the time, theories about this unnatural occurrence were rife. Hell, even Eccles Nimrod himself hinted at El Supremo's possible involvement!'

Rockwolf's bullish face softened, a delicious thought dancing in his eyes. 'And if that creature up there is Ssasky, and she's willing to testify that the blizzard was really a malicious attack on the king and that the inhabitants of Vlan were really murdered...'

'We'd have cast-iron evidence, strong enough to set before Captain Goldhorn,' finished Grogg. 'Enough to finally bring Baldizar before a court of law!'

'Yessss,' hissed Mudgutts. 'More than enough to chop his evil tin head off once and for all!'

Skatt grinned up at his brother, whispering. 'If these giant hairy fools believed that, then their ingrained dedication to duty and the law might just be our salvation!'

'Shouldn't we rescue her, then?' ventured Nogga daringly. 'And perhaps the spider too!'

'Tell me, thief,' asked Rockwolf, 'just how was breaking into the Waking Dream Vault going to help those two?'

'Er... Well... We needed to know what was going on up there,' blurted Nogga, 'so I was going to use the Seealloscope!'

'The Seealloscope,' hummed Rockwolf, stroking his bristly chin. 'I'd forgotten about—'

Without warning, the stone slabs beneath their boots trembled once again. Here and there, small cracks snaked out from corners and joints, whilst from above, several ghoulish plaster gargoyles crashed to the floor. The wrought-iron torch holders rattled in their mountings, and two glass doors, buckling under the sudden strain, exploded in a shower of tiny glass fragments.

All eyes turned to Sergeant Rockwolf.

Walking to the nearest wall, he placed a big hand flat

against the stonework. Even with skin as thick as a rhinoceros, he could clearly feel the aftershock still ringing in the heart of the stone. Slowly, he turned, not a hint of fear in his round black eyes. 'Methinks that the foundations of the great amphitheatre of Garrknock are not as strong as they used to be!'

'Time to go, Sarge?' offered Corporal Mudgutts.

'So... Er... So, we're working together, then?' asked Nogga sheepishly.

'For the time being, yes,' growled Rockwolf, reaching down and clamping a big hand about Nogga's piggy snout. 'But be under no illusion, troll dung. I found you two about to plunder the Waking Dream Vault, so as a sergeant chieftain, I should report you!'

Nogga felt his eye bulge as Rockwolf's huge fingers slowly squeezed his snout.

'Shouldn't I?'

Unable to speak, Nogga vigorously nodded his head in agreement.

'However, when we reach the arena and the fighting starts, which it will, I may be inclined to overlook your being here, if you cease being Baldizar's spies and swear your allegiance to me.' He released Nogga's snout and stood.

'Y-Y-You knew that we were Baldizar's spies all along?' spluttered Nogga, tenderly rubbing his poor snout.

'By the curly horns of Jagdar,' laughed Corporal Mudgutts, 'we've known that for many a moon. Snoopers are easy to spot!'

'Er, Sarge, I—'

Nogga shushed his brother, whispering, 'Shut it, bro. We're

not out of trouble yet.'

'Well, thief,' snorted Rockwolf, 'what's your answer? Are you with us, or shall we stretch your scrawny necks right here and now?'

'Yes, yes,' bleated Nogga, 'we're with you. Most definitely with you!'

'Blooming heck, bro, all I was going to say,' barked Skatt angrily, 'was that I can smell sewage again, and it's really blooming strong now!'

Nogga was about to tail-whip him when a panting minotaur came running up to them. 'Sergeant, that black stuff is surging up the tunnel at a good pace, and it smells fouler than ever!'

'The mutt's right. Time to go,' said Rockwolf. 'But first, let's have a look.' He strode into the vault, heading for a weird-looking metal stalactite that was in fact a statue of a big bat, hanging from the ceiling. With an odd familiarity, he pushed in both of the statue's glass eyes before folding down the creature's crossed wings. After a few seconds, they shined bright green and popped back out. From somewhere above, a soft humming could be heard.

'Jagdar's teeth, Sarge, is that the Seealloscope?' asked an intrigued Mudgutts.

'It is indeed. I heard Madspanner declare to Baldizar that with this, he could spy on any room or place in Fortress Hexx or the amphitheatre!' Inscribed around the bat's stubby nose were several words, and he turned it until it pointed to the word 'arena.' For several seconds, he hunched forward, his black eyes glued to the bat's mouth, then announced. 'The girls in chains on the stage, and two chieftains—veggies I presume—are lashing the bandit spider to the Devil's Butcher!'

'Oh well.' Nogga sighed indifferently. 'So much for Flip-flop Freddy. It's the Duster brothers for him!'

'Well, that's one criminal off our books,' announced Mudgutts.

'Sergeant Rockwolf, may I ask you a question?' asked Nogga bravely.

'One,' growled Rockwolf.

'How is it that you know the location of the most secret treasure vault in the entire genieverse? I mean, it's nothing like its description in the rhyme.'

Rockwolf's chuckle was like a rumbling from the bottom of a mineshaft. 'It's not meant to be,' he said. 'It was just a nonsense rhyme to mislead idiots like you!'

Nogga, peeved by his demeaning comment, was about to flaunt the fact that they had found the vault when another chieftain came clomping into view.

The young minotaur came charging out of the darkness, approaching Rockwolf directly. His chest was heaving, his body soaked with sweat, his skin raked with pus-filled blisters.

'*Sarge,*' he said between gasps, 'all the lower tunnels are full of that stinking blackness. Nothing's stopping it!' Rockwolf made to speak, but the minotaur continued anxiously. 'I don't know what's in that stuff, Sarge, but it's bubbling and fizzing like acid, eating away at the very foundations. I saw several stone columns fall, and a section of the lower tunnel has completely collapsed.' There was a flicker of fear in the young minotaur's eyes. 'And the fumes, Sarge... I could hardly breathe.'

Corporal Mudgutts reassuringly slapped his big hands on the shaking grunt's shoulders. 'Good work, Dango. Grogg will fix you up with something for your breathing and them blisters too. Off you go, lad.' He watched the young grunt jog over to the medic before declaring to Rockwolf, 'Well, that explains the tremors, then.'

Rockwolf returned to the Seealloscope, frowning as he viewed four other locations. 'Jagdar's teeth,' he growled, 'the lad's right. All the lower tunnels and several of the upper ones are flooded with sewage, and there are cave-ins everywhere.'

Nogga felt beads of sweat trickling down his cheeks as he remembered his clumsy handling of Madspanner's weird weapon at the sewer entrance. *Surely that wasn't me?* he thought anxiously.

'Something you wish to share with us, Mmicky?' asked Mudgutts, clocking the thief's sudden twitchiness.

'Oh, n-n-no, nothing,' stammered Nogga, trying to swallow. 'Just a bit hot, that's all. There's a lot of big bodies in this small room,' he joked pathetically.

'Sarge, even if the main sewer outlet is blocked,' offered Mudgutts, 'I'm sure the backup outlet, that one carved with the big ugly gargoyle face that looks out over the forbidden lake, will clear the backlog eventually.'

Nogga choked at the minotaur's words, his face flushing a vivid purple as he suddenly imagined everyone glaring down at his obvious guilt.

'Time to be off, lads,' commanded Rockwolf. 'We'll plan on the run.'

As the platoon trotted off, shoving the two moaning Mmickys aggressively before them, both Nogga and Skatt glanced wistfully at each other then back at the vault door. 'The greatest treasure horde of them all,' Nogga said, heartbroken, 'was almost ours!'

It might have been a sixth sense or the survival instinct of a battle-hardened chieftain, but something made Rockwolf turn for one last glance. Looking past the drama occurring on the stage, his attention was drawn to the top of the outer stalls, where he could plainly see Captain Goldhorn and Lieutenant Redhorn illuminated in the flickering torchlights.

The last of the twin suns of Hexx had just set, and in their fading radiance, he could see them staring at a strange glow on the far eastern horizon.

'So it seems I'm not the only one bent on ruining your party, Baldizar.' Rockwolf chuckled gruffly. 'Methinks that that yonder glow might just have something to do with that oddball maggot that everyone's been gossiping about!'

The still night air had turned colder on the last eve of Atunka Gaar. Ssasky thought sadly that the frost would be thick and full of sparkle come sunrise. It would be a beautiful diamond dawn, which she knew in her heart was to be her last.

Shivering, Ssasky found herself wishing for the thick, ugly coat that Archie had found. Even briskly rubbing her hands up and down her arms did little to help, for the tough, comfortable material her gambeson was made of may have protected her body from the rigors of wearing Baldizar's suit of armour, but it afforded little warmth. Worst still, the thick leather corset that Baldizar's goons had locked her into to prevent her from flying away sadistically chafed her waist and sides.

Archie, she mused with a tender sigh. She wondered how a boy from the ancient world, a boy who had freed her from Baldizar's bewitchment, could also steal her heart in less than one day. She wanted to see him once more, if only to tell him just how much she appreciated all that he had done for her, including freeing her from that insidious suit of armour then defending her from the chamelesquid's wrath. She felt her heart pounding, its thundering beat deafening. But it wasn't pain—it was joy. For the first time in her life, she felt truly free, alive, and happy, and it was all down to him. She grasped one of her chains with both hands and, gritting her teeth, pulled as hard as she could.

'Waste of time, Princess!' shouted Freddy. 'Your shackles may be wrought from spungold, but they're strengthened by genie magic!' The bright-yellow chain rattled as she threw it down, then he laughed when he heard her punch the rough wooden deck, crying out in pain. 'And getting angry won't help you either,' he added.

'I'm not angry!' she snapped. 'I'm... *frustrated!*'

It all suddenly seemed so clear, she thought bitterly as her past life, a lonely life of servitude and slavery, flashed before her. The yoke of oppression had started early. As the firstborn daughter and future Queen of Vlan, her life was that of a strictly organized and punishing regime of labour, discipline, and duty.

Then came Baldizar's blizzard. She had spent too many years imprisoned in that evil suit of armour, spellbound by his powerful, perverted magic, and unable to resist his bidding. She had slain many poor creatures, creepies, and mongrels throughout the genieverse in the name of El Supremo.

With the taste of freedom still wet on her lips, the hopelessness of her situation seemed to smother her like a blanket of lead. 'Oh, what I would give right now to be able to cast off my shackles and take up a sword.' Her voice was loud and proud, and her bright, sharp yellow eyes were full of anger. 'Vengeance would be mine, and none would be spared!'

A loud, rousing, malevolent cheer erupted about her, the deafening voice of the mob shattering the depression that manacled her mind. They were on their feet and claws, baying for blood, but it wasn't hers. To her side, she heard a different kind of laughter—it was Freddy, jibing and cursing at the chieftains as they tightened the last of the leather restraining straps that lashed him to that hideous torture machine, the Devil's Butcher.

'How can you possibly laugh at a moment like this?' she asked. 'They've finished your bonds, and the blade's bite is but seconds away.'

Freddy smiled, his wide mouth full of jagged, pointy teeth, his eyes bizarrely full of optimism. 'Don't worry about me, Princess. I can regenerate my limbs.'

'Your limbs, maybe... but not your heart.'

'Humm,' he muttered. 'Let's hope they don't get that far, huh?'

'There's no cavalry coming to rescue us, Freddy!' she cried. 'This is our last moon rise... *ever!*'

'Are you absolutely sure about that?' the spider said with a brazen chuckle, his hairy little face alive with laughter and his stalked eyes gleaming with confidence. 'Princess, do you remember when we were in the treasure room at the Tower of

473

London, back on Earth?'

'Yes,' she said. 'Why?'

'Well, I saw your boyfriend, young Archie Wilde, thrust a small black bag inside his vest just before Old Buckethead appeared.'

Ssasky felt her face redden at the mention of Archie's name, and unchecked tears rolled down her cheeks at the thought of never seeing him again. She wondered whether she could have fallen in love with him so quickly. 'I don't get what you're saying,' she said, brushing her cheek. 'What use is a small bag?'

'Okay, look at it this way, Princess. Why would someone hide an item in his clothing, when he knows that he is going to lose his head minutes later?' Freddy's smile became impossibly large. 'It strikes me that the boy obviously had a plan to beat old Buckethead's golden collar!'

This glorious thought exploded like fireworks in her head. 'Do you really think so?' she blurted joyously.

'I'll bet my stash of stolen booty on it. That's why we need to keep strong for at least the next ten minutes.'

'Ten minutes?' Ssasky's cat's eyes were suddenly vibrant, her blue swath glowing.

Six of Freddy's stalked eyes winked knowingly at her. 'Look yonder at that magnificent shining blush on the eastern horizon. *Someone* has dialled up the Storming Kaleidoscope Falls, which isn't scheduled to reappear for another day!'

Ssasky felt her body tremble with expectancy as, in her heavy heart, the flame of hope flared. She could almost feel her whole being sparkling with courage at the sudden prospect of rescue.

Chapter 34

THE NIGHT SKY ABOVE HEXX.

Captain Frostskarr, a cunningly cold-hearted cinnamon spider and captain of the *Crimson Raptor*, paced the bridge, silently overseeing the loading with his four long, thin, bony arms clasped behind his back. Below, an endless stream of labouring swizzer crabs lugged heavy green plastic containers up the forward gangplank, stockpiling them in the belly of Baldizar's mighty sky cruiser. The corners of his mouth were turned up in a devious, knowing smile—like all warship captains, he knew that boat size always came second to firepower. *With the contents of those boxes,* he mused wickedly, *my cruiser will be the most powerful predator in the genieverse!*

HMS Victory exploded out of the Storming Kaleidoscope Falls, taking everyone on the ground by surprise. Creepies, creatures, and mongrels alike fled screaming in terror as the hull of the huge mystery flying machine struck the hard, sandy ground with a grinding screech.

Archie felt every bone in his body rattle on impact.

The frozen desert sand had come up to meet them faster than Archie had expected, and it took all his strength to hold the Skyshark's flight control column back and steady as he desperately tried to keep the Victory's bow from digging in. Ramming the engine throttles forward, he grinned approvingly as he heard the Rolls-Royce engines roar.

Luckily, the Victory's massive two-and-a-half-thousand-ton wooden hull merely struck the ground with a glancing blow, although it still shuddered heavily under the impact. Its copper-plated keel gouged a deep channel, ploughing through the fairground and crushing tents, marquees, and rides as it went.

'New plan!' said Archie. 'Get us up high and fast, and head for the amphitheatre.'

Boff simply nodded as the boy handed control of the *Skyshark* over to him. He knew it wasn't a request.

'I need to check something.'

He watched the boy head for the hatch ladder. 'Heave to, youngling!' he shouted, swivelling one coned eye over his shoulder. 'If you're out there, how will we—'

Boff watched the boy open a large red locker to the left of the ladder. From it, he pulled out a small green tin box, which he waved at him. 'Can you hear me?' asked Archie.

'Well, hornswoggle me giblets, lad,' a bewildered Boff said with a chuckle, 'your voice is coming out of this here little round thing full of holes!'

'It's called a radio. We'll be able to use it to stay in contact with each other whilst I'm outside.'

By the time Boff had twisted his head around to ask why, all he could see were the soles of Archie's silver-and-blue moon boots disappearing swiftly through the hatch.

'Keep an eye on the radar for the Crimson Raptor!'

'*Radar*,' muttered Boff, scratching all his chins thoughtfully as his eyes roved slowly across the long flight control console. 'What in Jagdar's name is a radar?'

Archie's laughter was tinny and edged with crackling. 'Look at the middle orange screen. We are at the centre, the fuzzy circle ahead of us is the amphitheatre, and the square just beyond that is Fortress Hexx. Baldizar's flying machine will appear as a glowing dot moving toward us. If you see it, sing out, okay?'

'Well, trounce me trunnions,' Boff said. 'An eye in the sky that can see in the dark. Oh, how I could have led the revenue cutters in a merry dance with one of these thingamajigs.'

'Oh, and the rings on the radar screen are set at ten miles apart,' added Archie.

'Captain Frostskarr, sir,' said a junior officer, snapping to attention and handing him an ornate nearascope, 'disturbance reported down at the fairground, sir.'

Frostskarr snatched the optical device from the officer's trembling hands, slowly raising it to one of his twelve stalked eyes. Focusing on the motley collection of tents pitched on the far side of the great amphitheatre of Garrknock, he spied a strange-looking flying machine wreaking havoc there. He didn't need orders from Baldizar to know that the enemy was different and dangerous. Only moments before, he'd witnessed the arrival of the twin cyclones, announcing the imminent and unscheduled arrival of the Storming Kaleidoscope Falls.

The loading of the new weapons was only half complete, but he had a gut feeling that the disturbance immediately demanded his full attention. Turning to his helmsman, he ordered, 'Get us underway now. Take us straight up. When you're clear of the fortress, wheel hard to port then set course for the Storming Kaleidoscope Falls!'

'What about the loading teams, sir?'

Frostskarr shot him an icy glare. 'What about them?'

The helmsman's fear of his captain's wrath far outweighed the lives of mere swizzer crabs. So, jabbing a button, he started the Crimson Raptor's four massive electric motors. Even through the thick glass of the bridge windows, he could clearly hear the soft whooping of the four sets of eight forty-foot-long blades as they began to spin. Then, with no hesitation, he flicked the switch to close the forward gangway.

The sudden downdraft from the four mammoth lift fans, coupled with the unexpected movement of the gangplank, sent startled, yelling swizzer crabs spilling from its length. On the ground, with Baldizar's mighty sky cruiser quickly rising swiftly into the air, confused loaders, suddenly engulfed in darkness, ran for cover as all about them, it rained unhappy crabs and heavy ammunition boxes.

After wrestling the Victory free of the desert sands, Boff pulled back on the Skyshark's flight control column and aimed both ships towards the stars. Glancing at the round orange screen, he declared triumphantly into his microphone, 'Archie, me boy, we're skyward bound, and your radar thingy is dot less.'

Archie had just jumped down from the Skyshark's port wing and was heading for the powder room. 'Are you sure?' he quizzed. 'What about near the outer ring?'

Boff swivelled an eye at the screen. 'Boil me britches, boy,' he hissed, 'I may not be tech savvy, but I do know a moving dot when I see one!'

Archie chuckled as he ran to the gunwale and peered out into the dark night. Sure enough, the only moving lights he could see were on the ground. 'Well, in that case, full speed ahead for the amphitheatre.' He laughed, thankful for a lucky break at last. 'Let's go get our friends and save those silly genies!'

Peeking out of an archer's slit set in the perimeter corridor, four pairs of eyes studied the stage and arena. Three were large, round, and black, whilst the last pair, at the top, were small, piggy, and upside down!

'What's happening?' moaned Skatt, pawing impatiently at the dirt floor. 'All I can see are hairy legs!'

'Think yourself lucky, bro,' grumbled Nogga, holding his stovepipe hat on with one hand whilst hanging upside down from the corridor roof. 'All I can see are horns and dirty great hairy heads.'

One of the big hairy heads turned slowly, glaring threateningly at Nogga. 'Shut it!' snorted Sergeant Rockwolf. 'Or I'll give one of my minotaur's permission to do something nasty to the pair of you with his broadsword!'

'That's not nice, Sergeant,' croaked Nogga timidly. 'We're all on the same side now, aren't we?'

Rockwolf's thick hairy brows clashed together, forming a ten-inch angry caterpillar. 'Don't push your luck, Mmicky.'

'Could… could you at least tell us what's going on out there?' he persisted bravely. 'Plea—'

'By the horns of Jagdar,' cursed Rockwolf, punching the wall so hard that a storm of broken plaster rained down on Skatt's head, 'Baldizar's gone too far this time!'

'What's he done, Sarge?' asked his corporal from the rear.

'He's only gone and broken the first golden genie rule of Atunka Gaar,' growled Rockwolf.

Mudgutts muscled his way to the front, eager to see for himself. 'Jagdar's teeth, that numbskull is in full armour, and he's not wearing his cape!' He rubbed his hands with joy. 'That's an arrestable offence he won't be able to genie his way out of!'

'So, our El Supremo is expecting a fight,' Rockwolf said smugly, relishing the thought.

'What about the woman, Sarge?' asked Grogg.

'The two prisoners are on the stage. The bandit spider is strapped into the Devil's Butcher—they'll have fun with that one. The woman, the one you think is Ssasky, is in chains.'

'Look, Sarge,' a grunt said. 'Baldizar's holding up a dagger. Do you think that's the fabled Fangs of Jagdar?'

For the first time since he could remember, Sergeant Rockwolf felt a sense of dread welling up inside his cast-iron stomach. 'It could very well be, laddie.' He watched the supreme genie holding it aloft for the crowd to see, the red metal giant's mannerisms screaming triumph. 'From the way he's playing to the mob, *he* certainly thinks it is!'

'If it is, Sarge,' offered Mudgutts, 'we're the ones in trouble now.' He gestured to all the minotaur's packed into the long thin corridor. 'Our platoon will be no match for him and that dagger!'

'Let's not be hasty,' Rockwolf replied, a huge smile enveloping his large bull's face. 'He may have the fabled Fangs of Jagdar, but I've a sneaky suspicion that he doesn't know how to use it.'

Grogg cocked a curious eyebrow at his leader. 'What makes you think that?'

'Simple!' declared Rockwolf, slapping him hard on the back. 'If you had all of Merlin's magical powers, would you waste time entertaining the mob, or would you simply usurp the council of the power ten genies and seize power?'

Archie shouldered open the powder-room door, its warped ancient timbers scraping along in protest. His torch cast a rectangle of silver across the wooden deck, illuminating a huge pile of neatly stacked canvas tubes. Stepping over the raised doorframe, he grabbed the nearest and hurled it at a metal hook jutting from the bulkhead. To his dismay, it wasn't black powder that spilled out.

'Einstein's underpants!' he cursed. 'Sand!'

'What sand?' asked Boff over the radio.

'Maggy was right,' groaned Archie. 'We have useless cannons. All these bags are sand-filled dummies, just like me!' Before Boff had a chance to agree, Archie quickly continued. 'What if they don't know we're here yet? Do you think there's a chance that the Crimson Raptor might not even be airborne yet?'

'Oh yeah,' Boff replied, 'about as much chance as Baldizar winning a Nobel Peace Prize for being a really nice guy! And as for the Crimson Raptor... Jagdar's teeth, boy, the whole of Hexx must have heard us arrive via the Storming Kaleidoscope Falls and gate-crash the fair!'

'Okay, so we need to improvise a new weapon if we're going to beat Baldizar's flying boat.'

'Trounce me trunnions, boy,' said Boff, dumbfounded,

'you mean all the cannons are useless? And who in Jagdar's name is Maggy?'

'She's another spiv,' answered Archie casually. 'Zephyar sent her.'

'Scupper me,' growled Boff, 'you seem pretty tight with that demigod and his hairy little messengers.'

'I think he just wants to help,' offered Archie.

'Don't suppose he sent you a weapon of any kind? A knife or an axe perhaps?' asked Boff. 'Because if we're going to join the party below, then it's close-quarter combat for everyone!'

'Ruddy heck,' muttered Archie, 'I hadn't thought about that.'

'Egads, boy, you've lost your catapult,' hissed Boff, 'and Old Buckethead crushed your electric prod when you first arrived here, *remember?*'

'Oh yes.' Archie smirked. 'That electric prod was good fun.'

'Not if you're on the wrong end,' Boff said.

'Sorry,' offered Archie, turning to search the powder room for weapons. 'I promise I won't do it again.'

'Hornswoggle me giblets, boy,' growled Boff. 'You're damned right you won't!'

Chuckling quietly to himself, Archie knowingly patted his left boot then turned to leave. As he flicked off his torch, he suddenly noticed the soft pink glow that replaced it. His right hand flew to his eye patch, which was hot but not painful. He caught his reflection in a shiny strip of metal nailed to the bulkhead.

For a moment, he just stood, staring at his eye patch in silence. It was glowing brightly like a fading half-crescent moon on a clear winter's night. But the odd thing was, it didn't hurt anymore. Its soft glow felt reassuring, a bit like the comfort a child feels when hugging a favourite teddy bear.

Then the reality of his situation torpedoed the moment, and serenity gave way to fear.

'I'm going to attempt to rescue my girlfriend from the clutches of the evilest man in the universe,' he said to his reflection, 'who also happens to be the supreme genie as well as a ten-foot homicidal maniac in a suit of armour blessed with magical powers and who commands his own private army of bloodthirsty veggie minotaur's.' He banged his clenched fists against his thighs. 'And all I've got is Squid Boy, an unarmed flying sub, and an antique ship with useless guns!'

In his eagerness to obey Captain Frostskarr, the helmsman decapitated the fortress flagpole, sending a murder of crows squawking skyward as he wheeled the mammoth sky cruiser in a tight arc, bringing it to its new course. Anxiously, he watched the compass readout click agonizingly slowly towards eighty degrees, at which point, sighing with relief, he quickly swivelled all four of the forty-foot octet rotor blades simultaneously through ninety degrees before accelerating all four of the giant electric motors into forward flight mode.

'Course east by northeast, Captain,' reported the helmsman as the gentle hum outside turned into a whining scream. 'Storming Kaleidoscope Falls dead ahead.'

Frostskarr's smile was like fractured ice. 'Steady as she goes, helmsman,' he ordered, 'and pipe hands to battle stations.' Having the superior fighting ship, he was in no hurry, especially since Professor Madspanner had ordered the installation of his new weapons.

Archie sprinted to the bow, his desire to see Ssasky powering his legs. They'd crossed the Forbidden Wall and were quickly approaching the amphitheatre, its giant statue of Garrknock towering before them.

As he stared down, fleetingly lost in the surreal sight beneath him, a brutal shiver rippled through him. 'Blimey, it's cold,' he said, his teeth chattering.

Boff chuckled. 'Hornswoggle me giblets, boy, for a creature who considers himself to be intelligent, you can be a real dunderhead sometimes!'

Archie turned, frowning back at the Skyshark, annoyed by his friend's abrasive tone.

'We're on the frosty planet Hexx, it's night-time, and we're thousands of feet above the ground. Of course, you're naffin' cold!'

'Maybe I should have kept my coat.'

'*Scupper me!*' shouted Boff. 'A big orange blob has just appeared on your radar thingy!'

'How many rings are there between it and us?' asked Archie.

'One!'

'One?' He instantly forgot the stinging cold. 'Crickey, it must have been hiding behind the fortress all along!'

'So much for trashing old Buckethead's flagship, then,' whinged Boff. 'I was looking forward to that part!'

'If we can't outgun his cruiser,' offered Archie, 'perhaps we could outsmart him by destroying the gun in the statue first?'

'Tech savvy you may be, my boy,' said Boff, 'but as a combat tactician, you're a naffin' noodle!'

'Why not?' asked Archie. 'Surely if we destroy the gun, the power ten genie council will immediately side with us!'

'Scupper me, boy,' Boff said in disbelief, 'have you forgotten old Horatio "Guns" McTavish's wisdom already? He who has the high ground wins the battle, remember? If we go for the statue, we concede the high ground, and they'll pound us to bits. And if by some Jagdar-given miracle, we succeed in destroying that hidden gun, and that rabble of no-good genies does decide to help us, the second we drop anchor, the scurvy crew of the Crimson Raptor will tear us to pieces.'

'That outnumbered, huh?'

'Archie, they'll massacre us then barbeque our gizzards at their victory party afterwards!'

'But what about the council genies?' asked Archie.

'The power ten genie council are the ruling government,' hissed Boff contemptuously. 'No creature can trust a ruling government. They peddle their lies to get elected then steal your spungold!'

Seems politicians are the same everywhere, thought Archie, staring off into the inky darkness. 'Boff, I can't see any sign of the Crimson Raptor yet, but we're almost on top of the amphitheatre.'

'It's out there,' growled Boff, staring at the radar screen. 'I'm taking us up *now*!'

As the Victory's bow started to rise, Archie, gripping the gunwale with white knuckles and a pounding heart, strained to see the stage below. Even at a thousand feet, he could feel the heat from the mass of bright-yellow torches, and the stench of burning animal fat permeated the air. His heart sank as he spied Ssasky in chains, his happiness swiftly turning to anger. Next to her was Freddy, centre stage, strapped onto some weird bench mechanism. Archie knew a torture machine when he saw one, and from the swinging motion of its odd-looking pendulum, it was already in motion.

'Jagdar's teeth, boy,' growled Boff, 'I can't see a thing on these silly screen things. What's going on down there?'

'From what I can make out, Ssasky's shackled to the stage, and Freddy's strapped onto an old wooden bench,' reported Archie excitedly, 'but they're alive, and that's what matters.'

'Is old Buckethead there?' asked Boff.

'Oh, he's there, all right,' Archie replied. 'His red armour is positively glowing!'

'By the curly horns of Jagdar!' roared Boff furiously. 'You say he's wearing his naffin' armour?'

'Yes,' answered Archie, a little bewildered. 'Why wouldn't he be?'

'Egads, boy,' Boff growled, his voice seething with venom, 'this is the final eve of Atunka Gaar—all genies must attend *without armour*. Baldizar has broken a law that's as old as Jagdar himself! What blasphemy! The sooner the Fangs of Jagdar is thrust into his evil heart, the better!'

'Blimey,' exclaimed Archie suddenly. 'You should see the size of the black gorilla that's just lumbered onto the stage. It's huge, and it's got four arms!'

'Stuff the ape!' snapped Boff. 'If by some miracle we somehow manage to beat Baldizar's sky cruiser, how in

Jagdar's name are we going to destroy that secret machine gun hidden in the statue of Garrknock? We have no naffin' cannons!'

Archie laughed. 'Blimey, Boff, we've got a three-and-a-half-thousand-tonne ship. *We ram the beggar!*'

'And what about after we land?'

'Hmmm,' said Archie, whose mind clearly wasn't thinking that far ahead. 'Well, try and squash as many veggie chieftains as possible on landing, and from there on, we'll just have to wing it.'

'What in Jagdar's teeth is *wing it?*'

Ssasky and Freddy, along with every other living creature in the great amphitheatre of Garrknock, froze as the strange giant flying machine with its three tall masts in full sail glided silently overhead. The whole of Hexx seemed to catch its breath as the ghostly apparition sailed into view, momentarily blocking out the stars. The fearful eyes of the mob turned anxiously to their El Supremo for guidance, which came unexpectedly, in the form of a loud, incredulous laugh.

'Is that the best the Merlin's marauders could get!' cried Baldizar contemptuously. 'A decrepit old wooden ship?' His mocking laughter quickly revived the mob's spirit.

But whilst the supreme genie revelled in his moment of glory, laughing along with the cheering mob, Freddy gave Ssasky a sly wink. Her pale face blossomed into a bright smile as she suddenly realised that their salvation had arrived.

Although Boff had done a grand job wrestling the Victory free from the ground whilst keeping its aged timbers together, it was painfully obvious just how sluggish the combination was. With regards to aerodynamics, the Skyshark was perfect—sadly, the Royal Navy's flagship was a flying brick.

Ahead of them, framed by the stars, Archie could clearly make out the outline of the Crimson Raptor, a glowing red stain quickly approaching on the horizon. The spectral enemy was made all the more frightening because with no working cannons, the Victory was defenceless.

'Boff, they're gaining on us,' urged Archie over the radio. 'We need more height, and quickly.'

'Stop flapping your gums, shipmate,' said Boff boldly. 'That thing's only armed with bows and catapults. We're well out of range!'

From the centre of the crimson blur, a barrage of bright flashes lit up the sky. A second later, the still of the night was shattered by bursts of loud, sharp cracks, as the first volley of high-calibre bullets struck the Victory. All about Archie, everything suddenly exploded in a thousand tiny, splinter-filled eruptions.

'Einstein's underpants, they've got guns!' cried Archie, diving for cover. 'I thought you said that thing only had bows and arrows?'

Boff, shocked by the unexpected gunfire, initiated a daring evasive manoeuvre. With both engines roaring at full power, he yanked the flight control column back hard, sending the two-hundred-year-old wooden ship into a reckless, steep climb.

'Brace your britches, boy,' Boff shouted courageously. 'We're going vertical!'

As the Victory began climbing steeply, its aged timbers

creaking in agony, Archie lost his footing and fell tumbling across the wooden deck. Panic cramped his stomach and clouded his mind as his body slid towards the stern, towards the big gaping hole filled by the glowing white, yellow, and red cones of fire from the Skyshark's flaming engine exhausts.

Wildly, he threw himself towards the midship's deck gratings, flaying out with both hands, his fingers desperately trying to snare a grip in one of its many holes. But he'd thrown himself with such force that his roll was uncontrollable. Instinctively, he slammed both arms down flat, the painful manoeuvre luckily arresting his roll just enough for his fingers to jab through a hole in the aft grating. A stabbing pain shot through his left shoulder as his body jerked to a sudden halt.

'Is that your idea of tactical wizardry?' he wheezed between spasms of pain. 'This is a maritime relic you're flying; you know!'

'Absolutely,' agreed Boff, willing the slowly rising needle of the altimeter to move faster whilst watching the tiny radar dot slowly fall astern. 'And now there's a thick wooden hull between those lethal bullets and us!'

The Crimson Raptor's gunners loosened off second and third volleys, which smashed into the Victory's wooden hull with devastating effect. Even safe inside the Skyshark, the noise was deafening as more and more bullets found their way through, pinging off the Skyshark's Kevlar hull in all directions like metal rain.

Boff's head felt as if he were inside a giant bell on Christmas day.

Captain Frostskarr, outraged by the enemy's sudden cowardly manoeuvre, drew his cutlass and decapitated his steward. Then in a thunderous voice, he bellowed fresh orders at his master gunner. 'Open fire, all weapons. I want that sky cruiser pulverised!' His stalked eyes glared insanely at the quaking officer. 'Understand me?!'

'Y-y-yes, sir, pulverise it at once, sir,' he repeated, backing away nervously, trying not to trip over the headless body on the deck.

The Crimson Raptor gave chase, slewing wildly from port to starboard, firing off devastating broadsides when its guns came to bear. Archie, unable to do anything whilst they ascended, monkey climbed along the deck until he reached the main mast. He dropped, landing astride it, protected by its thick girth, a place of safety whilst he frantically tried to think of a new plan.

His aching head, confused and fearful, swam. Time was running out. Then a line of several cannonballs rolled passed him, and an ingeniously wicked idea was born.

Madspanner had designed the Crimson Raptor, and his warship had one obvious Achilles's heel. After all, Archie deduced logically, the professor was without doubt an egomaniac who, fearing nothing else in the sky, had arrogantly arranged all the Raptor's armaments to be downward firing.

Chapter 35

THE NIGHT SKY ABOVE HEXX.

Within minutes, HMS Victory was showing the enemy her stern light and gaining altitude fast. With Fortress Hexx and the amphitheatre rapidly shrinking, Archie stared off into space, fretfully biting his lip, hoping with every fibre of his shaking body that his new idea would work and that they wouldn't be too late to save their friends.

'What is that thing?' whispered Ssasky.

'That magnificent sky cruiser, Princess, is an Earth warship.' He forced a smile as he saw hope gleam in her eyes. 'It's armed with two hundred cannons.' He laughed, lying as best he could. 'It'll make mincemeat of old Buckethead's flying bug.' Then he turned away, knowing in his heart that the Victory belonged in a museum, not on the battlefield.

Suddenly, the shining stars were blotted out by a crimson blur, and with tears in her eyes, Ssasky dropped her troubled head in prayer. 'Almighty Jagdar,' she beseeched, 'as Serpentina, I did many barbaric things, and I know that I am not worthy of saving, but *he is*. I beg of you, if you are listening to my humble pleas, then save the youngling Archie, if not for my sake, then for his, for he has the courage of a lion and the heart of a saint.'

Jolting Ssasky from her prayers, red metal fingers grabbed her chin, prising her head back. 'Take a good look, my dear,' hissed Baldizar, his volcanic red eyes glowing with assured triumph. 'Your presumed rescue will fail.' He cast her head roughly aside, his tone cavalier and gloating. 'It seems that Boff, like you, also had feelings for the maggot Archie Wilde. Such a waste! Never mind, at least his valiant but oh-so-feeble attempt at a rescue will give the crew of the Crimson Raptor chance to play with their new weapons. A little extra entertainment, courtesy of Professor Madspanner.' He laughed, pointing to the crowd. 'One must keep that fickle mob of morons amused.'

'Never fear, Princess!' shouted Freddy, nervously watching Baldizar saunter his way. 'HMS Victory is a warship, second to none, and she'll blow that tin bug clean out of the sky.'

Baldizar stopped next to the Devil's Butcher torture machine and rested a gauntlet on top of a long wooden lever. With another, he flicked open the visor of his helmet, exposing his pale, sickly-looking leathery face. Freddy thought he was going to vomit as a ruthless sneer escaped Baldizar's thin cruel lips.

'A first-rate ship of the line, yes, two centuries ago!' Baldizar sneered and pushed the wooden lever forward.

Underneath the torture machine's robust wooden frame, a mechanism engaged, wheels creaked, and cogs began to turn. Directly in front of Freddy, suspended from a large A-frame, hung an evil-looking half-moon axe, its keen blade the length of a chieftain's broadsword. A length of rope attached to the blade snapped taut, grabbing Freddy's full attention. Slowly, the torture machine's hidden mechanism hauled it away to the left.

'You see, my dear,' continued Baldizar, whimsically checking his prisoners' bonds, 'truth be told, said warship is nothing more than a tourist attraction. The cannons of which this theft so eagerly boasts are made of wood, and its powder bags are full of sand.'

Something inside Freddy's furtive little mind suddenly popped like a bag full of odd thoughts, and outlandish notions suddenly fused together. *Old Buckethead doesn't know how to use the dagger!* Freddy's head snapped up as, with a loud click, the vicious blade was released, its keen edge swinging towards his toes.

Baldizar grinned at the blade then glanced at Ssasky. 'Fear not, my dear. I'll have Og scrub the blood off my toy before he straps you to it!'

As Boff levelled out the Victory, Archie staggered across to the gunwale and glanced over the side. The Crimson Raptor was a good two thousand feet below, its rim alive with bright flashes. 'You're out of range, you plonkers!' he shouted. 'But feel free to waste your ammo!' He took a breath. 'Okay, Boff,' he said over his mask radio, 'enough running. It's time to go on the offensive!'

'Hornswoggle me giblets, boy!' yelled Boff happily. 'You're alive!'

'Course I'm alive, you dope.' He laughed. 'What's our altitude?'

Boff glanced at the altimeter and flinched. 'Trounce me trunnions, will you look at that,' he cried in astonishment. 'We've only crested ten thousand naffin' feet!'

'Good, that'll do nicely,' Archie said. 'Now bring us about

and descend. We need to be directly over the Crimson Raptor, and close!'

'Jagdar's teeth, boy!' yelled Boff. 'We've just left a storm of bullets. If we go back down there, they'll blow us out of the sky!'

'If I'm right,' said Archie confidently, 'we just need to stay above them.'

'Jagdar, protect us. If you're right!' With trepidation in both of his hearts and small movements of the flight column, the storm raider put the Victory into a spiralling descent. 'Avast, you scoundrels,' he cried boldly. 'Bilge Rat Boff, commander of the Royal Navy's finest, is coming to bust heads and kick butt!'

Captain Frostskarr seethed with anger, barking new orders at his frantic crew. 'Look lively, you worthless scum,' he bellowed. 'I want all those guns dismantled and moved onto the upper deck. Now!'

In the world of predators, the Crimson Raptor was the highest flying and deadliest in any sky. It hadn't needed weapons on its upper skin before. 'A pox on you, human,' hissed Frostskarr spitefully, grasping the ship's wheel with two pincers. 'I'll have a few choice words for that Madspanner when this battle is over.'

'B-but, sir,' snivelled his first lieutenant, 'there are no mountings on the upper skin, sir. This cruiser was never designed to repel an attack from above.'

'Don't bother me with details, you lame-brained heap of troll dung! Just make it so!'

'Y-yes, sir, but first we'll have to—'

The keen edge of the captain's cutlass whistled through the air, striking the quaking officer with such speed that he saw his own body standing rigidly to attention as his head fell to the deck.

Frostskarr levelled his bloodied sword towards the others, calmly asking, 'Any other disbelievers amongst you mongrel-hearted cinnamon spiders?'

Instantly, the crew was an enthusiastic blur of action as they all scrambled toward the upper deck, as far away from their insane captain's blade as possible.

But Frostskarr was just as cunning as he was ruthless. He fully understood that he needed to gain some time before the new weapons were sited and could be brought to bear on the enemy. 'Master gunner!' He bellowed across the open gun deck. 'Have your catapult crews turn their weapons inward then get them to rip off the deck skin above them. Load them all with my special firebombs.'

Standing in the bow, Archie called out adjustments to port and starboard as Boff gingerly manoeuvred the Victory into position. There was a strong north-easterly wind, but Boff was compensating magnificently, keeping the ship directly above the Crimson Raptor. Below, the upper skin of Baldizar's ship was a hive of frenzied activity. Archie had never seen so many cinnamon spiders—they were everywhere, recklessly hauling high-calibre machine guns up through hurriedly hacked holes to their new, hastily prepared mountings. He watched the furious activity curiously for a few seconds before picking up a twelve-pound cannonball. It felt cold to the touch, but its weight made him smile.

The flat top of the wooden gunwale was ideal for launching. Holding it with both hands, he looked passed the iron ball and down at the Crimson Raptor's port-forward lift fan. Smiling wickedly at the whirling blades, he rolled it over the edge. The large iron ball whistled through the air as it dropped towards its target. Seconds later, much to his disappointment, it smashed harmlessly into the skin of the Raptor, creating nothing more than a neat hole.

Archie stepped two paces to the left and slightly readjusted his aim. 'That should do it.' He watched, grinning as the second iron ball dropped toward its target. Sadly, at the very last moment, an unsuspecting cinnamon spider inadvertently scampered into his line of fire, its scaly head taking the full force of the impact.

'Damn!' Archie quickly reached for a third ball and heaved it over the side. 'Yes!' he cried, punching the air as it struck the lift fan's spinning propeller blades with a resounding bong.

But his triumphant cry was short lived, as the iron ball was batted about for several seconds before falling harmlessly through the whirling blades.

'What?' He angrily kicked the gunwale. 'How the flipping heck did that happen?'

'Did we hit it?' asked Boff eagerly.

'Yes,' said Archie, 'sort of.'

'Either we did, or we didn't,' growled Boff.

'It fell right on target. Unfortunately, it bounced off.'

'Jagdar's teeth, boy,' Boff said in disbelief, 'you're naffin' joking!'

'If a single bird can destroy a modern jet engine,' stated

Archie, 'then a twelve-pound cannonball should easily have destroyed that lift fan.'

Angered by this setback, Boff listened as over the radio, he heard the boy grunting and groaning whilst muttering a volley of foul language.

'What are you up to now, boy?' asked Boff.

Strengthened by his anger, Archie quickly unshipping a nearby fifty-pound swivel cannon, staggered forwards and heaved it over the side. 'Bombs away.'

'Hornswoggle me giblets, boy, was that a small cannon?' asked Boff, grinning at the monitor.

Archie laughed. 'Yeah, and it's racing down to the Crimson Raptor as we speak!'

Archie watched the small hand cannon sail out of view. Seconds later came a mighty clang from the Crimson Raptor's port-forward lift fan. For a brief, wonderful moment, there was a really nasty rattling sound, accompanied by the shrieking of scraping metal. Sadly, apart from a brief change in the pitch of the lift fan's motor and a slight wobble, nothing happened.

'Einstein's underpants, what's that thing made of?'

The world about him suddenly exploded in a vicious blizzard of splinters. Fantastically, the storm of bullets from the hastily installed guns on the Crimson Raptor's upper deck hit everything but Archie. However, several struck the lower boom of the main mast, right above his head. The flying lead chewed through the thick wood, dividing it into four pieces, and the outermost one, still attached by three ropes, swung free of the rigging. Unseen by Archie, the shattered six-foot length of timber whistled down at great speed, striking him squarely in the chest.

Knocked breathless, Archie was sent staggering backwards before tripping over an eyebolt and crashing through a skylight. Shards of broken glass fell about him as he landed with a heavy thump on his back.

Captain Frostskarr arrived on the Crimson Raptor's improvised upper-gun deck, cursing and lashing out violently at any poor sailor within range of his claws and fists. 'By the fiery wrath of Jagdar, how dare they damage my sky cruiser!' he ranted. 'I'll skin those scrawny pirates alive and dip them in salt until they beg for mercy.' He rounded on the master gunner, his stalked eyes bulging with rage. 'Then I'll spit roast them and feast on their charred gizzards.'

The master gunner snapped smartly to attention. He tried to speak, but his pounding heart was wedged in his throat. Coughing forcefully, he quickly declared, 'Both catapults loaded and ready to fire, sir.'

'With my special firebombs?' hissed Frostskarr.

'Yes, sir. Each fifty-gallon wooden cask has been filled with fire oil *and* boom-boom nuggets.'

The boom-boom nugget was an unusual seedpod that, when warmed by the midday sun, would pop open, spitting out its seed. Quite by accident, it was found that tossing a boom-boom nugget into a fire would make it explode with the force of a hand grenade. His answer was good, but he could tell by his captain's crooked smile that it wasn't enough. 'I've also had twelve extra casks made up, sir, for the coming battle and for any other target you see fit to destroy.'

The master gunner's heart skipped a beat as one of

Frostskarr's bony hands shot out like a striking serpent, only to settle gently on the gunner's quaking shoulder. 'You've done well, Lieutenant Brongnaa, and I shall personally inform El Supremo of your dedication to duty.' Then he turned to the officer in charge of the firing lever. 'Out of my way.' He scowled, shoving the cinnamon spider aside. 'This is personal!' He snatched a speaker tube off the bulkhead, marked Bridge, and gave it a hefty blow.

On the bridge, a whistle sounded next to the helmsman. 'Bridge, helmsman speaking.'

'Helmsman, this is the captain. Bring the ship hard to port when we're broadside to the enemy. I want half astern on both port lift fans and full ahead on both starboards, understand?'

'Aye aye, Skipper,' replied the helmsman. 'How long should I hold the manoeuvre, sir?'

'Ten beats of the hortator's drum, no more,' he ordered. 'Then close on the enemy at full speed ahead.'

'Aye aye, Skipper,' said the helmsman.

Archie stared up groggily at the shattered, jagged edges of the skylight he'd just fallen through and then about the small cabin where he lay. Outside, he could hear gunfire—it sounded like a million woodpeckers trying to fell a redwood. His mind felt like a bowl of cold porridge, with a million unanswered questions all mashed together. And then there was that distant, irritating voice.

'Archie, where are you?' persisted the voice. 'You've vanished from the picture box.'

Archie shook his head, desperately trying to clear his mind.

'Speak to me, you dunderhead,' Boff said. 'Where are you?'

'I'm in some sort of cabin,' Archie said with a groan.

'Jagdar's teeth,' snapped Boff. 'Stop lollygagging about. The enemy's preparing to attack again.'

'Okay.' Archie moaned, rubbing his aching head. 'I'm on it.' Rolling off the bunk, he steadied himself for a moment then headed for the cabin door. The room was about ten feet square, with four plain wooden bunks. Hanging nearby were two portable glass lanterns, whilst a small but solid-looking table occupied the middle of the room. On top of the table was an array of tiny models. It was to these that his curiosity was momentarily drawn.

The detailed design and craftsmanship were first-rate. There was a replica of the Victory in the centre, with a ship's wheel and rudder mechanism, a main mast with all associated rigging and sails, an anchor, and a cannon and cradle.

As his appreciating mind surveyed the models, his eye suddenly fell on one in particular. 'That's it,' he cried, snatching up one of the models. 'The anchors. They've got to be big enough to do the job!'

'Archie, my boy, have you lost your marbles? We're far too high to drop anchor. The ropes will never reach.'

Archie kicked the cabin door open, suddenly stopping in his tracks. To the left of the doorframe, his eye fell upon an officer's sword. He eagerly grabbed it from its hook. The leather was old and worn, its ornamental gold filigree dull and tatty, but as he pulled it partly out of its scabbard, he smiled at the sheen of its lethal blade.

'Here's something I'd love to give to old Buckethead,' he chuckled, 'point first!'

Clasping it to his belt, he was about to leave when he spied a bright-red, two-handled fire axe. 'That's just what I need.'

As he lifted the axe, it revealed a small but fresh split in the wooden deck. His eye worryingly followed its snaking path across the worn planks, up the bulkhead, and along the thick oak doorframe. Sadly, as he felt Boff manoeuvring the Victory, he watched other splits flexing disturbingly. They were everywhere, accompanied by an alarming cacophony of unnatural creaking and groaning.

She's tearing herself apart, he thought, running his fingers tenderly over the ancient wood. *The stress of the flight here, the plunge into Niagara Falls, and now the fight... It's just too much for her old timbers.* Beneath his feet, he heard and felt another volley of gunfire hammer the ship's keel, several rounds passing completely through before chewing into the battered masts. *If the masts snap,* he thought anxiously, *Boff won't be able to control the* Victory.

'Archie, what in Jagdar's name are you up to?' barked Boff.

'Trust me,' said Archie, jumping through the cabin door. 'My new plan's a corker.'

'Jagdar's teeth, boy, I had a horrible feeling you were going to say that!'

Archie, axe in hand, sprinted back to the bow. Although the Crimson Raptor was still firing lethal volleys of bullets and gaining fast, their position directly overhead afforded them one last, slim chance of victory.

As he peeked over the gunwale, Archie was amazed to see that they were still almost on target. 'Well done Boff, try and keep us in this position,' he said excitedly, 'I'm going to give our friends down there a really big present.'

'A present?' retorted Boff, completely convinced that the boy was insane.

'Yes! If a fifty-pound cannon doesn't scratch the beast, let's see what a four-ton anchor will do!'

'Hornswoggle me giblets,' laughed Boff excitedly, suddenly understanding the boy's plan. 'That will mash their gizzards for sure!'

Archie vigorously attacked the six-inch thick anchor rope like a madman. Chopping wildly, he brought the axe blade down again and again with all the strength he could muster. Each of the six thick, twisted strands parted with a loud twang until only one remained. After a final glimpse at his quarry below, Archie took aim and swung the axe around in a wide, overhead arc, screaming in triumph as he brought it down with a loud thwack and severed the last strand. 'Take that, you scabby bunch of crabs,' he yelled jubilantly.

The sheer weight of the four-ton anchor tore itself free from the ship's side, falling as if in slow motion, its two massive iron flutes dragging it down in a kamikaze dive toward the enemy.

On board Baldizar's mighty sky cruiser, all eyes excitedly watched their captain as he ignited the first barrel of oil-soaked boom-boom nuggets. Like their captain, they cared little for Madspanner's fancy new weapons—they preferred the awesome destructive power of the firebomb. Their raspy, rousing cheers filled the gun deck as the barrel erupted in flames, and Frostskarr yanked the catapult launch lever hard.

Wound almost to the snapping point, the huge wooden catapult paddle sprang forward, hurling its deadly payload up towards the Victory with such force that the shock of its release reverberated throughout the whole craft.

'Blimey,' screamed Archie, staring wide-eyed at the blob of fire racing up toward him. 'What the flipping heck is that?!'

'It's a firebomb!' cried Boff as he jammed the Skyshark's flight column hard to the starboard, sending the Victory into a brutal, timber-creaking turn. 'Egads! I've been on the receiving end of those things,' he added venomously, 'and if those dastardly cinnamon spiders have added boom-boom nuggets to the mix, then we definitely don't want to be around when it explodes.'

Archie wasn't listening. His fingertips had frozen with fear, and he dug them into the top of the wooden gunwale like clenched claws as he stared in horror at the mass of raging fire whistling towards them. Luckily, Grizwold, who had glimpsed the danger through the boy's eye, took control. Quickly, he relaxed the boy's fingers muscles before twisting his body around and throwing him to the deck.

It was a heart-stopping moment as unfortunately, Boff's gallant attempt to outmanoeuvre the firebomb was just a smidge too slow. Archie, feeling as if he were being barbequed alive, instinctively curled into a tight ball, bracing himself for the coming explosion.

With a deafening boom, he was thrown into the base of the main mast, the impact knocking the breath from him. But as he lay dazed, gasping for air, staring up into the burning rigging, he swiftly realised that somehow, incredibly, he, Boff, and the indomitable old warship, had survived.

Miraculously, the firebomb had struck the Victory's

figurehead but didn't explode. However, in the resulting impact, the imposing eight-foot bust of George III and his shield, along with the bowsprit and all its rigging, had completely disintegrated. The firebomb continued on its blazing course, roaring up the front of the Victory, its crackling tail of fire merely scorching the very top of the foremast before arching over then falling clear. Sadly, the creatures in the fairground below didn't stand a chance.

'Are we hit?' crackled Boff's anxious voice over the radio.

Archie stared at the shattered, scorched hole in the bow. 'We were lucky. The firebomb didn't explode. There's a massive hole in the bow where the figurehead and bowsprit used to be, but the hull still seems to be intact.' He stared at the remains of the shattered timber, which oddly reminded him of a pair of giant gaping insect pincers.

On board the Crimson Raptor, the crowing cheers of triumph suddenly turned to howls of panic as the crew spotted the large object hurtling their way. With a thunderous clunk, the four-tonne anchor smashed into the port forward lift fan. The sky cruiser lurched heavily to port; the air filled with the sound of screeching metal. In one dramatic blow, the lift fan's electric motors, along with its eight, long whirling blades were all ripped violently from their hull mountings.

'Yes!' cried Archie, jumping and leaping wildly about the deck. 'Stuff that in your pipe and smoke it, Baldizar! You're totally fubar now!'

Unfortunately for Archie, the helmsman of the Crimson Raptor was a wily old cinnamon spider well experienced in flying sky cruisers. In a blur of movement, he danced all six of his claws expertly over the flight controls, quickly rerouting all electricity to his three remaining lift fans and accelerating them to maximum power whilst adjusting and compensating for the raptor's roll pitch and yaw with the tail rudders, elevators, and ailerons.

Before Archie knew what had happened, the Crimson Raptor had restored controlled flight. He flopped over the gunwale, clutching his head in dismay. 'Einstein's underpants, you have got to be kidding me!'

'Jagdar's teeth, boy, what's happening out there?' Boff asked. 'Are we winning, or what?'

'Bull's-eye! We totally destroyed the port-forward lift fan.' Archie sank to his knees. 'Unfortunately, it wasn't enough.' He suddenly sprang up again, his eye patch burning wickedly. Drawn back to the gunwale, he saw a second dreadful fireball erupting out of the Crimson Raptor. 'Incoming fireba—' he screamed.

But it was too late. As he dived for cover behind the massive anchor capstan, the firebomb hit the Victory's hull, port side, and midship. The explosion rocked the ancient warship from bow to stern, its three massive masts quivering like bamboo in the wind. Having withstood the ravages of sea, battle, and time, its centuries-old timbers disintegrated in a maelstrom of shattered debris.

Encased inside the metal Skyshark, the blast hit Boff like an express train. Multicoloured stars exploded before his eyes, whilst Satan rang hell's bells so loudly in his head that he surely thought it would split in two.

'Boff... Boff, talk to me,' cried Archie over his radio, his friend's screams tearing at his heart. 'What's going on? Are you okay?'

Boff's tentacle hands shot out, anchoring themselves onto whatever they could grasp in a sudden, desperate need for stability.

'Come on, buddy,' pleaded Archie, 'talk to me.'

'Argh,' came a weak reply. 'What happened?'

'We've been hit midships by a firebomb,' said Archie, jumping out from behind the capstan seconds before a mess of burning rigging and sail crashed down upon it. 'There's damage to the port side, fires are everywhere, and all three masts are ablaze!' With burning debris falling all about him, Archie weaved his way to the starboard-side gunwale. 'Is the Skyshark okay? Can you see any damage to the Victory on your end?'

'No,' answered Boff groggily. Archie was about to speak when he added, 'No, wait, that's not right. I can see stars!'

'It's a concussion,' said Archie reassuringly. 'You're a bit dazed. You must have knocked that big, thick head of yours!'

'Scupper me, boy, not that type of stars,' Boff snapped, sounding more like his old self. 'Twinkly naffin' stars!'

'Which camera is showing on?'

'The left-hand one. I can see a naffin' great hole out of the Skyshark's window!'

'Flippin' heck,' cried Archie. 'They've only breeched the flipping hull!'

'Scupper me boy, we're fish bait,' offered Boff in a weak, resigned tone. 'I've seen smaller sky cruisers tear themselves apart with less damage.'

'That's defeatist talk,' snapped Archie, spying the fire axe. 'We're not finished yet! With one lift fan knocked out, the enemy is crippled, so let's drop the starboard anchor as well and finish that flying heap of junk for good! Get us back above the Crimson Raptor. I'll guide you from here.'

Jumping over burning rigging, Archie swiftly snaked his way over to the starboard anchor, holding the fire axe above his head.

On the Crimson Raptor, captain Frostskarr was in a jubilant mood, scuttling about the gun deck, gearing up his crew. 'Come on, lads,' he said, slapping sailors heartily on their backs. 'We've holed her, the enemy is badly damaged. Concentrate all guns on that hole, and let's finish her off for good.' Grabbing a voice pipe, he bellowed yet more orders. 'Below, armoury, I want those other firebombs topside now!'

Frostskarr smiled with evil delight as the night sang with the rat-tat-tat of machine-gun fire as fifty crew members hurriedly moved high-calibre weapons then poured a lethal onslaught of flying lead into the gaping hole in the side of the enemy.

From out of nowhere, a third firebomb exploded above Archie, its burning boom-boom nuggets raining down upon the Victory like a hailstorm of hand grenades. Some bounced off the decking before exploding, but others decimated the masts and rigging, showering Archie and the main gun deck with splintered wood, burning canvas, and singed rope ends.

Several nuggets exploded about him, their concussive bangs and blinding flashes beating him to the ground. Their invisible punches covered him in bleeding nicks from a thousand tiny, jagged nugget-shell fragments. Dazed and bleeding, he crawled helplessly between two cannons, his hands clamped over his ears and his face pushed hard against the wooden deck.

Boff, frustratedly seated in the Skyshark, scowled at his own sense of uselessness. Through Archie's radio, he could clearly hear multiple explosions and the boy's pitiful cries.

Then, as dramatically as the firebomb storm had started, it finished.

'Archie, talk to me, boy,' he begged frantically. 'Say something, Archie, they're loading more firebombs!'

Not again, thought Archie as he slowly and with great effort dragged himself back onto his feet. 'I-I'm all right,' he groaned, swaying from side to side.

'Jagdar's teeth, boy, if you want to celebrate your sixteenth birthday, you'd better drop that last anchor naffin' sharpish!'

Archie stood zombielike, his battered body barely breathing, his concussed mind snatching at random thoughts. As he stooped to pick up the fire axe, his shaking hands missed its handle several times.

'Archie, I know just how you're feeling, shipmate,' Boff said reassuringly over the radio. 'I inked myself in my first battle. You must swallow your fear. Remember, we have a fight to finish if we're going to save Ssasky and Freddy.' Boff knew that Grizwold was doing his best for the boy, helping in whatever way he could. But the truth was that if they were going to beat Baldizar, Archie really needed to dig deeply and find his reserve of courage.

Archie's motions were like that of a robot. He saw himself snatch up the axe and then, wielding it with an executioner's aim, bring it down with a loud thwack, severing the thick anchor rope with one clean chop. The axe fell from his hands as he fell to his knees, the massive four-tonne anchor swinging free from the Victory's side.

Through a red, puffy eye, Archie smiled as he watched the anchor accelerating towards its target. The Victory was a mere five hundred feet above the Crimson Raptor, so close that he could hear the cinnamon spiders' screams of terror as the anchor hurtled their way.

The stalls of the great amphitheatre of Garrknock rocked with cheers as the swinging blade of the Devil's Butcher torture machine neatly sliced off the first two of Freddy's fingers. The bandit spider grimaced, knowing full well that he didn't have long to live. But the longer he refused to scream, the more he deprived Baldizar of his entertainment.

Sadly, for all of Freddy's dogged determination, Baldizar's eyes were not fixed upon his pain but on the glorious victory being won high in the skies above. 'Look up at the stars and see how your rescuers burn!' he shouted.

The council of the power ten genies had seen enough, and their simmering anger at Baldizar's outrageous actions finally boiled over. Eccles Nimrod, the genie of order, backed up by the genie of system, a huge cinnamon spider called Archibald Pinchwick, jumped to their feet.

'Enough!' Yelled Eccles, pointing a single accusing finger at Baldizar. 'You go too far. You have dishonoured the council and exceeded your authority.' The genie of order, although a good three feet shorter than the ten-foot supreme genie and shaking like a jelly on the inside, bravely took two paces forward. 'I demand that you recall your sky cruiser and desist from your fiendish actions at once!'

'The council of the power ten genies hereby revoke you as their elected leader,' growled Archibald through gritted, pointy teeth. Then he turned to the crowd, raising four long thin arms up high, bidding them be silent. 'On this, the third and final eve of the ceremony of Atunka Gaar, a new El Supremo, as dictated by the laws of the ancient ones, Merlin and Zeplin, will be proclaimed.'

It was a truly bold move on behalf of the council, especially because Baldizar's Hector's gift and magical powers were far stronger than all the council put together, and he possessed the fabled Fangs of Jagdar dagger too. His next move was totally unexpected.

With a zing of steel, Baldizar drew his six-foot broadsword with a right hand and strode resolutely forward. With a sideways action, he bashed the sword's pommel hard into the side of Eccles's head, the force of the blow spinning him off the stage. Still moving forward as if in fluid motion, he brought the tip of his savage blade close enough to Archibald's neck to pierce the skin.

The advancing members of the genie council became rigid with fear, gasping in horror at the trickle of orange blood dripping from the tip of his blade.

'Anyone else feel like trying to elect a new leader?' Baldizar bellowed.

Chapter 36

THE PLANET HEXX.
THE RESCUE.

I t was a detonation of gigantic proportions, a fireball of such intensity that it seemingly ripped the night sky apart, turning night into day. Its brilliant white flash momentarily blinded every creature, creepy, and mongrel on Hexx, whilst its thunderous boom struck like an exploding volcano. With ringing ears, all heads turned to the heavens, their shocked voices whispering in awe, spellbound by the maelstrom of red, yellow, and white fire that filled the sky.

The whole of the amphitheatre reeled in fright as fire billowed out of the incandescent, broiling storm clouds, then cooed softly in wonder just as quickly as it folded back in on itself, fading to nothing.

Yet not all creatures on Hexx at that precise second were gripped with fear, for standing alone in the darkness, atop the great amphitheatre of Garrknock's high wooden wall, one solitary figure was smiling with delight. 'Yes!' hissed Professor Ratchet Madspanner, ripping night-vision goggles from his face. 'Now that's what I call pest control!'

Staring with crazy, wide eyes at the small, insignificant figures playing out their last pitiful moments on the stage below, Madspanner declared with a loud, brazen laugh,

'Ladies and gentlemen, now it's time to use *my* ten-foot robotic puppet to fulfil my plan!'

Below, dominating centre stage, Baldizar gloated evilly up at the sky, his monstrous ego buoyed by his mighty sky-cruiser triumph. Raising two arms, he pointed towards the far away flames and shouted, 'See how your precious rescuers burn?'

Ssasky felt her eyes brim with tears at his taunting laughter.

'My mighty metal raptor has crushed the last of the Merlin's marauders. They, like you, will not feel the warmth of the coming dawn!'

Stunned by Baldizar's outrageous attack on Eccles Nimrod yet confused by his odd reluctance to use the dagger's power, the remaining council genies looked to Archibald Pinchwick for guidance. They took strength from the way the system genie, a cinnamon spider of unusual size and strength, bristled rebelliously. Standing as one, the genies formed a semi-circle of linked limbs, their sudden unity bolstering their sense of purpose. Then slowly, with Archibald leading and revenge shining in their eyes, they summoned the power of their Hector's gifts and advanced upon their El Supremo.

Baldizar stood silently like a red metal monolith, towering over all others on the stage. In the light of a thousand burning torches, his crimson armour, adorned with its ancient silver symbols and its lethal black horns, radiated menace. In his right upper hand, he held aloft his deadly broadsword and in his left, the fabled Fangs of Jagdar dagger. He wondered whether the display of power would be enough to fool the council.

Baldizar felt the stage creak behind him. Captain

Goldhorn marched directly towards him, his massive barrel chest heaving, his grim minotaur face set and determined. He clasped his huge law-enforcing broadsword in his left hand, whilst his right hand gripped his judgment-dispensing double-edged battle axe.

Stomping to a halt within a blade's length, the chieftain captain slowly turned his massive bull's head towards Baldizar, his coal-black eyes fixing El Supremo with a menacing stare.

Archie stared in horror at the flaming inferno below. 'Einstein's underpants,' he said in disbelief, 'that thing must have been a hydrogen airship!' As he picked his way carefully through the burning maze of wreckage back to the Skyshark, he should have been jumping with joy, but he wasn't. They'd won the battle, but strangely, he didn't feel good about it at all.

The Victory was well ablaze now, and the only thing louder than the crackling fire all about him was the creaking and groaning of her ancient timbers.

Boff swivelled an eye behind him as Archie dropped through the Skyshark's round hatch.

'Jagdar's teeth, boy,' he snapped as Archie jumped into the pilot's seat, 'why didn't you answer me? Your flying machine's on its last naffin' legs!'

'What do you—'

Boff pointed at the console. 'Look at your precious engines.'

Engine one was dead, and the RPM dial for engine two was spiralling down.

'Einstein's underpants,' cried Archie. 'We're not falling, we're crashing!' He frantically scanned the controls for engine two. But it didn't make any sense—it had electrical power, the air vents were clear, and the fuel tanks were still half full. More out of habit than procedure, he wrapped his knuckles on the glass front of the fuel gauge with a fingertip. To his horror, the small black needle dropped to zero.

'Stall point reached,' announced the female voice calmly. 'Altitude two thousand feet. Crash landing imminent.'

'That ground's coming up really fast Boff.'

'Think, boy, think,' said a pale skinned Boff. 'I can hear the Duster brothers calling our names.'

'I'm trying.' Archie frantically flicked the number-two-engine fuel tank open and shut, achieving nothing. He glanced at the altimeter, which read twelve hundred feet. 'But she's not getting any fuel.'

'What?' growled Boff, flushing an angry red. 'You mean this heap of junk's just thirst—'

'That's it!' said Archie, leaping from his seat. 'It's that stupid pump again!'

Cursing aloud, he raced to the back of the cockpit, throwing open the maintenance hatch for engine two. Snatching up a large wooden chock, he took aim then whacked the top of a grungy-looking fuel pump. The lump of wood bounced off the pump's metal housing with a dull thud, and engine two immediately regained its healthy growl.

'Don't just sit there, squid boy,' Archie said, jumping back in the pilot's seat. 'We're crashing. Grab your flipping flight column!'

For several heart-stopping seconds, the pair wrestled

514

desperately with the Skyshark's flight controls, but never once did Archie's faith falter. With seconds to spare, the spiralling altimeter needle finally began to slow.

'We're slowing down!' cried Boff.

'Pull harder!' yelled Archie, his arm muscles quivering with pain. 'We're still crashing.'

'I'm pulling as hard as I naffin' can,' cried Boff, 'and I've got ten tentacles!'

As the Skyshark fell on its suicidal three-hundred-miles-per-hour dive, the pair of them saw nothing but a grisly death staring them in the face.

Archibald Pinchwick, the system genie, had raised his four bony hands, ready to fight magic with magic, when he suddenly felt his quaking nerves dramatically bolstered by the timely arrival of the captain of the chieftains. He grinned with smug relief, armed by the fact that the minotaur's' hatred of Baldizar was legendary. Confidently, he raised a single hand, halting the advancing steps of the council of the power ten genies.

'Goldhorn, as captain of the chieftains and chief law enforcer, I order you to arrest Baldizar,' demanded Pinchwick boldly, 'for acts of treason against the council of the power ten genies and all species of the genieverse.'

Tense excitement rippled through the crowd as the minotaur's muscular body flexed like an oak tree in a storm, his big, hairy knuckles clenched white about his weapons. With eyes as black as coal, Goldhorn raised his broadsword then, in an outrageous act of betrayal, levelled its tip towards the council.

'What in Jagdar's name...?' gasped a dumbfounded Pinchwick as Goldhorn turned his aggression to the trembling genies. 'You're the captain of the chieftains. You hate Baldizar!' A brutal flash of realisation swept the confusion from his mind. Baldizar was using the power of the dagger to control the chieftains.

Pinchwick shuddered at the thought of what he must do. Mustering what little courage he had left, he slowly raised a shaking hand and beckoned the council forward. He tried to swallow, but the idea of war had baked his throat dry. If the great god Jagdar had deemed it to be the candle mark of their destruction, then so be it. At least future scrolls would tell that he and the council went down fighting.

Tensed and readied for inevitable one-sided slaughter, Baldizar suddenly shocked them all by simply lowering his sword. Whereas the council genies stood confused, only Pinchwick correctly interpreted the odd manoeuvre as a signal. The cinnamon spider's cluster of stalked eyes anxiously flicked in all directions at once. It was a signal, but he didn't know to whom or for what.

From the foot of the great statue of Garrknock came a loud creak of timber as Og, the big gorilla, acknowledged the signal and heaved back on a large wooden lever.

'Jagdar, protect us,' muttered Pinchwick. '*It's an ambush!*'

In a moment of unprecedented, murderous deceit, the great amphitheatre of Garrknock was ripped apart by the sudden, thunderous sound of high-calibre gunfire. The shocked mob cried out in horror as the first volley of bullets blew the huge carved face of Garrknock apart, its destruction revealing a high-powered Phalanx machine gun. In a howling mechanical rage, the ungodly weapon spat seventy-five 20mm shells a second. In one minute, it had unleashed a storm of forty-five hundred shells that chewed a gash three feet wide across the stage from front to back.

The stream of ear-piercing projectiles hit the stage with pinpoint accuracy, pulverising the old wooden planks and instantly stopping the advancing genies in their tracks. As they looked up, their bodies frozen in unified terror, from underneath the machine gun there came the clunking and whirring of cogs as a rudimentary mechanism redirected the monstrous weapon's aim directly at them.

Baldizar's thin lips smiled cruelly, rejoicing in the knowledge that the council of the power ten genies had but seconds to live. His assured ascension to leader of the genieverse was but a machine gun's breath away.

Archibald Pinchwick knew his time was at an end—his life candle was just a melted nub. But instead of quaking in fear at his own demise, he rather oddly found his ever-curious mind staring past Baldizar to a bizarrely growing blister of light beyond the theatre's eastern edge.

With the fury of a hurricane, HMS Victory, flagship of the Royal Navy, fully ablaze from bow to stern and keel to masthead, roared up from behind the statue of Garrknock like an avenging behemoth. The whole theatre cried out in shocked awe as, at the very moment the Phalanx machine gun opened fire, the fiery spectre rammed the statue, snatching both weapon and idol between the battered jaws of its bow. With the statue of Garrknock mashed there, the thick oak keel of the Victory scraped torturously over the crest of the chunky wooden outer wall before gliding down into the amphitheatre.

In the stalls, mayhem erupted as creatures, creepies, and mongrels shoved, clawed, and fought one another in a frantic bid to escape the burning phantom that was hurtling towards them. With the main exits choked with fleeing bodies, the desperate creatures hemmed in on the top of the stalls and soon began hurling themselves off the high wooden wall. For those who survived the sixty-foot leap, it was simply a matter of scrambling quickly onto the path of red lights that led them out of the forbidden zone and to safety.

However, for those who landed badly, hampered by broken limbs and bleeding wounds, escape was impossible. They became the menu special, as all about them, the ever hungry dreadlies homed in on their desperate cries.

Inside Archie's head, Grizwold, having recovered from the dizzying blast of the firebomb attack, marvelled at the boy's brain. It was now half the size of the cavity within which it sat, and the two scars that so closely resembled the mark of the rippling cross were perfectly aligned. Its chaotic growth had calmed, its flashing colours soothed. It flushed a deep, oxygen-enriched purple and pulsed strongly and steadily like the heart of a waking dragon.

Grizwold chuckled to himself as he watched the boy deftly handling his precious flying machine. *Oh, maggot of mine,* he thought light-heartedly, his smile lopsided but happy, *sooner or later you'll realise that you are keeping this metal-and-wood monstrosity aloft, not that silly mechanical-engine thingy you're so proud of.*

Through Archie's eye, he could see the cold, hard dirt of the arena floor racing up to meet them. Wrapping his tentacles about Archie's brain, Grizwold braced for impact. *Ready yourself, Archie Wilde of Earth,* he thought with a grin. *Your destiny is at hand.*

Their ship burning out of control, Archie and Boff also braced themselves as the Victory's keel ploughed into the arena floor, gauging a deep furrow towards the stalls. Juddering wildly, the ship's three masts promptly snapped and flew forward like giant spears of flame.

'Jagdar's teeth, boy!' yelled Boff. 'We're going to ram the stalls!'

'The Victory is,' Archie said, laughing, 'but not us.'

Boff gasped, swivelling both coned eyes at him.

Archie's mind rapidly calculated distance and speed as they skidded toward the chunky, solid wooden barrier that formed the front of the stalls. 'Nearly... Nearly... *Now!*' he shouted, smashing his left fist down on a big red button and yanking the flight control column back hard.

Amidst the terrible noise and confusion, unheard by anyone, came a small, sharp crack as two tiny explosive devices neatly severed the Skyshark's steel wire anchor cables, the only thing holding them securely to the old wooden galleon.

A heartbeat before the burning wooden ship smashed into the stalls, the panicking mob shrieked in terror as a mysterious shiny silvery creature burst free of the flaming wreckage, roaring up into the night sky.

Although shocked by the mystery sky cruiser's sudden and destructive arrival, those onstage were quick to react. The stunned genies fled, colourful coats swirling and ornate turbans falling. Baldizar, seemingly impassive to the chaos about him, acted with an unnatural calmness, simply stepping back out of harm's way, flanked all the time by a stone-faced captain Goldhorn.

From their hiding place, Sergeant Rockwolf and his minotaur's watched in amazement as the mystery ship crashed into the stalls. They were even more stunned to see the small, strange silver cruiser burst from the burning wreck and soar into the sky, gracefully looping before gliding back into the arena and skidding to a halt with its nose kissing the lip of the stage.

Rockwolf roared heartily as a small round hatch on the top of the craft popped open, and two familiar laughing figures emerged.

'Forward, minotaur's, to battle!' he yelled, sending the corridor wooden door flying off its hinges with one mighty kick of a huge iron boot. 'We're chieftains, so let's spill blood and break bones in the name of the law!'

Archibald Pinchwick leaped from the stage with all the vigour of a youngling cinnamon spider. Curling his long, bony arms underneath his body, he hit the ground and rolled before springing back onto his feet and scooping up the fallen Eccles Nimrod. Scampering clear of the stage, he quickly rejoined and reorganized the other dumbfounded genies into a more respectable fighting force.

Events had overtaken him, and his mind reeled as it struggled to comprehend what to do next. To add to his confusion, he saw Sergeant Rockwolf's platoon, which had strangely appeared from nowhere on the far side of the arena, inexplicably hurling themselves upon their fellow chieftains, kicking and hacking.

Even if we defeat Baldizar this night, his ever-scheming mind coldly calculated, *the genieverse has changed forever.* He glared across at the rainbow child standing brazenly atop the strange silver flying machine. *The council of the power ten genies must possess the magic of the fabled Fangs of Jagdar dagger, not that maggot!*

Archie and Boff stood grinning at the carnage about them. Half of the great amphitheatre of Garrknock was ablaze, the air thick with the sound of crackling wood and screams of terror. Above, heavy plumes of black blotted out the stars, whilst acrid, choking fingers of smoke snaked their way across the arena floor, lacing everything together with an eerie, post-apocalyptic feel.

'Not bad, huh,' offered Archie smirking, 'considering we've only just arrived?'

Boff swivelled a coned eye at him. 'So, this is your idea of a lightning smash-and-grab raid, is it?' he remarked, chuckling at the mayhem about them. 'In, out, *gone!*'

'Oh, come on,' laughed Archie, 'you of all people know how *my plans* always turn out, huh?'

'Well, hornswoggle me giblets, boy, you're right,' he roared, slapping Archie on the back. 'But who cares? I'm just an old storm raider who enjoys a good punch-up. Look, even the genies are getting stuck.'

'Crickey, so they are,' agreed Archie. 'Shall we join them?'

'It's a rum party we've crashed,' he roared, beating his chest excitedly with his tentacle pads. 'Be rude not to!'

'*YOU!*' raged Baldizar. 'You should be dusted!'

Archie pointed his sword contemptuously at El Supremo. 'Terribly sorry to disappoint you, Buckethead!' he said whilst casually smirking and flicking the crown of Avalon with a finger. 'You didn't really think that cheap, silly trinket of yours was going to stop me, did you?'

The pair roared with laughter, causing Baldizar to shake like an old boiler about to explode. 'It's impossible!' cried Baldizar furiously. 'No maggot has ever survived the golden collar. It's just impossible!'

'Well, obviously it's not... is it?' Archie calmly unhooked an object from his belt. 'Oh, and thanks for the use of your bog spinner, it came in very useful.'

'Kill them, Goldhorn!' screamed Baldizar, pointing his shaking broadsword at them. 'Hack them to pieces!'

Even though Archie stood before an evil giant, drastically outgunned on a chilly and hostile planet, with no coat and in shorts that exposed his cold, bare, red legs, his heart still pumped like a furnace. He should have been terrified, but things were moving so quickly that he didn't have time to be scared. There was no quaking or knocking knees, just a surging exhilaration racing through his veins and an unnaturally violent desire for revenge.

'Well, trounce me trunnions,' said Boff, wrapping a tentacle about Archie's shoulders. 'You've gone from geek to sleek in twelve candle marks. I'm naffin' proud of you, boy!'

'Knock it off Boff.' Blushed Archie.

'Yeah, well, enough mushy stuff,' Boff said, elbowing him in the side. 'What's say we kickstart this rescue, huh?'

'Sounds good to me,' said Archie, taking out his slingshot

and loading it with a large steel ball bearing. 'Hey, Buckethead.' he shouted, stretching the elastic to full length. 'I'm back for revenge and to rescue my friends.' With a twang, the ball bearing shot across the stage, striking Baldizar's helmet with a loud ding. 'Stand by to spill tin guts!'

Boff chuckled. 'Spill tin guts. I like it, boy.'

'You get Freddy, and I'll free Ssasky,' said Archie to the empty space next to him.

'Avast, you yellow-livered scoundrels.' yelled Boff, launching his battle-red body towards the stage, all eight of his zizzers zinging out in all directions. 'Bilge Rat Boff's my name, and dusting's my game.'

Archie, his logical mind blinded by the excitement of the moment, leapt onto the stage, brandishing his sword in one hand and his slingshot in the other. But his youthful courage faltered immediately as, dropping his sword in fright, he found his way barred by the massive hulk of Goldhorn.

Boff, whilst watching Archie with one eye, carefully aimed two zizzers at the thick supporting rope of the torture machine's massive crescent blade. *If this is going to work,* he thought anxiously, *I'd best get it right first time.*

'Freddy,' he yelled. 'Curl your fingers in tight. This is going to be close.' The crescent blade seemed to hesitate at the farthest reach of its arc before swinging back towards its victim. Freddy, struggling to pull his skinny legs up against his unrelenting shackles, started praying.

'Archie,' cried Boff. 'Hit the deck. Incoming.'

Archie dropped like a sack of spuds just as Boff loosed off two zizzers, his multibladed fighting yo-yos slicing through the thick rope holding the blade just as it reached the end of its arc.

Nogga and Skatt, hiding behind the shattered remains of the large wooden door, watched googly eyed as the huge, curved blade flew free, scything Goldhorn clean in half.

'Did you see that, bro?' Skatt asked. 'Old squid boys just diced up the captain of the chieftains.'

'By the curly horns of Jagdar, it's a green one,' barked Skatt, rearing up on his hind legs. 'He's one of them there veggie things!' Startled by the close clash of steel, the pair of Mmickys leapt aside as half a veggie chieftain crashed on top of the battered wooden door, his green guts spilling everywhere.

'Sarge,' cried one of Rockwolf's platoon, his left arm dangling, bloody, and useless. 'There are too many of them, Sarge.'

'Wow, that was close,' Nogga said. 'This fight's getting dangerous.'

'Hey, bro, look at that,' said Skatt from behind.

'If those veggie chieftains win,' said Nogga fearfully, 'old Buckethead will feed us to the dreadlies.'

'Bro, will you look at that.'

'Quit your yelping, Skatt, I'm trying to get us—ow,' cried Nogga as Skatt sank his teeth into one of his tails.

'Shut your pie hole, you dummy,' growled Skatt angrily. 'Took back there. That stinky black sewage is bubbling up into the arena.'

Boff unleashed several deadly zizzer strikes at Baldizar's head and chest. His punishing attack sliced off two of Baldizar's helmet horns, whilst the rest viciously pummelled his big iron chest. The furious pace of his attack sent the red giant staggering off balance.

Boff glanced backwards with one eye whilst deftly slicing off Freddy's restraining straps with a single zizzer. Archie, who had been watching the blistering attack with great joy, seized the moment and nimbly skirted around the tottering red giant to where Ssasky lay, quickly snatching up Goldhorn's discarded battle axe as he passed.

Ssasky jumped to her feet, her spungold chains rattling. 'Archie! Oh, Archie,' she cried, her bright-yellow eyes clouded with tears, 'you came back for me!'

'Of course I did my love.' He smiled roguishly, raising the axe up high then smashing it down on one of her shackles. To his dismay, the axe blade shattered into pieces. 'What the—'

'The chain and shackles are enchanted with genie magic,' she offered forlornly. 'Only Baldizar can lift the spell.'

'Really?' Archie laughed, producing a huge set of bolt croppers from a hidden pouch in the back of his combat vest. 'Good that I brought my spell breaker, then.' After snipping easily through the enchanted chains, he handed her a tissue from his vest. 'You didn't really think I'd leave you to that megalomaniac, did you?'

'Is this all really happening?' Archie heard her whisper, her eyes swollen with tears. 'Or has Baldizar finally driven me insane?'

With the battle raging about them, Archie put down his bolt croppers, took her head in his hands, and kissed her soft lips. 'You're not insane, my darling,' he whispered gently in her ear. 'I am!'

Baffled by his words, she pulled back, her golden eyes confused. 'I don't understand,' she said.

'I'm insanely in love with you, Ssasky,' he declared,

winking. 'Now what say we leave this party, huh?'

Behind them, Baldizar took advantage of a miscalculated move by Boff. Using his lightning reflexes, he unexpectedly swung his long broadsword around and up in a vicious arc, severing the strings of seven of Boff's eight zizzers.

'See how the tide of battle turns in my favour, Boff of Kromper?' snarled Baldizar. 'My plant chieftains have the real chieftains and the council genies outnumbered.'

Boff felt a stab of pain in both hearts as glancing quickly at the fighting about him, he realized that Baldizar's glib statement was true.

'Victory is mine,' roared Baldizar, 'along with the whole of the genieverse!' His voice suddenly became demonically calm, his glare as cold as ice. 'And along with all of your miserable lives!'

All about them, the pace of battle was slowing. Boff looked despondently across the arena at the tired, overwhelmed, and rapidly diminishing pockets of resistance. The sound of clashing steel was fading fast.

Rockwolf's platoon numbered but six still standing, and all bore savage wounds. He had watched his minotaur's fight heroically with glowing pride, but in the end, the enemy's sheer numbers were overwhelming them.

'Sarge,' spat Corporal Mudgutts from behind as he decapitated an advancing veggie chieftain with the last of his strength, 'it's looking grim back here. There's just too many!'

A blank-eyed veggie chieftain stormed towards Sergeant Rockwolf, brandishing his sword viciously.

'Aye, laddie,' the sergeant said, 'I fear the battle is lost, and the Duster brothers will be on overtime today.'

The rest of his platoon took courage from the complete absence of fear in his voice. After all, no minotaur ever really expected to reach retirement age.

'But by the fiery breath of Jagdar,' roared Rockwolf valiantly, 'I'm going to slay as many of these foul veggie creatures as I can before I fall.' Having lost his battle axe, gripping his mighty two-and-a-half-handed broadsword with both hands, he waited until the very last moment then dropped unexpectedly onto one knee. With the enemy towering over him, off balance and overreaching, he lashed upwards with lightning speed. His blood boiled, his heart pumped hard, and a war cry escaped his screaming lips as he brought his blade up, neatly severing the enemy's left arm from his body.

The veggie chieftain's face remained blank, as if his crippling wound hadn't even registered. But the creature did hesitate, just for a heartbeat, and that was enough for Rockwolf to recover. Swinging his sword around in a flying arc, he was about to strike when right before his astounded eyes, the vile creature's head began to melt, its blank eyes falling from their gooey, bubbling eye sockets.

In a few seconds, the enemy's head had completely dissolved, and it was then that he spied, off in the distance and directly behind the dying veggie chieftain, two shouting slugmen desperately trying to get his attention.

'Sergeant Rockwolf,' yelled Nogga excitedly waving his stumpy arms towards several large puddles of gooey green muck. 'It's the black sewage. It melts the veggie chieftains. Throw it at them and see.'

'It makes them fizz proper good,' barked Skatt, who was

happily flinging piles of black muck in all directions.

Rockwolf exploded into action. Inspired by this unexpected turn of events, he lashed out like a buzz saw, his broadsword carving a brutal, green-blood-splattered gap in the ring of veggie chieftains.

'Section one, follow me!' he shouted. 'Corporal Mudgutts, advance on the genie council to give them the good news.'

Baldizar went wild with anger, his cry of outrage echoing throughout the arena, his crippled ego barely able to comprehend just how dramatically events had shifted back into the enemy's favour. His long-awaited plan to possess and dominate the genieverse was in tatters.

'You! Maggot!' he growled with a voice like thunder, wheeling towards Archie with his broadsword raised. 'This is all your doing, boy!'

Flicking open a small pocketknife, Archie quickly cut free the leather brace holding Ssasky. 'Fly, Ssasky,' he beseeched over his shoulder, not daring to take his eyes off the advancing red giant. 'You're free. Go while you can.'

'Form a circle,' yelled Boff to everyone on the stage. 'He may have four arms and a sword, but he can't attack everyone at once.'

'Get the dagger!' shouted Freddy, who was vigorously poking Baldizar with two lengths of smashed timber whilst narrowly dodging the sweeping tip of his blade. 'It's the only thing that will dust him for sure!'

Archie, Boff, Freddy, and two of Rockwolf's minotaur's quickly surrounded the supreme genie, but no matter how they dodged and weaved, it was to no avail. At ten feet tall, with an arm's length of five feet plus his swords, the advantage was all Baldizar's.

Then out of nowhere, a huge dollop of black goo sailed through the air, hitting the supreme genie square in the face. 'Not a bad shot if I say so myself,' said Eccles Nimrod from the other side of the stage. 'Perhaps that silly Earth game of cricket has some merit after all.'

The band of heroes enthusiastically took advantage of Buckethead's temporary blindness, immediately lunging in for the attack. Freddy and the two minotaur's jabbed with their swords and makeshift pikestaffs. Boff, who had managed to repair one of his zizzers, frantically tried to dislodge the genie's wildly slashing sword, whilst Ssasky, flying safely above, gleefully bombarded him with rocks.

Dodging Baldizar's flaying iron gauntlets, Archie snatched up the bolt croppers, his eye fixed steadfastly upon the clenched fist holding the dagger. To and fro it wildly swung, whistling close to his face, but he kept his cool, waiting for that golden opportunity to knock it from his hand.

Whilst lashing out defensively, Baldizar frantically tried to scrape the foul, sticky black goo from his face. His darting red eyes were half blinded and stinging, as he desperately tried to focus on the next attack. But as he cursed at the united weapon-wielding creatures advancing upon him, haphazardly countering their jabbing with ever more daring assaults, he'd missed the young Earth boy crouching quietly at his side.

Springing up, Archie made his move, swinging the bolt croppers with all his might. But as he zeroed in on the dagger hand, from nowhere, an unseen flaying metal fist cuffed him hard on the side of his head. The impact sent him sprawling across the wooden stage, the bolt croppers slipping from his limp grasp, stars filling his one eye and clouding his concussed mind with explosions of colour.

Archie felt something warm and wet running down his cheek as he tried to shake the smothering fog from his brain, his stumbling efforts to kneel all but useless.

All about him, distant voices were shouting. They called to him, they begged him, but the ringing in his head muffled their words. Then a single, vaguely familiar, scratchy voice suddenly penetrated the chaos in his head.

The Tower of London, thalked the voice repeatedly, *remember what you did at the Tower of London, Archie. Use your Hector's gift. It's your only chance!*

Archie was sure the words were important. Tower, London, Hector's gift… he felt that they should link in some way. Maybe he was simply hallucinating.

No, you aren't! screamed his conscience. *Grizwold has thrown you a lifeline. Now grab it, you dunderhead!*

Archie doggedly began repeating the words. 'Tower, London, Hector's gift, Tower, London, Hector's gift,' he chanted, scolding himself for his own pathetic weakness. 'They're not nonsense—they mean something. Concentrate, Archie!'

In desperation, Grizwold swamped Archie's brain with an adrenaline cocktail.

Suddenly, a bone-creaking spasm enveloped Archie's whole body, as if he'd received a massive electrical jolt. And in that microscopic moment of painful clarity, he intuitively knew exactly what to do!

Semi-conscious, he began forcing every thought in his distressed brain into a giant, imaginary funnel. Ideas, notions, pictures, images—even his screaming, troubled subconscious slowly gurgled, twirling downward. Constrained yet guided by its tapering edges, he suddenly felt a soothing tranquillity spreading throughout his trembling being as all the befuddling noise and nonsense was slowly filtered away. One by one, the clamouring voices faded, as did the tendrils of chaos that fogged and hampered his actions. Slowly, he focused his thoughts into an ever-thinner stream, filtering until eventually, he held but a single concentrated beam of illuminated thought.

As the chaotic world about him slowly flickered to a halt, a calm clarity descended upon him. With his eye open, his mind was as clear as a bright blue sky, his purpose as powerful as the burning sun.

Boff and Freddy, deftly wielding their makeshift weapons, appeared to be suspended mid-jab, as did the bowling-ball-sized rock, which Ssasky, hovering above the stage, had just dropped. Baldizar, his goo-splattered malevolent face glaring with rage, stood motionless, his huge broadsword frozen in a sweeping arc, desperately trying to deflect the savage sword blows from the two heroically fighting minotaur's.

There was a palpable fearfulness about the supreme genie as his half-turned head acknowledged the huge, grinning figure of Sergeant Rockwolf charging towards him, battle axe and broadsword held high.

We're like flies attacking a tank, Archie thought despondently. *He's fully armed, and we're just several minor annoyances!*

Do something about it, then!

Grizwold? thalked Archie, stunned at hearing the mutmut's voice. *B-but I'm thinking to myself!*

You're babbling, thalking aloud, offered Grizwold. *You're still a little concussed—that's why I can hear you.* He chuckled, patting the boy's brain affectionately. *Oh, and congratulations on mastering your Hector's gift.*

It was you who put the thought of the Tower of London in my mind.

The thought was always there, Archie. I just nudged your analytical mind in the right direction!

Thanks, Grizzy. Right now, I need all the help I can get.

Yes you do, confirmed Grizwold, looking out through Archie's eye at the towering red figure dominating centre stage. *But that problem apart, tell me honestly. How are you feeling?*

Archie smiled. *Weirdly, I've never felt better. My mind feels sharper than a surgeon's blade.*

And your body?

Terrific. Archie reconsidered that statement as his hand wistfully touched the empty pouch on his belt. *No—my breathing's a bit laboured. I'm all out of Muzzberry pips, and I think I'm going to have one hell of a headache when this is over!*

And what of that annoying bubbly, gassy sensation in the pit of your stomach?

Oh, that's just hunger, Archie replied. *I've only eaten two jam-steam puddings all day.*

That's not hunger, young Archie. It's a rising tide of nausea. Only moments ago, Baldizar punched you in the head, which is the equivalent of being smacked with a ten-pound hammer.

Why do I not feel injured?

Your Hector's gift. It enhances the mind whilst overriding your injured body. Sadly, for you to be able to attack Baldizar, you must first return to the real world by relinquishing your gift.

Archie read between the lines. *Am I severely injured?*

Sufficiently enough to render you unconscious the moment you surrender your gift, Grizwold said regretfully.

Archie groaned. *Fully unconscious?*

Yes, almost immediately.

I might have a few seconds, then? Archie grasped at the positive.

Doubtful! So if you're planning some form of action, I suggest you make it swift.

You know what, Grizwold? He sighed. *Sometimes I feel like you're my own personal albatross.*

Oh yeah? Where's that cocky positive mental attitude you humans are famous for? After all, what's that saying you Earth creatures have? 'Every suit of armour has a fault or two.'

Not a fault, corrected Archie, clambering up onto his knees and staring at Baldizar's long tin legs, *a chink!* The word 'chink' resonated in his mind as he glimpsed something odd just below Baldizar's right knee. It was a thin strip, no wider than his little finger and about the same length, but there was a vague difference in both colour and texture.

Whereas the rest of Baldizar's armour glowed with an evil crimson hue, enhanced by a network of ancient, shining silver symbols, that one tiny spot was unquestionably paler and more importantly, devoid of hieroglyphics.

Archie grinned to himself as a cunning thought sparked in his mind. *Is this the break my friends and I so desperately need?* Reaching down, he slid the fingers of his left hand into the top of his left moon boot, grasping the top of something remarkably familiar.

What's that? thalked Grizwold.

Archie unzipped a roguish smile as he produced an eighteen-inch-long metal rod with a robust rubber grip on one end. *This is my reserve cattle prod.*

And just what do you intend to do with it?

This! he cried.

In a courageous act of defiance against overwhelming odds, Archie jammed his thumb down on the cattle prod's power button, relinquished his Hector's gift with a sigh, then rammed its shiny tip deep into the tiny and vulnerable chink in Baldizar's armoured right knee joint.

Archie watched the fabled Fangs of Jagdar dagger slip from Baldizar's hand as his knee joint exploded in a dazzling, brightly coloured display of fizzing sparks, his huge tin body jigging about like an electrified puppet.

As the dagger bounced tantalizingly close on the wooden stage before him, Archie felt a wave of nausea strike with the force of a tsunami, enveloping him in excruciating pain whilst smothering his head with a woozy darkening fog. Desperately dredging up the last of his reserves, he somehow found the strength to reach out and grasp the dagger, then, with the light of consciousness fading fast, hurl it towards Rockwolf.

'Give… to… Ssasky,' he said as the blackness rushed in and consumed him.

Sergeant Rockwolf lunged for the dagger, then in a rolling dive that made the stage planking creak to near breaking point, scooped it up whilst fending off Baldizar's wildly punching gauntlets. His colossal forward momentum enabled him to nimbly flip his twenty-five-stone body back onto his feet and, in a spine-wrenching twist, launch the dagger towards Ssasky with one hand whilst burying his axe into Baldizar's right knee with the other.

'Catch it!' cried Boff. 'Use the dagger before Baldizar recovers!'

For a few precious seconds, the world seemed to hold its breath. Sparkling in the torchlight, the fabled Fangs of Jagdar dagger flew as if guided by the invisible hand of Jagdar himself, straight into Ssasky's waiting grasp.

It fell into her open palms, her fingers lacing together about its spungold-filigree handle as if it had been made for her. Its smooth wooden sheath slid away, revealing the four-sided blade glowing with magical power.

Suddenly, her whole roller coaster of a life flashed before her, beginning with vivid images from her royal birth, through the great blizzard, including her capture by Baldizar, her imprisonment in his bewitched suit of armour, and all the following atrocities she committed under the influence of El Supremo.

Then, like a shaft of sunlight in the eye of a thunderstorm, came the image of her rescue by Archie, the strange yet enchanting human youngling who had in just twelve candle marks both saved her life and won her heart.

Abruptly, her kaleidoscope of conflicting thoughts was vaporised by an ancient voice speaking from deep within the recesses of her mind. The voice carried the authority of a king yet spoke with a tongue as sweet and enticing as honey, chanting a string of magical words. Within the flutter of a butterfly's wing, her pounding heart calmed, her raging thoughts cleared, and she obeyed the instructions emblazoned upon her mind without hesitation.

Baldizar, stunned by the massive electrical jolt, screamed with rage as he watched unbelieving while Rockwolf's axe cleaved clean through his right knee. Unbalanced, he unexpectedly felt the weight of his huge, armoured body begin to topple backwards, his frantic hands desperately trying to grasp anything to arrest his fall.

'Knock his block off!' cried the fickle mob, cheering as they watched the weary, bloodstained creatures circling their El Supremo. 'Give him to the Duster brothers!' roared others, clapping and howling as their new heroes moved in for the kill. Even as Baldizar fell, Boff, Freddy, and the others kept up their unrelenting assault, jabbing, hacking, parrying, and lunging again and again with broadswords, pikestaffs, rocks, zizzers, and axes.

The centuries-old wooden stage of the great amphitheatre of Garrknock groaned aloud as Baldizar's bulk finally succumbed. His huge metal body struck the decking with such a punishing blow that it bounced Archie's unconscious body up into the air, his limp head falling next to Baldizar's screaming face.

'Use the dagger,' yelled a red-faced Nogga. 'Stab him! Dust him!'

'Stab him in the head,' Skatt added. 'Free us from his evil!'

The two minotaur grunts attacked together, furiously wielding their swords over their snorting bull's heads, only for Baldizar to stop them with a clanging of metal, grasping their blades firmly in his upper gauntleted hands. Laughing at his growing vulnerability, Freddy swung forward with a long length of splintered decking, and as he did so, Rockwolf let his battle axe fly. Baldizar snared both weapons with his two free remaining hands.

'Now, Ssasky! Now,' cried Boff, waving his eight tentacle hands triumphantly. 'He's totally defenceless.'

'Go for it, Princess,' yelled Freddy. 'Revenge is yours.'

With each of his four arms pinned down by a grinning enemy, Baldizar could do little but stare up in desolate terror, helpless for the first time in his miserable, evil life. Suddenly at the mercy of Ssasky, who floated above him, his raging volcanic red eyes viewed her for who she truly was, not his onetime bewitched assassin, Serpentina, but the vengeful firstborn daughter of the House of the White Dwarf Star.

'Dust him, dust him!' Chanted the mob as thousands of creatures streamed back into the theatre, closing in on the stage in an act of open rebellion. 'Dust him, dust him,' they cried in unison, stabbing Baldizar's broken ego like a storm of merciless knives.

His helmet visor was open, and Ssasky glared down at Baldizar's ashen, leathery face, the venom in her golden-yellow cat's eyes piercing the trembling malevolence of his. With the fabled Fangs of Jagdar dagger clutched tightly in her hands, she fell upon him like an avenging angel, a lifetime of torturous imprisonment screaming from her hate-filled heart, her whole body seething with revenge.

'Knife him, Princess,' cried Boff, trembling and red with rage. 'Spill his gizzards!'

She clasped the dagger tightly in both hands, and the fate of the genieverse was sealed with one piercing thrust. But a howl of shocked anguish echoed throughout the great amphitheatre of Garrknock that dawn as at the very last moment, to the utter horror of every living creature watching, Ssasky plunged the lustrous, six-inch dagger blade deep into *Archie's* skull!

Epilogue

Through a bleary eye, Archie woke to see Boff holding a broadsword to Ssasky's throat. Her normally vivid-yellow eyes were pale and full of tears, and her stunning cascade of snowy-white hair hung like a straggly mop of filthy rat's tails.

'Boff,' he croaked weakly, 'be careful, my friend. Those things are sharp!'

'Well, trounce me naffin' trunnions,' cried the chamelesquid joyously. 'You're alive, boy!'

Archie tried to laugh, but it stuck in the back of his throat, causing him to cough harshly. 'Of course I'm alive. What else would I be?'

Ssasky slumped to her knees as Boff begrudgingly pulled the blade away from her neck. '*Try dusted*.'

'Me, dusted,' echoed Archie, grimacing as he struggled painfully into a sitting position. 'Why, I've never felt better.'

'Which is all the more miraculous, me boy,' growled Boff, shooting Ssasky's crumpled figure a withering glare, 'considering that the princess here tried to murder you by plunging the Fangs of Jagdar dagger into your head!'

Shaking away the last of the mist that clouded his mind, Archie rose unsteadily then crossed over to where Ssasky lay and knelt beside her. 'Thankfully, Ssasky did exactly what she was instructed to do,' he declared, smiling lovingly whilst clasping a comforting arm about her trembling shoulders.

'She was instructed to do it,' repeated Grizwold, using Archie's speech. 'Then I wasn't hearing things,' he added excitedly. 'I did actually hear *his* voice!'

'Y-you also heard the man who spoke to me?' stammered Ssasky, wiping away her tears. 'Then I wasn't hallucinating, and he really does exist.'

'Whose voice? What man?' Boff asked angrily. 'Scupper me, boy, talk sense. Who in Jagdar's name are you lot twittering on about?'

'Why, the main man himself,' replied Archie, chuckling as his friend flushed beetroot red with frustration, 'the sorcerer Merlin!'

'Well, hornswoggle me giblets,' declared Boff in amazement, 'you've actually spoken to the greatest naffin' genie of them all.'

Archie shook his head. 'Not so much spoken to—more listened. His words were merely echoes from the past.'

'How do you feel, Archie Wilde?' asked Grizwold, gently massaging his vocal cords. 'You've survived an ordeal that would have surely seen a lesser creature dusted.'

Archie took a moment to gather his thoughts, corralling them into some sort of order. Breathing in the frosty dawn air, he found himself calmed by its coolness, not chilled. He also realised with a smile that he no longer needed any Muzzberry pips.

'Oddly enough, I feel particularly good,' he said, his hands cautiously patting his arms and body for broken bones. 'A bit frazzled around the edges, but good nevertheless!'

'Aye, laddie, but do you feel any different?' asked a scratchy voice belonging to a hairy head that popped out from behind Boff's shoulder.

'Oh yes, Freddy, I certainly do feel different.' Archie grinned.

'Scupper me, boy, you look your normal nerdish self to me,' declared Boff.

'Perhaps on the outside,' said Archie, 'but in here…'—he tapped his chest with a finger— 'I feel like an Aston Martin Vulcan sports car that's just been fired up, its V12, eight-hundred horsepower engine ticking over with raw power!'

'Who's this Aston Martin fellow?' whispered Freddy into Boff's ear. 'And why does he need so many horses?'

'Beats me, shipmate.' Boff frowned, circling a fingertip to the side of his head. 'Methinks the boy's brain's still a bit crooked after that last blow.'

Archie raised his left hand, his fingers tentatively probing the open wound on his head. 'So that's where it went in.'

'It's where the voice told me to place it,' Ssasky said softly, relieved at knowing she did right but still ashamed of her actions.

'Thus, forging the link betwixt men and magic,' remarked an elderly voice, 'a conduit through which the rainbow child can receive all the magical powers once possessed by the great Merlin himself.'

Archie turned to see a grouchy, wrinkly, old face staring at him. He recognized the small, skinny man's pantomime costume immediately. 'You're Nimrod, aren't you?' he asked apprehensively. 'One of the council genies.'

'I am *thee* Eccles Nimrod,' declared the old man snootily. 'I am the System genie of the council of the power ten genies and second only to El Supremo himself!'

'Yes, I know,' said Archie, perhaps a touch too cynically. 'Grizwold told me.'

The old genie's face wrinkled like a prune. 'And you think you're now the living embodiment of all of the great sorcerer Merlin's magic, huh.'

'Well, if the dagger has been thrust into my head, then yes, I suppose I am.' Archie replied cheekily, watching the old genie's wizened face frown. 'My friend Grizwold also told me that you are the very courageous leader of the band of rebels that goes by the name of Merlin's marauders.'

Nimrod's displeasure at being spoken to in such a manner by a lowly maggot vanished instantly upon hearing his flattering words. 'I have that honour, yes.'

'By the curly horns of Jagdar,' Boff said with a laugh, 'what a corking disguise. Who would have ever guessed that a scrawny little runt like you could be the leader of a naffin' rebel army.'

The system genie bristled with anger at his demeaning remark. 'Careful, Boff of Kromper,' he hissed, his bent, aged body suddenly growing tall and rigid, 'your master and protector'—he glanced jubilantly to where Baldizar lay— 'is no more.'

'If anybody is going to threaten the storm raider,' snorted the deep voice of Sergeant Rockwolf, stepping forward with his unsheathed broadsword dramatically emphasizing his thinly veiled threat, 'it will be me.' His free hand shot out, grabbing Boff roughly by the throat, yanking him close. 'You

542

and your arachnid friend have been of great interest to us chieftains for some time now.' Rockwolf smiled at a sudden commotion to their side.

'Hey, careful. I'm injured, you know,' Freddy said as he was roughly thrown to the floor by two hulking, unsympathetic minotaur's. 'The princess is my friend you know, and she's the Queen now!'

'Is she really?' sneered the scratchy voice of a cinnamon spider scuttling up alongside Eccles Nimrod.

'My learned friend here, Archibald Pinchwick, has a valid point,' offered Eccles sceptically. 'Although this woman bears a passing resemblance to the late Ssasky, firstborn daughter to the House of the White Dwarf Star, looks alone cannot guarantee authenticity.'

'But you will of course be investigating her claim?' insisted Freddy.

Eccles Nimrod tried to hide his displeasure. 'The council of the power ten genies will of course investigate her claim.' He then added with little enthusiasm, 'In due time.'

'Jagdar's teeth, Freddy, me boy,' Boff said, glaring at the scrawny little man with both coned eyes. 'Sounds to me like someone's a mite reluctant to relinquish his power, huh?'

Ssasky, unsure of just what to do or say, cast her swollen eyes down and remained silent.

Archie, feeling every cut and bruise on his battered body, staggered forward. He coughed, annoyed by the growing hostility. 'I think you're all missing the point here, people,' he offered, walking over to the lifeless body of the red metal giant. 'Your dictatorial El Supremo has been toppled.'

'Archie's right,' Boff said, floating over to his side.

'Baldizar's dusted. We should be rejoicing, not sniping at each other.' A tiny series of flashes caught Archie's eye, and Boff suddenly realised that he was touching his eye patch. 'Something wrong, shipmate?'

'Yes,' he said, bending down to inspect the damaged knee joint.

'El Supremo has been dusted,' insisted Eccles Nimrod, pushing forward. 'I can sense it. There's no life in that body!'

'Blimey,' groaned Archie, 'you're right, Nimrod. There is no life in this metal body.' He looked up; his face full of fear. 'Because there never was. We've all been hoodwinked.' He held out the end of Baldizar's right leg. 'I'm afraid that old Buckethead is still very much alive and well!'

Horror rippled through the small gathering.

'*Impossible!*' screeched Pinchwick, 'his defunct body lies before you.'

Turning slowly, Archie displayed the damaged end of the leg to everyone.

'That's not blood and bone,' uttered Nimrod in dismay.

'No,' agreed Archie, 'what you see is a hydraulic piston, wire tendons, and electrical circuitry. This thing is a robot.'

As if joined by string, everyone on the stage suddenly gasped in shock, stepping or hovering back with revulsion.

'Jagdar's teeth,' declared Freddy nervously, 'if that tin thing's not old Buckethead, then where is he?'

'Egads, Freddy, me boy,' growled Boff. 'He'll have slithered away like the venomous snake he is.'

'That thing is the work of the black art of technology,' hissed Pinchwick.

'Sergeant Rockwolf, take your troop and search for the real

Captain Goldhorn and the other chieftains,' ordered Eccles Nimrod, hoping that the endorsement of his authority would somehow pacify the minotaur's seething hatred of him. 'Secondly, have your minotaur's throw that abhorrence on the fire yonder and keep it well stoked until nothing remains.'

'No,' countered Archie firmly. 'I need to study it.'

'Impudent pup, how dare you countermand my orders,' sniped the genie of order. 'Destroy it, captain. I command it!'

'Actually, *matey*,' insisted Boff, curling a restricting tentacle arm about the little genie's shaking shoulders, 'I think you'll find that young Archie Wilde there is now the ruling genie!'

'Nonsense,' barked Eccles Nimrod and Archibald Pinchwick in unified anger, outraged at the direct challenge to their established authority. 'We have no proof that the maggot actually possesses Merlin's powers.'

'Sergeant Rockwolf, as a duly appointed enforcer of the law,' said Archie, smiling up at the huge minotaur, 'and the highest-ranking chieftain here, I will obey your decision in this matter.'

Pinchwick shuffled forward, eager to speak, but Archie quickly cut him short. 'I'll be blunt, sir. I don't trust the genies. I fear that—' He hesitated just long enough to reel the minotaur in and unnerve Nimrod. 'They have their own secret agenda when it comes to ruling the genieverse.' He played on the sergeant's obvious distrust of the genies superbly. It only took one look at Rockwolf's frowning hairy brows atop his huge coal-black eyes for Archie to know that he'd just made a new friend.

'Why do you not want this metal man destroyed?' asked Rockwolf curiously.

Smiling, Archie turned back to the fallen body of Baldizar. 'This machine—'

'Should be destroyed now!' demanded Nimrod. 'It's an affront to creaturekind, the blasphemous work of the ancient black art of technology.' The wrinkly little genie glared across at Rockwolf, his eyes as cold as ice. 'And if you won't obey my orders, I'll—'

'Drogo, Orlac,' commanded Rockwolf, his big bull's head snorting with simmering anger, 'close quarter guard those two genies.'

Nimrod's frail body shook with indignation, his face flushing red with rage. 'How dare—'

'And if they speak out of turn again,' continued Rockwolf, grinning as he patted the pommel of his broadsword, 'feel free to separate their nagging heads from their scrawny necks!' Turning, he snorted in Archie's face. 'Now, human youngling, just why in Jagdar's name shouldn't I destroy that unholy thing?'

'This is highly advanced technology, sir,' said Archie, poking the end of the severed leg with a fingertip, 'and there's only one person here on Hexx with the knowledge to create such a thing. Professor Ratchet Madspanner.'

'Jagdar's fiery breath... *Madspanner.*' Corporal Mudgutts elbowed the minotaur next to him sharply in the ribs. 'I naffin' told you so, didn't I? Huh?'

The minotaur sighed. 'Yes, Corporal, you were right all along.'

'And another thing,' continued Mudgutts, 'if that's a machine, who's driving it?'

Rockwolf's huge hairy eyebrows meshed in thought. 'I

don't know,' he muttered, 'but I...'

Archie twisted on the spot, pressing a single finger against his lips. Then he took a small notepad from his pocket, scribbled several lines, and held them up for Rockwolf to read. In a flash of movement, Boff felt a slight breeze as the chieftain captain's double-edged battle axe whistled past his cheek before smashing down on the robot Baldizar's neck with a loud metallic thwack. So much strength had he used in his attack that not only did he sever the head, but he also buried its keen edge several inches into the stage.

Archie pointed to the head's volcanic red eyes, which seemed to glow violently for a few seconds before fading to black.

Away from the stage, high upon an undamaged section of the amphitheatre's great wooden wall, a lone figure in a ghostly grey suit watched the goings-on below with amused interest. As the first glowing fingers of dawn began creeping over the theatre's battlements, casting light upon the night's destruction, Professor Ratchet Madspanner slipped quietly away, along with the receding shadows.

'Whoever was controlling this,' said Archie, lifting the head admiringly, 'was listening to us.'

'But it was destroyed!' Nimrod said, instantly regretting speaking as he felt his guard's blade twitch against his throat.

'This is why I need to completely dismantle it.'

'And that will render it harmless?' ask Rockwolf.

'Yes,' said Archie, 'and it might also tell us where it was constructed.'

'Jagdar's teeth, Archie,' Boff said, chuckling, 'who cares, as long as it doesn't work anymore?'

Archie sighed. 'Boff, you can't just knock up something this technical in a garden shed. You need a factory complex.'

'I don't know what a factory complex is,' Rockwolf said, 'but I don't like the sound of it.'

'You're extremely perceptive, my giant friend!' agreed Archie. 'If Madspanner has a factory'—he shuddered at the thought of it— 'then there could be hundreds, possibly thousands more of these things just waiting to be unleashed!'

'The boy makes a good point, Captain,' conceded Mudgutts. 'I mean, just look at the destruction one tin Baldizar caused.'

With the first rays of dawn banishing the dark, the corporal gestured to the smouldering remains of the great amphitheatre of Garrknock about them.

The massive wooden entrance gates to the theatre, along with its two towers, were nothing more than ash and charred timber stumps. Here and there, small fires still glowed, their gently spiralling plumes of acrid smoke whipped away by a refreshing breeze.

As for the once-proud flagship of the Royal Navy, all that remained was its huge hull with a gaping hole in its port side. Its two bright, defining bands of yellow were smutty black, and its three towering masts were gone, along with its canvas sails and rigging.

Archie wondered just how their lordships at the Admiralty would explain its disappearance to the government and the world. Perhaps he should return to Earth one day to tell the story of just how the Victory won an epic battle against a modern-day flying dreadnought. *But why bother?* he thought sadly. *They wouldn't believe me anyway.* Still, the newspapers would make up their own stories based on speculation and artistic licence. They always did.

The Skyshark, although battered and scarred, had fared best of all. It was a tough little craft that had proven its worth in both flight and fight. *Perhaps,* thought Archie longingly, *with a large amount of TLC and two tanks full of my specialist fuel, it might fly again one day.*

The arena floor surrounding the Skyshark looked like a battlefield. On either side of the Victory's scorched hull was the wreckage of the stalls, littered with hundreds of charred bodies. In their attempt to escape the destruction and fire, the fleeing mob had trampled over those in the front rows, only to be confronted by a picket line of murderous veggie chieftains. Those who were lucky enough to escape the fire had been slaughtered by the veggie chieftains.

Archie frowned at Nimrod. 'I don't get it. Baldizar, or the robot Baldizar, had the magic dagger, right? So why didn't he use it?'

Nimrod glanced nervously at his guard, who looked questioningly at Rockwolf before nodding and fractionally lowering his blade. 'Thank you,' said the genie of order, physically relaxing. 'It is my belief that El Supremo had no real understanding of how to actually use the fabled Fangs of Jagdar dagger.'

'Well, hornswoggle me giblets,' Boff said, slapping Freddy hard about his hairy shoulders, 'after all the trouble old Buckethead went through to get the greatest source of power in the genieverse, he couldn't actually use it. What a tin-headed plonka.'

'So, what happens now?' asked Archie.

'For the time being,' began the genie of Order, puffing out his scrawny little chest, 'the council of the power ten genies, led by me, of course, will—'

'The council will do nothing,' proclaimed Ssasky, her voice suddenly strong with regal authority. Everyone turned, surprised to see her standing next to Archie. Gone were the tears and fatigue. A proud Freddy looked admiringly at her majestic figure, which radiated natural authority, along with her gleaming yellow cat's eyes, full of strength and courage.

'How dare you interrupt me, girl, when I'm—'

'Quiet, you odious speck of nothingness!' snapped Ssasky. Slowly, she raised a single long, slender arm and pointed to the western horizon. 'Behold, the Kalifar cometh.'

Every creature still alive in the burnt-out theatre dropped to their knees, except Archie. He just stood with one hand shielding his eye staring at the far-off apparition.

'Jagdar's teeth,' groaned Boff, 'show some naffin'-' Before the chamelesquid had chance to finish, the far away dot suddenly flashed up before them in a swirling cloud of glittering dust and lightening.

'What manner of creature are you?' commanded a large rhinoceros with the head of a shrimp wearing an ornate black and gold mitre and eight long waving tentacles. 'How dare you stand in the presence of a Kalifar, law speaker to the almighty Jagdar.'

'I'm Archie Wilde sir.'

The Kalifar floated nearer to the impudent youth. 'Do you know who I am?' He hissed intimidatingly.

'I know you're a Kalifar,' he replied rubbing his tired eye, 'but no more than that sir.'

'I am Lord Arkutor! Does that not make you tremble with fear?'

'Er… no, not really sir.' Answered Archie trying to be respectful.

'How dare you,' roared the floating rhinoceros, his squeaky shrimp voice making Archie chuckle, 'never have I-'

'Forgive me Lord Arkutor, for I mean no offence,' grinned Archie interrupting cheekily.' 'But well, this Jagdar fella, he's all that is good and wonderful in the Genieverse right?'

'Yes,' agreed Arkutor suspiciously.

'Well as you're his law maker, doesn't that make you a good friend to all the creatures of the Genieverse too. So instead of falling about trembling with fear, shouldn't we all rejoice at your arrival and welcome you with a big smile and a happy heart?'

'Huh… what an extraordinary youngling you are.' Declare Lord Arkutor smiling, which isn't easy when you have the face of a shrimp. 'Your words are cast in iron, and you possess a wisdom and courage beyond your age.' Snapping his head to the right he glared at the huddle of fidgeting genies. 'A wisdom and courage that some here would be wise to heed!'

On the front of the Kalifar's head two long and thin antennae uncurled, their tips floating across to investigate the youth. The tip of one tugged disapprovingly at his clothes. He tutted. 'Considering that you are the long-awaited Rainbow child, you're a scruffy irk, aren't you?'

After a few seconds, the giant turtle's bright-white eyes suddenly darkened, his head snapping towards Ssasky. 'I feel no blade, Princess,' he said, his suspicious tone edged with betrayal. 'If you have truly used the Fangs of Jagdar dagger, then where is the blade?'

'I-I don't know, Lord Arkutor,' stammered Ssasky.

Eccles Nimrod, with a twitch of his little finger, magically flung his minotaur guard across the stage. Sensing a dramatic turn of events that might go in his favour, the genie of Order edged boldly forward. 'Are you now saying that you didn't *actually* plunge the dagger into this maggot's head?' Nimrod asked Ssasky aggressively, hoping that Arkutor would follow his meaning. He watched the beak of the Kalifar move then quickly added, 'After all, in the heat of battle, even the best-trained warriors make mistakes!'

'When you heard Merlin's voice speak to you, Ssasky,' began Grizwold, choosing to ignore the genie's accusation, 'did you follow his instructions precisely?'

'Yes, I did!' she blurted anxiously. 'I did exactly what he told me to do!'

'Obviously, you didn't, *Serpentina*—I mean Ssasky,' hissed Nimrod, deliberately baiting her. 'As a trained assassin, you have dusted many creatures.' He paused, delighting in the tears welling in her soft yellow eyes. 'Perhaps, as a princess, you have lost your killer instinct.'

Outraged by his dastardly trick, Freddy hurled a smashed length of timber at the genie, but he brushed it aside with his Hector's gift. 'You scumbag, Nimrod,' he rasped. 'You know full well she was under an enchantment cast upon her by Baldizar himself.'

Eccles smiled as he raised his right hand then cried out in pain as a shiny silver zizzer whizzed out of nowhere and sliced it off at the wrist.

'Avast there, you scoundrel,' snarled Boff. 'Baldizar was one of your kind. I bet you lot were all in on it together.'

'Enough bickering,' ordered Arkutor, stamping a large, wrinkled old foot down hard whilst trying not to smirk at the old genie's shocked expression. 'Ssasky,' he continued in a more friendly tone, 'what exactly did Merlin tell you to do?'

Ssasky took a deep breath, trying hard to quell her trembling body. 'My Lord, when the sorcerer Merlin spoke, he bade me plunge the dagger into the top of Archie's head.'

Arkutor seemed to catch his breath as if suddenly disappointed. 'Nothing else was said?'

Ssasky thought for a moment, desperately searching her memory, as if trying to grab at something unseen.

'Is there something else you wish to tell me?' asked the messenger of Jagdar.

'I-I don't remember hearing his words,' she continued falteringly, 'but—'

'But what?' insisted Arkutor.

'Although there were no spoken words,' she offered, 'I felt that the sorcerer Merlin hadn't finished speaking.'

Paying no attention to the council genies as they hurriedly tended to Nimrod's bleeding wrist, Arkutor momentarily retreated in thought, his pristine white eyes frosting over like snowballs. Tense seconds passed as no creature on the stage dared move. As for Captain Rockwolf, he and his minotaur's stood motionless but ready to uphold the law, although unsure as to whose law it would eventually be.

'After you plunged the dagger into young Archie's head,' continued Arkutor, suddenly waking from his trance and addressing Ssasky, 'what happened to the blade?'

Ssasky looked down at her empty hands, her troubled eyes running through her actions. 'After I plunged it in'—she hesitated as if trying to quell a wild notion— 'one of Baldizar's metal hands flew up, knocking my hand backwards.'

'Jagdar's teeth.' Boff scowled. 'What happened to the dagger, Ssasky?'

'She speaks the truth, my Lord Arkutor,' ventured Grizwold. 'It must have been knocked out of her hand. I witnessed the blade enter Archie's skull only to be jerked out again.'

'And tell me, mutmut,' persisted Arkutor, 'did the dagger's tip actually pierce the human youngling's brain?'

'Yes, my Lord,' confirmed Grizwold without hesitation. 'Of that I am certain.'

Without warning, the giant rhino's shrimp head slumped, and he sighed heavily, his tone full of anguish. 'Then it is with great sadness in my heart, that I must inform you, Archie Wilde, Rainbow child and winner of the race, that your destiny has failed you. The Duster brothers have you marked in their ledger and will call for your soul soon.'

'*What!*' cried Ssasky, her yellow eyes cloudy with tears. 'This cannot be my Lord. I did as I was told.'

'Alas, Princess, you didn't fully fulfil your task.'

'Er... exactly what is going on, Lord Arkutor, sir?' asked Archie, his eye patch suddenly burning. 'And what's this about the Duster brothers?'

'Thrusting the dagger into your head,' explained Arkutor, 'is only part of the prophecy. 'Immediately after, Ssasky should have snapped the hilt off, leaving the blade embedded in your skull.'

'Okay, so she got that bit wrong. So what,' he smiled

554

comfortingly at her. 'Merlin's magic is safely inside my brain. Surely, that's all that matters, isn't it?' Archie felt himself tremble when he saw Arkutor's genuine look of sorrow.

'I'm afraid not, young Archie Wilde, for without the blade to act as a conduit for you to express the magic, Merlin's powers are useless.'

The chorus of cheers that rose from the genies was short-lived as Boff shot his last remaining zizzer a hair's breadth over the top of their laughing heads.

Archie groaned. 'Einstein's underpants, all that trouble for nothing. What a washout this birthday's been.'

'By the curly horns of Jagdar,' Boff said, sweeping Archie up in his tentacles and spinning him around, 'you started with nothing, and you've ended up with nothing, but who cares? We'll make your next birthday extra special, huh.'

'If only that could be so,' offered Arkutor sadly.

Boff's impromptu swirling stopped. 'Jagdar's teeth, Kalifar,' he hissed angrily, 'explain yourself!'

'Oh, it's quite simple,' interrupted Eccles Nimrod smugly, pushing forward, daring to speak for the messenger of Jagdar. 'You see, Archie may well have all of Merlin's power, but he can't use it.' He and the other genies began laughing like a pack of hyenas closing in for the kill. 'Tell me, young human, do you perchance have a headache?'

'Actually, yes, now you come to mention it,' answered Archie, taken aback by his odd question. 'How did you know?'

'Foolish youngling,' sneered Eccles, 'even with the wisdom to win the race, you still don't see the obvious. It's the pressure of all that magical power building up in your pathetic little human brain.'

Archie suddenly found himself sweating.

'In twenty-four candle marks, it will all become too much for your skull to bear.'

Only Boff was dumb enough to ask the obvious. 'Then what?'

'Why then, his head will explode, of course!' The genie seemed to take great joy in watching a world of horror descend upon Archie and his friends.

'This can't be!' cried Ssasky, her heart breaking as she clutched Archie's arm. 'Is there nothing that can be done?'

'Why yes there is,' teased Eccles Nimrod, cradling his bloody wrist.

'What?' demanded Boff. 'Tell me, genie, lest I gut you here and now!'

'Isn't it obvious even to a gutter-bred, brainless chamelesquid like you. You simply replace the dagger back in Archie's head and finish the prophecy.'

'And of course, remember to snap off its handle after!' added a cackling Archibald Pinchwick.

'Then that's what we must do,' cried Ssasky, her hope suddenly soaring.

'I admire your indomitable spirit, Princess, and the council of the power ten genies wish you good luck with your venture,' Eccles Nimrod announced in an openly mocking tone, delighting in the feel of the Fangs of Jagdar dagger nestling against his leg, concealed safely in a secret poacher's pocket in his gown.

'Now, all you have to do… *is find it!*'

THE END